"Well researched with captivating language...*The Garden of Lost Secrets* did not disappoint."
—*Fresh Fiction* on *The Garden of Lost Secrets*

"Kelly Bowen has written another compelling, dual-timeline, WWII/Present Day novel that sucked me in and refused to let go."
—TheRomanceDish.com on *The Garden of Lost Secrets*

"Kelly Bowen is quickly becoming a favorite author. With her beautiful settings and descriptions, exciting plots, and lovely characters, this book has earned a permanent spot on my bookshelf!"
—The52BookClub.com

"Bowen draws on the lives of Nancy Wake and Josephine Baker and the 2018 discovery of a Paris apartment untouched since WWII in this rich historical tale. The stories unearthed in the apartment pique from the first page in this magnetic novel full of tragedy and rich characters."
—*Publishers Weekly* on *The Paris Apartment*

"Kelly Bowen creates an evocative and thrilling glimpse into the lives of two heroic women risking everything in occupied Paris during World War II. A beautiful novel for fans of *The Nightingale*." —Karen White, *New York Times* bestselling author, on *The Paris Apartment*

"A beautifully written cast of characters unraveling the mysteries and humanity of war. Enticing."
—Mandy Robotham, *USA Today* bestselling author, on *The Paris Apartment*

"Kelly Bowen's *The Paris Apartment* is a compelling story of two women navigating the dangers of occupied Paris with bravery and compassion. Bowen paints a richly layered picture of glamour, intrigue, and sacrifice that is at once heartbreaking and hopeful. —Julia Kelly, international bestselling author, on *The Paris Apartment*

"A story of deep humanity and redemption, demonstrating the stunning beauty that can emerge from the darkest places. A true work of art." —Erika Robuck, national bestselling author, on *The Paris Apartment*

ALSO BY KELLY BOWEN

The Paris Apartment

The Garden of Lost Secrets

KELLY BOWEN

FOREVER

NEW YORK BOSTON

Copyright © 2024 by Kelly Bowen
Reading group guide copyright © 2024 by Kelly Bowen and
Hachette Book Group, Inc

Cover design by Lila Selle
Cover photo by Ilina Simeonova /Arcangel
Cover copyright © 2024 by Hachette Book Group, Inc.

Forever
Hachette Book Group
1290 Avenue of the Americas, New York, NY 10104
read-forever.com
@readforeverpub

First Edition: May 2024

Forever is an imprint of Grand Central Publishing. The Forever name and logo are registered trademarks of Hachette Book Group, Inc.

The publisher is not responsible for websites (or their content) that are not owned by the publisher.

The Hachette Speakers Bureau provides a wide range of authors for speaking events. To find out more, go to hachettespeakersbureau.com or email HachetteSpeakers@hbgusa.com.

Forever books may be purchased in bulk for business, educational, or promotional use. For information, please contact your local bookseller or the Hachette Book Group Special Markets Department at special.markets@hbgusa.com.

Print book interior design by Marie Mundaca

Library of Congress Cataloging-in-Publication Data
Names: Bowen, Kelly (Romance fiction writer) author.
Title: Tomorrow is for the brave / Kelly Bowen.
Description: First edition. | New York : Forever, 2024. |
Identifiers: LCCN 2023051335 | ISBN 9781538756935 (trade paperback) |
ISBN 9781538756942 (ebook)
Subjects: LCSH: Travers, Susan—Fiction. | World War,
1939–1945—England—Fiction. | World War, 1939–1945—Africa,
North—Fiction. | World War, 1939–1945—Participation, Female—Fiction. |
LCGFT: Biographical fiction. | War fiction. | Novels.
Classification: LCC PR9199.4.B68523 T66 2024 | DDC
813/.6—dc23/eng/20231107
LC record available at https://lccn.loc.gov/2023051335

ISBNs: 978-1-5387-5693-5 (trade paperback); 978-1-5387-5694-2 (ebook)

Printed in the United States of America

LSC-C

Printing 2, 2024

To Jhet and Lincoln, the two best teachers I've ever had. I am so proud to be your mom.

CHAPTER

1

Violet St. Croix was fifteen years old when she fell in love with something that would change her life forever. It happened on a Sunday afternoon, after an extra tennis lesson with the malcontent Monsieur Marceaux, who was renowned for his overly waxed moustache and his mean-spirited attempts to shame his pupils into better performance. It had been her father who had insisted on the lesson, disappointed with the report that Violet had failed to win her last tennis match against a younger opponent. Violet had accepted the consequences because nothing caused more strife than disappointing Commodore Robert St. Croix.

Yet the sun that afternoon had been just as merciless as Monsieur Marceaux, beating down on the exposed skin that her tennis whites did not cover and making her woolen stockings itch unbearably. By the end of the lesson, her ears ringing with shouts of contempt and scorn, Violet did not feel much improved. Instead, she only felt irritable, frustrated, and hot. Afterward, she'd waited at the tennis club for just over an hour before concluding that her mother had either forgotten to send a driver to fetch her or had, in typical fashion, simply fallen asleep with her favourite bottle of rosé before she could do so. So under a blazing August sun, Violet started the three-mile walk back to the St. Croix's villa.

As she wound her way home, Violet stuck to the shaded side of the streets as much as possible, avoiding the bright stretches where the pavement baked and broiled. Boulevard Gambetta was unusually empty for a Sunday afternoon but she took little notice of that, absorbed as she was in her own discontent, until a distant roar swelled and receded between the buildings that stretched toward the sea. A peculiar whine, like a swarm of a thousand angry hornets, cut through that sound and rose and fell along with the roar. Baffled, Violet stopped for a brief moment before she understood what she was hearing. And then, forgetting about her discomfort and frustration, she ran toward the source of all of that noise.

Violet had known that there was a car race today, an important one—everyone had talked of little else this past week and she'd seen some of the men who drove such cars arrive in town. She'd heard that over the last few days the drivers had been practicing for the Grand Prix de Nice, testing their cars through the course, though Violet had been forbidden to go and watch. Too long and too hot, her mother had told her, before pleading a headache and calling for more ice. Too dangerous and too crowded, her father had opined sternly over crackling telephone lines from his study in London.

But at the moment, neither her father nor her mother was here right now to deny her anything, and Violet hurried on until she reached the outer edges of the crowd. Yet guilt made her stop before she could join the crush. She wasn't in the habit of disobeying her parents—from the time she was little it had been made clear that, outside of tennis, school, picnics with girlfriends, and the occasional riding lesson, there was nothing in Nice suitable to entertain a young, impressionable girl. Her days were carefully scheduled, her evenings spent in the villa, all to mitigate the chance that a single poor decision on Violet's part would bring shame and scandal crashing down on the St. Croix name. And above all, Violet did not wish to be a disappointment.

But as Violet prevaricated, a rousing cheer went up, and she decided that it couldn't hurt to take a quick peek. She'd been forgotten at the tennis club, after all, and her mother would likely nap until it was time to dress for dinner, and Violet would be back home long before then. Ignoring the heady rush of rebelliousness that should have made her uncomfortable but instead felt rather thrilling, Violet joined the mob of spectators that lined the Promenade des Anglais.

The noise here was deafening, engines and tires shrieking their efforts as the cars slowed and accelerated. Around her, the crowd comprised mostly men, shouting and yelling with abandon. But there were women here too, some yelling just as loudly as the men, if not louder, some merely craning their necks for a better view. Violet edged and sidled her way through the press until she found a space at the front, just big enough to accommodate her wiry frame. It was here, against a canvas of azure sea, on concrete that was lined with straw bales, and beneath towering palms limp in the still air, that Violet got her first look at her first love.

The men driving the race cars were covered from neck to toe in overalls. Goggles covered the top halves of their faces, and leather caps were strapped securely beneath their chins. A short distance from where she was watching, down from the domed bulk of the Hotel Negresco, the course doubled back on itself, and the drivers had to slow and wrestle their cars into a hairpin turn, accelerating back in the direction that they had come. The drivers leaned and grimaced as they jockeyed for position. The car that appeared to be the leader, a bright red, low-slung model bearing the number 28 across the side, took the turn neatly, the engine growling and braying its capabilities as the driver expertly gunned his vehicle out of the turn.

Violet gaped. "Goodness," she breathed.

"Isn't he dreamy?" The voice was right in her ear.

"What?" Startled, Violet turned her head to find a girl standing beside her who couldn't be more than a year or two older than she. The girl was close enough that Violet could see the gold flecks in her brown eyes and the way her front left tooth protruded slightly over her bottom lip, which was painted a hue of crimson that her mother would never allow her to wear. She was dressed in a faded yellow frock that had a tear near the hem and a straw hat that was unravelling at the brim, though the girl seemed wholly unconcerned about any of that. Violet blinked, reflecting that Audrey St. Croix would succumb to a fit of the vapours should her daughter ever venture out in public with such disregard for her personal appearance.

The girl elbowed Violet with a wiry, darkly tanned arm and grinned at her. "Achille Varzi. He's Italian. We all think he's just the most handsome of them all, don't you?"

"Um," Violet managed, not sure what the correct response was but delighted at the idea that the comment was an invitation to be included in some unknown *we*.

The girl pulled a dented flask from the bodice of her dress and took a swig before offering it to Violet. Violet gawked before she shook her head, and the girl shrugged. "Varzi will win this year," she continued confidently, tucking her flask back into place. On the far side of Violet's companion, another girl squealed her delight as the second-place car slid through the hairpin.

"You've seen races before?" Violet asked, feeling acutely envious of this girl wearing a threadbare dress and ruined hat.

"We come to all of them. Everyone does." The girl jumped up and down and yelled something unintelligible in the direction of the track. "Don't you?"

Violet shook her head again, ashamed to admit to this worldly, uninhibited creature that her parents hadn't allowed her.

"Well then you've chosen a good one to start." The girl stuck out her hand. "I'm George."

"George?" Violet repeated, even as she took the proffered hand

and shook it like she'd seen American businessmen do regularly. The girl's palm was warm and callused, her grip strong and sure.

"Yes, George," the girl confirmed, looking amused, and Violet squirmed with embarrassment. She pulled her hand away, thinking she wouldn't blame this girl one bit if she was offended at Violet's gaucheness.

"I'm sorry. I've never met anyone named George. A girl, I mean. That is—" She stopped, wondering why she couldn't seem to just keep her mouth shut.

"It's my brother's fault," George told her. "My name, that is. When I was born, my brother was dismayed that I was a girl. My parents named me Georgette but my brother refused to call me anything other than George, as if that would somehow make me into the little brother he'd always wanted. It stuck."

"Oh." Violet tried to imagine what it would be like to have a sibling so headstrong. To have a sibling at all.

"And for his troubles," George continued with a gleeful smirk, "he got three more sisters after me." She adjusted the brim of her hat against the glare. "What about you? Do you have one?"

"No. No brothers or sisters."

"I meant, do you have a name?"

"Oh. Um. Yes. Violet. Violet St. Croix."

"Nice to meet you then, Violet St. Croix." George was still grinning with amusement, and Violet rather suspected it was now at her expense. "Tell me about the cars," she blurted.

A third vehicle was barrelling toward them, tires humming on the track, and the heat shimmering off the pavement made the car look like it was floating.

"The cars?" George turned her attention back to the race.

"What kind of cars are these?" The driver's teeth were bared as he slowed his car enough to manage the turn, accelerating away as though the hounds of hell were on his heels.

"Maseratis, Bugattis, Alfa Romeos," George told her. "You

know, if you'd wanted to see the cars, you should've come at the beginning. They parade them in front of the pits." She shrugged. "You might be able to see them at the end if you wait."

Violet digested that, wishing now that she had been here to see the beginning and wishing she could get a look at these pits. Cars weren't new to her—her family was wealthy enough to own one here in France and one back in England as well. From the back seat of both, she'd never given a great deal of thought to the lackluster, boxy vehicles that unfailingly delivered her to scheduled lessons and luncheons, other than that they were a fortunate convenience. But these cars on the track were something else entirely. Something wild and reckless, something powerful and potent. Violet wondered, for the first time, what it might be like to drive one. To know how to make such a machine work, to be able to make it fly on an endless choice of roads toward an endless choice of destinations.

To control all that power and all that possibility.

"How do they make them go so fast?" Violet breathed, watching the car vanish back up the track.

"Engines." George's eyes travelled the length of Violet's expensive tennis whites. "Not the kind your daddy probably has driving him around," she said, though not unkindly.

Violet fidgeted. "Oh."

"Varzi's is a two-nine S-eight," George told her. "Nuvolari's is a three-zero S-eight."

"Oh." Violet had no idea what that meant but she was too embarrassed to ask. "You know a lot about them."

"My brother is an avid devotee of all things on four wheels," George went on. "He talks about engines and the like a lot."

"Is he a driver?"

George snorted. "He wishes." She cocked her head. "You have a favourite?"

"A favourite?"

"Driver. Maybe Trossi? Villapadierna?" Her red mouth curled wickedly. "Someone you'd like to take home for a ride?" The deliberate innuendo was clear.

"Um." Violet couldn't find words though she was certain that she might simply burst into flame if her face got much hotter.

George laughed, her head thrown back, apparently entertained by Violet's obvious discomfiture. "You're adorable."

Violet didn't want to be adorable. Babies were adorable. Puppies were adorable. And neither were ever taken seriously.

"Have you ever driven a car like those before?" Violet asked, knowing the question was absurd and maybe a little spiteful, but it was the first thing that popped into her head as she flailed to change the subject.

George laughed again. "Never driven a car ever of any sort. But I think it would be a thrill, don't you?" She turned away from Violet as someone tugged on her arm from the far side.

"Yes," Violet mumbled. Her eyes followed the silhouette of a driver leaning hard into the turn, listening to the encouraging bellows of the men and admiring shouts of the women, all urging him on.

George was being pulled forward by her companion but she gave Violet one last crimson-coloured smirk. "It was nice to meet you, Violet St. Croix. I hope you enjoy your first race. You're bound to find yourself a favourite." She winked. A new cluster of competitors were approaching the hairpin turn, and amid a new wave of rousing enthusiasm, Violet's temporary companion pushed forward for a better look, leaving Violet forgotten and alone again in the crush.

Violet watched the new challengers navigate the course while the sun flashed off chrome and colour, numbers blurred past, and the throaty growl of the engines travelled through the pavement to reverberate in Violet's bones. When Achille Varzi sailed by the black-and-white checkered flag three hours, two minutes, and nineteen seconds after he had started the race, Violet St. Croix was there to see it. She saw the Italian driver mobbed by spectators and crew members alike, who hoisted him on their shoulders in triumph. With his cap and goggles off, she got her first glimpse of his handsome face, smiling widely. Violet couldn't help the answering smile that crept across her own face.

The girl with the yellow dress and the crimson lipstick had been right. Violet had watched long enough to find herself a favourite. To experience butterflies dancing in her stomach and enchantment singing through her veins. To fall in love. As the winner pushed forward, heading up the promenade, and the masses celebrated with abandon all around them, Violet turned away.

And headed in the opposite direction to follow a magnificent, bright red, dust- and exhaust-streaked Alfa Romeo that was being slowly rolled toward the pits.

CHAPTER
2

14 MAY 1939
NICE, FRANCE

Y ou should drive us to Paris next weekend." It was a command poorly disguised as a suggestion.

"Yes, you have to." Another voice chimed in immediately. "We have to go soon."

"I heard that they're going to start requisitioning railways." A third voice spoke with hushed urgency. "And they're calling up reservists. One of our gardeners left. Mother pitched an absolute fit. She's had to find another to look after her roses."

"Who cares about your mother's roses? It's the couture houses that I heard will close if the Germans threaten Paris. Could you just imagine?" There was a dramatic intake of breath. "It would be like being frozen in time. We'd all have to wear the same look for…" A hand accented with blood-red nails fluttered in the air. "…who knows how long? What if this is my last Balenciaga this year?" The hand brushed across the midnight-blue skirt of an evening gown. "I wouldn't be able to show my face in public. I have a reputation to uphold. That's why we need to go this weekend, Violet. To prepare."

Violet stood in the center of the small group, her fingers squeezing the stem of her champagne glass. Three sets of eyes, all lined and shaded and finished with artfully applied mascara, had her pinned in place.

She forced her fingers to relax before she broke the glass. She also forced herself to keep a pleasant smile fixed to her face and to summon the grace and patience required for such a conversation. She had grown up with these women—shared tennis lessons and music lessons and attended all the same parties and picnics—and while Violet could admit that they were often selfish and oblivious, she had to believe that they meant well. After all, they were here tonight to celebrate Violet's engagement and had brought Violet a small collection of gifts that sparkled and dazzled from their Cartier boxes.

"I can check to see if my calendar is free next weekend." Violet spoke to Gladys Durand first. The last thing Violet wanted to do was drive up to Paris. She knew she was prevaricating but she didn't want to argue. Not in the middle of this crowd where all eyes were on her. It was always hard to say no to Gladys. "Besides, you are too beautiful to worry about your reputation."

Gladys preened, pursed her ruby-painted lips, and looked slightly mollified.

Violet turned to Lydia and Florence Catroux next. "I am sorry your mother lost your gardener," she told the sisters, "but I'm sure he'll be back. Whatever hostilities might be on the horizon will be brief, I think. Saner minds will prevail."

Florence and Lydia still looked unhappy.

"I don't understand any of it but I hope it doesn't affect us," Florence pouted, twirling a chestnut curl around her finger.

"But it already is, Flo," Lydia protested. "We are supposed to go to Vienna in September on holiday, but now Father says we might have to wait. I hate waiting."

"Honestly, war is all everyone talks about anymore," Florence complained, letting her curl spring back into place. "It's so tedious. I, for one, am tired of it."

"I'm sure it will all be fine," Violet lied. She wasn't sure what was going to happen in the future but everything that she heard on the radio and read in the papers seemed to possess the same ominous thread—that the German leader appeared wholly uninterested in listening to any sort of protest or diplomatic exchange with France or Britain. "Surely no one has forgotten the tragedies and atrocities of the last war already. The soldiers and civilians who—"

"Speaking of atrocities, did you all see what Roselle Huberdeau is wearing tonight?" Gladys cut her off. "Honestly, I'm shocked that she even showed her face here."

Florence and Lydia craned their necks searching the crowd while Violet bit her tongue.

"A perfect example why we should go shopping this weekend," Gladys said, fingering the sapphires at her throat. "And Violet is the only one with a car and who can drive. It's the least you can do for friends." She fixed Violet with a look as though daring her to disagree.

"I'll check," Violet repeated, a little more sharply than she intended. "I promise." There was an inexplicable...restlessness needling her. Or maybe it was just impatience for such frivolity given the circumstances.

"You do that," Gladys purred. She reached for Violet's hand and pulled it up, examining the ring on Violet's finger. "I honestly don't know how you did it."

"Did what?"

"Managed to snare the most handsome man in the entire south of France. You've known each other for barely two months. And now you're getting married."

"I...um..." Violet had no idea how to answer. Gladys was making it sound like Violet had tricked him into proposing.

"You're not pregnant are you?" Gladys whispered.

"What? No. Of course not." It was an effort not to sound defensive and churlish.

"Well, that would be one way to end up with a diamond the size of a grapefruit on your finger."

"I can assure you that that is not the case."

"Hmph." Gladys tipped Violet's hand up toward the light. "I hope I get a diamond at least this big when I get engaged. You're so lucky."

"She knows that." A pair of arms suddenly wrapped around Violet's waist and squeezed.

Violet twisted and looked back at her fiancé, Augustino Leblanc, hoping that he hadn't heard the entirety of that conversation.

His face was flushed with heat or drink or both. "And speaking of diamonds," he said, releasing her waist, "turn back around, dear."

Violet did as she was asked and felt the brush of something cool and heavy settle around her neck.

Gladys gasped loud enough to be heard over the music.

"I was going to give these to you later," Tino said, his breath tickling the side of her ear. "But I couldn't wait." He lifted her hair from the back of her neck and fastened the clasp before releasing her. "There we go. Beautiful."

Violet raised her fingers to her throat and glanced down, the web of diamonds sitting against her skin in an intricate chain sparkling in the light.

"Oh, they're lovely, Tino. Thank you. You didn't have to do—"

"Of course I did. It's our engagement party."

"You're so lucky," Gladys said again, stepping closer to examine the necklace. She pushed her auburn hair back over her shoulder with a flip. "What a marvelous piece." The envy in her voice was unmistakable.

"Just wait until you see what I will gift her as a reward for the birth of our first son." Tino chuckled. "Leblanc men treat their women right."

"Indeed." Gladys' eyes narrowed. "I'd have a dozen boys if I could get rewarded like that." She sniffed and straightened. "Well, time to find another drink. Come along, girls." She lifted her empty champagne glass. "Congrats again. And Violet, do let's go to Paris next weekend, hmmm?"

"Of course." Violet forced a smile.

Gladys and the two sisters wandered away but not before giving Tino a flirtatious wave.

"I didn't know where you went," Violet said into the silence, for lack of anything else to say. *How many sons are you planning on having?* seemed like an awkward way to continue the conversation. Probably a conversation that they should have had earlier, but this courtship and engagement had been unexpected and a complete whirlwind, and Violet had been admittedly reluctant to venture into awkward topics.

"Doing what you should be doing, darling, and making the rounds." Tino came to stand beside her.

Violet tried another smile and this one felt more natural. Gladys hadn't been wrong when she'd called Tino handsome. With golden blond hair combed back and expertly styled, sharp cheekbones and an aquiline nose, a wide smile with straight, white teeth, and broad shoulders tapering to a narrow waist accentuated by an excellently tailored tuxedo, Tino embodied every desirable, masculine trait splashed across the pages of fashionable magazines.

"There are lots of people here tonight," he said to her. "Important people. Important connections that will be critical for both business and social success, but they need to be carefully cultivated. You can't just hide away here in the corner with your friends."

"I wasn't hiding away," Violet said. "I—"

"It's all right. No need to apologize. You'll learn. Once you're a Leblanc, you won't have much choice, I'm afraid." He carefully smoothed his hair with his fingers to make sure that it hadn't fallen out of place. "But speaking of your friends, you should listen to Gladys."

"Gladys?"

He stepped back and let his eyes roam up her body. "Drive up to Paris next weekend, darling. Do some shopping."

"Why?" Violet was confused.

"You look lovely, of course, but you've worn that dress before. And it's rather plain."

Violet glanced down at her dress. It was her favourite, made of pale rose satin that shimmered in sunlight and glowed in candlelight. It was draped across the top of the bodice, secured by narrow straps, and gathered at her waist before falling in a simple cascade of fabric to the floor.

"You'll need to dress better from here on out. And I'd encourage you to acquire a style that is more…dramatic. Modern. Schiaparelli will suit. And Lanvin, I think. Worth should also be considered, at least for formal occasions. I'll send you a list with colours and cuts that I think will best flatter you. Money is no object, of course. Have Gladys help you choose a few pieces. Once we're married, I'll accompany you and make my own selections." He paused. "As my wife, you deserve a new wardrobe that will make me proud to show you off. Appearances matter."

"Oh." Violet knew she should be pleased. Gladys would be squealing with hysterics at the prospect. Most girls would. Goodness, her own mother would be tripping over herself at such an offer.

"I'll think about it." She was prevaricating again because she wasn't feeling pleased at all. But she didn't know how to tell her fiancé that she didn't really like shopping all that much, nor did she particularly like the idea of someone else picking out her clothes for her like she was a child. But that seemed like another awkward topic, especially in the face of his generosity.

"Do better than think about it, darling." Tino took her hand and kissed the back of it. "And promise me you'll also get rid of those horrid work clothes you insist on wearing. I don't particularly like trousers on women and certainly not on my wife."

"I wear those when I'm working on my car," Violet said.

Tino patted the hand he held. "Ah, yes. Your car. I meant to speak to you about that."

Violet tensed instantly.

Tino laughed. "No need to look so worried, my dear. While I admit I thought it rather odd at first that a woman should wish to drive herself about, I have come around to the idea. Your father endorsed it years ago, of course, and it certainly makes you popular with your friends, which is never a bad thing. But rest assured, I will make certain you have a safe vehicle to drive and one that is maintained for you. Something new. And not quite as fast," he added with a rueful shake of his head.

"But I like my car. And I like working on it." Violet was aware her voice had risen and every muscle in her body was taught. The glass was cutting into her fingers again, only this time she didn't release it.

A few heads had turned in their direction, and she bit back the rest of her words, unwilling to make a scene. Certainly not in front of these people, all part of the Leblancs' carefully curated guest list and who all wielded wealth, influence, power, and notoriety like the weapons they could be. Violet had seen firsthand the damage that could be wrought by a bored, jaded society hungry for scandal to feed their amusement.

Tino glanced around, a shadow of irritation flickering across his handsome features. "Violet, be reasonable. While driving is one thing, gadding about like a common…mechanic is another. I only want the very best for you. You know that."

Tino told her that often, and he'd given her no reason not to believe him. He had certainly proven himself different from the men that Gladys and Florence and Lydia had always thrown into her path—desperate writers and starving artists, cynical socialites and disgraced royalty, whose sole ambition seemed to be their devotion to opium- and alcohol-fuelled debauchery.

Tino, on the other hand, had sought her out and spoken to her about Dumas and Hugo. He'd even gifted her with a first edition of *Les Misérables*. He had taken her to the theater and had listened to Violet's opinion when he'd asked if she'd liked the production. He'd fetched her drinks and asked her to dance when no one else had. He'd brought her flowers and never forgot a second bouquet for her mother when he called at their villa. He spoke often of his family and the responsibility he had inherited in assuming control of their manufacturing business. He seemed like a man in a mob of boys.

"You're right. I'm sorry. I know you only want what's best for me." Violet put a placating hand on his sleeve. The marquis-cut diamond on her finger flashed.

"Good girl." Tino bent and gave her a peck on the cheek. "Trust that I will take care of you. I'll make sure you don't have to worry about anything."

Violet made herself smile for the benefit of those around her. She would bring the matter of her car up with him later, carefully. Her car was not something that she would willingly give up but this engagement party was neither the time nor place.

Tino tucked her hand more securely under his arm. "Now, join me out on the terrace. There are some people that you need to meet. You've been with your friends long enough."

Something in Violet resisted though she wasn't sure why. She pulled her hand back. "I'll be right there," she told him.

His brows drew together in what looked like displeasure.

"Just have to visit the ladies' room for a moment," she continued. "I'd like to freshen up first."

Tino's expression cleared. "Of course. I'll meet you out there. Don't be long, darling."

Violet nodded. She watched him retreat, his handsome silhouette cutting a swath through the crowd amid happy bonhomie and congratulatory wishes. Still clutching her half-empty champagne glass, she slipped through the crowd, heading not toward the ladies' room but in the opposite direction. She made her way through the kitchens, generally ignored by the hired staff loading trays with food and sweets, and out into the darkened and deserted back garden.

The air out here, away from the heat and the humidity of the crowd, was cool, and Violet dragged in a few deep breaths. From the tall, open windows of the Leblanc villa, bright panes of light splashed across the stone walkways and manicured foliage. Music, mixed with peals of laughter and a hundred conversations, floated on the evening breeze, yet here it was mercifully muted. Violet tipped her head up to the sky, the stars and the moon partially obscured by patchy veils of clouds drifting across the dark expanse.

The nagging restlessness that she had been battling all evening still clung to the edges of her conscience. Violet closed her eyes, chastising herself. This evening should be one of the happiest of her life. It was a toast to new beginnings and all the wonderful things that still awaited her in a future full of... Violet opened her eyes.

A future full of what?

"Ditching the groom before you even get to the altar?"

Violet jumped, and the remaining champagne in her glass sloshed over the rim and across her wrist. She turned to discover that she wasn't alone in the garden at all.

"Lady Enid," Violet stammered shaking the droplets from her hand and arm.

"You know who I am." The woman in the garden with Violet was leaning casually against a stone pillar crisscrossed with clinging clematis.

She was tall, as tall as Violet, with platinum-blonde hair and piercing green eyes, and was wearing a white lace dress that clung to astounding curves and glittered with crystal tassels along the hem. A string of emeralds twinkled from her throat and more dangled at her ears. She held a slim, lacquered cigarette case that was open, her bejewelled fingers paused halfway to the neat row of cigarettes within.

"Everyone knows who you are," Violet said artlessly. It was the truth.

"Indeed? I suppose I'll choose to take that as a compliment," Lady Enid said.

"It is, I assure you." Violet cringed. "We haven't met but I knew you and his lordship were invited, of course, and—" She stopped babbling before she embarrassed herself any further. Lady Enid Furness was infamous among every social circle of southern France and probably the rest of the country too. She possessed money and a title. She oozed confidence and daring. She was assertive, seductive, unapologetic. Everything Violet wasn't.

The viscountess seemed to find Violet's blundering amusing. She selected a cigarette and offered the case in Violet's direction.

Violet shook her head. "I don't smoke."

Enid shrugged and snapped the case closed. "It's not too late to reconsider, you know."

"No, my father didn't want me smoking when I was younger, and now I don't really—"

Lady Enid laughed, a low throaty sound. "I meant it's not too late to reconsider the wedding."

Violet gawked. What a bizarre thing to say at an engagement party. "Why would I want to do that?"

"Why, indeed." Lady Enid set the case on top of the stone pillar and produced a lighter. "If it's the sex you're looking forward to, I can assure you that that can be had anywhere. At any time. And with any man of your choosing." Her lips curled. "One does not need a ring for that."

"Um. That's…um…"

"I'm on my third one. Husband, that is," she clarified. "Though they are not nearly as…necessary as people seem to think they are."

Violet wondered if the viscountess was trying to shock her on purpose. It was certainly working.

"Is it because of the war?"

Violet frowned. "Is what because of the war?"

"The wedding. Are you getting married ahead of the war? So many people are rushing to get married now."

"No. I mean, that's not the reason we're getting married." She stopped. "You really think we're going to war?"

"I think it's unavoidable. I watched the last one start." She seemed to be searching for the right words. "I think this one already has."

Violet shivered.

"I heard that you drive." The viscountess lit her cigarette, and the flame jumped.

"I beg your pardon?" The abrupt change in topic caught Violet off guard.

"Drive. Cars." She waved the lighter in a circular motion. "Not a common skill for a young woman."

"I do, yes. Drive, I mean." Violet hesitated. "You…er…"

"I what?" Enid demanded. "Good Lord, girl, say what you mean and mean what you say."

"You're actually one of the reasons I drive," Violet confessed.

"Me? How so?"

"I asked my father for driving lessons when I was sixteen. He refused at first. I pointed out that you drove, and if the wife of a viscount and a lady of the peerage did so, then it was perfectly acceptable for me."

"A title won him over, did it?"

"I suppose."

"Not your talent or ambition?"

"Well, I… That's not exactly what I…"

"How very British. Well, pleased to be of service, then." Enid put her out of her misery, and another low chuckle danced through the garden. "Do you enjoy driving?"

"More than anything," Violet enthused. "It's utterly...liberating."

"It is, isn't it?"

"Is it true that you drove an ambulance in the last war?" Violet ventured. She had heard someone say that. She had also heard that Lady Enid had slept her way through half a regiment during that same war, but she would never ask about that.

"It is. At the time, I had no idea what I was getting myself into. Those were some of the most terrifying moments of my life." The viscountess no longer sounded amused.

"Why did you do it, then?"

"Because I was good at it. I learned quite a bit about myself. Everyone always tells you that adversity and struggle builds character, but they're wrong. It doesn't build anything. It only reveals what was already there." Enid took a drag on her cigarette and exhaled. "Will you? Volunteer?"

"Yes." Violet's answer was immediate. "I want to do what you did. I think I'd be good at it too."

"You've thought about it, then." It was more of a statement than a question.

"Quite a bit. It's hard not to. It's all anyone talks about anymore." Florence had said that earlier, and the while the words were the same, the sentiment and gravity of this conversation could not be any more different. "I don't think I could do nothing if the worst happened."

Lady Enid was studying her keenly and unrepentantly. "When I first received the Leblancs' invitation to this party, I wasn't going to come, you know. It's a little...sedate for my taste, though I mean no offense by that. And while I am somewhat acquainted with your fiancé, I'd never met you." She brought her cigarette to her lips again and inhaled. "But then someone told me that they had seen you driving out by Cap Roux. Even more scandalizing, they whispered that they had seen you changing a tyre on the side of the road. By yourself." The viscountess blew out a stream of smoke. "And I thought right then that perhaps I should very much like to meet this young woman."

Violet felt a flush of pride.

"Will you be allowed?"

"I beg your pardon?" The pride evaporated at the question.

"I know who your father is. And I know who your fiancé is." She tapped ash from the end of her cigarette, and it drifted silently to the ground. "Will they allow you to volunteer?"

"I…" Violet stopped. "Of course they will," she said, knowing no such thing. Another awkward topic she had avoided with Tino, knowing that it was bound to cause at least some friction. But until war was declared, the point was moot, was it not? And why go looking to create conflict?

"Mmm." A perfectly sculpted brow rose. "Have you discussed it with them?"

"No. Not yet. But it won't matter. It would be my decision." She was lying again, and she knew it.

"I hope you're right." The viscountess shifted, and the crystals on her dress flashed. "The world needs more women who can change a tyre for themselves on the side of a road, Miss St. Croix. Now more than ever. Women who do not seek permission or apology to live."

"I don't," Violet said defensively. In her ears, it sounded like an accusation. Or maybe Violet was simply reacting to an uncomfortable truth.

"Then I'm glad to hear it. Tell me, how did you meet your fiancé?"

It was another abrupt change of topic though Violet was a little more prepared this time.

"At the tennis club." Tino had introduced himself to her after a tournament. She'd been sweaty and dishevelled yet the attention he'd lavished on her had made her feel like the most beautiful woman in the world. He'd complimented her on her play, on her grace, and on her success. He was the first man to make her feel special and esteemed, and she'd been smitten.

"Ah. So you are both tennis players."

Violet nodded.

"I've heard that you are very good," the viscountess said. "A tournament champion, even."

"I do all right."

"No need for modesty, Miss St. Croix. You should be proud of your accomplishments." Enid was back to looking amused. "And what does your fiancé say when you beat him on the regular?"

"Oh, we've never played each other."

"Why not? It's nice to have something in common with your spouse."

"He's…um…very busy," Violet said.

Enid chuckled. "He's not very good, is he? Doesn't want to lose to you?"

Violet bit the inside of her cheek, feeling like she would be disloyal if she were to admit the truth in that. "He's busy," she repeated. "Though he comes to watch me whenever he can."

"I'm sure he does." Lady Enid crushed out her cigarette on the edge of the stone pillar. "Let me just leave you with some marriage advice, then. I've been widowed twice, borne three children, travelled widely. I've seen enough of the world and learned enough about people that very little surprises me anymore." She reached for Violet's hand and lifted it gently, examining the engagement ring that glinted between them. "Don't become an accessory. Not to anyone." She tapped a manicured nail on the diamond. "You may lose your name but don't lose who you are when you become Mrs. Augustino Leblanc. Your greatest accomplishment in life should not be a wedding. Do not allow yourself to be reduced to a mere extension of another."

Violet was rooted to the ground, unable to move. "I won't. Of course I won't."

The viscountess shook her head. "It's an easy thing to say, but standing on your own two feet and becoming your own person will be the hardest thing you'll ever do." Her fingers fell away from Violet's. "It will take courage. People will tell you that you'll fail—and you might. Probably will. But that failure will be a necessary part of a greater success. And if you're lucky, your husband will be a partner and a friend first and not—"

"Violet." Her name was called from the far side of the garden.

Both women turned, and Violet watched as Tino marched across the stone clearing.

"I gave up and had to come find you. I dislike being made to wait—" He stopped just short of Violet and seemed surprised to find that she had company.

He recovered quickly. "Lady Enid, how lovely to see you this evening. You look stunning, as always. We're so very pleased you could come."

"Thank you," the viscountess replied politely though her expression was cool. "My congratulations to you both. You must be looking forward to the wedding. I do hope the current turmoil across the continent does not interfere with your plans."

"I am certain that it won't come to that," Tino assured her. His gaze strayed to the villa windows. "I apologize if I've interrupted anything important, but I must insist that my darling Violet joins me in—"

"Oh, we were just talking cars," the viscountess purred. "As women do. And the opportunities that will allow us to volunteer to serve our country if this unrest escalates into something more serious."

Tino's gaze snapped back. "I'm sorry?"

Violet winced.

"You should be very proud of your fiancée. She was telling me that she will indeed volun—"

Violet let her champagne glass fall, and it shattered across the stone. She ignored the burn of her conscience that labelled her a coward. "Goodness, I'm very sorry," she said. "I'll clean it—"

"Leave it," Tino said. "I'll send someone to take care of it." He turned back to Enid. "Forgive me, my lady, but while I can commend you on your patriotism, I should hope that there would be no need for you ladies to get involved, even if matters escalate, as you've said." Tino was frowning. "I'll endeavour to make sure Miss St. Croix is kept safely away from any unpleasantness. She means too much to me. There is no need to alarm her."

The viscountess retrieved her cigarette case and tapped it against her thigh. She slid her gaze to Violet, and to her shame, Violet looked away.

"A noble sentiment," Enid murmured, and it sounded like anything but a compliment.

Violet raised her eyes again.

The viscountess aimed a sudden, brilliant smile in the direction of Violet and Tino. "But you're right, of course. Such gloomy conversation on a night meant for celebration. I bid you both good night and felicitations." She brushed Violet's arm with her fingers. "Do think carefully on our conversation, Miss St. Croix."

Violet watched as the viscountess took her leave, her white dress swaying back across the garden.

"What on earth possessed you to come out here and speak to that woman?" Tino turned on her the moment Lady Enid was out of earshot.

Violet frowned. "That woman is a viscountess, Tino. I can't ignore her."

"A viscountess with a husband who has been forced to hire a private detective to follow her around because she can't be trusted on her own. Her behaviour is appalling. She sleeps with any man she pleases. Does whatever she wants with whoever she wants whenever she wants. She keeps a damn cheetah on a leash for attention. She is not the sort that I want you associating with."

"You invited her."

"I invited her husband."

The nagging restlessness was back, and Violet wasn't sure if it was Lady Enid's last words or Tino's that were causing such deep disquiet.

"Now please, Violet, can we just return to our party and enjoy it? There are still people waiting for you to greet them, and I cannot make excuses for you forever, darling." He tucked her hand under his arm and guided her away from the broken glass, back toward the villa.

"Of course," Violet mumbled. And as she was enveloped into the crush of well-wishers once again, the music swelling in a cheerful symphony, a new glass of champagne that she would never drink pressed into her hand, she wondered.

Wondered who was making excuses for whom.

CHAPTER
3

8 JUNE 1939
NICE, FRANCE

Y our father would like you to report to his study."
The message was delivered to Violet by a weary-looking
housekeeper holding a tray of empty glasses and assorted dishes left
scattered throughout the St. Croix villa from the alcohol-soaked
soiree her mother had hosted last night.

"Now?" Violet checked her watch. It was just after nine in the
morning, an implausible hour for her mother to be awake and an
unlikely hour for her newly arrived father to demand an audience.

"At eleven o'clock," the housekeeper clarified. "He is out on an
appointment at the moment."

"Oh. Thank you," Violet said, unnerved by the request. Her
father rarely wished to see her more than once on his annual visits
back to France. He expected a succinct debriefing each time he
returned to Nice, of course, and Violet had learned as a child that
a precise report on her performance in tennis, the classroom, and
the array of other lessons was all that was necessary. As she got
older and her lessons dwindled, her reports became briefer, which
seemed to suit them both. She'd already presented herself to her
father yesterday afternoon when he'd arrived distracted and harried from London, and she wasn't even sure he'd heard a word
she'd said.

Violet may not have been a commodore but she, too, could feel the change in the air—as if they were all standing on a cliff, waiting to see if the wind would rise to blow them over the edge or subside to allow a safe retreat. Fascist Italy and Nazi Germany had signed an alliance pact. The Germans had also tamed the Soviets with another. The Brits were still threatening to intervene if Germany were to invade Poland, and France was on edge, amassing resources to prepare for an attack that had seemed unthinkable only months prior.

Yet everyone here was still carrying on like none of that existed, arriving in decadent furs, sumptuous jewels, and expensive cars to an endless parade of evenings spent in extravagant villas, opulent hotels, and luxurious casinos. It seemed no one could get enough of the revelry, and if the continent was hurtling toward war and destruction, then all the more reason to make merry while they could. The absurdity of it all was difficult for Violet to grasp.

France was going to need men and women to help prepare for a war, not another party.

The conversation she'd had with Lady Enid about volunteering had weighed more heavily on her mind with each passing day, and with it, the conviction that she would not be able to stand by and do nothing should the very worst happen and France got pulled into another war. She hadn't yet broached the subject with her father or her fiancé because, deep down, Violet was already afraid she knew what their response would be. But neither man was here right now. And there was certainly no harm in simply asking questions and acquiring knowledge, was there? When she did present her father and Tino with her intention to volunteer, it would be better if she could present a clear, articulate case based on facts and research and not conjecture. It wasn't like she would need to sign anything or make anything official today. If she left now, she'd be back in plenty of time for her father's summons.

And no one would ever know.

★ ★ ★

The recruiting offices for the Red Cross weren't far from the military recruiting stations, and both were busy. Violet parked her car a street over and joined the queue outside the Red Cross station. She craned her neck, trying to get a better view inside, and wondered if this had been a mistake. She checked her watch anxiously.

"Got somewhere important to be, Violet St. Croix?"

Violet's head snapped up, a rush of momentary panic surging through her at the thought that someone had recognized her here. She met a pair of dancing hazel eyes and a wide smile that boasted a slightly crooked left front tooth.

Violet's memory jolted, and relief soothed her panic. "You're George. We met once at the grand prix."

"You remember?" George sounded delighted.

"I do." The day of that grand prix had been a revelation for Violet, and she remembered everything.

"I'm actually surprised," George mused. "That you would remember me, that is. That was a long time ago."

"I remember that you were very kind to me," Violet told her. "I remember that you took the time to explain about the cars and the engines and the drivers when you didn't have to."

"Well, I'm glad I left a good impression." George's fraying straw hat and bright lipstick from that day had been replaced by a neat braid and freshly scrubbed face, but the open cheerfulness of her expression hadn't changed. "What are you doing here?"

"I'd like to volunteer with the Red Cross." Not a lie.

"As a nurse? They're looking for many."

"Is that what you are volunteering to do?" Violet asked. "Become a nurse?"

"Yes."

Violet eyed the patchwork of posters that had been tacked all along the sides of the little office, all depicting a white flag with a crimson cross flying over what looked like dark images of barbed wire, guns, and trenches. "I don't know if I'd be a good nurse," she admitted. "I was hoping to volunteer as an ambulance driver."

"An ambulance driver?" George laughed.

Violet took a step back, every muscle in her body stiff. "I've been driving for a long time," she said. "Not ambulances, I mean, at least not yet, but I think I would be good at it once I had some hours behind the wheel."

George put a hand on her hip. "I'm sure you would."

Violet couldn't tell if George was making fun of her or not. Perhaps she thought Violet was simply being adorable again.

"That day with you at the grand prix opened my eyes. Introduced me to cars and driving, and I know not many people approve of me under the bonnet or behind the wheel—"

George smirked.

"What's so funny?"

"No one ever approves of women who do things that they're not supposed to do. Women who don't fit into the image that someone else has in their head about how she should act or work or speak. Eleanor of Aquitaine would probably tell you the same thing." She glanced at Violet. "Yes, we learned about her in our little school too."

Violet flushed. "I wasn't—that is, I didn't think that you didn't—"

George waved her hand, cutting off Violet's sputtering. "It's just a fact that you need to come to terms with or you'll be unhappy the rest of your life. We can't control how others choose to think. Best to just keep on living without trying to please everyone but yourself."

Violet absorbed her words and obvious conviction. "How do you know that?"

"I fish," George said simply.

"Fish?"

"Our family business. My father used to but he lost most of his vision four years ago. Everyone expected that my brother would take over the boat and nets, and he does help out, but I am good at it. Really good at it. Turns out the girls in our family have a knack for it. And so it's usually me and my brother, or me and at least one of my sisters, out on the water every day. It's a little different now, but in the beginning, I think we all heard just about every useless, unsolicited opinion." She held up four fingers of her right hand. "Fishing is a man's job, and my sisters and I have forgotten our place." She folded the first finger. "We can't possibly be safe on our own. Or competent. Or both." Another two fingers went down. "We would never be able to find husbands." She paused thoughtfully. "Never could quite figure out what being able to manage a boat and an outboard and a handful of nets had to do with us getting married."

For a moment, Violet wondered what sort of remarkable man was married to this remarkable woman. But she didn't want to ask because she didn't want to bring up Tino or have to confess that she hadn't even told him about her intentions to volunteer because she feared his reaction.

"My parents have always told me that everyone's place is not defined by the opinions of others but where they are happiest." George smiled at her. "I think that's good advice, don't you?"

Violet was trying to imagine the commodore ever encouraging her to ignore the opinions of others and couldn't. The opinions of others had always been like a living, fire-breathing dragon in her life, ready to snuff out her very existence at the merest hint of misjudgement. This picture that George so easily painted, where perspective was defined by happiness and capability, was utterly foreign. And utterly mesmerizing.

"But what about your boat? What happens if we go to war and they send you somewhere?"

"Then one of my younger sisters takes over." George shrugged again. "They're quite capable on their own."

Violet gazed at the women in line in front of her and wondered if these women also lived without apology like George rather than in constant fear of misstep like her. They were all dressed like George, in plain, serviceable dresses and solid, sensible shoes, and they all seemed to possess an unflinching aura of competency and capability.

"I didn't expect there to be so many people volunteering." George had followed her gaze and misread her thoughts. "But we should be in soon to see a clerk. In case you have somewhere to be, I mean."

"Not really," Violet murmured.

"Why don't you think you'd make a good nurse?" George asked abruptly.

The line inched forward, and Violet shuffled closer to the office door alongside George.

"I can't stand the sight of blood," Violet confessed in a whisper. "At all. That's why I don't know if I could ever be a nurse. What if I can't do it? What if I'm not good at it?" It felt strangely freeing to speak that fear out loud. "I've never told anyone that."

"Well, I'm certainly not going to tell anyone," George said with a shrug. "And you don't know that you're not going to be good at something until you try it, right?"

"I suppose," Violet agreed slowly.

"Besides, unless you're a vampire in one of those novels my brother reads, no one really likes the sight of blood," George reassured her. "Even nurses. Especially nurses, I would think."

"Maybe."

"You'll surprise yourself, you know. About how much you can really do."

Violet wondered if she would ever reach a point in her life

where she was as unapologetically confident as this woman standing beside her.

"You should come fishing with me and my sisters sometime," George offered. "I think you would like it."

"Oh, I'm not sure that I should—"

"What is there not to be sure about?" George asked, sounding amused.

If Violet was being completely honest, she would tell George that she wasn't sure that she would be allowed. It didn't sound like something the commodore would approve of, and her mother would never consider George suitable company.

But Violet also knew that neither one of her parents would approve of her being here, outside a Red Cross office, and yet here she was. And the sky hadn't fallen and a plague of locusts hadn't descended.

Violet nodded. "All right."

"Good." George linked her arm through Violet's. "We live just past Cap Roux. It's the yellow house up on the side of the hill, across the road from the beach. Do you know it?"

"Yes. I mean, not your house, specifically, but I've driven by there many times. I know where the beach is. I've seen the boats."

"You could come anytime, you know. I'm on the beach by dawn with our gear, out on the water shortly after, back in the afternoon with our catch to get it ready for sale in the markets. My sisters are out today, of course, so that I could be here to apply, but it's almost always me. Just ask for George Chastain and someone will point you in the right direction. You're always welcome."

Violet found herself grinning at George. "Thank you. I'd like that." She wasn't sure if it was the prospect of friendship or freedom or adventure or maybe all three that made her feel almost giddy inside.

"Good," George said again.

"Will you stay?" Violet asked suddenly. "While I talk to the

clerk inside?" She wasn't sure why she asked that, other than standing beside this woman made Violet believe that she might really be
able to do anything.

"Of course," George told her.

The line moved forward again.

George slanted Violet a mischievous look. "Did you ever pick
a favourite?"

"A favourite?"

"That day at the grand prix when I first met you?"

Violet smiled. "Yes."

"Who was it?"

"Alfa Romeo."

George tipped her head back and laughed, loud enough to turn
a few heads. "Ah, see, Violet St. Croix, I knew we were going to be
great friends."

★ ★ ★

The clerk tapped his pencil impatiently on the paper in front of
him. "No nursing experience? First aid training? Hospice work?"

"I'm afraid not," Violet replied, catching herself twisting the
edge of her lavender Lelong skirt with her fingers. She forced
her hand to drop. She deliberately did not glance at George,
who was standing loyally beside her, and instead squared her
shoulders.

"What about care of an elderly family member, midwifery,
tending children?"

"No, nothing."

"What about farm experience? Livestock?"

Violet shook her head. George had had an exhaustive list of
experience that had seemed relevant to the clerk, from tending to
her younger siblings as they suffered through the usual assortment
of childhood illnesses, to setting her brother's broken finger after
a fight, to even expertly gutting and cleaning the myriad of fish

that she and her family hauled in from the sea every year. Real-life experience that was all useful.

"Does it matter that I have no nursing experience?" Violet asked.

The clerk grunted. "Probably not. We're always short volunteers." He scratched at his thick grey beard and leaned back in his chair. "What else can you do?"

"I can speak Italian. And English. And Spanish."

"Mmm." He made a note on her application. "That's something I suppose. What about German?"

"A little."

"Hmph." His pencil scratched. "Are you willing to travel? Work out of country if it becomes necessary?"

"Um." Violet wasn't sure how Tino would react to that. "Yes." She'd worry about travel when she crossed that bridge, if in fact, it ever came to that.

The clerk recorded her response. "What else?"

"What else?"

"What else would make you a good nurse for the Red Cross?"

George nudged her subtly.

"I'm a good driver." Violet hesitated before she hurried on. "I wanted to volunteer to drive an ambulance."

"We don't need ambulance drivers. Certainly not women. We have men for that."

"But in the past, women have driven—"

"The Red Cross requires women to work as nurses." He was scowling at her as he said that. "And we will provide suitable training as necessary."

"I could do that." Even in her ears, it sounded uncertain. "Train as a nurse if that's what it takes to get into an ambulance."

"I don't think you're hearing me, miss. You'll never drive an ambulance. Women cannot be assigned to combat or field positions because they simply don't have the character or temperament.

Women are assigned to hospitals, where they will comfort and care for those men who fight on their behalf. Am I making myself clear?"

"Yes."

The clerk stamped the date on the top of her paper and shoved it in her direction. "Fill out the rest of this with your name and address and return it to the field clerk at the far end. You'll be contacted by mail at a later date. Expect to start training in early September." He waved in the general direction of the desk at the very rear of the office. "Next!"

Violet was jostled aside as the next applicant moved forward, and George caught her arm and steered her away.

"Here," she said, handing Violet the stub of a pencil. "I'll wait for you to fill out your form and hand it in. I already did mine. It doesn't take very long."

Violet made no move to take the pencil.

"Oh, come on," George chided. "He wasn't very friendly but he did kind of make sense."

"What do you mean?"

"Well, when you start driving ambulances, I think it makes sense that you have good first aid training. You're going to need it."

"He said that I wouldn't be allowed to drive—"

"And how does an old man sitting at a desk know what is going to happen in the future?" George scoffed. "He doesn't. Maybe you won't drive an ambulance. Maybe you will. Maybe we won't go to war. Maybe we will. He doesn't control any of that. But what he does control, at this moment, is the requirement for you to complete nursing training, which seems beneficial no matter what happens in the future, don't you think?"

"I suppose." George did have a point. "I—" She stumbled forward as someone bumped into her from behind.

"Let's go outside where it isn't so crowded," George suggested, sidling through the congested space and pulling Violet along behind her. "Fill out the rest of your application and then you can take it back in."

Violet followed George out of the little office and back into the sunshine. The day was already heating up, the sun brilliant where it bounced off the stuccoed buildings and glassy windows. She wiped the perspiration from the side of her face and above her lip and shuffled into the meager shade of a palm, away from the crowd.

"Here." George handed her the pencil, and this time Violet took it.

Carefully, she wrote her name at the top of the application, trying very hard not to dwell on the empty lines under the heading "Prior Experience." Up until now, volunteering had seemed like an abstract hope. Something that she had imagined in vague terms. But being here, surrounded by women and men in uniform, the prospect was very real. And holding on to the application, a tangible declaration of her intent, Violet hesitated, battling uncertainty. No matter how encouraging George might be, Violet still harboured deep doubt of her own abilities and reservations about the conflicts this may create with both her father and Tino. Maybe she should take a little longer to consider what she was doing. She had come here to gather information, after all. Not to make any hasty decisions.

"Are you done?" George peered over her shoulder.

"Not quite yet." Violet toyed with the pencil. Abruptly, she handed it back to George.

"But you're not finished filling out the top section," George said.

"I'm going to finish filling it out at home," Violet told her. That was true. "And then I'll bring it back." She wasn't sure if that was true or not, and that admission held an uncomfortable undercurrent of shame and cowardice.

"Why? This is what you came here to do, and you're already here."

"I don't want to make you wait." That was a poor excuse, and Violet knew it.

"I don't mind."

"I'll bring it back later," Violet repeated. She folded the application neatly into a square and made a point to glance at her watch. "Thank you anyway. But I have a meeting with my father shortly," she said. "And he does not tolerate tardiness. I really should go." The feeling of shame and cowardice grew.

"All right." George shrugged and tucked the stubby pencil into a pocket. "Well, I'm glad that I met you again."

"Me too." Violet meant that.

"I hope I'll see you on the beach sometime soon, Violet St. Croix." George gave Violet one of her wide grins and a brief wave. "The invitation is always there. Don't be a stranger."

CHAPTER
4

9 JUNE 1939
NICE, FRANCE

Violet had retreated to the upper floor of the St. Croix villa sometime past midnight.

The dinner party had reached the stage when the food had been long forgotten and the guests were fully foxed, unbearably loud, demanding more drink and music, and likely to depart sometime after the sun rose. So by all standards, a rousing success. Violet would undoubtedly be reading about the guests and the décor and the fashion in the society pages for days to come. Her mother would be thrilled at the attention. Her father would be pleased with the attendance. Tino would be satisfied with the high society names that would forever be linked to his in black ink, published for all and sundry to read.

Violet just wanted it all to be over.

The meeting with her father earlier that morning had been a perfunctory affair—nothing more than a review of the dinner party details. Violet had tried to summon enthusiasm but had failed, still bothered by a nagging sense of ignominy and cravenness that had followed her home from the recruiting station. She'd obediently agreed to everyone on the guest list, taken no interest in the menu, and not cared that the musicians that had been hired were extraordinarily talented. She hadn't even been able to summon an iota of defiance when Tino sent her back up to change after she came downstairs in her favourite rose satin gown. She had met the guests who'd arrived at their villa as expected, had smiled and kissed cheeks as required, offered compliments effusively, and carried shallow dinner conversation as was custom. And as soon as she could, she escaped upstairs.

It was blessedly quieter up here, away from the din of the party. It was cooler too, though the heat of the night still refused to relinquish its grip on the upper floors entirely. The windows had all been opened but there was little breeze to stir the air. She caught sight of herself in the long gilt mirror at the end of the hall and paused, thinking that the woman who stared back looked like a stranger.

Her flyaway honey-blonde curls had been tamed and styled into artful waves. Her grey eyes, which she'd never thought overly remarkable, seemed more dramatic lined with kohl and mascara. She wore a new Lanvin gown, selected by Gladys and approved by Tino, and the bronze satin clung to her shoulders, hugged her hips, and plunged almost indecently deep in the front of her décolletage. Tino's diamonds encircled her throat, a glittering collar, and the entire effect was one of sophisticated glamour. Yet Violet felt neither sophisticated nor glamorous.

The sound of raised voices distracted her from the mirror, and Violet turned in the direction of her father's study. From behind the heavy wooden door, she could hear the muffled sound of the commodore directing his wrath at someone or something, which was not unusual. What was unusual was that it was her mother's voice that responded. Violet couldn't remember the last time, if ever, she had seen Audrey St. Croix in the commodore's study. It must be dire, whatever it was that they were arguing about, if Audrey had left the party downstairs. Violet stood frozen with indecision over whether she should knock or retreat. Perhaps her father had had news from England. Perhaps something had changed, or something had happened that had inched France closer to war. Or perhaps they were just arguing over the last furrier bill.

The door to the study banged open, and Violet jumped. Her father took two steps into the hall before stopping short as he saw her.

"You're already here," he said. "Good. Saves me the trouble of sending someone to fetch you."

"I beg your pardon?"

"Join your mother and me in the study." He gestured for Violet to precede him.

Slowly, Violet entered. This room was her father's domain and where he held court when he was here. Unlike the rest of the villa, it was not airy and bright but ornamented with rich patterned burgundy wallpaper and ponderous walnut bookcases. Paintings of English thoroughbreds and hunting scenes from a century gone by hung in gilded frames, and an expensive Persian rug covered most of the floor.

Her mother was draped in a chair off to the side, a glass of cognac in one hand and the bottle in the other. She was drinking languidly with a familiar expression of resigned boredom stamped across her beautiful features, like that of an unrepentant pupil called to the headmaster's office. Violet's father followed her in and stood behind his polished ebony desk, looking like a very displeased headmaster.

"What's wrong?" Violet blurted, looking back and forth between her parents. "Has something happened?"

"Is Tino with you?"

"No. Was he supposed to be?" She wasn't even sure where he was in the melee downstairs.

"I had thought to include him, yes." Her father drummed his fingers on the desk. "But no matter. Just as well that we have this conversation in private. Close the door, Violet."

"Oh, for God's sake," her mother groused. "Just get this over with so we can go back to the party." She slurred her last word slightly. "This party was supposed to be for you, after all." She snorted into her glass. "The return of the prodigal husband—"

"There is no need for the servants or anyone else to hear any of this," the commodore snapped. "I can't abide gossip, especially about my family."

Audrey rolled her eyes and topped up her glass.

Violet retraced her steps and closed the door before returning to the center of the room.

"We're going back to London, aren't we?" Violet guessed. She'd heard more than a few people talking about getting out of France ahead of whatever political or military turmoil was coming their way. Perhaps her father had decided that they too should—

"No, we are not. While the Home Guard requires me back in London in two days' time, there is no good reason that you or your mother need to accompany me." He was speaking slowly and deliberately, as if keeping a tight rein on his patience.

Violet could think of a couple of good reasons, namely men named Mussolini and Hitler, and the trouble that they might be brewing, but she held her tongue.

"Then what is so important that you—"

The commodore brought a hand down on the polished surface of the desk with an angry thump. A pile of books next to his hand bounced slightly. Violet frowned as she noticed the stack for the first time. They were her books. More specifically, her collection of novels that she kept discreetly tucked away in her room.

And with a sinking feeling, she understood that this summons had nothing to do with the war or England or France, her wedding, or even the drunken, well-dressed crowd downstairs.

"How did you get those?" she asked.

Her father ignored her. "I believe I am owed an explanation, Violet."

"An explanation?" Violet kept her expression carefully blank and clasped her hands together behind her back so she wouldn't fidget. She hated the way the commodore was making her feel. Like she had done something inexcusably wrong.

Her father leaned forward from behind the desk, his cold gaze flicking toward the offending pile of books. "What are these, Violet?"

"They are novels, sir," she said.

"These are not novels," her father bit out. "These are garbage. A pile of garbage not meant for and not fit for consumption by a young lady." He picked up the novel on the top of the pile and sneered at the title. "*Venus on Wheels* by someone who calls himself Maurice Dekobra?" He tossed it to the side and picked up the others. "*Chéri? Madame Bovary? Les Liaisons Dangereuses?*" He let each fall back to the surface of the desk with a dull bang. "Filth. All of it."

An unexpected rush of anger and defiance threaded through her. It wasn't filth. Those novels were stories of romance and love—and, yes, lust—and tales of bold characters living in a bold world. Real emotions and real imperfections given to fictional people who enthralled and amused and captivated Violet.

The commodore swept the books from the surface of the desk and into the dustbin near the wall.

Violet started forward in protestation but was brought up abruptly by her father's glare. "If you are to spend time reading, Violet, then you will read things that improve the mind, not damage it. You have an approved reading list. The fact that you did not adhere to it has broken my trust. And broken trust is unforgivable."

"I finished everything on the reading list," Violet said.

"And then decided to select those for yourself?" He shook his head and turned his accusing glare in the direction of Violet's mother. "This is what happens when young girls do not have appropriate supervision, Audrey. I am starting to question whether you know or care what poor choices our daughter is making."

Her mother seemed oblivious to her husband's ire, watching the amber liquid swirl in the crystal tumbler. "How can I possibly be expected to know what she reads?" she asked carelessly. "She's not twelve, Robert."

"And therein lies the problem," the commodore said stonily. "This is the most important time in her life. When every action is judged. She cannot be found wanting. She is engaged, Audrey, but not yet married. Something like this, in the hands of an individual not as magnanimous, could be disastrous and cost her everything." He placed his hands on his desk again. "She is still your responsibility, so long as she lives under this roof."

She is standing right here, Violet wanted to shriek.

"How did you get my books?" Violet asked again, wrestling with her emotions. It was implausible that her father would have wandered into her rooms and stumbled across them.

The commodore scowled, and Violet thought that he wasn't going to answer. But he seemed to change his mind. "Your fiancé brought these to my attention."

Violet's hands fell numbly to her sides. "I beg your pardon?"

"It seems Tino came across you reading *Venus on Wheels*." Her father sounded angry again. "In public, no less."

She wanted to say something—anything—but her words were mired in disbelief.

"He had some grave concerns about the suitability of such a book," her father continued, "especially since he shared that you were exceedingly well-read in the classics. He feels that your substantial intellect would be better directed toward more challenging literary material."

That was the most backhanded compliment Violet had ever heard, and it did nothing to soothe her growing distress.

"He came across me reading?" she repeated, trying to determine when Tino would have done so. Violet did all of her reading in the garden or in her room. Had she left the novel somewhere?

"Yes," her father went on, "and I'm glad he brought the matter to my attention. I agree with him. I took the liberty of collecting any other unbefitting reading material from your rooms, though I left your collection of automotive engine manuals. While I recognize that those are unconventional, I equally recognize their use. Just ensure that you study those in private."

"You're glad he brought the matter to your attention?" Violet was repeating him again, but she couldn't seem to put her thoughts in any sort of rational order amid an unfamiliar rage that was rising like a white-hot tide.

"You are a St. Croix, Violet. Your actions are a direct reflection on myself and my name. It is profoundly disappointing that I should have to correct such deplorable behaviour at this juncture in your life."

"I hardly think my behaviour has been deplorable, sir." Violet managed to keep her tone even.

"No?" He opened his desk drawer and withdrew a piece of paper folded into a neat square and very deliberately smoothed it out on the surface of the desk. "Then would you like to tell me what this is?"

Violet found herself looking at the Red Cross application, her name clearly written across the top. She had secreted it between the pages of the Dekobra novel, thinking it safe. What a fool she'd been.

"I asked you a question." Her father's jaw was set.

"It is an application to become a nurse with the Red Cross," Violet said unnecessarily.

"And were you ever going to ask my permission? Or were you just going to betray my trust and stick your nose in matters that are not your concern?"

Violet rubbed her bare arms. Betray his trust? She wasn't entirely sure how she was betraying anyone but she was certain of one thing. "I rather think that the security of France is everyone's concern, sir. Including mine."

Her father's face darkened to an alarming shade of red. "I forbid you to volunteer for the Red Cross or anything else. I forbid you to even consider it further."

"But it is important to me." For a suspended second, Violet couldn't believe she had dared to push back, but her rage was still rising and she didn't seem to be able to stop it.

The commodore leaned forward over his desk so that his face was inches from Violet's. "More important than the future I have worked so hard to secure for you?"

"That's not what I—"

"Your entire life, you have been denied nothing, Violet. You have wanted for nothing. You have closets full of dresses and shoes, boxes of beautiful jewelry. You have an education, all the lessons you could ever want in tennis and riding and etiquette and languages and driving. You even have your own car because you wanted one."

Violet couldn't argue. That was all true. She did have everything.

"War is a nasty business. And not one that my daughter will ever partake in." He snatched the application from the desk.

"It's just that—"

"Let me make something clear, Violet. If you disobey me, you will cease to be a part of this family, do you understand?"

Violet stared at him.

"Do you still want to be part of this family?"

What a horrible, horrible question. But she only nodded, not trusting herself to speak.

He tore her application into small squares, letting them flutter to the floor. "Does Tino know about this?"

Violet watched as the flurry of torn paper scraps settled across the rug. "No."

"Thank God. All eyes are on you. A poor decision could jeopardize everything that I've done on your behalf, including your engagement."

Her anger abruptly cooled to be replaced with an icy disquiet. "What have you done that includes my engagement?"

From the corner, her mother laughed but it was a cruel sound.

The commodore continued to ignore her. "What every father is tasked with—ensuring you a safe and suitable future," he said to Violet.

"What does that mean?" The words felt wooden on her tongue.

Her mother laughed again. "Oh, dear God, Violet, you can't possibly be that naïve."

"What does that mean?" Violet repeated.

"It means that in exchange for the most eligible bachelor on the Côte d'Azure and acquiring the esteemed Leblanc name, your father gave him access to the fortune that I brought to our marriage." Each syllable out of Audrey's mouth was more bitter than the last. "You're not exactly a catch, Violet, with all your... oddities. And your height doesn't help, but it seems Mr. Leblanc is willing to forgive all of that because like everyone, he has his pr—"

"That's enough, Audrey." Her father moved out from behind the desk. "You're drunk and unhelpful."

Her mother made a mocking toast in his direction, cognac sloshing out the side of the tumbler.

Violet stumbled back a step. "I met Tino at the tennis club. You weren't even here then."

Audrey snorted again and refilled her glass. She set the cognac bottle down beside the chair, where it immediately tipped, amber liquid creeping across the parquet floor. "Who do you think told him to go to the tournament?" She pointed a finger at her chest and smirked. "I'll give you a hint. It wasn't me."

"You set me up." Violet pushed the words out. "Made me believe that I was—" She stopped, unable to finish that thought.

"I executed my duty," the commodore intoned.

"So none of our courtship was real?" She retreated a step

farther. "Did Tino even want to marry me in the first place? Does he even like me?"

"Don't be foolish, Violet. You're better than that. Everything was and is *real*. Augustino was at the tennis club at my suggestion, that is true. He has become extremely fond of you and has enjoyed your company. Has that not been obvious these last months? He is very much looking forward to marrying you, I assure you."

"Was this your idea or his?" It surprised her how calm she sounded, because a helpless panic was starting to batter her insides like a flock of starlings trapped within a glass house.

"Like I said, he is very fond of you."

"You didn't answer my question."

"Damn it, Violet, now you're just being difficult, and I blame it entirely on those abhorrent novels that make marriage seem like some unrealistic romantic fantasy. Ultimately, marriage is an arrangement, a contract, if you will, between two parties who find mutual benefit in such a union. In this case, you become a Leblanc, and I acquire a responsible, trustworthy son-in-law who I know will cherish and look after my daughter and all her needs. Augustino acquires an intelligent, well-mannered wife who will represent his family name with grace and class in society and access to the resources he needs to expand his family's business."

"His business?" She was back to repeating things like a half-wit but she couldn't stop. With a deep-rooted mortification, it dawned on her that she knew very little about the Leblanc business other than that they produced fine porcelain and that the Leblanc crest could be found stamped on the bottom of the best dishes in all of the best villas across the Riviera.

"Two of their northern factories suffered grievous damage during the war. Germans stripped all the tools and machinery out of each before they retreated. He is still trying to rebuild while expanding production. He will not have told you any of this because he will not have wanted to worry you." He paused to take a breath. "Does he mistreat you?"

"What?" Violet's head jerked up at her father's question.

"Does he treat you badly? Hurt you in any way? Hit you? Threaten you?"

"What? No. Of course not."

"Well then, you have nothing to complain about, do you?" He crossed his arms. "In fact, he has even told me that he intends to allow you to keep driving and enjoying your little automotive hobby after you are married. There are many men who would not be as indulgent as I have been with you. You are a very lucky girl."

Violet blinked. The helpless panic intensified, pushing up into her chest and throat.

You're so lucky. It's what Gladys had said too.

She was lucky. The rational part of her mind told her that. Yet in her heart, she didn't feel lucky at all. She felt…cheated. Deceived.

She retreated another step.

"Where do you think you're going?" the commodore demanded.

"I just need some air. I just need a minute to think." She withdrew farther, the door to the study at her back. Her skin felt clammy, and perspiration ran down her spine. "To consider—"

"You don't need to *think*," her father thundered. "You're acting like a child, Violet. You have no idea what it's like out there in the world for women who do not have a man to look after them. Everything I've done has been for your own good." He made a visible effort to soften his expression. "I've always done what was best for you. Done what was best for both you and your mother."

Violet's gaze slid to where Audrey St. Croix still sat on the gilt chair, her couture gown sliding off one shoulder, dainty gold lamé heels falling from her feet, and her lavaliere necklace twisted and bunched at her throat. One hand still gripped her crystal tumbler while the other picked absently at the velvet padding on the back of the chair. She no longer seemed to be listening to the conversation and instead stared through dull, bleary eyes at the spilled cognac that crept across the polished floor to soak into the edges of the priceless Persian rug.

"Nothing is changed." The commodore straightened his shoulders. "There are still three hundred seventy people who will be attending your wedding at the beginning of September. There is still a beautiful villa waiting for you and Augustino in Cannes where you will begin your married life, as well as a chateau in Reims where you will spend your summers. Once this tumult in Europe settles down, you will be free to travel as you wish. You will have children, raise a family. You have so much to look forward to." Her father stopped, seemingly satisfied he had made his point.

Violet fumbled for the door latch, the panic almost suffocating her.

"What do you think you're doing?" her father demanded. "You're not yet dismissed."

Violet yanked the door open, gasping for breath, feeling as though the walls were caving in around her. Afraid that if she stood there a moment longer she would never escape.

"Don't you dare walk away from me," her father ordered. "I have not yet decided that we are done with this conversation."

"But I have," Violet whispered.

And for the second time in her life, she disobeyed a direct order.

She fled.

CHAPTER

5

9 JUNE 1939
NICE, FRANCE

The night sped past Violet in a blur of shadows and impressions. Streetlights and traffic and pedestrians had been left behind a long time ago as she had raced into the darkness. On the driver's side of the vehicle, the cliff fell away into an abyss of yawning blackness. On the other side, a jagged rock wall loomed, streaked with russet and dotted with shrubs that clung stubbornly within the cracks. Neither side offered clemency to a driver hurtling through the night and guided only by a pair of headlights struggling against the gloom.

Violet gripped the wheel of the Spider with one hand and swiped at her eyes with the other. She shouldn't be crying but she couldn't seem to stop. She shouldn't be driving in such a state either, she knew, but couldn't bring herself to slow down. There was a terrifying certainty that every single emotion that she had ignored and suppressed and hidden had finally burst forth like a pack of wolves, snarling and snapping and howling, unchecked and uncontrolled, and if she didn't outrun them all, they would simply tear her into pieces.

Anger, disappointment, resentment. Maybe she was ungrateful. Maybe she was acting like a child. But somehow, she couldn't make the feelings or the tears stop.

Outcroppings of cliff and an occasional signpost flashed by faster and faster. Violet knew she was close to Cap Roux, though exactly how close she couldn't say. The road twisted and turned, descending now in places toward the sea. Buildings appeared out of the darkness here and there at odd intervals. She had pointed the Alfa Romeo in the direction of Cap Roux without really remembering that she had made a conscious decision to do so.

The invitation is always there, George had said. *Don't be a stranger.*

Violet couldn't explain why she was heading to a place where she might find a boat on the beach come dawn, tended by a woman who seemed to wield bravery and confidence and kindness without hesitation. Perhaps she just wanted to spend a few minutes in the company of such strength. Perhaps she just wanted, for maybe an hour or two, to be simply Violet and not another disappointment. Maybe she just needed a friend.

The sound of the ocean crashing against the rocky shore was now audible over the whine of the Spider's engine. Palms whipped by, their long foliage reaching toward the road like grasping fingers. The road blurred again through her tears. She wrenched on the wheel, the tires squealing their protest as she rounded a sharp turn.

She tried to calm herself. That her father didn't want her in a war was hardly unreasonable, was it? What parent wanted their child placed in danger? And that he would wish to have a hand in her future should never have come as a shock. Tino had been attentive and charming throughout their entire courtship. What difference did it make if her father had set them up? Introductions were set up all the time. It was how people met each other, how unions and partnerships were formed. Maybe she should just turn around and—

The Alfa Romeo swerved wildly as Violet hammered on the brakes.

She had only the briefest glimpse of a figure in the middle of the road under a pool of light, frozen in place behind something that resembled a handcart. She might have screamed, or maybe it was just the sound of the tyres trying desperately to find purchase on the pavement. The figure abruptly vanished, throwing himself to the side of the right fender of the Spider. The cart wasn't so lucky. Wood splinters exploded over the bonnet of the vehicle, and the car jerked and shuddered as it plowed over the remnants, finally coming to a stop on the shoulder of the road against a heavy tangle of bushes.

Violet sat for a moment, stunned, before she scrambled for the door handle.

"No, no, no, no," she whimpered, pushing the door open and half sliding, half falling from the car. Branches tore and clawed at her skin and gown. Her heart was in her throat, her stomach churning. Had she hit him? What if she had killed him?

She slipped on the loose stones on the side of the road running back to the place where she had hit the cart. A small, boxy building sat hunkered on the side of the road opposite the sea, and it was on this building that a light was mounted, illuminating the road and the wreckage scattered across it. Violet pressed a hand to her mouth as nausea washed through her.

Tossed across the narrow road were pieces of shattered wood, a broken wheel, and dented and damaged buoys webbed together with twisted ropes. In the patches of grass and scrub alongside the road, tangles of torn netting were strewn like a cluster of deflated ghosts. She stopped in the center of it all, looking around wildly. Where was the person? Was he lying dead in the darkness somewhere?

Out of the corner of her eye, she glimpsed a movement at the very edge of the pool of light. A young man had staggered up from the side of the road and was bent double, his hands on his knees and breathing hard. He was shirtless, dressed only in a rough pair of trousers rolled halfway up his shins, and even in the dim light,

Violet could see the ugly scrape on his right shoulder and arm. She couldn't move, her feet rooted to the ground, relieved beyond measure that she hadn't killed him and horrified that he might yet be badly injured.

He groaned, wincing as he examined his shoulder.

Violet forced herself to move and stumbled toward him. He must have seen her coming because he straightened and turned, and the expression on his face brought Violet to a graceless halt on the side of the road next to him.

"You almost killed me," he snarled. Standing straight, he was a good half head taller than she was. His bare chest rose and fell in uneven breaths, and his eyes flashed with fury as his gaze raked her head to toe.

Violet took a step back.

"What the hell were you thinking?" A vein was throbbing at his temple.

"I…" Words failed her. "I…"

"Wait, I'll tell you what you were thinking. Nothing. You weren't thinking about anything or anyone other than your joyride."

"I'm so sorry," Violet babbled. "So sorry—"

"You're not sorry. Your type is never sorry. You come to this place, do whatever you want for the sake of amusement, and none of you cares who or what gets destroyed in the process." He rolled his shoulders, the corded muscles under the skin bunching. A rivulet of blood trickled down his forearm from the scrape on his shoulder and upper arm, dripping over the back of his hand and onto his trousers. He cursed.

Violet shuddered.

"Are you all right?" she ventured and wanted the question back as soon as she had uttered it. Of course he wasn't all right. He was bleeding. Because of her.

She took another step back, afraid that her knees were going to betray her.

"Does it look like I'm all right?" he demanded.

"No," Violet whispered.

"Just look at this." He raked a hand through his hair and then gestured at the wreckage on the road. "Look what you've done."

"I'll fix it," Violet told him.

He laughed, a harsh sound devoid of humour. "You'll fix it? How are you going to fix anything?" He put his hands on his knees again and bowed his head in defeat. "You have no idea what you've done," he mumbled. "You've destroyed everything. Everything that I need. Everything that my family needs so that we don't starve. So that we have a roof over our heads. Not," he spat, "that I expect your sort to understand any of that."

"I'm sorry," she whispered again.

"How am I supposed to catch anything with no nets?" he asked as though she hadn't even spoken. "No gear or tackle? Or get my catch to markets without my cart?"

"I'll replace it all, I promise."

"No you won't." He turned his head to look at her, his eyes lingering on the bronze of her dress and the diamonds at her throat. "I already know how this will go. You'll tell your husband that I stepped into the road and endangered you. In two days' time, a lawyer or someone else on his payroll will demand that I pay for any damage to your vehicle. Demand that I apologize for causing you any discomfort. I know what money can do."

Violet felt her jaw slacken. "What? No, that's not—"

"Save yourself the breath. I don't want to hear it."

"It was an accident. It was dark. It's the middle of the night—"

"The middle of the night?" He jerked upright again and, in two steps, had closed the distance between them. Violet swallowed but resisted the urge to back up again. He crowded her space with his size, and she could feel the heat rolling off his skin. She tried not to look at the ridges and planes of bare muscle and sinew that were only inches away. This close, she could see that his eyes were a startling colour of blue, like the shallows of the sea, and right now they had her pinned in place with a glacial intensity.

"It is not the middle of the night, princess," he said, enunciating each word slowly. "It is almost dawn." He tipped his head toward the east without looking away from her. "The time when people who work for a living actually work."

Violet blinked. Over his shoulder, she could see the first faint layers of gold challenging the night on the horizon. He was right about dawn but wrong about everything else. What had happened here was not his fault. It was all hers.

She lifted her chin. She would make this right.

"Here." She unfastened the necklace from her throat and held it out to him "Take this. Until I can come back and fix this. Like a down payment until I can come to reimburse you." She wasn't entirely sure how she was going to do that or how much everything would cost, but she would figure it out.

He made no move to take the necklace.

"Please. Until I can come back."

"And get accused of stealing it later?" He made a rude noise. "Not a chance. Keep your baubles, princess."

Violet stared. "I would never do that." She had never met anyone so cynical.

"Not a chance I'm going to take."

"What were you doing in the road?" she asked, and then regretted that question because it sounded like an accusation.

"What was I doing?" He was almost shouting. With effort, he seemed to collect himself. "I live there." He pointed up the hill on the far side of the road. "My boat is moored there." His finger swung in the direction of the beach across the road. "Where I should be right now. Setting up to get on the water. With all the other fishermen."

"Oh." Violet realized that he was pointing to the same beach where George had said her boat would be.

"Oh," he mocked. "But I won't be getting out on the water to fish anytime soon now, will I?"

Violet took a deep breath. "What is your name?" Her thoughts were starting to reorder themselves. At the very least, she would need his name to find him again.

"Not a chance I'm giving you that."

"What? Why?"

"For the same reason I'm not touching your diamonds." He heaved a disgusted sigh. "Just go back to your husband and leave me be."

"I'm not married." Yet.

"Then go back to your daddy." He threw a hand in the air. "Or go back to whatever gilded castle you drove out of. I don't really care. Just go back and leave me alone."

She was not going to crawl away like a coward. She extended the necklace again. "Take it, please."

He scoffed and turned his back on her. He bent and picked up a buoy that had miraculously remained in one piece. "You can't eat diamonds, princess. And you can't repair anything with them either."

Violet stared down at the glittering stones in her hand. He was right. She spun, and on legs strengthened by purpose, she strode back to the Spider.

When she returned, she had her toolbox from the boot of the car in her hand. She set it down with a thump on the side of the road where he was making a pile of salvaged belongings.

"Take this, then," she said.

He stopped and stared at the heavy box and then back at her.

"What is all this?"

"My tools."

"Your tools?" His brows disappeared under the thick, sandy hair that had fallen over his forehead.

"You were right. You can't fix anything with my diamonds.

But you can with my tools. Keep them until I can come back. They're worth more to me anyway."

He laughed without humour. "Do you think I'm an idiot?"

"No."

"Those aren't yours."

"They are."

"So you're a liar and a bad driver."

"I'm neither."

He put his hands on his knees again and looked at the wreckage. "This is unbelievable."

"My name is Violet," she said quietly. "Violet St. Croix. I've lived in Nice since I was five. My father is British, my mother is French. I have no siblings. I like reading and hate tennis and love driving. Those tools are what I use to maintain this car." The words were tripping over themselves but she pushed on, unable to stop, feeling like she owed him this information. "In three months, I am supposed to be married, and tonight I left a party before I was supposed to and drove foolishly. At the moment, I'm just trying to make this right, I promise. Please let me."

The sun had emerged over the edge of the horizon, and everything around Violet was bathed in a wash of pale light as the sky lightened.

The man straightened, grimacing as he did, but the fury in his expression had faded. "The party or the wedding?"

"What?" She frowned in confusion.

"The reason you were driving foolishly. You strung those things together."

"That's not—" She stopped. "I don't—"

"You were crying."

"I was not." The lie was immediate.

He gave her a hard look. "Like I said. A liar and a bad driver. Your makeup is a mess, and your eyes are red and puffy."

Violet swiped at her face, her cheeks burning in humiliation. She had never felt so small, so miserable, so…useless.

The man kicked at a piece of broken board, sending it spinning off the road. He looked out toward the east, where a rim of gold had illuminated a thin ribbon of cloud in the sky with brilliant hues of tangerine and rose. Against the glow, his silhouette stood out in stark contrast, and Violet found herself unable to look away. She watched the steady rise and fall of his bare chest, the way his hands absently worked at a piece of torn netting, and the hard set of his jaw.

"I'm keeping your tools whether you do what you promised or not, so don't complain later. Those I could sell."

Violet nodded even though he wasn't looking at her. "Fair."

He scoffed and dropped the length of torn netting in the pile. He bent again and moved to retrieve more of the scattered wreckage. Violet joined him.

"I don't need your help, princess. Just go away."

"No." Violet surprised herself with her defiance. "I'll help you until this is all cleaned up." The knowledge that her actions could have ended in real tragedy weighed unbearably on her conscience.

The man hissed as he reached for a broken buoy with his injured right arm.

"Let me." Violet didn't wait for him to answer, simply picked up the buoy before he could.

"You're going to wreck your dress."

Violet glanced down at the bronze satin, suddenly very aware of the plunging neckline. "It doesn't matter," she said. "I don't even like this dress that much."

"Then why the hell are you wearing it?" he asked.

She opened her mouth to answer but then closed it. "I don't know," she finally said.

"Of course you don't."

Violet cleared her throat and squared her shoulders. "Make me a list."

"A list?"

"Of everything that you will need to replace. Write it down."

He stared at her.

"Can you write?"

"This lowly peasant can read and write just fine, princess. My mother made sure of it." He sounded furious again.

"It was a reasonable question."

He sneered. "I'm sure you thought so."

"I am going to replace everything. You have my word."

"I think you think you're serious."

"I am."

"And you'll what? Ask daddy for the money?" There was contempt in his words but Violet ignored it. She deserved it.

She added the broken buoy to the pile on the side of the road. "Maybe," she lied. She had no intention of asking her father for anything. If her father or Tino found out about this, she'd never be allowed to drive again.

"And if he says no?"

"I can always sell my car." The idea stung horribly but she knew that it was justified. And not only was it justified, it would be easy. She'd had no fewer than three offers to buy the car in the last month, mostly from men who'd told her that the Spider was too much car for her. Maybe they'd been right.

Violet returned to the road. She crouched and stacked a half dozen broken cart boards into her arms.

The man hadn't replied, only picked up a mangled wheel. Violet wasn't sure if he had heard her or if he'd dismissed her entirely at this point. Not that it mattered, really. Dismissal was not new but this was something that she was determined to see through.

The pair worked in silence as the sun rose higher and flooded the world with amber light. Two vehicles passed them as they worked, slowing down enough to stare but neither stopping. Violet ignored them both. Within a half hour, the road was clear.

"I'll be back tomorrow," Violet told him.

"Not if you sell your car you won't."

He had heard her.

"I will be back tomorrow," Violet repeated. "For your list."

"Whatever you say, princess."

"Where can I find you?"

"You can't. I'd prefer it if I never see you again."

"Do you know George Chastain?" Violet asked. Surely if he had a boat here, he would know George. Or at the very least, he would know of George.

He was looking at her strangely.

"Do you know her?" she pressed. She needed to make this right, in whatever way she could.

"Yes." His answer was curt. "I know who she is."

"Then leave it with her."

He shrugged, hefted the toolbox in his hand, and then simply turned and walked away, heading back up the hill.

Violet wasn't sure if that was an agreement or dismissal. But she would still be back tomorrow.

CHAPTER

6

Afternoon was sliding into early evening by the time Violet arrived at the yellow house on the hill that George had described.

The house was constructed of wood, not stone, and listed slightly to port, as if the prevailing winds off the sea were slowly pushing it over. It had been painted sometime ago, judging by the patches of faded lemon pigment that clung to the corners under the eaves and windowsills, but the majority of it had been reduced to a weathered grey. Yet bright red curtains hung in the windows, and a profusion of flowers draped from well-tended boxes beneath. The tiny yard was swept clean, and a handful of chickens pecked their way around a coop that looked to be in better condition than the house.

Violet had parked the St. Croix's serviceable Citroen on the side of the road and, clutching her purse, climbed the winding path that ended at the front door. She tried to take some solace in the thought that her fit of self-pity and self-indulgence had not killed anyone. Not that the thought made the guilt she had wrestled with for the last day any less unbearable. In the harsh light of day, the realization that all she had destroyed were things that could be replaced was a miracle.

She stood with her hand poised to knock, wondering what the man she had injured the night before might have told George, if anything. Maybe Violet would discover that George had no knowledge of what had happened that night and no idea that she should be in possession of a list of equipment to replace. Unlikely in this small community, and more plausible that Violet would find herself faced with another round of cutting, if deserved, wrath. Squirming inwardly, she tried to frame her explanation and apology in her mind, but before she could finish her thoughts and before she could knock, the door swung open, and a woman filled the space, her hazel eyes flashing with curiosity.

"Were you planning to stand there all afternoon?" George asked. She swung the door wide. "Come in out of the sun. It's much cooler in the back."

Violet blinked at the figure before her, taking in bare feet sticking out from beneath a pair of cut-off trousers, tanned arms with hands perched on narrow hips, and sun-streaked hair jammed under a straw hat.

"I was hoping you might've come earlier so I could take you out on the boat," George continued without waiting for Violet to reply. "But I'm glad you're here. Good timing, really. I'm mostly done for the day."

Violet winced. Clearly, George knew nothing about what had happened on the road. Clearly, the man had been quite serious when he had declared that he never wanted to see Violet again. Well, that was too bad. Violet was going to pay her debt to him whether he wanted her to or not.

Violet stepped inside and found herself in what appeared to be a kitchen, and the inside of the house was much like the outside—worn but well-kept. Recently washed dishes sat drying in a rack beside a deep, battered sink. A colourful print of a fishing boat bobbing on a sea of blue was hung on the far wall, covering the rough planking. More flowers sat in a glass jar on a long table that gleamed in the sunlight spotting through the curtains. A home that lacked all of the finery of her own villa yet somehow welcomed a stranger in a way that marble floors and crystal chandeliers did not.

"Would you like a lemonade?" George asked as she closed the door.

"I, um, actually came for a different reason," Violet started slowly. "I need to ask you for a favour." Violet would take the initiative with George to make sure the man was compensated, since he hadn't. "The other night, I was driving out here, just on the road above the beach, and it was quite dark, and I, ah, well—"

"Oh, I heard all about the crazy dame by the name of Violet St. Croix driving like a reckless, selfish child." George reached for a tin mug on the drying rack and poured herself a drink from a jug on the counter. "Sure you're not thirsty?"

Violet shook her head, her stomach dropping to her toes. "No. Thank you. Um." She swallowed. "So you know what happened the other night?"

George raised her brows at Violet over the rim of her mug. "I got an earful when he got home."

A new sense of dismay gripped her. "He lives here?" she said, and then cursed herself for her redundant, foolish question.

George lowered her mug. "Yes." She sounded a little puzzled.

"With you?"

"Of course."

Violet closed her eyes briefly, feeling quite wretched. This woman had done nothing but shown her kindness since the moment Violet had met her, and in payment, Violet had returned that kindness by almost killing her husband with an Alfa Romeo.

"He's right. I was driving like a spoiled, reckless child. The accident should never have happened, and it was entirely my fault. I feel horrible. I know I can't undo what I did but I'm here to make sure that your husband, and you, are recompensed for whatever I—"

"My husband?" George was staring at her.

"I almost killed him," Violet told her, overwhelming guilt tangling her words. "I almost left you a widow. I wrecked his— your fishing gear. Nets, buoys, his cart, and my actions were unforgiveable—"

"I'm going to stop you right there." George leaned back against the door and crossed her arms across her chest. "I'm not married to that man."

"Oh." Violet could feel her cheeks heat like a naïve adolescent's, just like the last time she'd spoken to George at the grand prix. "Forgive me. I should not have made assumptions. Not that it's any of my business who you choose to live with—" Violet snapped her mouth shut.

Inexplicably, George only looked amused. "I didn't really choose to live with him, so much as I haven't really chosen not to. None of us have, I suppose."

Violet twisted the handles of her bag. "I'm sorry, I don't quite understand."

"I'm not married. And the man that you could have killed but didn't"—George put emphasis on the word *didn't*—"is my brother. And on the very small chance that my brother can trick a woman into marrying him one day, may the gods help the poor soul." She was grinning wryly as she said it.

"Your brother?"

"My brother," George confirmed. "His name is Henri. He didn't tell you that, did he?"

Violet shook her head.

"Didn't think so. He doesn't like your sort very much."

"My sort?"

"I think the words he used were *entitled*, *spoiled*, and *rich*."

"Oh. Right." She deserved that.

"He told me what happened. He said that he didn't think you'd come back. I told him he wasn't being fair."

"How could you know that? How could you know that I would come back?"

"I didn't. But I didn't know you wouldn't either. I think every-one deserves a chance to prove who they are by their actions, don't you think?"

"My actions almost killed him."

"But they didn't, and you admitted your mistake and you're here to fix it." George paused. "That's why you're here, right?"

"Yes. Yes of course." Violet fumbled in her purse and rum-maged for the envelope she had tucked away earlier. A novel fell out and landed on the floor with a thump. Violet bent hurriedly to retrieve it but George was faster.

"This any good?" She turned the novel over in her hand, slid-ing a finger over Maurice Dekobra's name on the cover before offering it back to Violet.

"Yes." Violet stuffed it back in her handbag. It was the only one of her novels her father hadn't found in her room, and she wasn't taking any chances that he would find this one too.

"Henri reads too, you know. Mysteries," George said. "Always has one stuck in his back pocket."

Violet was having a very difficult time picturing the man she'd met last night reading anything, nor did she want to. "Your brother said he would make a list." She finally found the envelope and pulled it out with more care. "Of everything that I destroyed. There is enough money in there that should cover it. More than cover it." She thrust the envelope in George's direction.

George took it from Violet's outstretched fingers. She didn't ask where the money had come from, and for that Violet was grateful.

Instead, George reached into her trouser pocket and withdrew a slip of paper. "The list Henri made. You can look it over and see if it seems fair. Be thorough because, while Henri was ranting and raving this morning, he mentioned something about rich prin-cesses and fancy weddings and diamond necklaces, and I wouldn't put it past him to have slipped a new outboard motor onto that list given the state of our current one."

Violet would agree to anything at this point. Anything to make this terrible guilt ease. All she ended up doing was scanning the neat columns written in a strong, slanted, meticulous hand before giving the list back and nodding. "It looks fine." She looked around the kitchen warily. "Is your brother all right? His arm was injured badly."

"Pfft." George snorted. "Hardly a scratch. He's done far worse to himself doing far more asinine things. I cleaned it out and patched him up. He's fine."

"I don't know." Violet's fingers worried the woven handles of her bag. "He was bleeding."

"He's fine," George repeated.

"Is he here?" Violet wasn't sure what she would do if George said yes. Apologize again? Run?

George put the envelope on the table and the list on top of it. "Henri's down at the boat right now before he catches the train up to Italy for the week."

"Italy?"

"To work," George elaborated. "We're not at war with them yet. And he can still get work in the bigger ports along the coast. Loading and unloading boats."

"Because he can't fish now that I've wrecked everything," Violet said unhappily.

George made a face. "Hardly everything. We still have our boat. My sisters and I can beg, borrow, and steal some gear. Probably won't catch enough fish to sell but we'll get by until our equipment can be replaced."

None of this was making Violet feel any better. She rubbed her face in misery. "I don't know how to buy fishing equipment," Violet told George, "or where to buy it. I don't even know what everything is on that list. I want to help more but I don't know how."

George leaned back against the edge of the table and crossed her ankles. "You drove here, yes? In that Citroen?"

"Yes." Violet straightened.

"I know how to buy what we need and where to get it. Most of it, anyway. But some of it is heavy and bulky, and perhaps you could—"

"Yes." Violet didn't even let her finish. "Anywhere you need to go. Just name it. I'll take you to pick up anything."

"That would help. We could get started on Henri's list now. Save me some grovelling tomorrow on the beaches."

"Should someone come with us?" She hesitated. "Your father maybe?"

"What for?" George looked puzzled.

"He probably wants to make sure you get the right things for the right price?" Violet couldn't even begin to imagine Robert St. Croix entrusting her with the family's livelihood.

"My father trusts us to do what he can't."

"Oh." Violet looked down. "Right. I'm sorry."

"Believe me, so is he. For as much as he taught us everything he knows, he wasn't able to pass along his magical touch with motors, and we're all suffering for it. Damn outboard is as cranky and stubborn as a hungry mule," she scoffed as she snatched the list and envelope from the table and folded both in half. "Don't suppose you know anyone who's a fair hand with motors?"

"Yes." Violet said it before she could reconsider. "Me."

A pair of sable brows disappeared beneath the brim of George's straw hat. "You?"

"I mean, I could look at it. I started learning with small engines. Some outboards." Violet winced, bracing herself for the inevitable ridicule. "Worked my way up to bigger ones. Car engines, that is. I don't know if I can fix whatever is wrong with your boat motor but maybe—"

"No shit?" George was practically hopping back and forth

on the balls of her feet. "Let's do that now. See if you can fix the motor."

"What? Now?"

"Unless you have somewhere to be?"

"Um. N-no."

Her hazel eyes narrowed. "How good are you at fixing motors, really?"

You should be proud of your accomplishments, Lady Enid had once told her. Violet didn't have many accomplishments that she was proud of but this was one. She lifted her chin. "Good."

"Huh. It would serve him right. Henri, that is. To have him watch while his diamond princess fixes the very same motor that he hasn't been able to in four months." George looked positively smug. "This is glorious. Of all the perfect people to almost run down my brother in the road."

Violet blanched. "Oh, no, no, no." Her temporarily bravado fled. "I don't think that is a good idea at all." Presented with the idea of facing Henri again, the urge to run was definitely stronger than the urge to apologize. "It might need a part that I don't have, and I definitely don't want to aggravate your brother further—"

"When I was four, Henri cut my braid clean off while I slept because he thought it would help make me look more like a real George. When I was sixteen, he hid my only lipstick, then forgot he hid it, and left it in the bottom of the boat, where it melted and made a terrible mess. My father made me clean it up. Me. Like it was my fault." She scowled. "He steals my shoes weekly. I mean, he delights in tormenting all his sisters but I seem to be special. It's a wonder we haven't killed him in his sleep." George hurried across the kitchen and stuffed the list and the money into a cupboard. She returned to Violet and put her hands on her shoulders. "Trust me, Henri deserves all the aggravation. And then some."

"I think it would be better if I just drove you wherever you needed to go."

"You really want to help my family more?"

"Yes. Of course."

"Then make my father happier and more at ease and get that motor running better before Henri leaves."

"But—"

"But nothing." She linked her arm through Violet's and practically dragged her toward the rear of the house. "I've an extra pair of trousers. You need to change."

"I don't have my tools," Violet protested weakly.

"Sure you do. I hid them in the chicken coop yesterday in case my brother decided to sell them before he gave you a chance to come back. Also, I wanted to make sure there weren't actually diamonds in the bottom of the box."

"There aren't."

"I know. It was a fun thought, though. I always fancied that I would look good in diamonds. We'll fetch your tools on our way."

"I told your brother he could keep them. As part of my payment."

"Bah." George waved her hand. "He has his own. For all the good that's done him recently." She was back to looking smug.

In a matter of minutes, Violet found herself attired in a pair of borrowed trousers worn thin at the knees and had her shirt sleeves rolled up past her elbows. She left her handbag, skirt, stockings, and shoes on a kitchen chair and followed George back out into the sunshine.

"Much better," George decreed, eyeing the borrowed clothes. She set off down the hill.

Violet picked up her tools and welcomed the familiar weight back in her grip. Winding her way along the path, Violet followed, feeling a little like she was being led to her execution. She pushed that thought aside. Whatever penance she paid, she deserved it.

The beach had come into view, and with it, a dozen bobbing

boats anchored to a jutting pier and a dozen more pulled up on the beach. There were people on the pier, unloading boats and dragging equipment and ropes back and forth. A number of them appeared to be older men, but she was surprised to note than a number appeared to be female.

"There are so many women," Violet said without thinking. "I didn't realize." She'd never given much thought to how the fish delicacies the St. Croix cook prepared got from the sea to their kitchen in the first place.

"Since the younger men have been called up," George said, and for once her grin was absent. "Women step in to do what still needs doing. Was the same in the last war too."

"Oh." The reminder of the consequences of war sent a shiver across Violet's skin even under the heat of the sun.

"Come." George led Violet across the beach away from the pier and toward the line of beached boats.

Only one had an occupant. The sturdy boat was maybe twenty-five feet in length, crafted of wood and painted a bright white with red trim. To Violet's untrained eye, what looked like long boxes were built along the inside of the gunwales, and three wide planks that seemed to serve as seats spanned the width. At the rear of the vessel, an outboard was mounted, and it was over this that the boat's occupant was hunched. He had his shirtless back to them, his shoulders slicked with sweat, his trousers riding low on his hips. The sea hissed and foamed around the little vessel as it raced up and down the pebbly shingle, though it was not loud enough to drown out the occasional curse.

"It's going well then, brother?" George asked cheerfully.

Henri tossed a tool into a bucket in the bottom of the boat and straightened, rubbing his lower back with his hands. Violet could see the scrape on his upper arm now, no longer bleeding but still looking red and angry. She cringed.

"I wanted to have this fixed properly before I went." He turned

around and shaded his eyes with his hand. "But it's old and temperamental, and I can't seem to—" He stopped mid-sentence, his gaze
fastening on Violet. "What the hell is she doing here?"

His eyes were even more startling in the bright light and
against the blue of the sea, though they were flashing with the same
resentment that Violet remembered.

"Tsk, manners." George leaned against the bow of the boat
and adjusted the brim of her hat. "Mademoiselle St. Croix stopped
by to leave us payment for the damages. Just like she told you she
would do."

"Good. Now she can climb back into her shiny Alfa Romeo
with her conscience cleansed and return to the comforts of her castle. Her good deed for the day has been completed. I'm sure there is
a medal for that."

George gave Violet a long look. "You drive a Citroen."

"Not last night, she sure as hell wasn't," Henri snarled. "Hard
to keep track of all your cars, princess? One for every day of the
week?"

"I sold the Spider," Violet said tonelessly.

"You had a Spider?" George was looking at her askance.

"Yes, she almost killed me with it," Henri snapped.

"Why would you sell it?" George looked horrified.

"Because she didn't want to ask her daddy for the money that
she just gave you," Henri answered for her.

Violet looked at her feet. That was the truth.

"You sold an Alfa Romeo? Because of Henri?" George choked.

Violet lifted her head. "No. I sold an Alfa Romeo because of
me. Because of what I did. To all of you."

Ironically, selling the Spider had pleased both Tino and her
father. Neither had asked her why she had done it. Her father had
chosen to view it as an apology of sorts and as a sign she was matur-
ing and committed to settling down. Tino was already perusing
more suitably sedate automotive options. In the meantime, she

would drive the serviceable Citroen that languished in the St. Croix garages.

Violet squared her shoulders. She would see this through and then walk away with whatever tatters of her pride and composure remained. "It doesn't matter anymore. Let's just do this, shall we?"

"Do what?" Henri was looking between George and Violet apprehensively. "And why are you dressed like that, princess? Did you sell your fancy ballgowns too?"

Violet ignored him and heaved her tools over the side of the gunwale. She hauled herself up and over, not caring if she looked awkward and clumsy. Henri's mouth had dropped open.

"What the hell is happening, George?" he demanded.

"Please move aside." Violet rather shocked herself with her forwardness but she was not trying to make a favourable impression on this man. That ship had sailed long ago.

"Move aside?"

Violet might have enjoyed the look on Henri's face if she had been more confident that she would actually be able to fix whatever ailed the outboard. He'd taken the cowling off, and there were small parts and pieces laid out in neat rows across the bottom of the boat beneath the motor.

"She's going to fix the motor," George told him.

"She's going to fix the—" Henri stopped. "Look, I'm sorry about your shoes last week but this isn't funny."

"I'm not trying to be funny. She says she can fix it."

"This is the only motor we have." He was speaking to his sister through clenched teeth.

"And it's not working well despite our best efforts. Despite the hours that you have spent trying to make it run better. What do we have to lose?"

"What do we have to— Are you insane? Look what she did to our gear. That only took her seconds." He leaned over the gunwale, seemingly to better berate his sister.

"You're afraid that she will do what you couldn't," George suggested with a smirk.

Violet closed her eyes as the siblings bickered.

"You really are insane—"

"No, I'm trying to help."

"I don't need any more help from either of you—"

"Two hours." Violet opened her eyes. "Give me two hours. If I can't fix it, you will never see me again. If I wreck the motor beyond salvage, I have a very nice strand of diamonds that will buy you a new one. Yes?"

A pregnant silence followed.

"Get out of her way, brother," George finally said. "Let her try."

Henri cursed and leapt nimbly out of the boat, splashing into the surf and pointing a finger at his sister. "I want nothing to do with this. I'm going to catch my train. This is all on your head." He stalked back up the beach.

"Thank you," Violet said to no one in particular.

George joined Violet as she shuffled forward and crouched in front of the disembowelled outboard. "He's a good sort once you get to know him, I swear."

"If you say so." In truth, she couldn't really blame him.

George crouched beside Violet. "Can you actually fix it?" she asked. "Please say yes or I will never hear the end of this."

Violet looked over at the woman beside her, for the first time acknowledging the acceptance, forgiveness, and trust that George had placed in Violet when she had no obligation to do so. She couldn't remember anyone else ever doing the same.

"I'll do my best," she said.

CHAPTER
7

The brothel by the port was the spy's first choice.

It was dark and busy and anonymous, and the spy used brothels just like it often. Being located close to the port meant that the clientele was rarely regular and most often transient and almost always drunk. It offered a plausible excuse for any man's presence should that man become careless and be followed. Best of all, no one inside paid much attention to the clients who came and went with their needs and wants so long as they paid for it.

The spy had very few needs and wants, and he always paid for them. A prostitute who could lead him to a private room, preferably the room closest to a rear or alternative exit. A woman who, for a little extra, would then make herself scarce, happy to be reimbursed for her discretion and time and not her service.

The spy waited in one such room now, resting patiently on a wooden chair in the corner. The room was tiny and dank, and stunk of mildew, stale alcohol, cigarettes, and sex. An electric light flickered feebly overhead, concealing the farthest corners and crevices from view, which was probably for the best. Through the walls, the spy could hear the sounds of raucous laughter and shouts in the hallways and downstairs, and the noise mostly drowned out the moans and thumping from the room next door.

The spy lit a cigarette. The brothel was exceedingly busy tonight, far busier than the last time he had been here. It had cost him significantly more to secure this room, which did not please him. He hoped that the man whom he was meeting would remedy that by making it worth the price.

A sharp knock on the door interrupted his musings, and the spy rose to open it. A thin man stood on the threshold, looking uncomfortable and uneasy. The spy beckoned the German in, careful to ensure that the door locked behind them. In his experience, the number of men and secrets that had been compromised simply because one failed to lock the door behind oneself was staggering and unforgivable. ‑

"You are Schmidt?" the spy asked in French. That was the name that he'd been given for the low-level cipher clerk from the Wehrmacht who had been identified as holding information that had the potential to be valuable to the French and their allies.

The man nodded, his eyes darting about the room as though he expected an ambush. "You are Faucon? With the Deuxième Bureau?" His French was hesitant but precise.

"Yes." Today the Nazi spy posed as French intelligence. Tomorrow he would be someone else. "Did anyone follow you here?" he asked. He always asked, and he always had contingencies in place because, no matter the answer, he had to assume someone was watching.

"No. But there are soldiers everywhere." The man sounded anxious.

"None that concern us. They are merely Italian volunteers returning from the Spanish War. There was a public parade or reception or some such thing." The spy frowned, impatient. "I am told your message is urgent," he said, studying his visitor.

He was middle-aged, perhaps, what hair he had left around the periphery of his skull already faded to grey. His build was short and wiry, his movements abrupt and quick, and the spy didn't know if those mannerisms were normal or borne from nervousness. At the moment, Schmidt was pacing in a tiny circle, rubbing his hands together as if they were cold.

"Sit." The spy waved Schmidt into the chair he had just vacated.

In the next room, the thumping was reaching a fever pitch, and the moans had escalated into shouts. The man named Schmidt shifted fretfully on the chair.

"You have information for me."

"Yes." A crash reverberated through the adjoining wall, followed by a bellow, and Schmidt jumped.

The spy tapped his foot and crossed his arms.

"Don't waste time, do you?" Schmidt smiled weakly at the spy.

"I do not have much time. I will be missed."

"Right. Of course. Do you want to sit too?"

The spy glanced at the crumpled, stained sheets on the bed. "No. I'll stand."

"Er. Right."

"Show me what you have."

The diminutive man reached into the inside of his threadbare coat. He pulled out a piece of paper folded in four. "The Ardennes," he said.

"What about the Ardennes?"

"The Wehrmacht are proposing to come through Belgium and launch an armoured attack on France through the Ardennes. To invade France's northern borders."

"That's impossible. Everyone knows that. The terrain and the trees are impassable."

Schmidt shook his head. "That's not what they're saying at headquarters."

"I don't believe you." The spy's handler often directed would-be traitors to him. Usually they were men who fancied themselves

important but offered small, insignificant pieces of information, usually demanding payment. Sometimes they simply lied.

The spy was not yet sure about this man but there were alarms
beginning to ring in the back of his mind, if only for the reason
that money had yet to be mentioned.

"It's true." Schmidt flattened the paper out on his knees. *Fall
Gelb* was written in German, followed by lists of what looked
like names, dates, numbers, and coordinates. A rough map of the
northern border of France and the Somme valley was sketched
below. "France is exposed," he said, his words rushing out with
low urgency. "The Maginot Line does not protect this section.
Look, here, they will simply outflank it. The generals have been
arguing back and forth about it."

The spy felt the hair on his neck rise. This information was
not small nor insignificant. This was the type of information that,
should it prove true—and the spy suspected it was—had the potential to turn a war. And if this man was truly listening to his German
generals, who else was he listening to? Who else was he feeding
information to?

His handler had been right to direct this man to him.

"How do you know this?" the spy asked.

In the room next door, a set of high-pitched shrieks and giggles
filtered through the wall. A new, thudding rhythm started, hard
enough to knock a piece of rotted plaster from the corner of the
room to the floorboards by the spy's feet.

"I worked on the decryption of some of it." Schmidt was rubbing his hands together again, his leg bouncing erratically. "You
have to believe me. The French must be prepared. You have to tell
them. The Wehrmacht must be stopped."

"I believe you." That was the truth. An unfortunate truth. The
spy uncrossed his arms and let his hands fall loosely at his sides. "Why
do you do this?" he asked. "Inform against your own country?"

"Because I want my country to survive," the man cried. "And going to war again with madmen at the helm will be the end of us."

"Who else knows about this information? Other clerks, other employees?"

"No one. Well, not the whole of it. They have us decrypting in pieces. As a safeguard, I imagine, so that no one has all the information. I don't even have all the information but I have enough. This is enough, isn't it? For you to do something?"

The thudding in the adjoining room was increasing in tempo and more bits of moldy plaster fell victim.

"Indeed it is." The spy would need to do something, that much was true. "Can you get more information?"

"Yes, yes. The generals are not often careful. They think that the encryption makes them invincible. But I'm listening. Is there a way I can send information to you? We could meet here again—"

The spy held up a hand. "Who else have you told about this?" he asked carefully.

"No one."

"Are you sure? Think hard. This is very important."

"No one," Schmidt repeated earnestly. "Only you."

"And have you made copies of that document?"

"Of course not. This is the only one. I made it from memory tonight. I'm not stupid enough to carry around that sort of thing." He held the paper toward the spy. "Please. Show your generals this. Make them believe before it's too late."

The spy took the paper and refolded it. He tucked it in the inside of his own coat pocket. "You can count on me," he said.

Schmidt seemed to fold into himself with relief. "I fought in the last war. Fought for men who knew, at the end, that we could not win yet still forced us to the front lines and into death to salve their own egos and pride." He lowered his head, staring despondently at the filthy floor. "It's happening all over again. Germany will lose, and this time, we'll lose more than just our youth and our futures. This time, we will lose our humanity."

The spy grimaced. It was always distasteful dealing with veterans who had once done the right thing but had lost faith in their people and in their country. No matter.

The spy shifted under the pretence of peering around the curtain of the single, cracked window behind the cipher clerk. In the room next door, a woman was shrieking in either pain or pleasure, though both could be fabricated and neither was the spy's business. The bed continued its assault on the brothel wall, and the timing of the furor pleased the spy. Another reason he liked doing business in brothels.

With practiced movements, his fingers delved into his coat pocket. He extracted his wire garrotte and pulled it tight between his hands. The man's balding head was still bent. Without hesitation, the spy slipped the wire length over Schmidt's head and under his chin and pulled it tight.

The traitor's eyes bulged in shock and terror, and he grabbed uselessly and frantically at his neck where the wire had bitten deep into the skin. Blood welled and trickled into the man's collar. His booted feet banged on the floor in a frantic staccato as the spy twisted the garrotte and held it steady. The legs of the chair knocked against the floor as Schmidt struggled and twisted.

On the other side of the wall, a man was grunting now, loud enough to be heard over the hammering of the bed.

Schmidt's eyes were red and watering, and his complexion was a mottled purple. Spittle streamed from the corner of his mouth and across his cheek. The frantic pedalling of his feet slowed, and his attempts to dislodge the wire at his neck slackened, his arms dropping to his sides. The spy twisted the garrotte once more but it didn't matter. Schmidt would no longer be sharing information with the French or any of their allies. The job was done.

And so, it seemed, was the couple in the adjoining room.

Time was of the essence now, and the spy moved quickly. Under no circumstances could he leave a body in a brothel room, where it would be discovered quickly and make the spy suddenly memorable. The paid discretion of whores only went so far. He wiped the garrotte on the inside of his coat, recoiled it, and returned it to his pocket. He went through the man's pockets checking for anything else of importance that the clerk may not have volunteered, but all he found were Schmidt's papers and a few coins. He left the coins on the bed, shoved the papers into his own pocket alongside the map of the Ardennes, and then yanked the scarf from around his neck and wrapped it around Schmidt's lifeless one, hiding the damage done by the garrotte. The spy pulled his cap low over his forehead and bent, getting beneath the traitor's arm and pulling it around the back of his shoulders.

He stood and dragged the man to the door and out into the hallway.

There were a handful of people at the far end, near the main landing, but no one took any notice as the spy turned in the other direction and headed down the steep, narrow stairs that led out the rear of the brothel. The cipher clerk was diminutive, which helped, but by the time the spy reached the ground floor and pushed open the door into the night, he was sweating.

An Italian soldier was urinating on the wall right next to the door and yelped in surprise as the door banged open against the brick wall. The spy cursed inwardly and adjusted Schmidt's arm around his shoulders, the man's chin lolling on his chest.

He kept his head down but gave the soldier a grin. "Can't hold 'is fuckin' liquor," he slurred in broken Italian. "Missed all the fun."

The soldier swayed drunkenly and laughed.

The spy kept going without looking back. The night air was a cool relief after the rankness of the brothel. A few groups of men wandered about the narrow alleys and streets though no one took any notice of the spy and his silent companion. The lights here were sporadic and anaemic and petered out the closer they got to the wharves.

Closer to the water, the scents of salt and rotting wood, and the faintly metallic tang of fuel and chemicals sat heavy and pungent. Ships lay moored as darker shapes against a dark sky, the deep water lapping and sucking faintly around their hulls. Buildings jutted up, a ramshackle, shadowed collection of sheds and warehouses. The spy had selected this space the evening before because the spy always planned ahead. Contingencies made him very good at his job.

He dragged the dead clerk to the edge of the water, taking the time to take a good look around him, but as he expected, there was no movement, no lights, no sounds. The spy let Schmidt go, and the man slid limply over the edge of the wooden platform into the water. He watched as the body bobbed on the surface for a few seconds, the outline of the man's head just visible with the distant lights of the city. Within a half minute, the body had completely disappeared. It would take a few days before it surfaced again, if it ever did, exposed to marine scavengers, and by that time, the spy would be long gone and long forgotten.

The spy pulled his cigarettes and his lighter from inside his coat and lit a cigarette, inhaling deeply. The papers in the opposite pocket against his chest crinkled slightly with the movement, and the spy pulled those out too. The map of the proposed armoured attack through the Ardennes was the first to burn, and the spy held it gingerly in his fingers until the flames bit at his flesh. He let it go, and the ashy remnants twirled and burned their way to the ground. Bloody arrogant generals, the spy thought idly, as the embers slowly died at his feet. If a man like Schmidt could piece a plan like that together, then so could someone else. The spy would be sure to mention that in his report, and he had no doubt that there would be reprisals. But those were not his problem.

The cipher clerk's papers were the next to go, once the spy had committed them to memory. Those details would also be included in his report because his handler liked details like that, and the Abwehr liked being proven right. But the spy's training had taught him to never, ever travel with anything incriminating because chance was an unforgiving enemy and the spy had developed a healthy respect for the unexpected and the unpredictable. It was a fortunate thing for the Wehrmacht toiling under the Third Reich and the Nazi regime that France did not seem to share the same.

And it was only a matter of time before the world knew it.

CHAPTER
8

1 SEPTEMBER 1939
NICE, FRANCE

Y ou're in the newspaper again."
Violet didn't look up from where she bent over the outboard. The sun beat down on her back, the heat making perspiration drip from her forehead and off the end of her nose. The sound of seabirds shrieking overlapped with the gentle slap of the waves folding themselves against the hull of the fishing boat. The breeze shifted lazily off the water, carrying salty perfume that couldn't quite mask the distinct odours of fish, oil, and petrol. Out here, on the blue expanse of the sea, Violet had discovered a place she enjoyed almost as much as the open road.

"You told me you hated tennis," George remarked.

"I do."

"It says here you won a tournament last Saturday in Marseille."

"I did."

There was a rustle of paper somewhere off to her left before she felt the air stir near her shoulder. "If you hate it, why do you play?"

Violet turned her head and squinted up at her friend. "Because it's important to my father," she sighed.

Behind George, Henri Chastain snorted.

"Ignore him," George said imperiously. "He doesn't seem to have anything to add to this conversation besides judgement."

Violet almost smiled. She'd repaired the Chastains' outboard that June day, much to the delight of George and her sisters and both their parents. The tiny fishing community had seemed even more delighted to have a capable mechanic in their midst that could be consulted on the rare occasion that an ailing motor stubbornly defied their own skill. By the time Henri had returned, Violet had become a regular fixture on the beach and on the boat, slipping from the St. Croix villa before dawn and returning in the afternoons before her mother even thought to look for her. As long as Violet was promptly and properly attired and presentable for whatever social engagement the evening brought, both Tino and her mother seemed wholly uninterested in how she spent her days.

Henri, on the other hand, had cared very much how she was spending her days, but his early protestations had been largely ignored and regularly dismissed by his family. When Violet found herself in Henri's company, which was often since he had returned, she made a decided effort to forge a truce of sorts. Enduring his glowering silences and barbed comments was a small price to pay for the extraordinary freedom and friendship she had found. Out here, in George's company, she was simply Violet. She did not need to manage expectations or measure her words or filter her opinions. George certainly didn't.

"When I was younger, tennis was something that my father and I had in common," Violet felt compelled to explain. "Maybe the only thing. Something we could talk about when he called or visited."

"And now?"

Violet shrugged and shook her head. "He still likes to hear about it. Playing is easier than arguing."

"Is that what you're telling yourself about your wedding too? That getting married is easier than arguing?" It was Henri who asked from the bow.

"Henri!" George admonished.

"A reasonable question for the princess."

Violet bent over the outboard again. "Not that it is any of your concern, but no, that has nothing to do with it. And I don't want to talk about my wedding." Not now. She just wanted to enjoy the sun, the company, and the puzzle that was a badly running outboard. When Henri had called the motor old and temperamental, he hadn't been joking.

"You were already miserable the night I met you, princess," Henri muttered. "And that was only a dinner party with the family and the fiancé. I'll be sure to stay off the roads the day of the wedding."

"God, Henri." George sounded exasperated. "There's no call to be rude."

Violet tightened the last nut before she straightened. "Look, my father isn't perfect. Tino isn't perfect either, but then who is? Certainly not me. Maybe they both have more traditional views or opinions than you or I. But that doesn't make them bad people." Violet stopped, trying to order her reasoning. "Life is about accommodating and bending for the greater good. I have a duty to my family. Expectations and responsibilities that I cannot simply walk away from. Same as you. Same as everyone."

"Let's see what else is in the newspaper, shall we?" George interjected tactfully, rattling the pages.

Violet busied herself replacing the cowling. "Good idea."

Henri didn't bother to answer. George squinted at the tiny print, her finger moving slowly across the headlines. Violet glanced over at Henri to see if he would snatch the paper away from his sister in impatience, but he had closed his eyes and was leaning back on the narrow gunwale, his hands behind his head, his face tipped up toward the sun.

"Any more news on Germany?" Violet asked.

George didn't seem to notice, intent as she was on the

newsprint. "There is always more news about Germany, though none of it is ever good."

Henri opened one eye but remained silent.

Violet cleared her throat. "I feel horrible for those who are being persecuted. Who've had to leave their homes."

"The world backed Germany into a corner after the last war and then punished them." Henri leaned forward and put his hands on his knees. "What did you think was going to happen, princess?"

"What?"

"Between the reparations and rules, political instability, and an economy that suffered and kept so many mired in poverty...that Germany is spoiling for a fight should surprise no one who's been paying attention. All it took was someone with a vision for change to give desperate, angry people a reason to hope and a reason to hate. All it took was someone to understand that both of those are powerful, powerful things."

"You sound like you approve of what the Nazi party has done." Violet scowled.

"I didn't say I approve, princess, but I understand."

"How?" Violet demanded, still unwilling to accept his answer. "How can you understand?"

"Henri was born in Berlin," George said.

"Berlin?"

"Leave it alone, George," Henri warned.

"No. You brought it up and this is important. What you and mother experienced is important." She lowered the paper and faced Violet. "In actuality, Henri is my stepbrother. After the last war, our mother found herself a penniless widow with a child to look after, trapped in the same violence, unrest, and starvation as so many others. She hadn't planned on ever leaving Berlin but she felt she had no choice. She was one of the lucky ones. She had a cousin here to help. Who took her and Henri in."

Violet glanced at Henri but his eyes were fixed somewhere on the distant horizon, and something in his expression gave her a glimpse of the little boy he had once been.

"She met our father not long after. Remarried." George shrugged. "And here we are."

"How old were you?" Violet asked Henri. "When you left Germany?"

"Five." He didn't look away from the horizon. "Old enough to remember what it feels like to be cold and hungry and scared all the time."

Violet toyed with the edge of the toolbox. "I can't imagine."

"No, you really can't." His words were curt.

"Have you and your mother ever gone back?" She wasn't sure where that question had come from. Or if she had any right to ask.

"Does it matter?"

"It isn't unreasonable to think that maybe you wanted to go back home."

He finally looked away from the horizon. "This is home now. We built a new life here. I'm glad she remarried. I'm glad to have sisters. I'm happy here."

George reached out and gave Henri's arm an affectionate squeeze. Violet met his eyes but it was he who looked away first.

"Is the motor fixed?" he asked abruptly.

"Yes."

"Yes?" There was a healthy amount of derision in his voice and whatever vulnerability Violet might have sensed was long gone.

"Yes, it's fixed."

"Just like that?"

"Just like that."

George groaned and picked up the newspaper again. "My God, Henri, I think the words that you are looking for are *thank you*."

"I'll say thank you when she proves she's actually fixed it."

"The inlet water connection was partially blocked this time," Violet told him.

"Not the carburetor?"

"No. The carburetor is fine. The cleanest carburetor I've seen, in fact."

"Because I cleaned it out three times. I was sure that was the problem."

"Not the problem the first, second, or third time." She was deliberately mocking him, and she knew it.

Henri scowled and stood, the boat rocking, and shuffled away from them toward the bow, busying himself with the net lines that extended into the depths.

"I confess, Vi, that I hope your fiancé doesn't mind grease under your nails when you are married," George said cheerfully over the top of the newspaper. "I think my brother has finally met his match. The two of you together is almost more entertaining than a grand prix. I could watch the pair of you all day."

Violet tried not to think about the inordinate amount of time she spent scrubbing her hands every afternoon to erase the evidence of the mornings. "I'm not sure that I'll...that I'll have time. I'll have different responsibilities once I'm married."

George's smile slipped. Her fingers worried the paper, and she made a series of small tears along the edge before she spoke. "I'm to report to the hospital in Poitiers by the end of the month," she said. She hesitated again. "It's not too late, you know. There is still time to go back and apply at the Red Cross. You could still come with me."

Violet couldn't meet George's eye.

"You told me what your father said, and I know your fiancé agrees with him, but maybe they'll change their minds. A lot has happened over the summer. More and more people are volunteering."

"Maybe after I'm married I'll go back and volunteer. Once the wedding is behind us and things settle. Perhaps Tino will be more receptive to the possibility then."

"Right."

Violet couldn't tell if George believed her or not, though it didn't matter. Violet didn't even believe her own words. A silence stretched, the cry of swooping birds and the drone of a distant motor the only sounds.

"You don't have to live like that," George said suddenly.

"Like what?"

"You don't have to live every moment trying to make everyone happy. Trying not to disappoint everyone but yourself. Accommodating and bending for others until, one day, you won't recognize yourself anymore."

"You don't understand. It's not that simple—"

"It is exactly that simple. And everything you've ever told me about Tino makes me think that he's not just old-fashioned or traditional or overbearing. He needs you to be less so that he can be more." George stood. The boat rocked once again.

"Where are you going?"

"I'm going to help my brother pull nets."

Violet felt George's absence keenly as she moved to the bow. Slowly and mechanically, Violet began tidying her tools, placing each back securely in the box. When she was done, she stared out at the horizon, battling the feeling that she had just lost something terribly important. In the distance, other fishing boats bobbed across the water, earning their keep, while bright triangular sails of expensive sailboats glided between them, merely entertaining. Back and forth the pretty sails went, weaving their way aimlessly through a waterscape of purpose, drifting whichever way the wind took them. Maybe she was like those pretty sails—

"I'm sorry."

Violet started. She hadn't heard George return.

"I thought you were pulling nets."

"We're almost done." She grimaced. "A slow fishing day."

How long had Violet been staring out at nothing? "What are you sorry for?" she asked, confused.

"For speaking to you like that. That's no way to treat a friend."

"Don't apologize," Violet said. "The truth is not something you should ever apologize for. Since I was young, I've always been afraid of disappointing people."

"I stand behind whatever decision you make. So long as it's yours and only yours. Not your father's, not your fiancé's, and certainly not mine. Do you understand?"

Violet nodded.

George gave her an impulsive hug. "Also, don't let my brother bother you. He's just grouchy that you figured out what he couldn't. I told him he owes you an apology too."

"He doesn't bother me. And he doesn't owe me anything." She hadn't exactly been a paragon of grace.

"If you say so." George straightened. "I'm going to finish, and then we'll head back."

"Of course."

Violet bent and rearranged tools that didn't need rearranging, feeling that familiar restless unhappiness that, until this moment, had never followed her here.

"I should have said thank you."

Violet looked up to find Henri crouched beside her, bracing himself with one hand on the gunwale. His expression hovered somewhere between belligerence and chagrin.

"What?"

"My sister was right. The words I was looking for were *thank you*. For fixing the motor. Again. I'm sorry."

"Oh. You don't need to apologize because George said so."

"I'm not. I'm apologizing because I want to."

She'd had two apologies now in as many minutes, and neither really felt warranted. "Apology accepted, then."

He didn't move.

"Is something wrong?"

"I got this for you." He held out a plain, brown paper–wrapped package tied with twine. From the outside, it looked like it might be a book.

Violet made no move to take it. "What for?"

"For…being a good friend to George. And…for helping my family. For your help fixing stuff. You've been…ah…useful."

"*Useful*? That's an improvement from *entitled*, *spoiled*, and *rich*."

"I admit I may have judged you a little harshly when I met you."

"Ah." Violet was tempted to needle him further but checked the impulse. "I don't need a gift. Friendship with George is a gift enough. And I mean that."

"Just take the damn package, princess. And I think the words you're looking for are *thank you*."

Violet hid a smile and took the package from his hand. "Thank you."

"Open it." A muscle worked along the bottom of his jaw.

Violet carefully undid the string and peeled back the layers of paper to reveal a book. She stared at the battered cover, temporarily at a loss for words. She looked up at him. He was watching her with an unreadable expression on his face.

She ran her hand over the red-and-white cover, the title emblazoned across the front. "*The Madonna of the Sleeping Cars*."

"George said that you liked Maurice Dekobra."

"I do."

"I'm sorry that it's a used copy. It was all that I could find. Actually, it was all that I could afford," he corrected himself.

An unexpected lump had formed in Violet's throat, and she swallowed with difficulty.

"Have you already read it?"

She shook her head.

"I read the inside cover. And the first page. It's not written by Doyle, of course, but it still sounds like a really good story."

Violet nodded, horrified to find that her vision had blurred.

"Thank you," she whispered again. "This is the most wonderful thing anyone has ever given me."

Henri scoffed. "You have a fiancé who gives you ropes of diamonds."

Violet clutched the book tighter. "I don't really like diamonds, if I'm being honest."

"Don't let George hear you say that."

"Maybe I'll give the diamonds to her."

Henri was quiet for a moment. "An exceptionally stupid gentleman."

"I beg your pardon?"

"The title of the first chapter of that book." He rubbed his face with his hands. "And the perfect way to describe Leblanc, I think."

"That's not fair. You haven't even met him. And I already told you I don't want to talk about my wedding."

"Too bad. We're going to talk about it, because I would have this conversation with any of my sisters if they found themselves in the position you're in."

"The position I'm in?" Her words were stilted. "Was this George's idea too? It's now your turn to tell me that I shouldn't spend so much time trying not to disappoint people?"

"What?" He looked genuinely confused. "No. I'm not here to tell you that."

"Then what?"

He met her eyes. "Don't marry him."

Violet nearly dropped the book in her hand. "I beg your pardon?"

"Don't marry him."

"I don't know what George told you but—"

"If George were standing in your shoes right now, I'd be saying the same thing. Don't settle for someone who will hold you back."

"He's not holding me back. He isn't."

Henri wasn't smiling. "Tell me what Leblanc admires most about you."

Violet bristled, inexplicably defensive even though it was an easy question. "He pays me many compliments."

"For example?"

"This is stupid—"

"Humour me."

She set the book down on the seat. "Fine. Just last night, he told me I looked especially lovely."

"You look especially lovely all the time."

Violet glanced pointedly at her grease-stained trousers torn at the knee and her sleeveless blouse that was missing a button. "Please. I don't need you to pay me false compliments. I'll still fix your motor without fabricated flattery."

Henri's brow furrowed, and he looked as though he wanted to argue. Then his expression cleared, and he crossed his arms. "Tell me what he admires most about you then, princess. And not your appearance."

Violet opened her mouth and closed it again, trying to think of an answer that would satisfy Henri. The seconds ticked by.

"That you can't answer my question is my answer," he said quietly. "And it should be yours too."

"You're not being fair," she gritted again through clenched teeth.

"Probably not." He jammed his hands into his trouser pockets. "Your laugh."

"What?"

"Your laugh makes everyone around you smile. Your kindness is contagious. Certainly with my sisters—just ask George. You listen, really listen. My mother commented on that. You admit when you're wrong. That seems like a small thing, but in my experience, very few can do that. You're a talented mechanic, and you light up when you have a problem in front of you to solve. That's just the first five things that come to mind. I could easily go on."

Violet gaped at Henri, flummoxed. She would have liked to accuse him of dissembling but his expression was serious. No one had ever spoken about her like that. She tried to find words but her mouth had gone dry.

"What the hell?" Henri grunted.

She looked up, and it took her a handful of heartbeats to understand that Henri was no longer talking to her. Instead, he was glaring out at the water, his brows knitted and his forehead creased.

Violet followed his gaze and saw two speedboats flying across the water, sending up plumes of spray where they bounced over the waves. Both boats were low, sleek models, crafted of polished mahogany, chrome accents flashing silver in the sun. She could hear the whine of their motors as they approached, weaving wildly between the sailboats and fishing boats and carelessly sending a wash of wake in all directions, dangerously rolling and tipping the other vessels.

"Damn fools," George yelled from the bow. "Slow down!"

Each speedboat had a driver and a passenger, and as they raced past Violet, she could hear them laughing maniacally as they tried to outmaneuver each other to stay ahead. Henri cursed and grabbed an oar, digging it into the water to turn the fishing boat bow-first into the oncoming wake. George had dropped to her knees so she wouldn't go over the side.

Violet braced herself against the heave and pitch and stared after the boats, squinting. "I think that's Gladys," she mumbled. The passenger in the second boat had long auburn hair whipping wildly in the wind.

"You know them?" Henri growled.

"One of the passengers, I think," she told him unhappily. The motors buzzed louder as the boats increased their speed.

"They're going to kill someone. I hate it when they do this."

"This happens often?"

"Often enough." He was almost yelling over the noise. "Not the same boats but others just like them. They treat the fishing fleet like marker buoys, racing in and out with no regard for—"

A sickening thump boomed across the water, and the whine of the motors was instantly snuffed. The lead boat had cut too closely in front of the one behind, and the second powerboat had buried its bow into the port side of the first. Violet watched in horror as pieces and splinters were hurled into the air, and both boats flipped over the wake and capsized.

"Shit," Henri cursed. "Start the motor, princess. George, I'm going to need you to drive."

He flung the oar aside as Violet yanked the small outboard to life, praying that she had, in fact, fixed it. It coughed and sputtered and then caught, and Violet adjusted the throttle. George was clambering to the back of the boat, and Violet shifted so George could take the tiller.

"Get us there quick but careful," Henri said tightly to his sister. "Princess, get to the bow. You'll be her eyes. I'll get the ropes ready. We'll need to get them out of the water. If we're lucky, they were all thrown clear. If we're not, then this is going to be bad."

Violet crouched low and felt her way forward as George turned the tiller and throttled up. The little boat leapt ahead in the waves. Another fishing boat was starting to turn, coming to assist the capsized vessels, but they would get there first.

"Tell me what you see, Vi," George shouted from behind her.

Violet leaned over the bow as they drew closer. The first boat was barely visible above the water line, and only the fact that it was still impaled by the other boat was preventing it from sinking to the bottom of the sea. An oil slick was spreading around the overturned hull of the second vessel, dark, greasy rainbows creating an ominous shadow. Bits and pieces of the speedboats were floating around them, and Henri slowed to a crawl as they approached.

"I can't see anyone," Violet said, looking desperately across the water. "I can't see—there! To starboard." She could just make out a head, someone struggling feebly to stay afloat.

"I see." George expertly guided the boat as Henri coiled a rope. Their boat idled closer, and George cut the motor. In the next breath, Henri dove over the side, swimming toward the drowning man.

"Toss the rope," he called back, and Violet obeyed, wrapping the end around her hands securely.

Henri had reached the driver and was giving him curt instructions as he wrapped his arm around the man's shoulders. "Pull us in," he called, and Violet heaved on the rope, dragging them toward the fishing boat as quickly as she was able. They reached the side, and Henri released the man. "Pull his arms. We need to get him out of the water."

Violet and George both leaned over the sides and grasped the man's wrists. He moaned in pain but Violet ignored him. Henri reached up and grasped the gunwale with one hand and, with the other, grasped the back of the man's belt. He strained and heaved the man up and out of the water as the women pulled with all their might. The man rolled awkwardly over the side and into the bottom of the fishing boat, coughing and groaning.

"Help us." The panicked, high-pitched plea made them all turn.

Two women were clinging to the capsized hull, working their way around the ruined boat. They must have been on the far side when the fishing boat arrived. Violet focused on the woman closest, her red hair dark in wet, tangled coils around her face. She'd been right when she'd recognized her but Violet had no idea who she was with.

"Gladys?"

The redhead twisted in the water, confusion and panic stamped across her face. It took her a moment to focus. "Help us, please," she sobbed. "God, Violet, you have to help us."

Henri pushed off again into the water, the end of the rope in his hand, heading toward them. In short minutes, they had both women in the boat.

Of the fourth man, the other driver, there was no sign.

After long minutes searching the water around the wreckage, Henri finally returned to the boat, and both Violet and George helped as he hauled himself in, spent and defeated. George returned to the stern and frantically set to work restarting the motor. On the third pull, her efforts were rewarded.

"He's dying. Oh, Jesus, he's dying. You have to do something," Gladys wailed.

Violet turned to find Gladys crouched over the prone figure lying in the bottom of the boat. The second woman was sitting huddled on the bench at the bow, crying hysterically.

"Do something," Gladys wailed again. "He needs a hospital. He's going to die."

Violet blanched as she registered the blood that had pooled beneath the rescued driver, spreading outward in pale pink tentacles where it mixed with water. She forced herself to crouch beside him, and it didn't take a doctor to see the extent of his injuries.

A gash had been opened up across his chest, deep and ragged and bleeding profusely. Violet swallowed as she registered that, beneath the ruined skin and muscle, she could see a shard of white where a rib seemingly had been broken. He had lost consciousness, and his head lolled to the side, his hair plastered to his forehead and his skin a pasty white even beneath his tan. Violet looked away.

"I'll get us to shore," George said grimly, settling at the tiller. "Then you can take your car to the hospital."

Violet nodded. She grabbed a rag from her toolbox, the cleanest one she could find. "Here," she said to Gladys. "Put that over the wound and press down. You have to stop the bleeding." So much blood, she thought with a shudder.

Gladys shook her head. "I can't," she snivelled.

"Fine." Violet pressed the rag across the wound and leaned down as hard as she was able.

The motor throttled up, and the fishing boat once again raced forward, bouncing over the waves.

"What about David?" the other woman sobbed. "He's still out there. We can't leave him, Gladys. We can't. You have to find him. You have to save him."

"He's dead, you fool," Gladys shrieked at her. "This is all your fault."

"I wasn't the one who wanted to race," the other woman screamed back.

"You distracted him—"

"Shut up, the both of you," Henri snarled. He was still dripping wet and breathing hard.

A crowd had gathered at the beach by the time the boat nosed through the shallows, those who had seen the accident and those who wanted a glimpse of the aftermath.

"Get out of the way," Henri barked at the throng as his sister cut the motor again. The boat rode up on shore. He pushed unceremoniously past Gladys and the other woman, both now silent and presumably in shock, and grasped the injured man under his arms. "Get his feet, princess," he instructed Violet.

She stood, releasing the pressure she had been applying to his chest wound. Immediately, new blood bloomed under the edges of the rag. They pulled the driver from the boat, and one of the gawking onlookers rushed forward to help.

"Dear God, he needs an ambulance," the man stuttered.

"No time," gasped Violet. "I'll get my car. It'll be faster."

"Go with her, Henri," George urged. "I'll stay with the boat."

"Take his feet from me," Violet commanded the onlooker, and shockingly the man didn't argue. He grabbed the driver's feet from Violet as she raced ahead, across the beach, and up the trail onto the side of the road where she had left her car. She yanked open the rear doors, then the driver's, and slid behind the wheel. The Citroen roared to life as Henri and the good Samaritan loaded the unconscious man into the back.

"Drive, princess," Henri said as he clambered into the passenger seat, leaning over the back to reapply pressure on the man's wound. "And drive fast. I don't think he's got many minutes left."

Violet jammed the car into gear and hammered the gas, sending the Citroen racing back down the road in the direction of the town.

★ ★ ★

Henri and Violet had waited.

It had seemed unthinkable to simply abandon the bleeding man after they had made it to the hospital, so they had remained long after a doctor and a small army of orderlies had pulled the injured boater from the back of the Citroen and vanished into the maze of antiseptic-smelling hallways. They had ignored Henri and Violet's barefoot, blood- and water-soaked appearance, the doctor only grunting his appreciation that the patient had been brought to the hospital so quickly.

A stream of people had arrived at the hospital sometime after that, most with frantic, worried looks written across their faces, and Violet could only guess that they were family members of the man they had brought in, or maybe the man they had not. They milled about, asking hospital staff questions and demanding answers. They ignored Violet and Henri.

Violet was relieved. The adrenaline of the last hour was wearing off, and the thought of a hot bath and quiet room was vastly appealing. The palms of her hands were throbbing where the rope had burned welts into her skin, and her knees were scraped and raw from the bottom of the boat.

"Should we go?" Violet asked, edging farther away from the knot of expensively dressed people. She didn't know any of them and had no interest in involving herself in a conversation that they might not want to hear.

"I think we should," Henri murmured. Someone had given him a towel, and he had it draped over his bare shoulders. "I don't think anyone in that group wants to hear what we're going to say." He had echoed her own thoughts.

Violet led the way outside then came to a stop and blinked in the harsh afternoon sun, trying to get her bearings. The pavement was hot beneath the soles of her feet but not unbearably so.

"If he lives, it's because of you." Henri came to a stop at her side. "Getting him here so fast."

"It wasn't just me, it was you and George too. You were both so calm." She blew out a breath, glad for the fresh air and the heat of the sun soaking into her bones. She glanced down at her hands, crusted with dried rust-coloured streaks, and wiped them on the front of her still-damp shirt. Her efforts only left discoloured streaks across the fabric and did little to clean her hands. She shuddered. "Let's get out of here. I'll drive you back and then—"

"Violet?"

She jerked and spun in surprise. "Tino? What are you doing here?" she stammered.

Tino was standing in front of the hospital's main doors. He was dressed impeccably in a white suit, not a hair out of place, but he was slightly breathless, as though he had just been running. "Gladys telephoned me," he said. "She said you had been in an accident and that you had gone to the hospital. She was crying so hard, it was difficult to understand her. I got here as soon as I could."

"No, no," Violet assured him. "It was Gladys who was in the accident. I was just close enough to help."

"So you aren't hurt?"

"No." She put a hand on his arm. "Thank you for coming."

He glanced down at where her blood-crusted fingers lay on his sleeve and seemed to register her appearance. "You have blood on you," he said, his lip curling slightly.

"It's not mine. It was from—"

"What are you wearing? I thought you'd agreed to get rid of your trousers."

Violet looked down at her clothing.

"Where are your shoes?" He sounded aghast. "My God, Violet. You're in public."

"What? Tino, there was an accident. There wasn't time to change—"

"I'm Henri." Henri shouldered past Violet with his hand outstretched. "Henri Chastain. You must be Miss St. Croix's fiancé."

Tino looked down at Henri's outstretched, callused hand, then the towel draped across his darkly tanned shoulders, and finally his damp, salt-crusted hair. He made no move to shake Henri's hand.

Violet frowned.

Henri shrugged and let his arm fall back to his side.

Tino had already turned back to Violet, dismissing Henri altogether. "What happened? How were you close enough to help? I don't understand."

"They were racing out past Cap Roux. They crashed their boats."

"I'm still not understanding why you were there," Tino said impatiently.

"I was on Henri's boat when the accident happened. We were close enough to offer assistance."

"On his boat?" Tino's head swivelled between Henri and Violet. "Doing what, exactly?"

Violet took her hand from his sleeve, very much disliking the insinuation in his tone.

"Fixing an outboard motor," she said coolly. "His sister was there too, helping me." Irritation was rising with each passing minute. Aside from his appalling treatment of Henri, he did not seem to care that a person had died and another was badly injured.

"Jesus." Tino pinched the bridge of his nose in agitation. He muttered something under his breath and pulled his suit jacket off. He glanced around surreptitiously as he draped it over Violet's shoulders. "I'm taking you home before someone sees you like this."

Violet resisted the sudden urge to rid herself of the coat. "That's not necessary. I'll drive myself—"

"You're not listening to me. Do you know how this looks? You show up here, dressed like a beggar, in the company of a half-naked grifter. What sort of conclusions do you think people will draw? We need to get you out of here before someone recognizes you. Or me."

"I beg your pardon?" Irritation ignited into anger. Resentment congealed to sit heavy and greasy in the pit of her stomach.

Tino was scowling. "The police will want to ask you questions at some point. Too many people saw you to keep your name out of the report completely. We need to come up with a story that explains why you were there at the accident." He reached into his trousers pocket and extracted a money clip. He peeled off a number of bills and extended them to Henri.

"What's this for?" Henri had been silent for the entire exchange, letting Violet speak. Now he sounded merely curious. He made no move to take the offered currency.

"To stay the hell away from my fiancée. To tell the police whatever it is I tell you to say when they ask about the accident, because eventually they will." Tino's face was flushed. "Tell them Violet was on the boat with Gladys. At least that's believable. That's better than the alternative."

Violet was too stunned to reply.

Henri had no such problem. "No," he said pleasantly. "I don't think I will."

"Fine. Tell them she was driving by and happened to see the accident."

"No."

Tino peeled off another bill. "It's going to be like that, is it?"

"Keep your money, Leblanc. I'm not for sale." He met Violet's eyes, and she felt the force of those words all the way down to her toes.

Tino's fingers bent around the bills, crumpling them. "Have it your way." He stuffed the currency back in his pocket. "It matters not whether you take my money because it changes nothing. You change nothing. You'll only regret being a little poorer than you might have been a minute ago."

Henri looked between Violet and Tino, his jaw set.

"Do it," Tino dared him. "Take a swing. Come after me. I'll have you arrested. I will ruin you."

"Stop." Violet finally found her voice. "God, what are you doing?" She pulled Tino away from Henri. "You're embarrassing yourself," she said, lowering her voice.

"I'm embarrassing myself?" he whispered furiously. "That's rich considering I'm trying to fix a problem you have created." He pointed a finger at her. "You have been given far too much freedom, Violet. Your actions today make me wonder if I can trust you to make good decisions in the future."

Violet knew she needed to say something—anything—but she couldn't seem to make herself speak. The feeling that she'd experienced that fateful night in her father's study, standing in front of a pile of novels, was back. Alongside the anger and resentment sitting heavy in her gut, a suffocating panic was descending again, and the sensation that the walls were collapsing in on her was almost overwhelming. Only this time, she was having a hard time dismissing it as childish behaviour. This time, in the stark sunlight with blood on her hands and torn knees in her trousers, she was having difficulty believing that this feeling was simply immaturity.

A commotion near the entrance to the hospital distracted her. A knot of three older, well-dressed men were talking and gesturing in agitation or perhaps excitement. One of the men glanced over.

"Leblanc?" the man asked, recognizing Tino. He had a straw boater hat in his hands and he was twirling it around and around with jerky movements. "I thought that was you."

"Jesus, this is the last thing I need," Tino muttered. He offered an awkward wave and stepped in front of Violet as if to hide her from their scrutiny, but the men seemed wholly uninterested.

"Did you hear?" the man called.

"About the accident? Yes, I—"

"Accident?" The man frowned. "No, no. I'm talking about Germany invading Poland this morning. Just heard it on the radio. We're in for it now."

A chill chased itself across Violet's skin.

"We'll be declaring war on the bastards any day now," another man predicted. "Damn inconvenient. Going to impact your interests in the north, I would imagine, Leblanc?"

"Go home immediately, Violet," Tino growled without turning around. "I'll meet you there, and we'll finish this conversation. And I'd like to remind you that we've an important dinner in a few hours, in case you've forgotten your social obligations. Clean yourself up and please don't talk to anyone about what happened out on the water, understand? I will take care of that. I'll be by at five to fetch you." He started toward the men, heading them off.

Violet backed away, stopping only when she felt the steady pressure of Henri's hand at her back. She turned to look up at him.

His expression was grim. "It's started."

"Yes."

"I'm going to go now," he said. "I have somewhere I need to be."

"No. Wait. I'm sorry."

"For what?"

"For Tino. He should never have said those things about you—"

"I don't care what he said about me. I care how he spoke to you." He gave her a hard look. "And so should you. You're better than him, princess. Start believing that before it's too late."

Violet felt like she was going to burst into tears, and she shoved that urge down ruthlessly. She would not crumble, not now. "Can I at least drive you back—"

"I think it's best if you don't." He glanced over her shoulder toward the front of the hospital and the group of men in urgent conversation. "Take care of yourself, princess."

He didn't give her a chance to reply, only slipped his hands into his pockets and strolled away with all the casual confidence of a finely dressed gentleman on the promenade.

He didn't look back.

CHAPTER
9

1 SEPTEMBER 1939
NICE, FRANCE

Violet returned to the villa but not right away. She had a bath and washed the blood and salt from her skin and hair but she did not dress for dinner. She did not speak to anyone about the accident but instead sat on the edge of her father's desk and listened to the radio in the empty study as more ominous information trickled in. The man at the hospital had been right. There was very little doubt that France would declare war on Germany in the coming days.

"What are you doing in here?"

Violet turned to find Tino standing in the doorway. He had swapped out his white suit for a black dinner jacket, complete with a bow tie and polished leather shoes. As always, he looked striking.

He glanced at his watch. "It's five o'clock. You're not dressed yet."

"No," Violet agreed. "I'm not."

His lips thinned in annoyance before his expression cleared. "Just as well, then. We need to talk about what happened this morning before we go anywhere."

"I agree."

"Good. I'll start by saying that this cannot happen again."

"They didn't mean for it to happen. Gladys and her friends

were horribly reckless, and they'll have to live with the conse-quences. I doubt they'll be as irresponsible again."

Tino frowned. "I'm speaking of your behaviour."

"Mine?"

"We're to be married in three weeks, Violet. Have you forgotten?"

"No, I have not forgotten. But I don't understand what you're trying to say."

"Are you fucking him?"

Violet crossed her arms across her chest. "Don't be vulgar."

"That's not an answer."

"No, I am not—I am not." She took a steadying breath. "Is that what you really think of me?"

"Doesn't really matter what I think, does it? Only matters how it looks. It's humiliating and I will not tolerate it."

Violet closed her eyes briefly and tried to keep her voice com-posed. "He is the brother of my friend. That's all."

"That sort of people aren't friends, Violet. That sort of people are the hired help at best. Do not confuse the two. You will not see them again."

The ball of resentment that had not gone away since she'd returned home was changing into something quite different. It wasn't stagnant and leaden anymore but was now writhing and smoldering, pushing up into her chest. "I'm not confused—"

He held up his hand. "The good news is that the announce-ment about Germany and Poland has dominated almost every conversation I've had today. We are staring war in the face, and this incident will likely blow over and be forgotten quickly. You are very lucky that I am willing to pretend that this entire episode never—"

"I've volunteered."

His brow creased. "Volunteered for what?"

"For the Red Cross."

He left the doorway and walked into the room. "Don't be absurd. We've talked about this. I know it seems noble and exciting but you are not going anywhere near a war if it comes. It's much too dangerous. I forbid it."

"It's too late. It's done."

"It can be undone," Tino said flatly. "Believe me."

"No. This is something that I need to do."

"Oh, for pity's sake, Violet." He ran his fingers through his hair and then patted it neatly back into place. "Is it because of the uniform?"

"I beg your pardon?" Violet uncrossed her arms and pushed herself away from the desk.

Tino adjusted the cuff links at his wrist. "*The uniforms are so fetching,*" he mimicked in a falsetto. "*And just think of all the young men who will just adore us.*"

"I've never said that."

He scoffed. "I've heard all your friends talking about it. Lydia, Florence. Gladys too."

"They are not really my friends." That was the first time she'd spoken that truth out loud.

"Of course they are your friends. You're going to need the right people if you'll ever have a hope of managing our social calendar once we're married. It doesn't matter if you don't like them." He looked up from his cuffs. "Now go get changed."

"I don't care about the uniform, Tino."

"Oh, for God's sake. If you want to help, hold a bake sale. Knit some socks. Roll some bandages or something. I don't think you have any idea what it is you've signed up for, but I can assure you that you're not cut out for it."

Violet twisted the belt of her robe. "You're wrong."

"Look, while I can commend you on your concern, war is very ugly, Violet, and is not for you to involve yourself in. Trust that these are things that are beyond your understanding and comprehension.

I know what's best for you." He patted her arm. "Now, run upstairs like a good girl and change into something appropriate for our dinner. The yellow Worth, I think. We're already late."

"No."

He blinked in astonishment, as though she had unexpectedly slapped him. His eyes narrowed. "I beg your pardon?"

"Tell me, Tino, what do you admire most about me?"

"What?"

"You heard me."

"I don't believe this. You angling for compliments now? Have you lost your wits as well as your judgement?"

"I just want to know. One thing that you admire."

"I don't have time for this. We don't have time for this."

Violet tied the belt into a deliberate bow. "One thing, Tino."

"Fine. You are very pretty."

"Not what I look like. What do you like about me?"

"This is utterly asinine. I'm not playing these games. Now get upstairs and change or I'll go without you. I will tell everyone you have a headache. Maybe that's for the best anyway."

Violet's hands dropped from her robe. She had her answer, and she swallowed against the burn at the back of her throat. "I'm not going to hold a bake sale."

"What?"

"I'm not going to hold a bake sale or knit socks, not because those things aren't worthwhile, but because I'm going to train as a nurse. Just because I lack experience doesn't mean I can't learn."

He laughed, a callous, mocking sound. "You wouldn't last a day in a hospital."

"You don't know that."

"God, Violet, stop being stupid. You're afraid of blood. You don't even like having to bandage your own blisters."

I don't even like you. The thought burst through her mind with absolute clarity.

The jumbled inferno of anger and bitterness and resentment that had put so much heat behind her words abruptly cooled. A calm, cold certainty replaced the disorder.

This man, whom she was scheduled to marry in three weeks in a ceremony that was not planned by her, in a dress that her mother had chosen and others would judge, and attended by people she felt no real connection to, was supposed to be her biggest supporter. He was supposed to be a partner with whom she was expected to create a life with, if not out of love then at least strategic contentment.

I don't even like you.

Contentment seemed like a stretch. A vison of what her future would look like when attached to someone she didn't like, much less love, stretched out before her, like she was watching a film roll past her eyes, all hues of grey and devoid of sound.

With sure, deliberate motions, she twisted the diamond off her finger.

"What the hell are you doing, Violet?" Tino's jaw had slackened.

"This doesn't belong to me." She held out the ring. "The right thing to do is to give it back."

"Don't embarrass yourself." An angry flush had crept into his cheeks. "I'm not taking that back because you're throwing a childish tantrum." He crossed his arms over his chest. "Now collect your wits, get dressed, and meet me downstairs. There are important people expecting us."

Violet shrugged. All the emotions that had clung to her for so long—the anger, the bitterness, the resentfulness, the unhappiness—were gone, cut free and untethered and no longer dragging at her. In their place was a wild, reckless sense of freedom, accompanied by not a small amount of terror. She embraced them both because they were exhilarating.

She placed the ring on the corner of the desk. "I never should have accepted this in the first place. And for that, I apologize. But I apologize for nothing else."

"You don't know what you're doing," Tino snapped. "Other than making a fool out of yourself. And me. I will not be humiliated, Violet."

"The good news, Tino, is that the announcement about Germany and Poland will dominate almost every conversation, and this will likely blow over and be forgotten quickly." She used his own words. "Besides, the people who are waiting for us will be too consumed with worry about how difficult it will become to buy caviar if we go to war. They won't want to talk about me. They will be whining about the inconvenience of ordering a new gown or a bottle of *Je Reviens* should Germany set its sights on France next. They will still show up to parties in diamonds and furs and moan that the lights must be extinguished or the curtains must be closed when the sun goes down."

"Don't do this, Violet," Tino snarled. "Don't make a rash decision you're going to regret."

"I'm not making a rash decision. I'm making a decision I should have made a long time ago." Violet clasped her hands together, feeling almost drunk with that truth. "There are many women who come from wealthy families who would much better suit your needs." She walked steadily to the door. "You can show yourself out, Tino. I wish you the best. Honestly."

He lunged toward her, stopping only a breath away. Violet did not flinch, and she marvelled a little bit at that. Not very long ago she would have.

"You're picking...that penniless bastard from the hospital over me?" His face was an angry red.

"I'm not picking him," Violet said clearly. "I'm picking me."

"Think carefully." Tino's finger was inches from her face. "Your father and I had an agreement in place. Your father has promised to disown you if you go ahead with this, and he does not make empty promises. He will not tolerate disobedience. You will cease to be his daughter. You know this."

For a moment, Violet faltered before stiffening her spine. "I have tried to please my father my entire life, and for my entire life, I have been nothing but a disappointment. I suppose I should be thankful that I can stop trying so hard now." The words were braver than she felt but no less true.

His hand dropped. "You are throwing everything away, Violet. Your friends will cut you from their lives too. If you leave me, you'll be a pariah until the day you die, I will make sure of it."

"You do that, Tino. Make me as small as possible so that you can remain big. You would have done that anyway, but now I won't be there to see it."

"Don't you dare walk away from me, Violet."

"We would have made each other miserable, Tino. I am not what you want. And you are not what I want either."

"You won't last a day," he sneered. "You'll quit before you even get started. You don't have it in you. You are not brave enough or strong enough or clever enough. You think tennis lessons and dance lessons and the ability to choose the right dessert fork will help you in any of this? To prepare you for a war?" Tino laughed. "You are nothing but a spoiled little girl who has read too many novels that have filled your head with foolish dreams and goaded you into making reprehensible choices."

Violet paused, one hand on the doorframe. "At least they are my dreams and my choices."

CHAPTER
10

8 FEBRUARY 1940
KUHMO, FINLAND

The blood will not clean itself from the floor, Nurse St. Croix."
Violet started, nearly dropping the scrub brush she held in
her hands. She looked back over her shoulder at the head nurse who
was filling the doorway. Nurse Michlen had her hands on her hips
as she glowered at Violet.

Violet turned back and resumed her efforts, blinking away her
fatigue. Her shift had ended hours ago, but now she was complet-
ing her penance for wasting an entire carton of new bandages on a
patient who had survived not even thirty minutes after his arrival
at the hospital. Violet had been subsequently lectured about limited
resources. She had been harangued for her failure to perform even
the simplest of triage evaluations. And then she had been ordered
into the school kitchen, currently being used as the surgery, to
clean the thick, sticky, crusted puddles of blood from the tiled floor
before night fell and the next wave of patients arrived from the aid
posts.

Nurse Michlen sniffed from the doorway. "You should save
yourself and the rest of us some trouble and quit, St. Croix," she
said. Her English, the language that seemed to bridge the gap
between the Swedes and the Finns and the assorted other national-
ities that passed through, was harsh and abrupt.

Violet set her brush to the side and sluiced the floor with a bucket partially filled with cold water. "No."

"You're not cut out for this," Nurse Michlen added.

"I'll do better."

"Work faster then, St. Croix. It's almost dark."

"Yes, Nurse Michlen."

The head nurse snorted before Violet heard the sharp rap of her boots retreating down the hallway.

You won't last a day. Tino's last words rang just as sharply in her head.

Violet flexed her fingers, raw and reddened from cold and work. On days like this, it was hard to shut out the voices of doubt. It was hard, too, to remember that she wasn't doing this to prove Tino or Nurse Michlen wrong, but that everything she did was to prove to herself that she could do this.

But Nurse Michlen was right about one thing. It was almost dark. And with the cover of darkness, hidden from the constant threat of Russian bombers, a new wave of casualties would arrive. She picked up the brush again and set to work.

The floors weren't entirely clean by the time the first patients were being hauled into the surgery, but at least they were no longer gummy. Violet slipped from the surgery with her brush and bucket, largely unnoticed and entirely exhausted. She left both outside in the school hallway and headed back in the direction of the classrooms being used as wards. She would seek her own cot shortly, but before she did, she needed to check on one of her patients. She might not be skilled at bandaging or triage or anything else that every other nurse here seemed to have mastered, but she could at least be good company to the souls stuck here, injured, afraid, and alone.

She ducked into the third room on the right. She shivered in the chilled air as she moved carefully through the rows of cots. Most of the men were dozing in the early darkness of winter, but some were awake. She made a point to smile and acknowledge each of them before she reached the last bed. Her smile slipped.

The man lying under the rough wool blanket had his eyes closed and a pale, drawn face whose lower half was covered by a thick grey beard.

The patient that had been here this morning was only eighteen years old. Violet didn't recognize this man.

"Where is Private Virtanen?" she asked a nurse who was hurrying by with an armful of blankets.

The nurse paused and shot Violet a harried if somewhat sympathetic look. "He was…moved," she said carefully in her heavily accented English, glancing around.

"Where?" Violet asked. "Was he sent home?"

The nurse frowned and gave a small shake of her head.

Violet blinked, her heart plunging to her toes.

The other nurse was already walking away, heading toward the door. Violet hurried to catch up, her stomach churning. She waited until they had reached the hallway before speaking.

"I don't understand," she said to the nurse, who was stacking her load on a wheeled cart.

The nurse shrugged. "I'm sorry. Shrapnel wounds are unpredictable."

"But I saw him this morning. He had a letter to his family that I told him I'd help mail today. He was getting better."

The nurse finished her task and moved behind the cart. "Sepsis. It can arise suddenly and progress quickly. There's not much we can do. But you know this." She patted Violet's arm. "You can't get attached. You know this too. You treat them and move on to the next."

"I wasn't attached. I just…" Violet trailed off miserably. There was no point in lying. She had become attached, and this nurse was right. She knew better. "Did he give anyone his letter before he died?"

The nurse shrugged again. "Don't know. Sorry. Sometimes they leave the small personal things wrapped with the bodies. You could go look." She pushed the cart forward and started down the hall, but not before giving Violet another sympathetic glance.

Violet leaned against the wall, fighting the urge to burst into tears. That Private Johannes Virtanen, age eighteen, with a mother and father and three little sisters and a Fjord horse he called Halla, had died did not make him special. Many patients brought to this hospital died. Violet knew this. She just couldn't seem to get used to it.

Perhaps Nurse Michlen was right. Perhaps she wasn't cut out for this.

★ ★ ★

Violet found Private Virtanen in the shed at the far side of the schoolyard awaiting transportation to wherever they were burying the dead. He was stacked with six other bodies, and in the frozen moonlight, his skin was a waxen white, nearly as pale as the snow around them. His eyes were closed, the lines of pain gone, but that small mercy did nothing to hide just how horribly young he was. He'd been stripped of whatever clothing he'd worn, wrapped in a thin sheet, and the thick band of dressings that had been secured around his abdominal wound was easily visible.

Violet found the letter to his family tucked in the top of his bandages against his lower ribs, along with the worn photograph of his parents he'd once shown her. She left the photograph where it was but extracted the letter and tucked it deep into the pocket of her coat. Posting letters was nearly impossible at the moment but she would find a way and do what she had promised.

She closed the shed door and rested her forehead against the rough timber planks. She ignored the cold that was seeping in under her coat and through the soles of her boots. The hospital was always cold anyway. They couldn't risk heating it in daylight hours in case the smoke from the chimneys caught the attention of a Russian bomber.

Violet turned and leaned her back against the shed and looked up at the sky, framed by the snow-laced silhouettes of the evergreens that stood like silent sentinels around her. Her breath rose in crystalized clouds in the perfect stillness. She wanted to scream in frustration. Or maybe kick something.

She did neither because that would change nothing.

The sounds of crunching snow under footfalls made Violet straighten.

"Vi?" A figure stepped into the clearing, bundled against the cold.

"George? What are doing out here?" Violet asked. "Isn't your shift supposed to start now?"

"It is. But I heard about Private Virtanen." She crossed the clearing and enveloped Violet in a hug. "I'm sorry." She pulled back to look at Violet, her scarf frosted beneath her cheeks. "I came to see if you are all right."

Her friend's sympathy was somehow making her feel worse. "I'm fine."

"I know you and don't believe you," George said gently.

"I'll be all right, really. I knew better than to get that invested."

"You cared, Vi. That's not a bad thing."

Violet sighed, her breath clouding the air, and stepped away from George. "You should get back inside before you're late and Nurse Michlen has you scrubbing floors too. Now that would be a terrible waste of your talents. Another eighty, maybe a hundred casualties coming in from the aid posts tonight. Won't do them any good if you're out here playing nanny to me."

"Oh, Vi." George linked her arm through Violet's. "There is a reason we chose to do this together. To come here together. None of this is easy. But having a friend makes the truly hard things bearable. Having you here has made these months away from home bearable."

Violet heard the slight catch in George's voice. "I can't even imagine how much you miss your family. Have you written to them?"

"I write a letter almost every day. To my family at home or to Henri. Not that I have any way to send them but it makes me feel like I'm still connected." She paused as if deciding whether to go on. "You could too, you know. Write to my family. Even Henri. They would write you back."

The offer was made with kindness, Violet knew, but it still hollowed out her chest and made her stomach hurt. Her parents hadn't spoken to her since the day she volunteered. Her early letters had been returned unopened. Tino had been right. Her father had kept his promise to disown her.

"I don't think your brother needs or wants a letter from me." Violet looked up at the treetops. She hadn't seen Henri since that day at the hospital. George had told her that he'd enlisted that afternoon and had been gone from Nice the following day. "He has all of you."

"You have all of us too," George said. "I think everyone needs as many reminders as possible that there are people who care. Especially when none of us know what will happen tomorrow."

Violet thought of the letter currently in her pocket, and a new wave of debilitating sadness assailed her. "Private Virtanen was only eighteen, you know. He didn't even have a chance to live. To build his own family."

"I know. But Vi, you can't save everyone."

"I can't save anyone." Violet's voice broke. "I'm a horrible nurse."

"You're not a horrible nurse. Patients die. It happens to the best of us despite our best efforts. Go find something to eat and get some sleep, and maybe you'll feel better—"

"No, I just... I can't..." Violet made a fist in her mittens and winced as her raw, chapped hands reminded her of the deserved punishment she had just completed. "All the sleep in the world won't change my shortcomings."

"You are being overly hard on yourself—"

"I'm not, and you know it."

"Vi—"

"Remember when I once let a patient wake up during his surgery during training?" Violet asked, her suppressed frustration and helplessness and self-pity spilling out. "I was so afraid of killing him, I couldn't even manage to administer chloroform and ether properly. I didn't give him enough, and when he woke and started flailing about on the table, his insides exposed for all to see, I froze. One of the surgeons had to operate the machine." Violet dragged in an uneven breath, the cold burning her lungs. "The smell of an infected wound makes me nauseated," she continued. "I can't tell if I've applied dressings and bandages too tight or too loose. I have a hard time using a needle. I don't know whether to lie to patients or tell them the truth when they ask me if they're going to die. I spend every hour feeling useless. Incompetent. Powerless." She stopped, humiliation abruptly trumping all of those things and ending her rant. "I'm sorry."

"Don't be sorry."

"It's just...I watch you, and you're incredible. You always know what to do. You move through your days with this...complete confidence and utter authority. In the hospital. Out in the field. I hear the nurses and the soldiers talking about how brave you are."

George ducked her head.

"I wish I were more like you. I'm not brave at all."

"I don't, you know." George dug the toe of her boot into the snow.

"Don't what?"

"Always know what to do. And I'm not always confident. There are many days when all I feel is terror. And the same helplessness and powerlessness as you."

"I don't think I believe you." Violet leaned her head on George's shoulder. "I think you're just trying to make me feel better."

George was silent for a moment. "Do you remember when we got here?"

"Ten minutes ago?"

"No, not this clearing. To Finland."

"January." It seemed like a lifetime ago that they had volunteered to come with the armed French forces that had been sent to join the fight against the marauding Russians.

"You've had a long time to quit. You could have gone home anytime. Others have."

"I'm not quitting."

"You're doing your best. And your best is better than those who never tried. Or those who quit when it got hard—"

"Nurse Chastain!" George's name bounced around the clearing, oddly muffled by the snow.

"I told you you shouldn't be late." Violet started pushing George back in the direction of the school. "Michlen's out looking for you now."

"That's not Michlen." George frowned.

"Nurse Chastain?" The urgent address cut through the stillness, much closer now.

A small, spectacled man wearing a coat that had been hastily thrown over his uniform came to a stumbling stop in the snow. One of the military clerks, Violet thought, though she couldn't remember his name.

"Yes?" George asked.

"The road from one of our aid posts was bombed," he said rapidly. "Caught two of our ambulances. I'm told you are our only nurse at this hospital with field experience. I need to know if you can—"

"Of course I'll go." George was already hurrying in his direction. "The drivers?"

Violet followed her through the packed snow.

"Don't know. Presumably dead. Not sure if the ambulances are still functional. Report brought to me only says there are still patients alive."

"They won't be alive much longer left in the cold, will they? We'll have to hurry."

"I must tell you that it's quite dangerous out there, Nurse Chastain." He fell into step beside George. "Aside from the Russian bombers, there could be artillery or snipers or—"

"Yes." George cut him off. "I'm aware. Every day, I see men who have been taken apart by one or more of those. Every day, we try to put them back together."

The clerk tripped over an exposed root sticking through the snow. "Right."

George had reached the hospital. "Two ambulances, you said?"

"Yes. It is imperative that we recover them if they are salvageable. We already have pitifully few ambulances. We cannot, under any circumstances, abandon them to the Russians."

"Then you'll need drivers. And first aid kits for any patients that might have survived."

"Kits are ready." The man scrambled to keep up with George as she stalked through the building. "I've got my assistant out searching for more ambulance drivers now. We'll have to wait for him to return."

"Wait? For how long?" George's question rang off the walls.

The clerk shrugged helplessly. "Don't know. There aren't many men here who have any experience driving something not pulled by a horse."

"We can't wait." George stopped without warning and gracelessly yanked Violet forward. "This is Nurse St. Croix. She is a qualified ambulance driver."

The clerk stared at Violet.

Violet stared back.

"Is that true?" he demanded.

"Yes?" Violet squeaked.

George elbowed her.

"Yes," Violet repeated loudly.

"Better," George muttered. "She'll drive if there is an ambulance left to be driven and show me how if there are two."

"I don't know." Beads of perspiration dotted the clerk's forehead. "This is highly irregular. We don't generally allow women to—"

"Do you want your injured soldiers left for dead or fetched back here?" George demanded. "Your choice."

"Right. Um. Here, of course."

"Glad we agree. Now where are my kits?"

The clerk looked at both women, and for a moment, Violet thought he would argue further. Instead all he said was "This way."

★ ★ ★

The road had indeed been bombed.

In the ghostly light, there were deep craters scattered across the silver landscape and the carcasses of splintered trees lay shattered like matchsticks. The section of the road that had been hit had disintegrated into a deep pit of frozen earth and debris lit by tiny embers in places. The two ambulances that they had been sent to find rested at drunken angles on the side of the road. The bombs that had struck appeared to have hit one ambulance but spared the second. The closest ambulance had been reduced to a burning skeleton of twisted metal, and the flames sent a column of acrid smoke curling into the cloudless night sky and eerie orange shadows flickering over the canvas of snow.

There would be no survivors in that vehicle.

The second ambulance, however, looked intact. From the outside, the big, boxy vehicle did not look irreparably damaged, though the front tyres were buried in the snow. The back doors of the ambulance gaped open and a man sat propped up against the bumper. From where she sat, Violet couldn't tell if he was still alive.

George was already clambering down from the horse-drawn sledge that had brought them out here, barking orders to the painfully young soldier who had been sent with them to salvage what they could and transport what survivors might exist should the ambulances be a lost cause. Violet climbed down from her perch on the other side, frozen suddenly by fear. She jammed her hands deep into her coat pockets, hating how they shook, even as she glanced up at the sky, knowing that there would be more bombers out there somewhere, aided by the moonlight. She had never felt quite so horribly vulnerable in her entire life. In front of the sledge, the team of horses pawed the ground and shifted in their traces, as if they, too, could sense an impending threat.

A shout snapped her out of her immobility. The man who had been sitting against the ambulance was now staggering through the snow, waving an arm. He reached the edge of the road and stumbled to his knees. George and Violet hurried toward him.

He appeared to be a soldier and was wrapped in a blood-stained coat. His head had been bandaged all the way around his skull and over one eye, and his right arm was secured against his body with a sling.

"Help," he gasped, out of breath. "You have to help. They'll be here soon."

"Who?" George demanded.

"The Russians. Air or ground. There is a company advancing on this position behind us. I don't know how far but they will reach us at some point. If the bombers don't circle back to finish us first, that is."

Violet looked up at the sky again and then at the dark shadows surrounding them. The urge to run, to flee back the way they had come, to the relative safety of the hospital was almost suffocating.

George seemed to be ignoring the possibility of danger. "How many are still alive?" she asked instead.

"Five," he rasped. "Our vehicle was mostly spared."

"Mostly?"

"I think the driver is dead. And one of the other casualties that was in the ambulance with me doesn't look very good. Not breathing well. I moved them all out, under the trees, where the Russians won't see them if they come back." He couldn't seem to get the words out fast enough. "The ambulance makes too much of a target where it is. They'll come back to take it. The fire will lead them right to us, either infantry or bombers looking to make the road impassable. I tried to dig the ambulance out, but my arm... I couldn't—"

"Shhh." George cut him off. "You did all you could." She had her fingers on the man's wrist, measuring his pulse. She seemed satisfied with the results. "Where are the men you moved?"

The bandaged soldier pointed in the direction of a depression on the far side of the road mostly concealed by low-hanging branches that had survived the bombing. "They're over there."

"Very good. Wait here," she told him.

The man nodded weakly.

"See to the ambulance, Vi," George said briskly. "You have less than five minutes to evaluate the vehicle and determine if it is drivable. Otherwise, we'll use the sledge." She beckoned to the young soldier who had come with them.

"Go with Nurse St. Croix. Do exactly what she tells you. When she no longer needs you, join me. We'll need to move the patients."

The young soldier nodded, looking just as nervous as Violet felt.

George hefted her medical kit over her shoulder. "I'm going to evaluate the surviving patients and see what we're dealing with. Now go." She said the last words with enough force to spur Violet into action.

Violet hurried toward the second ambulance, stumbling over the uneven ground and breathing heavily. The stench of burning flesh and rubber filled her nostrils. Drawing closer to the ambulance, her initial impressions were confirmed. The driver's-side window had been smashed, but other than the broken glass, it looked like the ambulance had slid from the road but escaped any real damage to the body or chassis. Whether or not it still ran was a completely different question.

Violet made her way through the snow to the front of the vehicle and wrenched the driver's door open. The driver toppled lifelessly from his seat, the front of his uniform dark with blood. A thick splinter from one of the shattered trees had penetrated the windshield and lodged deep in the driver's chest. Violet cursed and automatically checked the man for a pulse, but the wounded soldier had been correct in his assessment. She grasped the shoulders of the driver's uniform coat and pulled him the rest of the way out, laying him on the frozen ground away from the ambulance.

She climbed into the cab and looked around. The fire from the burning ambulance lit the interior with a glow that flickered and faded, but it was enough light for Violet to see that, aside from the broken side window and the punctured windshield with cracks webbing across the upper glass, the cab appeared intact. Holding her breath, she started the ambulance.

The vehicle coughed and choked and then roared to life, the sound of the engine overly loud in the muffled stillness of the night. Violet cautiously turned the steering wheel left and then right, just enough to feel certain that the steering was also still intact. She jammed the ambulance into reverse and slowly eased up on the clutch but the tyres only spun in the snow. She put the truck back into neutral and thought quickly.

"Is it stuck?" The young soldier had followed her and hovered near the open door, casting anxious glances at the darkness surrounding them.

Violet slid down from the cab. "Yes."

"Then we should leave it and get away from—"

"No. It's too valuable. We'll get these men back far faster with the ambulance than with the horses. And we can't lose it to the Russians."

"But what if they—"

"Can you drive?"

"Me? N-no," the young private stuttered. "I mean, I never have but maybe I could—"

"Get the ropes and unhitch the horses," she said. "We'll use the team to pull the ambulance out and back onto the road. And do it quickly."

"But—"

"Quickly." Violet snapped. "The faster we do this, the faster we leave."

The private swallowed audibly but nodded and hurried away. Violet ran to the side of the ambulance where a shovel had been secured under the painted red cross. With deft hands, she yanked it from its fastenings and set to work. As quickly as she was able, she dug snow out from under the front tyres and undercarriage.

The soldier had returned and was hitching the team to the rear bumper of the ambulance. Violet tossed the shovel in the back and closed the rear doors so that they wouldn't swing and bang and spook the horses once the ambulance was moving.

"Take it nice and careful," she told him breathlessly as she ran by. "Get the team at an angle so that we can pull it back and keep at least one side of the wheelbase on the slope. As soon as it's up on solid ground, you can unhitch. I'll be in the cab to steer us out."

The young private nodded, still casting anxious glances around them.

Violet ran back to the front of the ambulance and slid behind the wheel.

"Go now," she yelled out the window in the direction of the soldier and the team.

The ambulance jerked and rocked, and she could hear the man urging the team forward. She kept the steering wheel set, and inch by inch, the ambulance rolled up the gentle slope and back onto the road.

"That's good," she shouted from the cab. Beneath her hands, the ambulance's engine rumbled reassuringly. She put it into gear and was rewarded as it rolled forward obediently. It was big and boxy and far more unwieldy than anything she'd driven before but she'd figure it out. She braked and brought it to a stop.

George appeared at the door to the cab. "It can be driven."

It was more a statement than a question but Violet answered anyway. "Yes." She exited the cab again. "Let's get the patients loaded into the back. You can ride with me, and the private can drive the horses back."

George gave her a curious look but only nodded. "Very good."

They were helping the last of the patients into the rear of the ambulance when they heard the first plane. It was a distant drone, and at first Violet didn't understand what it was, until the patient in the bloody coat yelled a warning. He yelled in Finnish, and Violet couldn't understand him but what she could understand was the urgency and panic in his voice.

Comprehension and icy fear lanced through her simultaneously.

She turned to where the young private was standing frozen on the road, holding the team that still hadn't been rehitched to the sledge.

"Get the horses off the road," Violet yelled at him. "Into the trees. As far from the road as you can get."

The soldier blanched.

"Go!" Violet shrieked, and he finally jerked into action, leading the animals into the safety of the dark shadows.

"Those planes will be on top of us before we can unload the patients again," George warned, and for the first time tonight,

Violet heard fear in her friend's voice. "We're going to have to run if we're going to survive this."

"I know."

George slammed the rear doors shut and bolted toward the passenger door of the cab.

Violet scrambled around the other side and into the driver's seat. She put the truck in gear, forcing herself to concentrate so she didn't stall it. She had to hunch low to see through the cracked windshield. The growl and rumble of the truck's engine temporarily drowned out the sound of the approaching planes. Violet geared up as fast as she could, putting as much distance between them and the bombed clearing as possible. The burning ambulance was like a damn beacon, she thought frantically. And the full moon, while providing her the ability to navigate the road, was not to their advantage either.

"Do you know what you're doing?" The patient with the bloodied coat and bandaged head had braced himself in the interior opening behind them. "We should stop. We can't drive like this."

Violet shook her head. "If we stop, we'll be like a sitting duck for those bastards overhead."

The ambulance gained speed, and trees whipped by them in the silver darkness. The cold air lashed her exposed cheeks through the open window.

"Can you even see?" he shouted.

"I can see just fine," Violet told him. Not a lie, exactly. She could see enough. She shifted gears, pushing the truck as hard as she dared.

"I really don't think—"

"It is not your job to think right now," she snarled. "It is your job to let me do mine. So cease talking, sit down, and get yourself secure because it's about to get rough."

Violet didn't look back to see if he'd complied but focused all her attention on the road ahead. The whine of approaching planes could now be heard over the sound of the labouring ambulance. She didn't dare turn on the headlamps, and the truck jolted and bumped over the frozen, rutted road. She was driving far too fast for the conditions, she knew, but if she could just get the ambulance up another kilometer or maybe two, the trees thickened enough that she might be able to get off the main road and hide down one of the smaller lake tracks scattered in the area.

Beside her, George sat grim and silent, and they both ignored the cries of pain and shouts of alarm from the back.

The first bomb fell somewhere behind them, a dull, crumping noise that ignited the darkness and shook the ambulance. George gripped the side of the ambulance door, and Violet gritted her teeth but didn't slow. The second bomb detonated in the trees on the passenger side and threatened to send the ambulance careening. Trees exploded, and rocks and wood fragments rained down on the ambulance in a deadly shower. Violet eased off the gas while she fought the wheel, careful not to overcorrect, and cajoled the heavy vehicle from the edge of the road back to the center.

The third bomb hit the side of the road ahead of the ambulance, and Violet had a brief impression of an eruption of earth and fire on the driver's side before everything went dark in front of the windshield. The ambulance shuddered and lurched, and Violet tightened her grip on the wheel. She squeezed her eyes shut and fixed in her mind a vision of the road as she had seen it seconds earlier. Letting the ambulance slow some more, she steered by instinct, terrified that, at any second, the vehicle would simply lose traction and be swallowed by the crater that no doubt existed somewhere to her right.

The engine protested the reduction in speed, and Violet opened her eyes and geared down, registering three things at once. First, the planes were no longer audible over the sound of the ambulance. Second, a pale, silver light now struggled through portions of the windshield. And last but most important of all, the ambulance still bumped and rolled forward. Violet fumbled for the wipers and turned them on. Twin crescents of moonlight appeared as the wipers swept across her view, clearing George's side and pushing bits of soil and ice through the hole in the windshield on her side.

Violet brushed the debris from the top of the dashboard and risked a glance at George. "You all right?"

George cleared her throat. "Yes." She was still gripping the door with a force that had turned her knuckles white.

"The patients?" Violet geared back up and increased speed again. The ambulance rumbled and growled as if it too wanted to get off this road as soon as possible.

George craned her head to look behind them into the interior. "Still alive, I think."

"Good" was all Violet could think to say as she focused back on the road and stepped on the gas. She lifted a hand from the wheel and flexed fingers that had gone stiff. She rubbed her palm against the hem of her coat, trying to generate some warmth, and then did the same with her other hand.

It wasn't until she put both hands back on the wheel that she realized that they were no longer shaking.

★ ★ ★

The soldier with the bloodied coat and bandaged head was the last to exit the ambulance. He had waited until the first three casualties had been unloaded and hustled away on stretchers and caught Violet near the rear ambulance doors. He looked her up and down through a single, narrowed eye beneath the bandages on his head.

"What is your name?" he demanded.

Violet suffered her first twinges of misgiving. He was speaking now with the same imperial tones that her father had always used. A man used to being in command and used to being obeyed. She tipped her chin up. "Nurse Violet St. Croix."

"Nurse St. Croix. A nurse?" he repeated. His accent became heavier as his voice rose.

"Yes. Sir." She added *sir* belatedly because she had a sinking feeling that it was called for. She winced inwardly, recalling that she had told this man at one point to *cease talking* and *sit down*. She was fairly certain she hadn't said *please*, either.

"You're not a driver."

"No. I mean, yes, sir." She refused to fidget. "That is, I was only asked to drive tonight. Because of the circumstances. The bombings." She straightened and stiffened her spine a little further. "I'm to go back to the aid post now to fetch more patients—"

"You're going back out?"

"Yes, sir. There is no one else to do it. The major at the hospital has just signed off on it." The military clerk that had sent Violet and George out earlier had been waiting as she'd parked the ambulance, new orders prepared for Violet on the chance she made it back with something drivable. "But it's just for tonight—"

"Why are you a nurse?" he demanded.

Violet blinked. Was this a trick question? Had Nurse Michlen reported her for poor performance? "I'm a volunteer, sir."

He scowled and made an impatient chopping motion with his hand. "You are not understanding."

"No."

"Why are you not driving our ambulances?"

"Oh. I applied as a driver but they said they only need women in the hospitals and not—"

"Idiootit." He spat the word, and Violet didn't need a translation. "Do you know who I am?"

"No, sir." She cringed, trying to remember if she had been even remotely respectful when she had snapped at him that *your job is to let me do mine*. He was probably a captain or a major or—

"I am Lieutenant General Jokinen, Nurse St. Croix."

Violet's twinge of misgiving deteriorated into full-blown

regret. It was worse than she'd thought. But what was done was done, and if she was to be dismissed or sent home, then she would deal with that as it came.

"I apologize, sir, for my insubordination in the ambulance." Being her father's daughter had at least taught her to take responsibility for her actions and accept the consequences. "It was a difficult, er, situation—"

"You think what we just survived was difficult?"

"Yes, sir. It's not an excuse, sir, but—"

"It wasn't difficult, it was near impossible. Terrifying, if we're to be honest. There are entire regiments of men who could not do what you just did and keep their wits about them. Without you, we'd be dead. You're the reason these men survived. That I survived."

"I was just doing my job." Violet had braced herself for a reprimand, and the praise had left her floundering.

"You must be one hell of a nurse."

"I am a terrible nurse," she told him.

"Good."

"Good?" She stared at him. "It's not good at all. The head nurse keeps telling me to quit."

"Good," he said again. Beneath the swath of bandages, he wore an expression of grim satisfaction. He reached into the inside of his coat pocket with his good hand, grunting in momentary pain. He pulled out a small field journal and, against the ambulance, scribbled something in pencil. "I think we can oblige her." He ripped out the page with awkward movements and held it out to Violet.

"Come see me tomorrow. Here is my direction. And your new transfer orders for whoever you need to give them to."

"Sir?" She took the crumpled paper from his hand and stared at it. One of the edges was stained with blood.

"Your talents are wasted in a hospital. I need you driving tomorrow and the next day and for however long this damn war goes on. Ambulances, yes, but also military dispatches. Personnel." He shifted his shoulder and flinched, his expression contracting with pain. "So don't die out there tonight, St. Croix."

"No, sir," Violet replied dumbly. "I won't, sir."

Jokinen slid his journal back inside his coat with another grumble of pain. Behind the ambulance, Violet could see George and more hospital personnel hurrying back to fetch the last two casualties and, presumably, the lieutenant general as well.

"You should get your shoulder and head examined," Violet told him. "Unlike me, Nurse Chastain is an excellent nurse."

"Yes." He exhaled, suddenly looking exhausted. "Thank you for saving my men. And me. I am in your debt."

"You can repay me," she said before she could reconsider her boldness. She withdrew Private Virtanen's letter from deep in her coat pocket. "Can you mail personal letters?" She handed him the creased envelope.

"For you?" He frowned at the address on the front.

"No. For Private Johannes Virtanen. His family deserves to know that he did his job too. That he did everything he could to come back to them but that, today, everything was not enough."

The lieutenant general nodded slowly and looked up at her. "I will see it done."

"Thank you, sir."

Violet watched as he joined the last two of his men being carried toward the hospital and allowed a nurse to assist him as he followed.

Violet tucked the lieutenant general's orders in the same coat pocket that Private Virtanen's letter had occupied.

"What happened out there?"

Violet spun. George had paused and was watching Violet thoughtfully.

"I beg your pardon?"

"On the way out to those men, I thought you were going to

faint from fear. Or vomit." She said it without apology. "Yet on the ride back, which, by the way, was the single most terrifying experience of my life, you transformed into...Brynhild." She held out her hand, and Violet could see that her fingers were trembling. "I still haven't stopped shaking."

"I just drove."

"No, you drove and ordered a lieutenant general to shut up and sit down while Russian planes bombed the road." George's voice had risen.

"I didn't know he was a lieutenant general."

"That's not the point." George made an effort to lower her voice again. "What the hell, Vi? What changed out there?"

Violet latched the rear doors of the ambulance with care. The back of the vehicle was streaked with dirt and dented where it had been struck by flying debris. She ran a finger over one of those dents. She tried to come up with something profound that would explain her actions because George was right—something had changed.

"I..." She trailed off, the words not coming.

"You what?" George's eyes had narrowed further.

"I was doing my job." It was what she had told the lieutenant general, and Violet wondered if that sounded simplistic. Too simplistic. Trite, even.

Yet those were five words that carried a peculiar weight and a peculiar conviction that Violet had never before experienced. *I was doing my job.* Five words that settled into her being with a solemn certainty. Five words that came with an unequivocal confidence and impenetrable knowledge that she would do so again.

Tonight, behind the wheel, with people depending on her, Violet had not had time to doubt herself. In those few minutes of danger and chaos, she had reacted with all the assuredness and instinct that George had maintained that she possessed.

Violet hadn't believed her until now. Not really.

"I thought we were all going to die," George told her. "We were being bombed."

"That wasn't within my control," Violet said. "The only thing that was in my control was the ambulance."

George opened her mouth as if to speak and then closed it. "Not within my control," she muttered under her breath. She suddenly launched herself at Violet and enveloped her in another one of her hugs. "You were extraordinary out there," she whispered in Violet's ear. "The bravest person I've ever seen."

"Thank you," Violet whispered back.

George pivoted away and looked toward the hospital. "You coming?"

Violet shook her head. "No. I've been ordered to continue driving."

"Ah." A wide grin split across George's face. "Good" was all she said.

CHAPTER
11

2 MARCH 1941
BERLIN, GERMANY

It had been a long time since the spy had been in Berlin, but even a child could recognize the shift in energy.

It was a city of hope now, a city of passion, and optimism. Maybe it was the flags that hung from corners and balconies, brilliant slashes of black and crimson that snapped in the wind, unremorseful. Maybe it was the groups of soldiers he passed throughout the city, dressed in immaculate uniforms, their bearing just as unrepentant. He'd seen photos of the victory parade of the Wehrmacht after the fall of France, stunning images of men and military might passing beneath the Brandenburg Gate. The photos sent electricity crackling through his veins, and he wished fervently he'd been there to see the welcoming crowds, to feel the reverberations of the drummers in his bones, and to hear the unyielding rhythm of unified boots on pavement.

As it was, the women he passed did not offer kisses or flowers for his lapel. He was not feted by old men with tears in their eyes or cheered by exuberant children hopping up and down in excitement. No one gave him a second look as he followed the canal west along Tirpitzufer, but that was the fate of a man who worked for the Abwehr. That no one gave him a second look meant that he was doing his job well.

The street was lined with broad-leafed trees, bare of their foliage and still in the grips of winter. Their naked arms rose up toward a cloudless sky, and the watery March sun reflected off a new dusting of snow that clung to the edges of each branch. The wind had a bite to it today, and he shivered within the thickness of his coat, realizing that he'd become accustomed to a much warmer climate. He picked up his pace.

Within minutes, he had reached his destination. He wondered how many people passed this building, with its pale grey stone, orderly rows of windows, and strong, angular lines that rose up stories above their heads, and wondered what went on behind its doors. It's blocky, rectangular shape and jutting center façade was as imposing now as it had been when he was younger—the years had done nothing to diminish that. But now there was a difference. Now he belonged here.

The spy strode into the building and headed directly for the stairs without acknowledging anyone. The energy in this building, where the Abwehr conducted their rapidly expanding business, was treble that of the streets. Men and the occasional woman hurried back and forth, up and down, sometimes in urgent conversation, other times silent. Very few made eye contact, and those that did, did so furtively, something that the spy found infinitely ironic and markedly amusing. Spies acting like the stereotypical spies he sometimes read about in novels.

On the fourth floor, he made his way down the hall and knocked twice on a painted wooden door to his left. Without waiting to be admitted, he simply opened the door and admitted himself.

"You're early." The man seated behind the small, modest desk in the small, modest room didn't look up from his writing as the spy entered.

"Early is on time," the spy said, shrugging out of his coat and hanging it on the hook behind the door. "You taught me that years ago." He wandered over to the window and peered down at the view. From up here, he could see the reflection of the building in the still waters of the canal, a mirror image warped on occasion by the wind.

The man's pen continued to scratch across his paper for a moment more before it stopped. The spy heard a drawer slide open and closed.

"Care to have a seat?"

The spy turned away from the window. "I'd prefer to stand."

"Very well."

The spy studied the man behind the desk. He knew him as Major Hugo Beck, though there was a strong possibility that the man was neither a major nor named Beck. Of the five sections of the Abwehr, the one that directed foreign espionage seemed to be the murkiest, and that troubled the spy not one bit. Because while the details might be vague, the directives issued by this man never were.

The major was older than the spy, a few inches shorter, and a few pounds heavier. His hair was cropped close to his skull and had run to grey. A beak of a nose dominated his face, and he had piercing blue eyes that missed nothing. Most people would likely dismiss him, just another middle-aged military man who had been relegated to a desk in the twilight of his career, tasked with busywork and paperwork in equal measure. Most people would just as easily dismiss the notion that this man controlled a small army of men just like the spy, espionage experts deployed to watch and learn and, whenever necessary, quietly kill.

It was Beck who had recruited the spy long ago, finding a capable soldier in the displaced German who was loyal to the Reich and its rightful ascent to supremacy in Europe. The work tested the spy like he'd never been tested before, pushing the limits of his patience and restraint, yet the rewards for a job well done made him feel powerful and fulfilled. The spy had learned and seen much over these last years, including the consequences that were levied should one think to disobey Major Beck's orders. Without rank and file, without orders and men to carry them out, the Reich would not have achieved what it had started and what it was poised to finish.

"Welcome back to Germany." The major sounded almost cordial.

"It's good to be back."

"Some differences I would imagine since you were here last."

The spy didn't answer. It wasn't really a question.

"How are things in France?" Beck asked.

"You have my reports. Were they not clear?"

"On the contrary. You are one of my best." He steepled his fingers. "Thanks to you, the Fuhrer had his photo taken in Paris inside of two months from the time we first crossed the border."

"I saw the photos."

The major leaned back in his chair. "There are many in the Nazi Party—including, I think, the Fuhrer himself—who refuse to comprehend just how close they came to having everything crumble from beneath them at the hands of a lowly clerk in High Command's cipher office."

"That intelligence came from you. I simply did my job." It was best to remain humble. Besides, the internal politics of the Nazi party did not interest him that much. Only the results. To that end, he asked, "What happened at Dunkirk?"

The major's face tightened. "Incompetence. Petty arguing. Poor communication. Overzealous egos. A combination of all of those things. A perfect example of what happens when High Command ignores our intelligence."

"Perhaps then High Command should have been there like I was to watch three-quarters of those forces slip away across the Channel. They could and should have been annihilated, because dead soldiers can't fight again." This failure still bothered the spy, even after all this time.

"I know this. But there is nothing to be done about it now." The major sat forward and traced his fingers around the green blotter on the desk's surface, adjusting it so that it was perfectly centered. "What was it like?"

"What was what like? Dunkirk?"

"No. Forget Dunkirk. What was it like watching France fall from the inside? I want to know about the intangibles that didn't come with your tallies and coordinates and photos."

"A nation of panicked rats fleeing a sinking ship," the spy told him. "Their precious Maginot Line protected them about as well as their antiquated beliefs about how a war should be fought."

"Mmm." This seemed to please Beck. "I need you to chase some of those fleeing rats," he said.

A thrill of anticipation hummed through his veins. He lived for the hunt. "And exterminate?" One of the things he did best.

"No."

The anticipation dimmed slightly but the spy ignored the sensation. He was committed to doing whatever the major needed. Whatever his country needed.

Beck slid an upper drawer of his desk open and withdrew a black-and-white photo. He placed it on his desk aligned neatly with the left edge of the blotter. A soldier with a long nose, high forehead, and intense eyes stared back from the glossy surface. "Marie-Pierre Koenig. Served with distinction as a junior officer in the French infantry during the last war."

The spy studied the image.

"Koenig is of special interest to us. He was a problem for us in Narvik—a notable leader. After the fall of France, he retreated back to England, where he cowered with de Gaulle. Unfortunately, he is no longer cowering."

The spy picked up the photo of Koenig.

"De Gaulle's puppet government in London formed something that they are calling the Free French forces," Beck continued.

"In England, de Gaulle was a king without a kingdom, his forces left with nothing to fight for, and all lacked a certain amount of credibility. However, those forces have since been dispatched to North Africa in an attempt to gain control of large territories and repulse our own efforts in that region. They are trying to forge and reinforce a new kingdom, as it were. This is where I am going to need you."

"It sounds disorganized at best." The spy was dubious.

"I'm not so sure. It is a significant military unit that will liaise with other allied forces. It has already absorbed what remained of the French Foreign Legion. Over half of the Legion refused to pledge loyalty to the Vichy government and instead intend to fight. Which means that they are still a significant problem."

"The Foreign Legion is a collection of mercenaries who have nowhere else to go."

Beck turned a bottle of ink on his desk so that the label faced outward. "The Foreign Legion might be a collection of mercenaries, but they are mercenaries who swear allegiance to no one but the Legion itself. They are brothers, loyal unto death, and if the Legion asks that they fight, fight they will. And they will inspire others to do the same. Only a fool would underestimate them. And I am not a fool."

The spy said nothing. The warning in Beck's tone was blatant.

"The English continue to hold Cairo and the canal," Beck went on. "This is unacceptable."

For the first time, the spy heard frustration in the major's tone.

"Without the canal, victory cannot be realized."

The spy lifted the black-and-white photo to the light. There it was—the entire North African campaign boiled down to a handful of words.

The Suez Canal was the key to control of the Middle East. Control of the oil fields, control of the resources, control of the trade ports and everything that went in and out. The Brits and

their allies would be cut off from India and the Far East. Russia
would starve. England would not be far behind. Both would fall.

Germany would rise.

Beck cleared his throat. "I don't need to tell you that the
Wehrmacht's success—the Reich's success—depends on us keeping
them informed at all times in all areas. Knowledge keeps men alive.
Knowledge keeps men in power. Knowledge wins wars."

"I understand."

The major considered the spy. "I've had three of my agents ask
to be assigned to units outside the Wehrmacht of late. To SD units,
to SS Einsatzgruppen units, to other Wehrmacht battalions and
brigades. They have all told me that they are done hiding in shadows and wish to go to work in the light. Not unreasonable requests
but disappointing all the same. The greatest threat to an enemy is
the one he cannot see."

The spy studied the image he still held in his hand.

"You've been away from Germany for a very long time. You
have been required to hide your true self for a very long time, to
pretend to be someone you are not. This assignment will likely be
lengthy as well."

The spy placed the photo back on the desk and turned to the
window to gaze down at the street.

"Is there something happening out there that I should direct
my attention to?" Beck's voice was like cut glass.

"When you recruited me, what did you see?" the spy asked
without turning around.

"Is there a point to this?" The question was biting.

"You are asking me if I am committed to this mission, are you
not?"

"Yes."

"Then yes, there is a point."

The major's chair creaked behind the spy. "Very well. When I
recruited you, I saw a man very skilled with a knife. A patriot. A

believer in a higher order. A man who had lost much at the hands of others and who sought to balance the scales."

It had been a fight in a Berlin tavern. The spy had taken exception to a man who had been drunk and loudly critical of Hitler's and Goring's plan for the rearmament of Germany.

"Balance the scales," the spy repeated softly. He ran the pad of a fingertip along the pane of glass, cold beneath his touch. "I was here once as a child," he said. "On the street below. It wasn't long after we came to the city. We'd lost our farm—the milch cows and sheep and even the pair of goats we had were seized and sent to France as part of war reparations. I was four, maybe five. It was a winter day like this. But colder. January, I think. We hadn't eaten in days. My sister and I were sent to scavenge along the edge of the canal." His finger stopped at a corner of the window, where the frame hugged the glass. "An old man had a cart, hitched to a horse. And right as he was passing this building, right in front of the east door, the horse collapsed. And all of a sudden, there were people everywhere." The spy looked out at the stark canopy of the trees along the canal. "Desperate, starving Germans with knives who tore that mare to pieces. Tore each other to pieces too, fighting over the scraps. In fifteen minutes, maybe less, all that was left were blood on the road and an old man sitting beside his cart, crying in the filthy snow." The spy turned back to the major. "My sister tried to get me a piece of meat that day. Someone slashed her arm with a blade in the fray."

Beck had reclined back in his chair. He made no effort to interrupt.

"Within a week, she was wracked with muscle spasms. Fevers. Trouble breathing. Within three, she was dead." The spy leaned against the window, letting the cold soak into his back. "I don't blame the person who cut her. I blame the French and their allies. They killed her. Stole our way of life. They reduced us to dying animals and killed more still with our own desperation."

He paused. "So to answer your question about the length of this assignment, please know that there are no concerns. I will do whatever is needed to balance the scales."

The major stood, and the chair scraped against the floor. "Very well," he said briskly. He offered no condolences or sympathy. The spy expected none.

He opened his desk drawer again, withdrew a second photo, and laid it out in a careful grid on the blotter with the other. "Commandant Lavigne," he said. "Your target."

"And where does the commandant fit into North Africa?" the spy asked, reaching for the new photo. A bespectacled man with a round, cherubic face stared back at him. He didn't look like a soldier. With his bushy white beard, he looked like St. Nicolas on a Christmas postcard.

"Dr. Charles Lavigne is the French Foreign Legion's divisional medical officer. He is responsible for organizing and facilitating the care and evacuation of the wounded and keeping the British and their allies' medical stations organized and functional."

The spy frowned. "I am not sure I follow. He is but a doctor. Not that important from a military perspective. Would my—our efforts not be better applied to a general or colonel? Someone with more power?"

If the major was annoyed by the spy's impertinence, he didn't show it.

"With power comes protection. With power comes careful attention to those who surround such men." Beck smiled but it did not reach his eyes. "Commandant Lavigne travels extensively through North Africa to execute his duties. With him travels a cache of information. Material dedicated to supply lines and staffing and resources committed to moving casualties from dressing stations to clearing stations to city hospitals. Buried in all of that information, should one think critically and extract reasonable conclusions, are plans not just for where troops have been but for where they are going to be." His fingers tapped in a staccato rhythm on the edge of the blotter. "Additionally, by way of logistics and necessity, he carries dispatches between cities that the English and French generals may not be willing or able to broadcast over the radio. Detailed orders and maps. Targets, artillery strength, air support, supply dump locations."

"Then he travels with a company of men?" The spy had visions of an armed motorcade.

"He travels with a driver."

"A driver," the spy repeated. "A single man?"

"Yes. And the cache of information he travels with will most often be secured in his officer's vehicle." The tapping stopped, and Beck interlaced his fingers. "I trust that you can manage the locks on a car."

"Yes." It seemed too easy. But then, the spy reflected, men saw what they wanted to see. Believed what they wanted to believe. Fell into traps of perceived safety without much of a push.

"You will do nothing to cast suspicion upon yourself or foster distrust. You must be compelling and invisible together." Again, the warning in the major's tone was palpable. "Your role, for now, is to mine information and report back, but that is all, am I clear?"

"Understood."

"Very good." Major Beck leaned over the grid of unfamiliar faces. "Let's talk about how you are going to present yourself, and when you're going to leave."

CHAPTER
12

20 JUNE 1941

SOMEWHERE NEAR DAMASCUS, SYRIA

Can you keep driving?"

Violet blinked against the glare and the dust as she fought the sand and rock beneath the Humber's nearly bald tyres. The old car strained and laboured up the slope as steam poured from beneath the bonnet.

"I'm going to have to stop soon, sir," she said, shaking her head. "I'll need to refill the radiator and let the engine cool if we're going to make it to the next dressing station."

"Do what you must. I trust you to find the best place."

Her passenger, the French Foreign Legion's divisional medical officer, peered out through the windshield, seemingly unconcerned at the state of the hissing, rattling car. She'd been Commandant Lavigne's assigned driver for four months now, since they'd left for Eritrea, and they'd chalked up thousands of miles together as she transported him between never-ending strings of advanced dressing stations and hospitals. Violet's only job was to keep Dr. Charles Lavigne alive and the old Humber running. That she had managed to do both for this long was something of a miracle. On the day Violet had been assigned to him, the doctor had happily admitted that he knew nothing about cars or driving and had put the entirety of his trust in Violet's skills.

"You heard that Colonel Monclar resigned?" Lavigne asked Violet conversationally. "Refused to fight the Vichy."

"Mmm," she answered, grimacing as the Humber slid sideways on a sandy slope. The sand was the worst. It swallowed vehicles on flats and tipped them on inclines. Violet despised sand almost as much as she despised the swarms of flies that materialized from it.

"I suppose I can't blame him," the doctor mused. "There are Legionnaires on the Vichy side that were once his own men. Bosches must be pleased. Can't fight them if we're fighting ourselves." He seemed oblivious of the alarming angle of the Humber that Violet righted after a few agonizing seconds.

"Mmm."

"You meet the new colonel yet?"

"No." She glanced at the fuel gauge. At least they had enough petrol to get to the station. Water would be the trick though. Water was always the trick. Hopefully, there would be a wellhead close to the station where she could—

"Those are his men in the trucks behind us," the commandant continued, looking in the mirror out the passenger window. "From the First Free French brigade. Headed to the front. Good men. I'm glad they've been with us."

"I'll take your word for it." Every week she promised herself she would try to take some time to be more social in the mess tents. Every week, she spent the bulk of that time threatening and cajoling the Humber, tools in hand.

"I met him the other day, in fact. The new colonel, I mean—Dmitri Amilakhvari. I found him in my tent, if you can believe it. It seemed that he had been erroneously directed to his new quarters. An upstanding gentleman, I must say, and I can see why he is exceedingly well-regarded. He's a Georgian prince or some such thing, though a man of the people, as it were. Not given to airs."

Violet didn't really care who the new colonel was at the

moment. Her biggest concern was keeping the bulky Humber rolling forward toward their destination. The drivers of the three troop and supply trucks behind them, the vehicles all in varying states of disrepair and strung out in the dust on the appalling roads, were relying on her to lead the way as they struggled through the terrain. In their path lay anti-tank walls, craters, and abandoned vehicles. And sand. So much sand.

"I'd regard the colonel very well too if he brought some better vehicles with him," she muttered beneath her breath.

Lavigne found this funny. "If he did, I'm sure the Brits and their sticky fingers will have already snatched them clean away by the time we get back," he said good-naturedly.

"I'm glad you can laugh, sir."

"It's really the only option left to us, I think. The alternative is just too grim."

"I suppose." Violet winced as the Humber's front tyres rode up on a rocky crest and thumped back down. She slowed to minimize the impact of the rear.

"You know one of their lieutenant colonels tried to assign another driver to me when they arrived?" the commandant said.

"What?" Violet's head snapped around to stare at the doctor.

"He suggested I might want a male driver."

Violet returned her attention to the road and eased off the brake as the rear tyres rolled over the crest.

"And what did you tell them, sir?" she asked cautiously.

"I told him to sod off." He grunted in satisfaction. "Told them I had the most capable driver in the whole damn Legion."

"Thank you, sir."

"I think he knew that," Lavigne said with a snort. "Think he was looking for an upgrade himself."

"I'm glad to be driving you, sir," she said with feeling. The man in the passenger seat was one of the best she knew.

"They were also asking about something else."

"Something else?" Violet guided the Humber around a deep crevice.

"Have you heard…" The commandant trailed off, sounding uncharacteristically uncertain.

"Heard what, sir?"

"I heard the chief of staff mention some concerns about intelligence."

"Mine or yours, sir?" Violet gently accelerated, worriedly eyeing the steam still leaking from beneath the bonnet.

"Very funny, Adjutant St. Croix." The doctor pushed his spectacles back up his nose. "No, he was speaking of intelligence breaches. And Koenig is not often wrong. He suggested that Allied information is leaking to the Wehrmacht somehow."

"About what?" Violet was really going to have to stop soon. There was an outcropping just ahead—

"The last offensive to Halfaya Pass last week was a disaster. I heard the Brits lost almost a hundred tanks and a thousand men, and they never even got to their objective. Tobruk is still besieged. Like the bosches knew exactly where they'd be and were waiting for them."

Violet rolled her shoulders and adjusted her grip on the steering wheel. "Maybe the Germans just got lucky."

"They seem to be getting lucky a lot. I think maybe Rommel is making his own luck." The commandant shifted his bulk in the front seat.

"I don't know anything about planning military offensives, so I can't speak to any of that, sir," Violet said. "But I do know that I'm going to pull over just ahead. There's a bit of an outcropping, so at least there will be a little shade for—" She broke off as a familiar noise reached her ears.

A sound that never failed to send ice through her veins even on the most scorching of desert days. And crawling along roads at speeds that rarely exceeded five miles per hour left them only one survival option.

"Air raid." She brought the car to a shuddering stop and threw open her door. "Get out! Hurry!" she yelled at the commandant.

Lavigne was already halfway out of the vehicle when the first bomb hit the ground. It struck a distance behind the Humber, close to the last of the supply trucks. The truck toppled onto its side, rolling down the sandy incline that Violet had navigated earlier, tossing men and crates in all directions.

"Goddammit." Violet hadn't heard the planes approach over the rumble and clatter of the Humber. And the desert wind often swallowed sound, but she should have been more vigilant. She should have kept a more careful eye on the heat-washed expanse above. She'd become an expert in identifying the individual threats—the high-pitched whine of Stukas and Messerschmidts that dove with terrifying speed and the lower drone of the big Junkers that were still just as fearful but not as fast.

The Humber was much too low to crawl beneath, so Violet yanked the commandant toward the outcropping. "Get beneath, cover your head," she yelled unnecessarily. This was far from the first time that she and the doctor had had to flee a Luftwaffe attack.

Both Violet and Lavigne crouched beneath the rocky ledge, arms clasped over their heads. A Messerschmidt, Violet guessed without looking up, based solely on the shriek of its engines. The ground shook as bombs fell and the plane's guns strafed the road, sending rows of sand into the air in small puffs. Dirt and sand and dust and rock pelted all around them, and Violet winced as a shard struck the back of her forearm. The plane roared overhead and away.

Violet took her hands from over her head. "You good, sir?" she asked Lavigne.

"Splendid" came the breathless answer. "It's like the bosches have a goddamn written schedule every time we need to move." He frowned. "You're bleeding."

Violet glanced down at her stinging forearm. There was a deep gash just below her elbow, and blood had run past her wrist. She looked away. "It's nothing."

"You will get that looked at as soon as we get to the dressing station, yes? If there are small shrapnel or shards, I don't want you getting an infection out here."

"Yes," Violet agreed, distracted. She stood slowly and assessed the damage. The Humber still steamed but all four tyres were intact, and the machine gun rounds seemed to have missed it entirely.

"Only one?" Lavigne asked, brushing the layers of dust that covered his uniform. He wiped his face, covered in a chalky, gritty mask. "How very odd. Those bastards usually travel in packs. It must be our lucky day."

Violet searched the sky and, in seconds, found what she was looking for. The glint of sun on wings of at least three more planes, all dropping from a high altitude, approaching from behind their column. "It's not."

Her gaze flew to the trucks that had been following them. The last, toppled truck was on fire, black smoke rising into the hot air. The second had driven off the road into a dune. The first had stopped in its tracks on the edge of the road. But that wasn't what put Violet's heart into her throat. Men were emerging from the trucks, some sliding down the incline to help their wounded comrades and others milling aimlessly and confusedly on the road. A few were pointing at the single Messerschmidt that was curling away from the destruction it had left behind. No one, it seemed, was aware of the danger dropping out of the sky behind them.

"Oh, dear heavens," Lavigne muttered under his breath as he joined Violet. "They don't see the planes. They're going to be cut to ribbons."

Violet stood and waved her hands, trying to get their attention. No one took any notice. Without considering what she was doing, she sprinted from the outcropping in the direction of the trucks. She ignored Lavigne's shout of alarm behind her. If the men in those trucks did not see those planes, did not take cover, they would be, as the commandant said, cut to ribbons. Before they could even arrive at the front lines, they would be reduced to bullet- and shrapnel-riddled casualties, and the doctors and nurses at the dressing stations would be left trying to patch together the pieces.

The men closest to Violet saw her coming. They stared, gawk- ing, and Violet could only imagine what they saw. A crazed appari- tion in a filthy, sweat-stained Legion uniform, covered head to toe in dust, pinwheeling her arms at the sky.

"Take cover," she gasped as she reached them without slow- ing down. "Planes." She didn't check to see if they obeyed but kept running, heading toward the stranded second truck and the wounded men near it.

"Planes!" she choked, out of breath and barely able to form the word through the dust that coated her throat.

There was no rocky outcropping here to afford cover, and the men here were too far away to reach one before the Messerschmidts would be on top of them. The only cover was in the uneven depressions of the ground or beneath the surviv- ing trucks. Someone else must have finally heard the approach of the planes or seen the glare of the sun off the cross-painted wings because shouts of alarm went up.

The men scattered then, most diving beneath the undercar- riages of the trucks and digging out hollows in the sand wherever it was possible. Others threw themselves into sandy, rocky depres- sions or fissures in the ground to take what cover they could. The men who had been dragging their wounded comrades to safety drew them into meager shelter where they were or pushed the wounded soldiers under the trucks. The whine of the planes turned into a scream as the Messerschmidts started their assault.

Violet reached a man labouring to roll a wounded soldier beneath a truck's undercarriage. She dropped to her knees beside him, focused on scooping out armfuls of rocky sand, scraping her palms. "Push him under," she wheezed, blinking furiously at the dirt stinging her eyes. The injured soldier screamed in pain.

The first bomb dropped somewhere near the burning truck behind them. A second and third followed, detonating in a punishing pattern.

"Now us. Hurry," Violet wheezed. On her belly, she wriggled under the truck. She was vaguely aware that the soldier she had helped was doing the same. She curled into a ball and put her hands over her head just as the guns opened fire. If the truck was hit by a bomb, they would all die, but at least here they had protection from the guns. She squeezed her eyes shut, her arms clamped over her ears, as the bombs continued to fall and the guns chattered. The truck above her shuddered as bullets thumped into it, and bits of sand and rock stung her exposed skin. It was over quickly, the rational part of her mind understood, though the seconds ticked by like hours. The whine of the Messerschmidts faded. She waited long minutes more but the planes did not return.

The wounded soldier was moaning and coughing but Violet ignored him for the moment. Cautiously, she opened her eyes and raised her head toward the daylight. She stretched out her limbs, finding everything still working, and twisted out from under the truck. Her heart was pounding in her ears and the back of her uniform was soaked with sweat.

A pair of hands pulled her forward as she staggered to her feet, and she found herself looking into the worried and slightly blurry face of Commandant Lavigne.

"Are you hurt?" he demanded, out of breath. His round spectacles were askew.

Violet shook her head and a shower of dust and sand rained down around her. "No." Her voice was hoarse.

"Are you sure? You're barely recognizable under all that dust. You could be bleeding to death, and I wouldn't be able to tell."

She blinked and rubbed at her watering eyes, trying to clear the grit from them. "I'm not." After a moment, her vision cleared, and she gazed around at the damage left by the Luftwaffe attack.

The last truck was still burning furiously. The truck under which she had taken cover, the one that had driven into the dunes, was steaming almost as badly as the Humber, the bonnet and cab punctured and torn by bullet holes. Around the trucks and along the road were soldiers strewn everywhere, many that were beginning to stir but some that were not. Violet exhaled heavily, trying not to feel defeated.

"Please do not do something so foolish again, understood? I do not wish to explain how I lost the best Legion driver because she ran into a hail of German bullets." Lavigne paused and patted her arm. "Even if it was very brave."

Violet only nodded.

"Well, what's done is done," the commandant sighed. "Nothing for it now than to get the casualties collected and to the dressing station as soon as we can. Those who are unhurt will have to either walk or wait, I'm afraid, until we can return. These two trucks are a loss but the first one up there is still drivable." He gestured with frustration at the damaged vehicles. "Even you cannot fix this."

"No." The desert was already littered with carnage of the Allied efforts to push back against the surging Afrika Korps. Violet would know. She passed the heaps of wreckage on a regular basis.

Lavigne grunted and then strode purposefully toward the men now attending the wounded. Wearily, Violet watched him go and then turned back to the bullet-riddled truck. The soldier that she had taken cover with, the one who had rolled his wounded comrade underneath, was now trying to extricate the man. He was on his hands and knees, his head beneath the undercarriage, trying to pull the patient out by his arms. Violet dropped down near the rear bumper.

The wounded man still beneath the truck was whimpering

with a wet whistling sound. Immediately, Violet could see why. The lower part of his jaw had been hit, his chin reduced to a bloody, pulpy mess. The front of his uniform was spattered with blood, and more bubbled and dripped with every breath he took.

"Goddammit, I hate blood," Violet croaked as she crawled back under the truck and grasped the man's belt.

"Everyone hates blood," the soldier mumbled without looking up, his voice rough. "Unless you're a vampire."

The unexpected comment reminded her of George, and she found the thought oddly comforting.

"On three." Violet gripped the man's belt and braced her feet against the undercarriage.

Together they slid the wounded man out from under the truck. She struggled to her feet and straightened. And looked directly into a pair of sea-blue eyes, made that much more startling by the dust and dirt covering his face.

"Henri?" The word was barely a whisper.

"Princess?"

He looked the same but different. He was still darkly tanned from the sun, though the skin on his arms and legs was lined with dust and grime. His hair was still sandy blond, though it was no longer shaggy but cut short, and he had at least a few days' worth of stubble on his jaw.

Without thinking, she reached out to touch him, brushing his sweat- and dust-stained uniform shirt with the tips of her fingers. He was warm and solid beneath her touch.

He took a step away from her, nearly stumbling.

"A little help here?" The barked request came from a dark-haired soldier that had appeared and was struggling to wrap the injured man's head with a length of gauze dressing. The man was thrashing and groaning in pain. Blood dripped and spattered everywhere. Violet flinched but moved quickly and lowered her weight across the man's knees. Henri knelt and pinned the wounded man's arms.

The patient's struggles lessened, and she received a grateful glance from the soldier bandaging his head.

"I was going to warn you not to try holding his feet," the dark-haired soldier said, winding the bandage quickly and with deft hands.

"I like my teeth where they are," Violet replied. She was staring at the back of Henri's filthy uniform as though she half expected him to vanish like a desert mirage.

"You've done this before," the soldier was saying to her. "Held down a man, that is."

She tore her eyes away from Henri's back. "Too many times. You a medic?"

"No. Just first into the crate of gauze." He looked up at her with a tight smile before returning his attention to his work.

He had kind eyes, she thought. She liked him immediately.

"You a nurse?"

"No. Well, sort of."

"Ah." He didn't seem to find her answer strange but then he hadn't seemed to find her appearance strange either. He tied off the bandage and stood.

"You can let him go," he said to Henri and Violet. "Let's get him in the truck before the bosches come back for another round."

Violet stood, her muscles protesting. Henri stood as well, watching her.

"How far away are we from the dressing station?"

"Five miles, maybe?" Violet forced herself to focus. "We'll need to get all the wounded loaded. There will be room in my car for three, maybe four if they can sit. The commandant says the first truck is drivable but the supplies might have to come out of the truck to make room for casualties. We'll have to come back for the crates." *And you*, she almost added but didn't. One thing at a time.

"You're Commandant Lavigne's driver, aren't you?" Henri's dark-haired companion asked.

Surprised, Violet nodded mutely.

"I've heard of you," he told Violet. "Well, at least heard that there was a fearless dame who was the personal driver for the Legion's medical officer. Didn't actually realize that it was you up there driving that car."

"I'm not fearless." That her pulse still hadn't returned to normal was proof of that.

"Says the woman who ran toward German planes for our sakes." He gestured at the prone man. "Your warning probably saved half these men."

Violet ignored the praise. She should have seen those planes earlier than she had. It was part of her job. "Let's get this man off the ground, out of the sun, and loaded into the first truck."

She could still feel the weight of Henri's silent gaze on her, and it was a disorienting experience, carrying on a separate, necessary conversation with a stranger when Henri was standing right there. If not for her stinging palms, the biting flies at her ankles, and the heat of the sun searing her skin, she might have surrendered to the notion that she was hallucinating.

Her words seemed to have spurred Henri into action, and he bent to the wounded man's head, gingerly getting his arms under his shoulders. "Take his feet, Gasquet," he ordered the dark-haired soldier.

The soldier called Gasquet handed Violet the bulky box of gauze and medical supplies and did as he was ordered, and the two men lifted and carried the moaning man toward the first truck, where soldiers were already loading more wounded. Violet followed them.

"Not many women out here," Gasquet told her as he navigated the ground, grunting under the weight of the wounded soldier. "Men tend to talk about the ones who are."

They had reached the truck, and Gasquet and Henri were relieved of their burden as their patient was lifted up into the rear.

Gasquet wiped his bloody hands on his shorts and extended one to Violet.

"Corporal Christophe Gasquet, at your service."

Violet shifted the box and shook his hand. "Adjutant Violet St. Croix."

"Ah, that makes sense now," he said. "A flower in the desert."

Violet had no idea what he was talking about.

Gasquet released Violet's hand and took the box from her. "A pleasure, Adjutant St. Croix. You know each other?" The question was directed at Henri.

"Yes," Henri replied faintly.

"Huh. Lucky you." Gasquet grimaced in the direction of the burning truck. "We should keep going. Poor bastards." He tossed a packet of gauze to Violet. "Here," he said. "Looks like you might need this."

Violet caught the packet awkwardly as Gasquet hurried away.

"You're hurt." Henri took a step toward her.

Blood was still dripping sluggishly down her arm.

"I'm fine," Violet told him. "It's nothing."

"It's bleeding a fair bit. Let me wrap it for you."

"You don't have to."

"I know I don't have to." He took the gauze from her without waiting for an answer.

Violet let him. "I heard you'd joined the Legion."

He tore the packet open and wrapped the binding tightly around her wound, his hands sure. "You sound surprised."

"No. Not surprised at all. I just…"

Violet looked away, trying to find something to say in the silence that had fallen. It had been almost two years since she had watched Henri walk away from her under a blistering sun. Two years since she had decided to listen to herself. To stop bending. To stop accommodating. In that time, she'd occasionally thought about what she might say to Henri, should she ever see him again. And now that the moment was here, her mind was an utter blank.

All she could focus on was the feel of his gentle but sure fingers on her skin.

"I saw your sister two weeks ago," she blurted.

His fingers stilled. "George? She's here?"

Violet nodded, grasping the topic with alacrity because it was easy to talk about George and she could offer him a ray of happiness amid the death and destruction that plagued this hostile land, battered by the enemy and abused by the conditions.

"She's at one of the dressing stations northeast of here. There are only two nurses there. Not many volunteers for the very front lines. Before that she was working in the Spears hospital in Gaza. She calls herself a Spearette. All the nurses there did." Violet was babbling but didn't care. It was better than awkward silence.

"Was she all right?" Henri demanded. "How did she seem to you?"

"She was the same as always. Caring. Unfailingly positive." The hour that Violet had been able to spend with her friend had been like a restorative balm to her soul. "It was nice to be able to just...talk." For a tiny window in time, they had ceased to be two women caught up in a war and were simply two friends sharing confidences and secrets and fears. "She worries about you—"

"Was she safe?" he pressed, apparently more concerned with her welfare than her worry.

"As safe as any of us are out here. She's really good at what she does, Henri. You would be so proud of her. She's an incredible nurse."

"I was always proud of her. She didn't need to become a nurse for that."

Violet swallowed, reminded that there wasn't much that Violet had had to be proud of the last time she'd seen Henri. "You haven't heard from George in a while, then."

"No, not for months. It's been almost impossible to send and receive letters," he went on. "We're on the move too much."

"Well, she's fine," Violet reassured him again. Another silence fell. "What about your parents and your sisters at home?" she ventured. "Are they well?"

"Haven't had a letter from home in months either. But they were doing all right last I heard from them. Still fishing, still keeping food on the table."

"That's good. I'm glad."

"And your parents? Are they managing?" His question sounded very perfunctory.

"Um." Violet bit her lip, hating the sadness that still came every time her parents were mentioned. She should be tougher by now.

"They must find the reduced access to champagne and truffles a real hardship." Henri secured the end of the gauze.

"I wouldn't know. Since I volunteered, they no longer speak to me."

Henri's hands stilled. "Shit. I'm sorry."

"Don't be. I made my choice knowing the consequences."

"No, I'm sorry for my snide remark. It was uncalled for." He regarded her steadily. "Your parents can apologize for their own foolishness."

Violet nodded, afraid her voice would break if she spoke.

Henri busied himself tucking the roll of bandages in his pack. "Will you wait for me?"

"What?"

"At the dressing station. Will you wait for me to get there?"

"Yes. Of course." Her answer was immediate, and she wasn't sure if it was the tenuous connection to George through Henri, or maybe to a time and place that had once brought her joy, or Henri himself that was leaving her so breathless. She didn't care to examine that too closely. "I mean, if I can," she added. "I'll try my best. The commandant might order me back out—"

"*If you can* is good enough for me." He stopped and looked at her with all the intensity that she remembered from those hot summer days spent in a little fishing boat out on the sea. "Adjutant St. Croix."

CHAPTER
13

The hospital, if a handful of canvas tents patched together could be called a hospital, was already in a state of organized chaos by the time Violet and the casualties from the air raid arrived. The wounded were unloaded from the vehicles, and the truck was immediately sent back to collect the men and supplies that had been left behind. Violet had volunteered to accompany them—argued vehemently, in truth—but Dr. Lavigne had ordered her to the hospital to have her arm attended. They would need to be on the road again within two hours, headed to the next station. She was ordered to look after the Humber and then look after herself in that time. Once he was satisfied that Violet had acquiesced, the doctor vanished into the chaos to offer his assistance.

And so Violet had parked the old Humber in a low-lying area on the very outer edge of camp that had the potential to offer a modicum of protection should the station be bombed. She wedged stones underneath the tyres to keep it from rolling since the handbrake no longer functioned. She repaired the leaking radiator as best she could and topped it up again. She fetched a jerrycan of petrol from the supply dump and filled the tank. She cleaned the grit and grime from the windows and wiped the blood from the back seat and doorhandles. And as she worked, she kept one eye on the road leading into the station, hoping to see the familiar bulk of a returning supply truck.

The road remained empty.

Her tasks on the Humber completed, Violet made her way into the hospital and sat impatiently until a harried doctor prodded, cleaned, disinfected, and stitched her wound. By the time he was done, the sun had reached its zenith, and the heat became oppressive, like a heavy, weighted blanket that made every movement an effort. The terrain around the camp had melted into a shimmering, hazy tableau and the sky had been washed a pale, tired blue. And still the road remained empty.

The anxious anticipation that had winged through her stomach dissipated and turned into anxious knots. Worry began creeping in despite her best efforts. She forced herself toward the mess tent and wolfed a meager meal she didn't taste, washed down with a tin of tepid tea. The practical side of her knew that there was no telling when she would next get a chance to eat and she was of no use to anyone while faint with hunger—

The rumble of an engine and the shouts of men had her bolting back outside. The familiar truck had pulled up nearest the hospital, and men were now swarming around the back, handing down any remaining casualties first and the boxes of supplies next. Violet stumbled to a stop. Frantically, she searched the milling faces, but there was no sign of Henri. She pushed her way into the crowd, standing on her tiptoes, grateful for her height.

Someone touched her uniform sleeve, and Violet spun, but it was Commandant Lavigne whom she found in front of her.

"Adjutant St. Croix." The doctor was sweating heavily and the bottom of his uniform shirt was stained with blood and iodine. A thick folder of documents and communiques that he would deliver to the next station was jammed under his arm.

"Sir."

Lavigne gestured at her wound. "You get that taken care of? Properly cleaned and stitched?"

"Yes, sir."

"Good. You've had something to eat and drink? You're feeling all right?"

"Yes, sir. Thank you, sir."

He waved his hand. "You do such a wonderful job of looking after me, Adjutant. I want to make sure that you are looking after yourself too. You're the best there is, and I don't know what I would do without you." He cleared his throat. "Is the car fit to travel again?"

No, she wanted to tell him. *Not yet.* "Yes, sir."

"Excellent. That is very good news." Lavigne handed the folder to Violet. "See that this is secured with the rest of my private papers and dispatches in the car, along with my luggage."

"Of course." Violet took the documents without question. The commandant's belongings and communications were her responsibility.

"We need to depart north in twenty minutes." The commandant removed his spectacles and polished them on the cleanest part of his uniform sleeve before putting them back on. "Please bring the car around, and I'll join you shortly."

"Yes, sir." She paused. "You are not needed here any longer?" She wondered if that question sounded as desperate as it felt.

Lavigne gave her a curious look. "No. The medical staff have everything well in hand here, as much as that is ever possible. Our tanks and armoured divisions are starting a push against a roadblock in the Barada Gorge. I need to get to the station nearest the position as soon as possible."

"Of course, sir."

"I have another...request for you, Adjutant. One that is more delicate in nature."

"Anything, sir."

He guided her away from the crowd and lowered his voice. "There is a British intelligence officer at a post a mile past the dressing station near Barada Gorge. With, apparently, a small company that is waiting for the advance into Damascus, if we ever get there. I would like you to pay him a visit."

Violet rubbed her forehead in puzzlement. "Me, sir?"

"Yes. I am relying on your discretion." He pulled a small square of paper from his uniform pocket. He unfolded it and smoothed it flat against his thigh. *Restricted* was written across the top of the page, beside a round stamp that was smeared and impossible to read. A series of letters and numbers had been noted in the top right corner and beneath all of that was a neatly typed paragraph.

"This report was generated by British intelligence. It seems that the communications men at British High Command have indicated that they have intercepted some unusual radio signals from this quadrant."

Violet frowned. "I'm not sure what that means."

"It means that somewhere out here, someone other than the French or British, is sending out radio signals."

"But there is an entire Axis army out here too," Violet pointed out in confusion. "And Vichy forces too. Probably all using radios as much as we are."

"I'm aware," Lavigne answered. "But our people whose sole job it is to listen in and decode such transmissions have flagged these ones for a few reasons." He consulted the report. "These particular messages are not considered regular military correspondence but consistently encoded in a manner that suggests a single German field operative."

"A field operative? A German spy, you mean?"

The commandant grimaced. "Yes. Further, they have not been able to decipher the code being used. It is different from the encryption being used by the Wehrmacht, though I don't pretend to know how they have come to that conclusion." He creased a corner of the paper. "I need you to follow up with the Allied communications and intelligence officer who sent this."

"Why me, sir?"

"Because I fear that the intelligence officer will be gone by the time I attend my duties at the dressing station, which must be my priority. You can proceed directly there once you deliver me to the station and report back to me. I trust you completely."

"Of course. Thank you, sir."

"The concern is that this particular operative is working within our own ranks. Find out if this is truly a significant threat or if this is a case of paranoia by men looking for ghosts in places they don't exist." He scowled. "Koenig managed to conceal this before anyone else here saw it. We cannot have communications like this coming from Command and floating around here without knowing for certain if they are legitimate."

"Understood."

"I'm sure that this will amount to nothing, but a lie can travel halfway around the world before the truth can even put its boots on."

"Sir?"

"Something I once heard someone say." He stared hard at Violet, his eyes unnaturally large behind his spectacles. "The morale of the men out here cannot be shaken if we are to survive the fight that I believe is coming for us. And in my experience, nothing, and I mean nothing, destroys morale and courage like the loss of trust between a soldier and the man standing at his side. Once that darkness worms its way into a man's thoughts, it will fester until men begin to turn on their own." Commandant Lavigne rubbed his face, the whiskers of his beard making a raspy sound. "Sun Tzu once said that the supreme art of war is to subdue the enemy without fighting." His spectacles had slid, and he pushed them back up the bridge of his nose. "And while I breathe, I will not allow the goddamn Nazis the pleasure."

Violet only nodded, uncertain what to say. The entire situation seemed unsettling, and maybe even a little doubtful, but then again, Violet had no experience with spies. She would do as she was asked and keep an open mind.

"Take this." Lavigne handed her the report. "And again, I cannot stress enough the need for your discretion."

"Of course." Violet refolded the paper and slid it deep into her own uniform pocket, buttoning the flap securely closed.

He checked his watch. "Twenty—no, make that fifteen minutes, Adjutant. I'll see you shortly."

Violet watched helplessly as Lavigne headed off. The conversation with the commandant had distracted her from the return of the troops but now she looked around again, searching for a familiar face. The truck engine was cut, and the sound of men's voices replaced the growl of the idling engine. Where on earth could Henri have gone? He'd asked her to wait. But maybe something had happened. Maybe Henri had been taken into the hospital—

She was jostled by a passing soldier and stumbled awkwardly. A pair of hands steadied her. A peculiar sense of déjà vu descended, and though she wasn't standing in front of a Nice hospital or a bullet-riddled truck, a silent clock was ticking all the same as she looked up at Henri Chastain.

He was still just as dishevelled and filthy, exhaustion stamped across his features. His uniform was torn at the shoulder, and his knees were scraped beneath the hem of his shorts. Sweat had tracked rivulets through the dust and grime clinging to his skin, running from his temples down the sides of his face and neck.

"Are you hurt?" she managed around a mouth that had gone completely dry. He hadn't let her go.

"No."

"I thought something had happened to you. The truck—"

"Overheated about a mile out. But they were able to get it running again."

Violet fumbled for her canteen slung across her shoulders. She held it out to him. "Do you need something to drink—"

"I'm fine."

She dropped the canteen. "Can I get you something from the mess—"

"No. I'm good."

"Maybe some tea—"

"No."

"I don't have much time," she said. "I have to fetch the car, and the commandant needs me to—"

"Violet."

At the sound of her name, she fell silent. She wasn't saying anything she wanted to but she had no idea how to start. It seemed so strange, so…insurmountable that so much had happened in the time since she'd seen him last. It seemed illogical that they could simply pick up where they had left off.

"How long do you have?" His hands tightened on her arms.

"Five minutes. Maybe a few more before I need to get the car."

"Right." He released her and reached into one of the leather pouches at his waist. "This is yours. I should return it." He produced a book and held it out to her.

Violet stared at the book in his hands but made no move to take it. The familiar red-and-white cover was significantly worse for wear but she recognized it instantly.

"You saved it."

"I did." He cleared his throat. "I confess I read it. I liked *The Hound of the Baskervilles* better, to be honest."

Violet was still frozen. "I haven't read that."

"You should. And *A Study in Scarlet* too."

"Why did you keep it?"

He rubbed the back of his neck with his hand. He seemed to

be debating his answer. "I like books. And it was, as it turns out, a good story, despite my biases. You should read it," he finally said.

Violet shifted the dispatch bag under one arm and took the book from him. She ran her fingers up and down the spine. "Thank you. For saving it. For keeping it."

"You're welcome."

"I volunteered that day," she said abruptly. "Did it on the way home from the hospital. I still hate blood, and I'm not really a very good nurse, but I am a very good driver. I wanted you to know that."

Henri didn't say anything, only jammed his hands under the leather pack straps that ran over his shoulders. She couldn't read his expression.

"I went back to find you the next afternoon," she said. "To tell you that. But you were already gone."

He stared at her, the force of that azure gaze travelling all the way through her. "Why?"

"Why?"

"Why did you go back?"

She'd asked herself that question often. Why had Henri's opinion mattered to her as much as it had? She'd yet to come up with a satisfactory answer. "I don't know. Maybe I—"

"Corporal." The address was hurried, somewhat breathless, and wholly apologetic. "I'm so sorry to interrupt but the colonel is looking for you."

A young man appeared beside Henri. He was of medium height and build with a broad forehead and earnest brown eyes.

Henri closed his eyes briefly. "Thank you, Picard."

"You probably shouldn't keep a colonel waiting," Violet said.

"Colonel Bennett is the American military attaché," Henri told her. "The chief of staff has asked me to assist him provisionally."

"Why is there an American attaché here?" she asked, momentarily diverted. "And what are you assisting him with?"

"Bennett reports directly back to Washington. He decided that if he is going to convince the powers in America to join this war, then his daily reports would be best if they originated using his own eyes at the front and not secondhand from an embassy office in Cairo. He's been with us since the beginning but he relies on me to get the details right."

"Oh. I guess that makes sense. Will they help us, do you think? The Americans?"

"Don't know. The chief of staff is hoping so, thus his direc-tive." He stopped, making an impatient gesture with his hand. "I don't have much time with you here, and I don't want to spend it talking about—"

"Corporal Chastain. There you are. I didn't know where you'd hared off to." Another man appeared, this one speaking fluent French but with what was very clearly an American accent.

Colonel Bennett, Violet surmised, studying the attaché. He was short with wide shoulders and a thick chest. He had curly, dark hair and a wide moustache and beneath that, an equally expansive smile. He stopped just short of Henri and the man called Picard.

"My superiors will want details on the air raids like the one this morning. Aviation specifics, numbers, munitions, strategy. Because that was hair-raising, and I'm not afraid to admit it. Also details of the German armoured light reconnaissance units we spotted later on. Thought I'd get a supplemental report out before evening," Bennett boomed. "Easier to transmit when I'm not fumbling in the dark."

"Of course," Henri replied, sounding painfully polite. He turned to Violet. "Adjutant St. Croix, allow me to introduce Col-onel John Bennett, American attaché. And Private Remy Picard, batman."

"A pleasure." Violet stepped forward and shook each man's hand. Picard still looked apologetic.

"Heard a lot about you, Adjutant St. Croix," Bennett said as he released her hand. "You're quite the novelty out here."

"I aim to be more than a novelty, sir," she said evenly.

"Adjutant St. Croix is one of the best drivers in the Legion." It was Private Picard who spoke. "When she is not on assignment for Commandant Lavigne, her services are sought by senior officers from the Levant to Cairo."

Violet gave the young man a small smile. She didn't need to be defended but she appreciated it all the same. And she was still painfully aware of the time slipping away like sand through her fingers.

"Well, then, perhaps you might speak to me sometime about what you see out there in your travels, Adjutant St. Croix," Bennett exclaimed. "Enemy sightings, allied positions, terrain conditions, that sort of thing. Could be mighty useful in my reports. Get a clear picture of what we're up against."

Violet nodded noncommittally. She wasn't entirely convinced that reporting such details to a country reluctant to become involved would be useful to anyone.

"I'll be with you in just a few moments," Henri told the American. "I have a matter to finish with Adjutant St. Croix."

"Very good," Bennett said. "I'll get set up. Again, a pleasure to meet the flower of the desert, Adjutant." He gave Violet another friendly smile and moved away, whistling a tune beneath his thick moustache.

"'The flower of the desert'?" Violet asked no one in particular. It was the second time she'd heard that.

"It's what the troops are calling you, Adjutant," Picard told her. "Sometimes just La Fleur."

Violet blinked. "Why?"

"Because you are an inspiration to the men," Picard said.

"How am I an inspiration?" she asked incredulously.

Picard blushed furiously and looked at Henri. Henri only shrugged and gestured for the batman to answer.

"Just by being out here. Enduring what they endure, fighting the same fight." The batman stumbled over the words.

"I'm just doing my job. No more and no less than anyone else, including you."

"But you are beautiful and kind and brave." The private twisted his hands together. "And you remind the men of their wives and daughters and sisters. You remind them of home and what they are here fighting for."

Violet bit the inside of her lip, not at all sure that she deserved that sort of veneration. "Thank you," she said awkwardly.

"Are you quite finished, Private Picard?" Henri asked, though it wasn't unkind.

The private blushed again. "Um. Yes, sir. Apologies. And I'm sorry that I couldn't stall Colonel Bennett for longer even though you asked me to head him off."

"It's all right. You did what you could. Find Corporal Gasquet and ask him to get the colonel started on his report until I can get there. There's nothing that I know that Gasquet does not. You may begin without me."

"Of course." The batman nodded fervently and hurried after the attaché, leaving Violet and Henri alone, surrounded by a hive of activity.

Violet desperately searched for the right thing to say. How, with precious seconds slipping by, could she not seem to string a meaningful sentence together?

"Private Picard seems like a good sort," she blurted.

"Private Picard is smitten."

"I'm sorry?"

"You have an admirer."

"Don't be ridiculous. I met him less than a minute ago."

"Doesn't matter. But you're right, he is a good sort. I'd trust him with my life. I have, on occasion, in fact. He was with us at Dunkirk."

"You were at Dunkirk? Was it as bad as I heard?"

"Yes." His answer was tight. "And yes. But I don't want to talk about Dunkirk either. Not now."

Another silence descended between them. Violet looked down at the book she still had clutched in her hand and struggled for the right words. "Where are they sending you from here?" she asked.

"Don't know yet, exactly. We'll find out shortly. Not far. Lots of fighting in the hills still in and around Damascus. I expect we'll be deployed there until we can take the city."

"Promise me you'll be safe," she whispered, pressing the book to her chest.

"I promise," he said, even though they both knew that that was a promise that no one could keep.

A trio of soldiers brushed past them hurriedly, waving their arms and arguing something among themselves. Henri waited until they had passed before he spoke. "I had heard about La Fleur, you know. Corporal Gasquet was right when he said men talk about women in a place where there are few."

Violet didn't know what to say.

"I heard the stories. About a woman in the Free French Legion with great courage and resilience. I had no idea that it was you. That you were La Fleur."

"Thank you?" The words ended up sounding like a question because she still wasn't sure how to respond.

"I don't want your thanks. The point that I'm trying to make here is that I think Violet St. Croix finally decided who she really is."

Someone shouted in the distance, and the truck roared to life again, belching exhaust. The gears ground, and the truck rolled toward them. Henri and Violet stepped to the side. Men were hurrying across the station, and Violet was reminded again that her time was almost up.

She didn't want to go. She wanted to capture these seconds that were tumbling away. But she couldn't do that. "Henri—"

"Did you marry him?"

His question jarred Violet out of her own thoughts. "What?"

"Adjutant St. Croix." He emphasized her last name. "Did you marry him?"

"No."

"Are you planning to?"

"No."

"Mmm." She couldn't read his expression again. Whatever he was thinking, he kept it hidden. He reached out and brushed a hank of stiff, dusty hair from the side of her face. "I'll see you again soon, princess. Be safe."

And in another peculiar state of déjà vu, Violet watched him walk away.

CHAPTER
14

20 JUNE 1941
ADVANCED DRESSING STATION, BARADA GORGE, SYRIA

The dressing station near Barada Gorge looked like every other dressing station that Violet had been to. A collection of tents assembled in much the same way that the last dressing station had boasted. This station, however, was closer to the front lines that were still heavily engaged, and a row of recently unloaded stretchers with their wounded was lined up in the shade of the main hospital tent, waiting to be carried inside. Men from the medical corps moved between them, offering assurances and tins of water.

Violet dropped the commandant off in front of the hospital tent and then guided the Humber over the rough, rocky ground, past the edge of the encampment, and on to the post where a British company and intelligence officer presumably waited. She followed the map Lavigne had provided and found the small cluster of tents right where he'd said they would be. She looked for the safest place to park, as she always did. The Humber had survived another journey, starting to steam only for the last two miles. She'd deal with the radiator again in the morning. If she was lucky, she would find a mechanic here who could assist her.

The sun had sunk low in the sky, lighting her surroundings with a golden orange hue and stretching the shadows into long, thin silhouettes. The distant hills were starting to turn lavender in the encroaching dusk, making the bleak emptiness of their profiles look almost inviting to those who didn't know better. At the bottom of the gorge, just visible from where Violet stood, a dark row of stubborn trees clung to the edge of the narrow ribbon of water carving through the stone. For a fanciful moment, Violet imagined navigating the heights all the way down to the bottom, if only just to lie in the water for a minute. Instead, she spared the mess tent a single, longing look before heading in the direction of where she hoped she might find the English intelligence officer's quarters.

She was pointed toward a pair of tents dug into a slope by a handful of soldiers. They studied her first with disbelief, then curiosity, and finished their perusal with a few low whistles. Violet ignored it all and thanked them for their time. She was hot and tired and hungry and thirsty and her sense of humour and tolerance were wearing dangerously thin. She moved on, retrieved the folded paper from her pocket, and checked it before ducking into the first tent the soldiers had indicated. It took her a moment for her eyes to adjust to the dimness and for her to see the officer who stood frozen, gaping at her.

"Excuse me," she said in English. "I'm looking for Major Scott."

"Dead," came the stammered response.

"I'm sorry?"

"He died," the officer told her.

Violet consulted the order in her hand. "Can you tell me who has taken his place, then?"

"Try Captain Lipton. He's in the next tent over." He was still gawking at her.

"Thank you." Wearily, Violet ducked back out into the evening and silently entered the next tent, where her eyes struggled to adjust all over again. Inside, a British officer was standing at the very rear, behind a long table covered in boxes and stacks of paper, giving orders to two other personnel. They hadn't seemed to notice her.

"Captain Lipton?" she asked.

All three men's heads snapped around to stare at her.

"Who's asking?"

"I am Adjutant St. Croix." She held up the missive. "I was to contact Major Scott regarding an intelligence matter."

Captain Lipton said something to the two men that Violet couldn't hear, though they departed quickly, eyeing Violet with some incredulity as they went.

"Have a seat," the captain ordered, gesturing at a lone wooden chair near the table.

Violet did as she was bid, struggling to find level footing for the chair, while Captain Lipton sorted papers that lay on the table at a hectic speed. A typewriter sat on the far edge of the table next to an ashtray that was barely visible under a mountain of cigarette butts. A flat board had been mounted behind the table with a map pinned to it, spidery red ink marking points of interest.

"What can I do for you, miss?" he asked without pausing his task. His English was clipped and precise and exceedingly posh.

"Adjutant," Violet corrected.

"Adjutant," he amended, albeit with a clear lack of enthusiasm.

"I was supposed to see Major Scott, but I understand that he has...er, passed?"

"Yellow fever," the captain confirmed. "Died last week. Wasn't well for a long time." He glanced up at her over a pair of wire-framed spectacles. He was a slight man with a gaunt face and permanent worry lines etched across his forehead. "Perhaps I may be able to assist you?"

"Major Scott sent this report to General Koenig of the Free French." Violet passed him the message.

Lipton paused to read it and then handed it back without

looking at her. He added a stack of papers to a box on the corner of the table.

"And what, exactly, does the general have issue with?" he asked.

"He would like to verify the authenticity of the message."

Lipton's hands hovered over a document. "If Major Scott sent it, and as far as I can tell, he did, then it will be genuine." The document went in a different pile.

"I think the chief of staff was hoping to get some clarity on how likely it might be that there is, in fact, a spy in his ranks. He does not wish to cause paranoia over an unfounded claim."

"Unfounded?" The captain slammed the stack of paper he held to the tabletop and braced his hands along the edges. "Let me make this clear, Adjutant. There are spies everywhere. Cairo is crawling with them." He pointed at the box of papers. "That pile alone is individuals who are under suspicion as foreign agents working against us. It is impossible to follow up on all of them. We have countless cases of suspected sabotage and murder and espionage but evidence is often very difficult to collect."

"Major Scott indicated unusual radio signals in this case."

"The Abwehr has agents embedded everywhere. We know this, yet to find and identify them is a different kettle of fish entirely. All we can do is report any anomalies that we come across." He frowned and resumed his sorting. "And speaking of anomalies, who are you attached to, exactly, Adjutant St. Croix?"

"I am Commandant Lavigne's driver, sir."

"Driver?" His brows rose over the tops of his spectacles. "Not a nurse?"

"Occasionally," Violet allowed. "I serve with the Free French Foreign Legion."

"The Legion?"

"Yes, sir."

"Well, if you're looking for spies, you probably don't need to look much farther."

"I beg your pardon?"

"The Foreign Legion is called the Foreign Legion for a reason, Adjutant. There are men with all sorts of ties to Germany and Italy in that bunch, and it would not be difficult for any one of them to conceal a small wireless. Honestly, I've never understood France's love affair with—and reliance on—a band of foreign mercenaries. It's like inviting the bloody fox into the henhouse."

Violet blinked.

"If unusual radio signals were detected, then perhaps start by looking at those who have reasons to be loyal to Germany or Italy. Those who grew up in either country. Those who have family from either country. Those who have reason to hate France. In my experience, there are always threads to pull that will unwind the whole damn knot. You just have to find them."

Violet folded Major Scott's report in her hand, once, twice, and then a third time, feeling faintly nauseous. She had hoped that this matter would amount to nothing but now Violet wasn't so sure. The thought that one of their very own, someone whom she might have spoken with or eaten with or even cared for in a hospital, was a traitor was difficult to accept. There were many Free French Legionnaires who had ties to Germany.

Including Henri.

She recoiled from that thought, refusing to even consider the notion. "I'd like to have a look at Major Scott's files. I'd like to see for myself the...anomalies that he came across that prompted him to send this report."

Lipton put down the papers in his hand and scowled. "You don't have clearance for those files, Adjutant. And I don't bloody well have time for this. As you can see, I have more pressing matters."

"What could possibly be more pressing than preventing Rommel's Panzerarmee from overrunning Egypt?" Violet asked.

Lipton's face went red. "You are walking a perilously fine line of insolence, Adjutant."

"Have you destroyed them already? Major Scott's files?"

The captain huffed and resumed his sorting with jerky movements. "Is General Koenig here? I would speak with him directly."

"No. He sent me here on his behalf." Not entirely true, but Violet resented Lipton's dismissive pomposity. They were on the same side, after all. "And if there is a spy in our ranks who is feeding our enemy information on our positions, our strengths, and our weaknesses, then the next time Rommel's Mark Fours crash through our defences, I need to know that I've done all I could to prevent that. And if that means I must walk perilously close to insolence, then I do so without apology. Sir."

The captain huffed again but left the documents he was holding on the table and hauled a box of documents from the ground up onto the table. He was muttering under his breath as he thumbed through a tall stack of dusty, discoloured folders and selected one from the middle of the pile.

"This is all that Major Scott left behind," he said, opening the folder and reading rapidly. "Unidentified radio traffic from areas surrounding Damascus. Regular encoded transmissions since early May." He peered at Violet over the top of the folder. "The pattern indicated here follows the movement of your Free French forces, hence his conclusion that the transmissions were originating within your ranks." *And not ours*, he didn't say, though the implication was clear.

Violet absorbed that unhappily. "Is it possible that that is an error? That whatever radio transmissions being sent could be ours? Or just a coincidence—"

"I'm not done." The captain resumed his reading. "Transmissions sent only at night, distinctively short, and with a consistent call signal in each transmission, which led the major to conclude a single operative."

"Call signal?"

"What the operative uses to identify himself." He frowned. "Or herself. It indicates here that *Liesl* is used in each transmission. Not encoded, it appears. Or maybe it is a code for something else."

"Are you suggesting that the spy is a woman?"

"It's a call signal, Adjutant. It means nothing other than a series of letters that identifies the transmitter. I cannot begin to guess what it does or doesn't mean. Maybe a woman. Maybe a man." Captain Lipton's lips thinned. "The file says nothing more but I can assure you, Adjutant, that nothing about any of that information suggests that the sender is one of ours. Quite the opposite, in fact, and I would hazard a guess that there is indeed a traitor within your ranks. For all I know, the spy, whoever he or she is, might be entrenched in the very upper order of command or in the medical corps or in the communications ranks." He tapped his fingers on the tabletop. "You come across any suspicious deaths? Sabotage?"

"I don't think so," she replied slowly. "When was the last noted transmission, sir?"

Lipton consulted the folder again and then snapped it closed. "Ten days ago. But that was when this file was last updated, just prior to Major Scott's death. If the major had any other information, he took it to the grave with him," Lipton said with an air of finality. He tossed the folder into the box with the rest of the suspected foreign agents. "I can't help you any further, Adjutant." His jaw was set.

Violet recognized that the conversation was over. "Thank you for your time, Captain. I wish you well."

"I would hope, Adjutant, that you will soon come to your senses and recognize that your place is not here." His words were heavy with censure.

Violet stood slowly. "And where is here, sir?" she asked.

"On the front lines of a bloody war," Lipton said slowly, as though he were speaking to a toddler. "Women should be at home, where they are safe."

"Home?" Violet steadied the chair. "You mean France? Where swastikas fly from every corner?"

Lipton scowled. "I'm only trying to think of what is best for you, Adjutant."

"Ah. What's best for me." For a moment, the table and boxes of paper and tent walls wavered, to be replaced by a vision of a desk and heavy oak bookcases and richly panelled walls. Yet it was curious, Violet thought, that hearing those words for the first time since she had left France no longer elicited a reaction from her the way it once had. The anger and resentment and guilt and shame that had once accompanied that phrase were entirely absent. Instead, Violet felt only a vague sense of pity for this officer.

"War came to my home first, Captain," Violet said. "I did not want it, and I did not choose it. But I can tell you that what is best for me is to fight the only way I know how." She made her way to the entrance of the tent. "And I do not apologize for that, either."

CHAPTER

15

The spy wanted to enjoy Damascus.

It was a stunning city that appealed to the spy immensely, though he would be hard pressed to put a finger on which facet he enjoyed the most. Maybe it was the warm, sun-washed stone or the clean lines worked into domes and turrets and augmented by intricate patterns and bright, turquoise tiles. Perhaps the brilliant blue of the sky that served as a canvas for the emerald expanses of palms or the silver-touched foliage of the olive groves. Possibly the sweet, sensual scent of the abundant jasmine that often suffused the air, a welcome respite from the noxious mixture of dust, exhaust, and gunpowder. Or maybe the simple fact that the constant, maddening, delirious thirst no longer plagued him in this city of plenty.

The only thing that extinguished his true enjoyment of this extraordinary oasis was the knowledge that he was here for the first time as part of the Allied offensive. Perhaps, when the war was over and the Reich claimed this city as its own, he would return. Yes, he decided, as he picked his way across rue Beirut, avoiding vehicles and burros and carts. He would make an effort to come back.

The sun was in its death throes as he sidestepped a small crowd of Australian soldiers laughing uproariously. The streets were starting to fill with the evening crowd—soldiers with a few hours' leave heading out for an evening of entertainment and locals who were in the business of supplying it. No one gave him a second look. The victory parade that the Free French generals had organized upon the fall of Damascus had been a silent affair—most Damascenes watching with unhappy resentment. Yet the inevitable necessity of business continued, as it had for millennia, in a city that had been conquered by a never-ending queue of empires. The Free French and their allies were only the latest.

The spy turned south and stopped in front of the New Royal Hotel, admiring the stone architecture that he so loved. With his hands in his pockets, he strolled around the entirety of the building, heading east down avenue Victoire and returning along the narrow alley to the north. He was looking for a familiar vehicle, yet the Humber was nowhere to be found. He hadn't expected to see it—he had observed Commandant Lavigne at the French hospital less than an hour earlier, but one could not be too careful.

Since the French had taken control of Damascus, the officers had been billeted in hotels across the city. Private papers, dispatch bags, personal luggage, and all manner of communication were no longer temporarily stored in cars or trucks or left unattended in sun-bleached tents. Such things had since found more permanent homes in locked rooms, tucked away in desks and drawers. This development had made access more difficult and forced the spy to adjust his approach, but he was enjoying the advantage of knowing exactly where and when he would have that access.

Hanging back, he waited until a small knot of officers approached and entered the hotel. He slipped in behind them, careful not to draw attention to himself. It had been ridiculously easy to identify which French officers had been billeted in which rooms. A bank of wooden cubbies with labelled room numbers was built into the wall behind the desk in the foyer—one needed only to present a written message to the concierge and watch in which cubby it was placed. The spy had presented a number of benign messages, at different times, to different concierges over the last three days, and the officers billeting at the New Royal Hotel were mapped clearly in his mind.

Unnoticed, the spy made his way up the stairs behind the group of officers. He slowed on the first-floor landing to distance himself as they continued to climb the flights to the upper floors. He did not want to be put in a position where he might be expected to strike up a conversation. Conversations were remembered, and the spy did not want—

The hotel room door closest to the stairs swung open, and a man exited, whistling a jaunty tune as he locked the door behind him. The spy jerked into action and bounded silently up another half flight and then waited. Below him, the American colonel appeared on the landing, still whistling to himself as he headed downstairs. The spy hesitated but only for a moment. He hadn't realized that the American attaché was staying in this hotel. And while Bennett certainly wasn't part of his planned mission for the evening, the opportunity that had just presented itself was too intriguing.

The spy descended quietly and stopped in front of the door the American had just exited. He knocked gently. There was no response, nor had he expected one, but again, the simplest things were often the undoing of men like him. Glancing up and down the deserted hallway, he opened his shoulder pack and withdrew his lockpicks. He set to work on the door, and within a half minute of working on the old, simple lock, the spy slipped into the attaché's room, closing the door noiselessly behind him.

He paused inside the room, assessing and studying. The American had conveniently left a small lamp on in the corner and the tasselled curtains were already drawn across the arched window. A double bed with a crimson coverlet was placed against the wall on his right, a table and chair opposite. A heavy, carved armoire dominated the space next to the window.

The spy went immediately to the table. A shaving kit, a canteen, and a small stack of documents sat on the surface. The spy rifled through the papers with practiced efficiency. Lists of itemized troop rations, records of daily temperatures, an inventory of the hospitals and their capacity in Damascus. Nothing useful. He turned his attention to a battered briefcase sitting on the floor next to the table. It was empty save for a packet of pencils, a pocket watch, a photo of an unsmiling woman in a high-necked dress, and a thick pad of blank paper. The spy held the paper up to the light looking for indentations that might have been left by the colonel, but there was nothing to see. He examined the briefcase next, looking for a false bottom or concealed pockets, but there were none. He carefully replaced everything as he had found it.

He went to the armoire and opened it. Uniforms and clothing had been neatly hung inside, boots and shoes lining the bottom. With deft movements, the spy searched through every article of clothing and the depths of the wardrobe. He found nothing aside from a handful of coins. He ran his hands along the bottom and sides but there were no hollow compartments or hidden spaces. He closed the wardrobe and put his hands on his hips. He'd been hoping to find at least a few of the lengthy, rather pessimistic encoded radiograms that the American composed for telegraph transmissions across the Atlantic. The spy was not a cryptanalyst by any stretch of the imagination, and he didn't pretend to understand how those individuals managed to decode and solve those sorts of riddles, but it seemed plausible that a copy of a message, coded or original, would be valuable to the Abwehr. Provided, of course, that he could actually find something.

Had they been in Cairo, the spy would have expected the attaché to have secured any documents he hadn't destroyed in an embassy safe. Except they weren't in Cairo, and there wasn't an embassy, and the colonel had obviously secured the more sensitive documents he carried with him somewhere else. The spy scowled.

This opportunity, while it had seemed like a good idea earlier, was taking too long. Wasting more time here would cost him precious seconds that he had intended for his primary objective. It was why the spy usually resisted impulsive decisions. He would give himself a minute more and then revert back to his original plan.

His eyes roamed the room, examining the minute details. The walls were smooth and adorned only with decorative tile and swirling stencils along the tops. The tiled floor was equally as bare. There was no safe, no strong box, and there were very few places to hide documents. He got down on his hands and knees and checked under the low bed, feeling a little foolish. As expected, he saw nothing save a gecko that scurried away in alarm. He rocked back on his heels, frustrated, and watched the little reptile dart up the leg of the headboard and over the rumpled coverlet on the side. The spy pursed his lips in consideration and lifted the disturbed bedding. At the corner, the mattress was overhanging the bedframe, which could mean nothing. Or something. He lifted the edge of the mattress and blinked.

Between the mattress and the slats of the bed frame lay a file folder. The spy extracted the folder and opened it to find a dozen radiograms and two slim, bound books, both with black covers. With utter disbelief, he thumbed through the volumes. He didn't need to be a cryptanalyst to understand that he was looking at codebooks and super-encipherment tables. An entire set of instructions that would enable the Abwehr to listen in on any encoded transmissions sent across the Atlantic by the American attaché. An electrifying thrill coursed through him but he immediately tempered his excitement. He had decisions to make.

He glanced at his watch. Stealing these books was useless. And this was not information that he could radio along with his usual reports to Germany. The only way this sort of intelligence could be valuable was if the colonel did not know that it had been found and if the spy could get a copy back to Berlin.

Working as quickly as he could, he laid the open volumes on the bed. He withdrew a tiny Minox camera from his pack and began taking photos of each page. He changed his film twice, even though the film was all he possessed and would be difficult to replace. The possibility that this intelligence would prove exceedingly valuable could not be ignored.

When he had finished photographing each page, he lifted the mattress and set the books and folder back with extreme care in the exact position that he had found them. He left the mattress overhanging the frame and left the coverlet rumpled in the identical way he had discovered it and went to the door, listening hard for any sound in the hallway. When he was satisfied that he was alone, he left the room as quietly as he had entered, closing the door behind him and working the lock with his tools until he heard it click, before retreating back to the staircase.

He paused on the landing and glanced at his watch again, wincing. He had planned to be back on the street by now, in and out and undetected. Leaving the hotel without a search of Commandant Lavigne's room and whatever dispatches and documents he might have brought back with him from Cairo was an unpalatable option. Rommel was poised to dislodge the Allies for once and for all from Northern Africa, but to do that and manage his tenuous supply chain, the generalfeldmarschall needed to know what the Allies had planned.

Thus far, the Allied officers had used an astonishing lack of discipline in their radio and written communiques out on the battlefield, and Commandant Lavigne had proven no different. La Fleur did an exceptional job of ensuring that all of Lavigne's private papers were secured, but she could not be in all places at all times. He'd verified that the pair would be back on the road at dawn, headed to Beirut for a day, perhaps two, before they returned, and the spy couldn't risk waiting until tomorrow to search the commandant's room. The most valuable information and dispatches would go with them.

Decision made, he took the stairs two at a time to the third floor and hurried down the empty hallway to the commandant's room. He would be in and out in minutes. He knocked again, out of habit. When no one answered the door, he made quick work of the lock and entered the darkened room.

The commandant had not been so courteous as to leave a lamp burning, and the spy had to work with the light filtering in through the open window. This room was almost an exact replica of the colonel's, and he was already familiar with the way Lavigne liked to organize and store his personal papers. To that end, he ignored the wardrobe and went directly to the heavy leather dispatch bag that he already knew would be resting on the chair. With care, he pulled the files and documents from the bag and laid them out on the table. From his own pack, he extracted a small torch and, shielding the light with his hand, began reading.

The sound of a key in the lock made the spy spin. He extinguished his torch and melted away from the table into the shadows of the wardrobe even as he chastised himself bitterly. Sloppy, sloppy, sloppy. There were no proper hiding places in this single room, and he would not fit under the bed. He was too far away from the window to escape. He had taken far too long in the colonel's room, and he had no one to blame for his poor choices but himself.

And now there were regrettably few choices left.

Lavigne closed the door behind him and walked into the darkened room. The spy couldn't see much, only listen as his booted feet came farther into the room and stopped. The doctor yawned noisily, heaved a tired sigh, and shuffled forward. The spy willed him back out of the room. Or simply into bed. Instead, he listened to the commandant fumble for the switch on the lamp.

Goddammit, he did not want to do this. The attention and the commotion that this would cause was unfortunate and would reflect poorly on the spy's competence. Berlin would be furious.

Beck would be livid. But the past was the past, and all he could do now was try to ensure that his earlier success in the attaché's room was not compromised. The spy slid his hand into his pocket.

Light flooded the room. The commandant froze where he was, staring down at the documents spread across the table's surface, and the spy could almost hear the bewilderment and confusion echoing through his mind.

The spy surged from his hiding place and slipped his garrotte over the head of the commandant. Lavigne gasped and struggled, his hands clawing at the wire around his throat. The spy was somewhat relieved. The doctor was a similar height, and had he thrown back his head or pulled the spy forward, it might have made things difficult. The spy pulled harder, and Lavigne's feet went out from under him as he kicked uselessly. A booted foot connected with the chair, sending it toppling with a crash, and the spy flinched.

Within two minutes, the spy was staring down at the prone, lifeless body of Lavigne. He left it where it was and, working quickly, dumped the contents of the dispatch bag on the floor. He regretted that he would not be able to properly peruse the contents, but he could not steal them without causing suspicion, and he could no longer afford to linger. He opened the wardrobe, pulled a few garments out, and left them in a haphazard pile. He went through the commandant's pockets and took whatever money he could find, as well as his watch and silver cigarette case. A robbery gone wrong was the best the spy could do in this situation, and he had to hope it would simply be accepted as such. He would discard the case and the watch as soon as he left here.

For the second time that night, he went to the door and listened hard for voices or feet in the hallway. The sounds from the street below filtering through the open window made it difficult to hear. He risked opening the door a crack and then a little farther. The hallway seemed deserted. He slipped from the room and closed the door soundlessly behind him. He was in the process of fumbling for his lockpicks when a door at the far end of the hall opened. The spy cursed inwardly and pulled away from the commandant's door, walking casually toward the stairs before he could be seen, leaving the door closed but unlocked. He straightened his uniform and smoothed his hair as he descended the stairs. His intent had been to lock the door behind him, but the more he thought about it, the more he realized an unlocked door set the stage much more convincingly for a robbery. Yes, the spy decided as he reached the ground floor. An unlocked door would invite all sorts of conjecture, and probably none associated with subterfuge. How very fortunate.

In the hotel lobby, his good fortune continued as the concierge desk was deserted. The spy strolled through the front doors, out onto the street, where night had definitively descended and the stars had emerged to twinkle in the desert sky overhead. His sister had known all the constellations by heart. She had once told him that he was born under the luckiest of signs. That the Aquarius constellation contained the stars believed by ancient astrologers to possess the luck of luck itself. Despite the regrettable and ill-timed return of Commandant Lavigne, the spy fancied that she was right. The notion that perhaps his sister was watching over him from those very constellations above comforted him enormously.

And with just a little more luck, the doctor wouldn't be found until the morning.

CHAPTER
16

Violet sat behind the wheel of the Humber idling outside the New Royal Hotel and waited for the commandant to return from his room. He'd promised her that he would only be a few minutes, that he needed only to fetch a set of orders that he had forgotten in his dispatch bag, but a few minutes were starting to stretch into many.

She rubbed her eyes, willing herself to stay awake. She'd been up since four that morning, working with an equally exhausted repair crew to fix the Humber's ailing starter, and then she and the doctor had been on the road by seven. Ten hours of navigating the terrain back to Damascus, and all she wanted now was to retreat to the staff quarters, find something that resembled a bed, and sleep until next week.

But before she could do any of that, Violet needed to return the commandant back to the French hospital. She rested her head on the driver's-side door, wishing he would hurry. A vendor somewhere nearby was grilling meat, and the tantalizing smell made her stomach rumble hungrily. Maybe food and then a bed—

Violet straightened at the sight of two familiar figures walking toward the Humber. She wasn't sure where they had come from or where they were going, but they were crossing the street right in front of the car. For a moment she wondered if she was dreaming, but the sweat trickling down her back and the grit in her eyes dispelled that notion. She opened the door and scrambled out gracelessly.

"George?" she called.

George turned at the sound of her name. Her arm was linked with her brother's and Violet could almost believe that she had just stopped them as they strolled down a road in Nice.

"Vi!" George disentangled herself from Henri and hurried to Violet, hugging her fiercely. She pulled back and studied Violet critically. "You look terrible," she declared. "Like you're about to fall over."

"I might," Violet admitted. "I think I'm just hungry."

"I saw the commandant at the hospital earlier but you weren't with him. I was worried something had happened."

"The damn car happened," Violet grumbled. "Specifically the starter. It gave me problems between Acre and Beirut and again when we got back to Damascus. I'm afraid to turn it off now in case I can't get it started again."

"Forget the car. You need to take care of yourself," George chided, "or you're going to get run down and sick. I don't want to see you as a patient in that hospital, you hear me?"

"I hear you." With George working in the French hospital here, Violet was able to visit her friend whenever she could. It was George's opinion that Violet worked too hard and travelled far too much, though that didn't ever stop her enthusiastic questions about the cities Violet had come from or the people she had met.

Though tonight, Violet didn't have the energy or inclination to talk about her last excursion. "They let you out for a night?" she asked George instead.

"Yes." George grinned. "Two of the other Spearettes and I were hoping to avoid the mess tent for dinner. We were on a search for the most delicious shawarma in all of Damascus." She gestured behind her in the general direction of Henri. "And then I ran into this big oaf in front of the hotel, so I sent the girls on ahead of us." The delight in her voice was unmistakable.

Violet glanced at Henri, who was standing to the side, his hands in his pockets, watching them. She hadn't seen him since that day at the dressing station though she had thought about him often. She'd read the Dekobra novel three times now, mostly for lack of anything else to read, but every time she opened the book, she envisioned him as he had been the first time he had handed her the book. Violet attributed the pang of intense longing that always accompanied that memory to home-sickness for the azure blue sea and salty breezes. And maybe a little loneliness.

"How are you, Henri?" she asked. It wasn't lost on her that in a different life, that question had been nothing more than a trivial and breezy social convention that Violet had asked and been asked a thousand times. And the expected response was always gay and light because no one was really interested in an honest one. Here, that question carried a sobering weight.

"I'm all right, princess."

His hair was a little longer and his uniform and skin no lon-ger caked in dust and blood. Which made the purple scar that ran across his elbow to disappear under the short sleeve of his uniform that much more visible.

She stepped away from George, closer to Henri, and assessed the puckered skin dotted with tiny scars where he'd been stitched. "What happened to your arm?"

Henri glanced down at his elbow. "It wasn't as bad as it looks."

"Shrapnel?"

"Yes."

"Shrapnel is always as bad as it looks. Usually worse."

"Now you sound like my sister. Always worrying. But there is no need. I'm fine."

"You are an idiot," George scolded. "I will always worry about you. The fighting before we took this city was awful. In case you've forgotten, I saw the cost incurred by the Italian and Vichy refusal to surrender firsthand. God, when I saw your name on that casualty list, I just about—"

"What casualty list?" Henri was frowning at his sister. "You never said anything about a casualty list."

George's gaze cut warily to Violet and then back. "The one that Vi showed me."

"You showed her a casualty list?" Henri held Violet's eyes with such a fierce intensity that Violet felt herself flushing.

"I work for the divisional medical officer, Henri. I asked him if I could look at them as they came in." Why was she defending herself?

"You were looking for my name?"

"Yes."

"Why?"

"Because I... Because George is my friend." That was the truth if not the whole one. "I thought it was better that George hear it from me if something happened to you."

"And the commandant let you?"

"Yes. Because he is kind and he knows that not knowing is worse. And there were so, so many losses. On both sides."

For the first time, his gaze dropped. "I didn't sign up to shoot countrymen. No matter if they were Vichy."

"There never should have been two sides. Just France," George said.

Henri yanked his hands from his pockets. "It's done. And we're here now. Waiting for someone to send us somewhere where we can do what we came to do and fight Nazis."

Violet exchanged a look with George. "Where? When?"

"I don't know. No one seems to know. It sounds like the Brits and their Commonwealth friends think that they can beat the

Germans all on their own out here. Their generals seem content to leave the Free French here and keep us on the sidelines."

"Good," George said with feeling. "You're safe here."

Henri ignored his sister. "There are rumours that if they won't let us into the fight, de Gaulle might offer to send us into Russia to help them fight the Nazis there."

"Russia?" Violet echoed. She shrank back and leaned against the bonnet of the Humber. The commandant had told her horrific things about the fighting in Russia. "You can't go there."

"We haven't gone anywhere, princess."

"Yet," she mumbled unhappily.

"Tell me about you."

"About me?"

"Where you've been. What you've been doing when you haven't been scouring casualty lists and spying on me."

The mention of spying sent a wash of disquiet through her. She had dutifully reported the details of her visit with the captain, but without any real physical evidence, Lavigne felt that there was little that they could do. He hadn't brought the matter up again, yet there were still moments when the intelligence officer's words nagged at her.

"She's been driving the commandant back and forth between here and Acre and Beirut." George answered for her like a proud parent. "Meetings and strategy and planning. Helping to keep our troops supplied, our casualties taken care of, and the politics managed." She made Violet sound like a general.

"Indeed?" Henri said. "You've been busy saving the world."

Violet couldn't tell if he was amused at George's loyal enthusiasm or mocking her.

"Ignore him." George grasped Violet's hand. "Come to dinner with us. I want to hear your stories about the people you've met and the cities you've seen even if this boor can't appreciate them."

Violet shook her head. "I—"

"Don't say no. You said you were hungry. I can't fix this war but I can fix that you're hungry."

"I wasn't going to say no. I was going to say that I can't. I'm waiting for the commandant." Violet paused and frowned.

"What's wrong?'

"He's been in the hotel a long time," she said, checking the time on her watch. "He said he'd only be a few minutes."

"Maybe he fell asleep," George guessed. "He looked just as done in as you."

"No. He wouldn't do that. Not when there are people waiting for him at the hospital. Maybe I should go to check on him."

"Is that a good idea?" It was Henri who asked.

"What do you mean?"

"Some superior officers are a little prickly about their privacy. Maybe he wouldn't like you following him. Infringing."

"The commandant's not like that." She glanced up at the empty windows of the hotel. "I think I should go check on him."

"If you like, I can send Corporal Gasquet up to do that so you can wait with the car," Henri offered. "I just saw Gasquet in the lobby of the hotel and I'm sure he wouldn't mind fetching the doctor for you."

"Um." Violet waffled in indecision.

"Speak of the devil." Henri waved at someone behind her. "Corporal."

Violet turned to find the dark-haired corporal with the kind eyes approaching the rear of the Humber. He sidestepped a man hustling across the road with a cart piled high with fruit and joined Violet and Henri. Henri's earnest batman, Private Picard, was with him.

"I thought that was you. A pleasure to see you again, La Fleur," Gasquet said with a flourish and a bow that wouldn't have been out of place in Versailles. "Especially in these much-improved circumstances."

Violet found herself smiling back despite her worry. "And you, Corporal." She turned her gaze on the batman. "A pleasure to see you as well, Private Picard."

The private ducked his head bashfully.

Gasquet had turned to George with a warm smile. "Christophe Gasquet. I have not yet had the privilege of an introduction..." He let his words trail off as a question.

"My sister," Henri growled. "You can save your charm."

Gasquet's smile faltered slightly.

George sent Henri a scathing glance and stepped forward. "Georgette Chastain," she said. "Though everyone calls me George."

The corporal's smile retuned in full force. "A pleasure to make your acquaintance." He gestured at his companion. "I found Picard heading up the street," Gasquet said cheerfully to Henri. "The bar in the hotel was especially crowded, so we thought we'd find ourselves a drink elsewhere. Would you all care to join us?"

"I can't," Violet said before Henri could answer. "I'm waiting for the commandant to drive him back to the hospital. But he's taking a really long time in the hotel, and I'm a little worried. I need to go up to check on him."

"Would you like us to wait with the car while you do that?" Gasquet volunteered immediately.

"Yes, please. That would be helpful—"

"I'll come with you," Henri interrupted. "Picard, can you wait with the car? Make sure a pack of Aussie soldiers doesn't take it for a joy ride? Or a local doesn't strip it bare of parts and pieces until we can get back?"

"Of course, sir."

"Corporal, you and I can escort Adjutant St. Croix into the hotel. I'll get you to check the bar downstairs. Maybe the commandant stopped in and lost track of time." He paused. "Is that all right with you, Adjutant?"

Violet thought it unlikely that Lavigne would have stopped for a drink and lost track of time but she would happily accept the help and the company.

"I'm coming with you," George said. "I've always wanted to see the inside of the hotel and bar."

Henri looked like he might argue for a moment but Violet turned and hurried toward the entrance, unwilling to wait. In a moment, Henri fell into step beside her.

"Do you know his room number?" he asked.

"Yes. It's on the third floor."

The four entered the busy lobby, and Gasquet and George veered off to check the busy bar tucked into the rear of the hotel. Henri and Violet continued up the stairs. Somewhere above their heads the sounds of an argument reached them, voices rising and falling before they abruptly stopped as a door closed.

"This floor," Violet said, and led Henri down the hall. She reached the commandant's room and knocked.

There was no answer.

"I don't see a light on under the door," Henri said. "I don't think he's here."

Violet knocked again. "Commandant Lavigne?" she called. Maybe he actually had fallen asleep by accident. She had almost fallen asleep waiting for him in the Humber.

There was still no answer. Half-heartedly, she turned the knob on the door, expecting it to be locked.

It wasn't.

"The door's open," she said to Henri.

"Then he must be in there, no?"

Cautiously, Violet opened the door a crack, mindful of Henri's comments about commanding officers and their privacy. But even if he had fallen asleep, he would likely be grateful that she had woken him. There were people who depended on him still waiting. "Commandant Lavigne?"

The only answer was the sounds from the street below drifting in through the open window.

Violet pushed the door wider, letting the light from the hallway flood into the room. "Sir, I'm just checking—" She froze, for the barest of seconds, before she shoved the door wide open and flew in.

The commandant was lying on the floor amid a blizzard of loose papers with a chair toppled on its side near his feet. A rapid list of medical possibilities raced through her head as she stumbled toward him. Heart attack, stroke, seizure, dizziness, heat sickness, dehydration—all things that her medical abilities, however inept, might have prepared her to identify and treat.

What she wasn't prepared for was Lavigne's wide, bloodshot eyes staring lifelessly at the ceiling, his spectacles lying broken beside his head, and an unmistakable, bloody welt around his neck. She fumbled for his wrist but couldn't find a pulse.

She lurched away until the backs of her legs banged painfully against a table. She was gasping, her breaths coming in jagged sips, and an icy sweat pricked at her skin. Her head pounded in time to her racing heart, and her stomach churned.

Henri had turned on the lamp and moved to the commandant's side, where he crouched.

"Someone killed him," she said dully, trying to calm her breathing. It seemed impossibly unfair that after all the terrifying roads and lethal landscapes, the doctor should have had his life snatched from him here, in what should have been a safe place.

"Yes," Henri agreed, though his voice seemed like it was coming from a distance.

"I don't understand." Violet was trying to think, trying to make her mind work, but all she could see in her head was the doctor's reddened, sightless eyes. "I was just with him. It couldn't have been more than thirty minutes ago."

"I'm sorry, Vi."

"He was a doctor." Violet pressed her hands to her forehead, looking away from the body. "He was kind and good and helped save so many lives out here. Why would someone do this? Who could do this?"

Henri straightened. "I'm sorry," he said again.

"Jesus." Violet turned to find Corporal Gasquet standing in the open doorway, George beside him.

George shoved by him, dropping to her knees beside the doctor. She bent over his body, searching for a pulse in much the same way Violet had. After a moment, she gently ran a hand over the commandant's eyes and closed them. She stood and came to stand beside Violet, reaching for her hand and squeezing it tightly. "I'm so sorry, Vi. I can't do anything for him. He's gone."

"What happened?" Gasquet had stepped into the room.

"The commandant has been murdered," Henri told him. "Strangled."

"What? Why?" Gasquet looked as stunned as Violet felt.

"I don't know."

"His watch is missing," Violet said abruptly. She had searched for his pulse on a wrist that was barren of the watch he always wore. The watch his wife and daughters had given him for his forty-fifth birthday. He never took it off and touched it fondly every time he spoke of his girls, which was often.

"You think he was robbed?" the corporal croaked. "You think someone killed him for a watch?"

"I don't know." Violet found herself perilously close to tears.

George gave her a quick hug, and Violet swallowed a sob.

"The door was open when we got here," Henri told him. "That his watch is gone means you might be right, Gasquet. Vi, is anything else missing?"

Violet looked helplessly at the mess in the room. "I don't know." She tried to focus. "His dispatch bag is still here. That's what all these papers will be from." She glanced at the open wardrobe. "His boots and uniforms seem like they are still here. I don't know if anything else from his personal effects is missing. I just don't know," she repeated, sorrow squeezing her throat.

"We need to report this immediately," Gasquet said. "My God, when we didn't find him downstairs, I didn't for one second consider that this...that this..." He trailed off. "Jesus."

"Go," Henri said. "Tell Picard to stay where he is. Then telephone HQ and tell them what's happened. Go there directly if no one answers. We'll wait here."

The corporal nodded and vanished, and Violet listened as the sound of his pounding boots receded down the hall.

"You should wait outside, Vi," George said gently. "You don't need to be in here. None of us do."

Violet nodded numbly and allowed her friend to guide her out of the room. She leaned against the wall in the narrow passage, her stomach still unsettled and her skin still slicked with perspiration. She closed her eyes but still couldn't get the image of the doctor's body out of her mind. His spectacles had been broken in the struggle, and she wondered if he had even seen—

Her eyes popped open. "What was he strangled with?"

"What?" Henri was hovering near her, his expression a mask of worry and concern.

"He wasn't strangled with a rope or a belt. He was strangled with something that cut into his skin and made it bleed. Like a wire or a very thin strip of cord."

"I'm not sure what you're trying to say."

"It wasn't beside his body, and I didn't see it in the room. Whatever it was that the killer used."

"I'm still not sure what you're getting at."

"Whoever did this must have followed Lavigne to his room or maybe they were already here and he surprised him, but the person who did this came prepared. Someone garroted the commandant and took the evidence with them."

"We don't know that for sure," Henri said slowly. "That room is a mess. HQ will send intelligence officers to go through everything. If something is amiss, they'll find it."

"But it doesn't sound like a simple robbery, does it?"

"Who knows why people do what they do? So many have lost so much from this war, and desperate people do desperate things. You and I both know that."

"I might have seen the person who did this," Violet mumbled. "I might have watched them walk into that hotel behind the commandant. If I had gone up with him, if I hadn't waited in the car, or if I had gone earlier to check, then maybe—"

"This is not your fault." George grasped Violet's shoulders and pulled her around to face her. "There was nothing you could have done."

"It feels like it was my fault. It feels like I let him down. My job was to keep him safe."

"And you did that, Vi," George told her fervently, letting her hands drop. "For a long time, through some really horrible and dangerous situations. But this was out of your control."

Violet pressed her fingers to her closed eyes, making spots dance behind her lids. Her thoughts were tumbling in a tangled mess of misery. "I just... I shouldn't... Maybe..."

A strong arm curled around her shoulders. Violet opened her eyes and stiffened before she leaned against the solid wall of Henri's chest, defeated and heartbroken.

"George is right, princess. This could not have been predicted or prepared for."

The tears that had been burning at the back of her throat were now hot on her cheeks, and she no longer cared. Over Henri's shoulder, through the doorway, she could still see Lavigne's discarded dispatch bag where it lay on the floor. She could still see where a handful of scattered documents had come to a rest over the booted foot of the dead commandant.

You come across any suspicious deaths? Captain Lipton has asked. *Sabotage?*

She remembered Lavigne's concern that there were intelligence breaches. She recalled the doctor's worry that Allied information was leaking to the Germans and, in the next breath, wondered if Henri was wrong.

That this could have been both predicted and prepared for.

CHAPTER
17

6 DECEMBER 1941
DAMASCUS, SYRIA

Violet sat alone in the villa, the sum total of all her belongings in a canvas duffel at her feet, save for her tools, which she kept locked in the Humber. The space she had been shown into had been a living room at some point before it had been appropriated by the military and turned into an office. Ornately carved tables, long low couches, and pretty gilt mirrors had been pushed to the side to make room for a desk and a series of serviceable chairs. The air in here was cloying, the small electric fan in the corner of the room doing little to move it, let alone create a cooling breeze, and it was heavy with the scent of baking earth laced with traces of cloves and coriander, suggesting someone was cooking. Through the open windows, she could hear the haunting, mournful trill of the doves that sat in the branches of the plum trees beyond.

It had been months since Commandant Lavigne's death, and since then, Violet had been shuttled back and forth between division officers requiring a driver within the city of Damascus or transportation to and from the coastal city of Beirut. She was glad for the distraction it provided. And even though the parade of officers that she had been driving were perfectly polite, professional, and courteous, she missed Lavigne dearly. And now, with rumours swirling that the Free French Legion would be shipping out shortly,

Violet found herself in a peculiar no-man's-land, uncertain where and when her next assignment would take her.

A door opened behind Violet, ending her musings. A tall, reedy officer with thinning red hair, a pockmarked face, and pro-truding eyes strode in. Violet stood immediately though he waved her back to her seat as he circled the desk and sat down heavily in his own chair.

"Adjutant St. Croix?" he asked.

"Yes, sir."

The officer pulled a thin file from the top of a stack on his desk and opened it, mumbling under his breath as he skimmed the documents in front of him. His fair complexion was sun reddened above the khaki of his uniform collar, and his nose was peeling slightly at the tip.

After a moment, he looked up at her. "I am Major Tremblay," he announced. "Of the First Free French Brigade."

Violet remained silent, waiting for him to tell her why she had been summoned.

Tremblay placed his hands flat against the surface of the desk on either side of the folder. "It seems you have become quite the celebrity around these parts."

It did not sound like a compliment.

"I am just a driver, sir," Violet answered carefully. "Not a celebrity."

"Mmm. You were the French Foreign Legion's divisional medical officer's driver, yes?"

"Yes, sir."

"A nasty business, that. A real shame. I read the report."

Violet pinched the hem of her shorts, rolling the fabric between her fingers while debating whether her next words would be out of line and then deciding she didn't care. "Forgive my forwardness," she said, "but was there anything in the report that you could tell me? If it was determined who killed Commandant Lavigne? Or why?"

The major gave her a look imbued with faint annoyance. "I was told that one of the commandant's personnel has been harassing headquarters regularly these last months with questions about his death. I must assume that was you."

"Not harassing, sir. Merely inquiring. The circumstances surrounding his death were not entirely—"

"I cannot give you a different answer than the one you had yesterday or last week or last month, as much as you might wish it, Adjutant. The thief was never caught, and this far on, it is unlikely that he ever will be. The hotel staff were questioned thoroughly and their possessions searched but to no avail. It could have been anyone, and unfortunately, he will be long gone by now."

"Are they sure it was a thief who killed him?"

His annoyance transformed into clear displeasure. "It was determined that his watch and silver cigarette case were the only items missing. Can't trust the locals here. Opportunists, the lot of them. You should know that, Adjutant."

"What about the dispatch bag? The communiques and private papers inside?"

"All accounted for by military intelligence." Tremblay's thin lips thinned further. "What, exactly, are you suggesting?"

"Has anyone considered that perhaps it is possible that it wasn't a simple robbery? Perhaps he was targeted or perhaps he had information that was targeted. He was killed in a very unique manner. I was there. I saw it—"

"I'll stop you there, Adjutant. It will behoove you to leave investigations and deductions to those persons more qualified than yourself, yes? We know what we're doing. And the last thing we want is unfounded rumours getting out that we have spies or vigilantes of some sort running amok in places like this."

"But—"

"It's bad for morale, Adjutant. And wild speculation like yours will not be tolerated."

Violet stared at him. Bad for morale?

"Look," Tremblay said, scratching at the peeling skin on his nose, "I know you want a better answer than that but there isn't one. Commandant Lavigne was well-liked and well-respected but this is a war, and sometimes you can't control the tragic randomness of it. The commandant was simply the victim of bad luck."

"Did anyone follow up with British intelligence?"

"I beg your pardon?" Angry red splotches were crawling up the major's neck.

Violet pushed on, unsure about how much she should reveal to preserve the commandant's confidence. But the commandant was dead, and maybe, just maybe, if she had pressed harder or dug deeper, she could have prevented that. "British intelligence suggested that there was a spy within—"

"British intelligence are a collection of paranoid fools who refuse to accept that the Germans seem to be beating them with superior weaponry and tactics. They believe that there must be Nazi spies on every street corner because that makes a convenient excuse for their failures—" He seemed to catch himself and took a deep breath. "You will not speak of it again, do I make myself understood?"

"Understood, sir." Violet shifted in her chair, and the backs of her thighs stuck uncomfortably to the seat. She wanted to argue, but in truth, she realized she had no good reason to do so. If all the communiques and documents that had been in the dispatch bag had been accounted for, then perhaps she really was seeing things that weren't there. There had been no unusual occurrences since that night, and she hadn't heard whispers of any either. Perhaps she was being paranoid. Perhaps the initial shock and sadness had impaired her ability to be objective. Perhaps Major Tremblay was right.

"Good. Let's get down to the real reason you were called in today." Major Tremblay straightened his collar and then tapped the file on the desk in front of him. "The First Free Brigade, which now

includes all nine hundred and fifty-seven of your fellow Legionnaires, has been ordered to mobilize. The brigade will be attached
to a division of the British Eighth Army headed into North Africa."
He sniffed. "It seems that, after telling us for months to stay out of
the way like good little children, the British have finally embraced
reality and realize that they need our help after all."

Violet absorbed this. There had been the rumours of course,
churning and eddying like dark, fast-moving currents through the
city, but hearing the stark confirmation was different.

"There is nothing dishonourable about remaining behind,"
Tremblay said to her. "It will be a harsh, brutal campaign."

"I'm sorry?" Violet wasn't sure that she had heard him correctly.

"You are not required to accompany the Legion west. You
may remain here. Or in Beirut, if you prefer, where you'd be much
more comfortable. The sea is quite lovely, all things considered.
And I'm sure we could find you a position in one of the hospitals if
you wished."

"I'm not required..." Violet trailed off. Once again, the desk
and tasselled tapestries and hand-painted tiles and brass chandeliers
of the villa wavered, to be replaced by a vision of a different desk
and heavy oak bookcases and dark wood panelling and paintings of
old English racehorses. "Will you be remaining behind, sir?" she
asked before she could stop herself.

"I beg your pardon?"

"Not accompanying the Free French west."

Tremblay's brows furrowed. "Of course not."

"Then I'm not entirely certain why you would believe that I
would."

"Adjutant St. Croix, I'm not sure that you fully understand
what you may be facing in North Africa. I'm only trying to think
of what might be best for you."

"Ah." It was still astonishing, really, just how many men in this
world assumed that they knew what was best for her.

"Do let me know which city you might like to reside in," Tremblay continued. "I can have a villa made available to you and—"

"Seventeen."

Tremblay looked confused. "Is that a street address?"

"No. Not an address. Seventeen is the number of times I've been bombed or fired upon while driving since I joined the Legion. I didn't count the times in Finland, though I could add them to the tally."

"Adjutant, I—"

"Seventeen times I could have decided to quit. To run back to somewhere where I would have been more comfortable than, say, beneath the undercarriage of a vehicle while a Messerschmidt strafes the road."

The major spluttered. "I think you misunderstand me. No one is questioning your capabilities or bravery."

"What then, exactly, are you questioning, sir?"

"I… That is…" Tremblay opened and closed his mouth twice like a carp. "Very well," he snapped after a moment. "But do not say I didn't warn you."

"I thank you for your concern. But I am not abandoning the Legion. Not now. Not ever."

The officer returned his attention to the thin folder that was on his desk. He seemed to read and then reread whatever was in the document in front of him. "You are fortunate, Adjutant St. Croix. Commandant Lavigne wrote several letters of commendation during your service with him that appear in your file." He looked up at Violet with a slightly sour expression. "While I would prefer to see you reassigned back to your role as a nurse, far from the front and far from where you might be a distraction to the men, it appears that the late commandant's submissions have caught the attention of my superiors, who believe you should remain in your current position."

Violet closed her eyes briefly and sent a silent thanks to the doctor for his kindness even from beyond the grave.

"It seems that Colonel Clement has made a formal transfer request on your behalf."

Violet swallowed. A colonel? Driving a colonel was no small thing.

"Colonel Clement's regular driver was killed some time ago," Tremblay said. "And he has yet to permanently replace him, until now. He has specifically requested you for the upcoming campaign."

"I am grateful for the colonel's confidence," Violet replied.

"Well, I hope you fare better than his last driver."

Violet wondered if she was imagining the grim spitefulness in his tone. "I am happy to serve where I am needed, sir."

"As the colonel's chauffeur, you should know that you will not be sharing his orderly as is custom, for obvious reasons," Tremblay went on. "Nor will there be any special treatment or private quarters for you with the men. You will be on your own and be required to improvise."

"Of course, sir."

"Hmph." Tremblay looked unimpressed. "Here," he said, shoving a paper and a pen toward Violet. "Sign this."

Violet reached for the paper and read it carefully. There was a paragraph of brief instructions detailing where and when she should report and a list of personal items she would be required to bring with her. Colonel Clement's name was typed on the bottom, a messy signature scribbled on the line above it. *Adjutant V. St. Croix* was typed beside that, and Violet signed her name above it.

She passed the form back to the major.

"I would suggest that you report immediately to the colonel's camp," Tremblay told her. "You'll not have any time to waste, and I do not wish to be blamed for your dillydallying."

Violet bit her tongue. "Thank you, sir."

The major waved his hand in her direction and selected another folder from the pile on his desk without looking at her. It would seem that she was dismissed.

Violet hefted her duffel from the floor and slung it over her shoulder. She let herself out of the room, closed the door quietly behind her, and leaned back against the wall. For the first time, she realized just how close she had come to being relegated back to scrubbing blood from sticky floors on her hands and knees. Or worse, idling away her days in some seaside villa, consigned to writing letters and waiting for answers that might never come as the war passed her by. She blew out a heavy breath and sent another prayer of thanks to her dear doctor. He could no longer fight but he had made sure that she could.

In the hallway, a long bench had been placed on one side. An officer who had been sitting near the end rose and turned toward Violet.

"Good morning, La Fleur," Corporal Gasquet said.

Violet's duffel fell unheeded from her shoulder. "Corporal. What on earth are you doing here?"

"Waiting for you. Colonel Clement asked me to collect you." He paused with a crooked grin, his green eyes dancing.

Violet couldn't help but return the smile. "One does generally not say no to a colonel."

"I'm sure old Tremblay tried to talk you out of it. But sending you back to the hospitals would have been a terrible oversight. The colonel agreed with us." He bent and picked up her duffel with ease. "Is this all you have?"

"Yes. My tools are in the car." Violet shook her head. "I'm sorry, I don't understand. Us?"

"The colonel needed a driver. Corporal Chastain suggested that the best might be available. That Clement already knew your name made it easy."

"Hen—Corporal Chastain recommended me to the colonel for this promotion?"

"Officially, yes. But we were all pleased as punch at the thought that you would be with us when we ship out."

Violet was still trying to comprehend this turn of events. "How did the colonel already know my name?"

"His jaw was broken, his chin still needs dressing daily, and he lost most of his lower front teeth, but there is nothing wrong with his memory. And he threatened to string up anyone who tried to ship him home. Turns out a man can still give very effective orders through a bandage."

It took Violet a heartbeat to understand. "The man you helped that day under the truck in the air raid."

"*We* helped," Gasquet corrected. "And you and Chastain saved. Colonel Clement is back now, returned from terrorizing the hospital staff in Beirut after he'd had enough of convalescence. Or they'd had enough of him. It wasn't entirely clear," he mused. "Though my money is on the latter."

"I didn't know who he was," Violet blurted. "He didn't have his own car. If I had known he was a colonel, I would have—"

"What? You would have done something differently?"

"No," Violet admitted, feeling a little foolish. "I'm just… surprised, I guess."

"His driver had just been killed. He had chosen to ride with his men that day. That's Clement for you, though." He twisted the strap of her duffel. "He sends his condolences for the commandant. He was sorry to hear of his death. But moving forward, he very much wanted you alongside us at the front and not emptying bedpans at the rear when we leave for the Western Desert because he will have his own car again. And he wants you to be driving it."

"It's an honour."

"That you earned. The colonel does not suffer fools, and regardless of what you did for him in the desert that day, or what Chastain suggested, he requested you solely because of your ability. Nothing more and nothing less."

"Thank you, Corporal."

"I'll warn you that he's a taskmaster," Gasquet said as he started back down the hall. "But always fair."

Violet fell into step beside him.

"You've heard about what's happening in the west?" He was no longer smiling.

"The Germans are advancing on Cairo. The officers who I drive don't say much but they say enough for me to know that they're worried."

"We're all worried. In less than two weeks, Rommel has destroyed entire armoured brigades and retaken Antelat, Agedabia, Msus, and Benghazi—almost everything the Brits once had in their control. It will be Tobruk and Cairo next." Gasquet scowled. "It's like the same strategy they used against us in forty all over again. A blitzkrieg, a lightning-fast strike that's caught the British generals with their pants down. If the Brits had asked us, if they had let us into the fight before now, if they had listened to our warnings—" He stopped abruptly and glanced around but the hall was deserted. "I'm sorry. Complaining helps nothing. But it's so very frustrating."

"I understand what it's like not being let into a fight," Violet told him as they stepped into the courtyard, shaded by plum trees. "My father and fiancé forbade me from volunteering."

"And yet you're here."

"And yet I'm here. And I wouldn't want to be anywhere else."

Gasquet stopped. "It must have been hard. To defy your family's wishes, I mean."

"It was at first," she told him honestly. "But all you need is one person who believes in you." It was surprisingly easy to talk to this man, though Violet couldn't have put her finger on why.

"Was it Chastain?" he asked. "The person who believed in you?"

Above their heads, the doves still serenaded them with their mournful song. Violet weighed her answer.

"I'm sorry, that was too personal," Gasquet said, shaking his head. "I just wondered, since you already knew him—"

"Sort of," Violet told him. She wasn't sure if Henri really believed in her but he had certainly pushed her. "His sister, George, was the person who first believed in me. She still does."

His eyes lit up. "She is extraordinary."

"She really is." Violet rather thought that Gasquet was blushing. "Tell me about the person who believed in you," she said.

A shadow of pain flickered across the corporal's face before it was gone.

"I'm sorry." It was Violet's turn to apologize. "That was also a very personal question. You don't have to answer that."

"No, it's all right." He scuffed the toe of his boot in the earth, sending up chalky puffs of dust. "I had a sister once too. And she was also the person who believed in me the most. She was my whole world." He looked up at her. "She died when I was young."

"I'm sorry."

"She was the one who inspired me to fight for what I believe in." He paused. "I think she would have liked you."

Impulsively, Violet reached out and touched his arm. "If she was anything like you, then I think I would have liked her too." She let her arm fall back to her side. "Thank you, Corporal."

"For what?"

"For reminding me how much goodness is still around me. How much I still have to be thankful for. Sometimes, especially lately, it's been hard to see."

Gasquet exhaled heavily and seemed to shake himself free of the solemnity. "Well, I have more good news then," he said, his face splitting into a grin. "That you will definitely be thankful for."

"Oh?" She let him guide the conversation away from family. "What is it?"

He reached into his pack and withdrew a book. "First, Corporal Chastain asked me to give you this." He handed it to Violet.

It was an English copy of *The Hound of the Baskervilles* with a note tucked between the pages. Violet pulled it out. *I told you so* was scrawled across the slip, signed simply with the letter *H*.

"He tells me that you will not be able to put it down," he advised.

"Hmm." Violet's lips curled. "We shall see."

"And there is something else."

"Something else? Better than a new book?"

"I'll let you be the judge of that," Gasquet said with another wide smile. "It's parked out front."

★ ★ ★

Violet adjusted the small brown paper–wrapped package she carried under her arm and hesitated at the entrance to the compound. She was uncertain how she was going to find Henri in the organized chaos of preparations for their journey west, but it turned out she needn't have worried. Two Legionnaires stopped and greeted her by name, inquired how they could help, and then insisted that they escort her to the far side of the barracks despite her protestations. She still wasn't entirely comfortable with the recognition and found herself almost stammering as she inquired after their well-being and then thanked them profusely for their assistance, which only seemed to delight them even further. They left her at the entrance to a low stone storage building, the wide doors propped open and stacks of crates and boxes visible inside.

"I'm wondering if perhaps General Koenig should consider making you a general also."

Violet turned to find Henri leaning against the doorway, wiping his hands with a grease-stained rag as he watched the two Legionnaires depart. The soft, golden light of the setting sun gilded his skin and the worn khaki of his uniform.

"What?"

"I'm fairly certain that any and all of these men would follow you to hell and back if you asked them."

"That's not—I don't—" She stopped and started again. "I haven't done anything to deserve this sort of…mythical regard."

"Doesn't matter." Henri pushed himself away from the door. "You know just as well as I that soldiers are a superstitious lot. For whatever reasons—though saving a much-respected colonel certainly caught some attention—you have become something of a symbol for them."

"A symbol?"

"These are men who have lost their country, but they have not lost their belief in what their country once stood for and might again. Bravery, perseverance, honour, freedom. It's what the Free French see in you. It's what they are fighting for."

"Um." Inside the storage building, she could hear the sounds of men speaking and crates and boxes being moved. "I came here to thank you," she said, deflecting the conversation from herself.

"For what?"

"Corporal Gasquet said that you recommended me to Colonel Clement."

"He wasn't supposed to tell you that."

Violet bit her lip.

"It doesn't matter," Henri said. "If I hadn't, someone else would have."

A soldier carrying a stack of wooden boxes exited the storage building, nodding at Henri and smiling broadly at Violet.

"Did you sign the papers?" Henri asked once he had passed.

"Yes."

"You didn't have to. No one would have thought less of you if you had stayed here."

"I would have thought less of me."

Henri nodded, his expression hard to read. "You've met the colonel then."

"Yes."

"He's a good man."

"Yes," Violet agreed. "He is direct and blunt and has made clear his expectations for me. And I get to drive a Ford utility car now. It has a heavier frame and is built more like a truck than a car, with an enclosed rear for storage. But it shouldn't take me long to get used to it. The Humber was really on its last legs."

"Good." He tossed the rag onto the top of the nearest crate.

Another man exited the storage building, loaded with an armful of wooden boxes. He too nodded at Henri and acknowledged Violet with a grin.

"I brought you a present," she said, thrusting the package from under her arm in his direction.

"What is it?"

"A thank-you."

"You already thanked me."

"Just take the damn package and say thank you."

Henri's lips twitched as he reached for it. "Thank you." He pulled the paper away. "You got me books."

"Have you read them?" she asked.

"I have not." He balanced both books in one hand, turning them over. "*Murder on the Orient Express* and *The Secret Adversary*," he read aloud. "By one Agatha Christie."

"Not Doyle," Violet said. "I thought it was time for you to expand your mystery horizons."

He opened the top volume to a random page and started reading. Violet reached out and snapped the book shut. "You can't do that. You'll ruin the suspense."

"You're telling me how I should read?"

"Yes. Clearly, it's warranted."

"Where did you get these?"

"I found them in a market in Beirut. I've read them and now

I'm giving them to someone who will appreciate them. Returning the favour, as it were."

He smoothed his fingers over the hard orange cover, staring at the black lettering. "That's…" His words seemed to stall.

Violet clasped her hands behind her back. "Well," she said after long seconds had ticked by in silence, "I should go. I've kept you long enough from your duties."

"It's no bother." He still hadn't looked up.

"Right. Um. Well, thank you again and—"

"It was selfish, what I did," he said suddenly.

"What was?"

"Recommending you to the colonel. I did it because I wanted you with us. With me, when we headed west."

Violet's breath caught.

"I should have asked you first."

"It was still my choice, Henri. Major Tremblay gave me all sorts of opportunity to say no, believe me."

"The truth is that you would be safer here—"

"Don't you dare do that to me," she said, a flash of anger sparking. "If I wanted safe, I wouldn't be here at all. If I wanted safe, I would have gotten married the way Tino wanted me to and crawled back to England the way my father wanted me to. This was my choice."

He met her eyes. "I know."

"Last I saw George, she was also packing up to head west. Seems there were very few nurses who volunteered."

"I'm aware. I saw her this morning."

"Did you tell her that she'd be safer here too?"

"Of course I did."

"And what did she say?"

"That she loved me and to please get out of her way."

Violet found herself laughing. "I should have led with that. To get out of my way, I mean." Her cheeks suddenly felt overly warm.

"Don't worry. I'm sure you'll get another chance." Henri looked amused.

The two Legionnaires who had exited the building were now returning with empty arms, their loads delivered. Henri tucked the books against his side. "I thank you again for your dedication to my intellect," he said as they approached. "And I'll see you in the Western Desert, La Fleur."

"Oh, it's La Fleur now?" Violet's brows climbed. "Whatever happened to princess?"

"That girl is gone," he said, and he no longer looked amused. "That girl became a Legionnaire. One I'm proud to serve with."

The two soldiers had almost reached them, and Henri stepped away from her. "Drive safe."

CHAPTER
18

The spy had been ordered into the souk. He remained alert as he traversed the sights, sounds, and smells of the market. Each vendor promoted their wares enthusiastically in a cacophony of chatter, and one could find nearly anything to barter for. The spy, however, was not interested in spices or furniture or brocaded silk. Not this evening, at least. This evening, he was visiting a tailor.

The tailor was near the northeast corner of the souk. The transmission the spy had received, like all transmissions, had been brief. A date, a location, and a series of code words or phrases that would guide him. The spy ignored a group of soldiers who were crowded around a vendor's stall, making drunken fools of themselves, just as he ignored the locals who were casting angry, resentful looks in their direction. Up ahead, he had spotted a sign hanging above a vendor's stall front, a crimson background against a black depiction of an antelope's head, with two long, spiral horns. The spy stopped in front of the stall where the vendor was hanging an eclectic collection of brightly coloured kaftans next to an assortment of bland khaki uniforms.

"Do you use yellow silk embroidery?" the spy asked.

The vendor turned slowly to look at him. He was short and thin with black hair almost completely covered by his keffiyah. He had small, narrow eyes that darted left and right, twin pools of dark suspicion. .

"Never yellow," the tailor answered in heavily accented French. "Only purple."

"Very good," the spy replied. "Then I have come to the right place."

"Yes." The tailor glanced up and down the busy passage. "Give me but a moment." The man barked a rapid torrent of instructions in Arabic toward the rear of the stall, and a young boy appeared. Another set of instructions was delivered, and the boy vanished.

"Come," said the tailor, switching back to French. "I have what you need in the back."

The spy surreptitiously checked his surroundings but all the attention seemed to be on the soldiers, who continued to sway and laugh uproariously. He followed the tailor, ducking under rows of hanging belts and shelves lined with spools of thread, jars of buttons, and cushions bristling with needles. In the back, away from the noise of the souk, two sewing machines were mounted to small tables, bits of cloth and thread littered beneath them. A narrow door was framed between bins of fabric bolts propped against the wall. The tailor waved the spy toward a stool at the nearest machine.

"I'll stand, thank you," the spy said.

The tailor shrugged and turned away, reaching for a bottle of arak amid what looked like the pattern of a traditional dress. Without asking, he poured two small glasses of the milky liquid and handed one to the spy. The other he left on the table opposite, and without saying anything further, he returned to the front of the stall, leaving the spy alone.

The spy raised his glass and sipped. After being in the desert, he would never not accept a glass of anything liquid ever again.

The narrow door between the stacks of fabric bolts opened, and a man entered. He was tall, his flowing white kaftan making him look even longer. He had an angular face with a deep bronze complexion and impenetrable eyes that hovered somewhere between brown and green. The man crossed the room and picked up the second glass of arak, making himself comfortable on the stool the spy had declined.

"It always surprises me what friendships are forged when one faces a mutual enemy." He spoke quietly and in German. "Our tailor would as likely slit the throat of one of your Free French comrades as he would sell them a new uniform. He was quite distraught to see the Vichy go." He took an exploratory sip of his arak and grimaced.

The spy studied the man he knew only as Otto. He had been in this very place the first time he'd met him, at the end of summer. An Abwehr courier of sorts was how Major Beck had described this man when the spy had requested assistance getting the film out of Syria and into Germany. The spy suspected this man was far more than a mere courier but those were not questions he needed to ask. Questions like that got people like him killed.

"Berlin sends their regards," Otto said. "They were exceedingly pleased with the film. Turns out the Americans made themselves useful after all, though not in the way they probably wish. Those were Black Code books, used by all of their military attachés."

The spy said nothing.

"Berlin was less pleased with whatever incompetence led to the termination of a previously steady source of intelligence. The commandant's private papers were consistently useful. You were under orders to observe and report only, in case you have forgotten."

The spy had seen firsthand what happened when agents disobeyed orders and went rogue. He'd witnessed those men lined up against concrete walls, hoods over their heads, hands tied behind their backs, branded traitors or double agents.

"I have not forgotten," he said. "It was a regrettable circumstance. I had no choice." He had been obediently and faithfully observing and reporting for a very long time, and the spy did not appreciate being reminded of his mistakes.

"The Abwehr does not have patience for regrettable," Otto said.

The spy wondered if that was a threat. He leaned back warily, letting one of his hands drop so that it rested closer to his knife. He still didn't know why he had been summoned here by his superior back in Berlin, but he wasn't naïve enough to believe that he wasn't expendable should he have been deemed an incompetent liability.

Otto placed his glass down on the edge of the cutting table amid the scraps of fabric. "We are poised to take Tobruk and Cairo. There is no room for errors and regrettable circumstances."

"Understood."

"I must ask…" Otto toyed with his glass, tipping it in a slow, circular motion, seemingly considering his next words carefully. "The late commandant's driver, this woman that they are calling La Fleur. I have heard that she is quite clever. I have heard that she is still asking questions about the manner of the commandant's death."

"She's not asking questions to anyone who matters."

"Mmm." Otto stroked his chin thoughtfully. "I have also heard that you are quite taken with her."

The spy suppressed the anger that rose hot and fast. How dare this man suggest that he would lose focus and have his head turned by a pretty girl.

"Every man in Damascus is taken with her," the spy said evenly, refusing to rise to the bait. "I have made sure that I am no different. It has never been a chore to be in her company."

"And if she starts asking questions that we don't like to people who matter? Who are likely to look beyond what we want them to see? Then what?"

"Are you asking me to kill her? Because you just reminded me that I am under orders to observe and report."

"No, no. At least, not yet. It was merely raised as a possibility."

"Then I will do what needs to be done. She won't be difficult to kill because she will never see it coming."

Otto studied him from beneath dark brows. He seemed to reach a conclusion.

"Good. I'm told that they've already started burning papers in Cairo," he said. "The Brits are terrified of us. But we are going to need more to finish them. More from you."

"I am willing to do more," the spy told him. "There are many officers within my reach who would never see it coming either. The death of one French general could save the lives of many German soldiers."

Otto frowned. "You're suggesting the assassination of General Koenig."

"I'm suggesting that I could do much more than observe and report. And I'm suggesting that it would not be that difficult."

"And then what?"

It was the spy's turn to frown. "And then he's dead."

"And will be replaced with someone else."

"Less cunning. Less skilled. Less respected."

"Perhaps. And perhaps not. Regardless, that someone else will be suspicious of everyone and everything. The access that you currently enjoy will be restricted." Otto pulled at a loose thread on his kaftan. "Short-term thinking applied to a long-term problem is never beneficial."

Anger once again spiked but the spy kept his expression blank. "Merely a suggestion."

"Your orders from Berlin remain as they are. Observe and report for as long as they require you to. No more, no less. Without orders, and men to follow them, the world falls into anarchy." Otto's voice was silky.

The spy gritted his teeth. "Understood."

"I have brought something for you." Otto stood and crossed

the tiny room, stooping to extract a bundle of fabric tied with a string that had been piled on a dozen others just like it. He placed it on the table amid the pattern pieces.

"What is this?"

"Your new radio."

The spy untied the string and unwrapped the rough fabric. Nestled inside were three boxes that looked very much like small biscuit tins.

"You leave shortly for the Western Desert. A lot of open space out there. The model you are currently using does not have the range that this one does. Inside the top unit you will find instructions and the frequency ranges to be used once you are west of Cairo."

"Very good."

"Remain in General Koenig's camp and maintain your cover. It is expected that the Brits will try to establish a defensive line south of El Gazala, or perhaps Tobruk, and that the Free French will be part of that line. Berlin still expects regular communication from you, especially when we are so close." He tapped his finger against the edge of the fabric pile. "If we take Egypt, we take the Suez. And then no one will stop us."

The spy rewrapped the radio, tied the string tightly, and tucked the bundle under his arm. "The Brits are badly overextended in the west."

"And yet they cling like a tick to a mongrel. It's why any and all sources of intelligence are so valuable now. Our supply lines are our biggest challenge, and knowing what the enemy plans will be the difference between defeat and victory. We do not have resources to waste."

"I understand."

"There cannot be any more...regrettable occurrences. Certainly not now."

The spy fumed inwardly. He imagined correcting such superciliousness with any one of the weapons he had at his disposal, if only to make himself feel better. Instead he answered in a flat voice devoid of emotion. "Contrary to what the Abwehr believes, the death of the commandant was not regrettable at all. And La Fleur is far more valuable alive than dead at the moment."

Otto raised a single, dubious dark brow. "You sound very sure of that."

"I am." The spy adjusted the weight of the radio under his arm. "Because the late commandant who once rode in La Fleur's car has just been replaced by a colonel."

CHAPTER
19

14 FEBRUARY 1942
BIR HAKEIM, LIBYA

The word *fort*, as it was applied to the fort at Bir Hakeim, was a misnomer.

Violet wasn't sure what she'd expected when the Free French were ordered to defend Bir Hakeim, but it wasn't this. She supposed that, in her imagination, she had conjured a vision of a crusader castle with high stone walls and robust, sturdy towers. The word *bir* meant "water" in Arabic, and around the fictional crusader fort in her imagination, she also envisioned an island of palms and lush greenery surrounding a lake that would reflect the blue of the sky.

Yet as she carefully steered the Ford across the expanse of desert, all she could see was a slight rise in the sand on the horizon and a handful of crumbling concrete shacks. Above them, the sun beat down with a punishing intensity, and farther south, past this slight rise in the earth, the undulating expanse of the Sahara stretched out infinitely. For a horrifying moment, Violet wondered if she had navigated incorrectly and they were miles from where they were supposed to be.

"Is this it, sir?" Violet asked without thinking.

"Yes." Colonel Clement's answer was terse and grim. "The very end of the defensive line. The twelve square kilometers we've been ordered out here to defend. Perhaps we should have gone to Russia after all," he muttered.

Violet wisely kept her mouth shut. There was nothing that she could say that would improve what faced them.

She kept the Ford steady, and as she drew closer, heads suddenly popped up from the ground. She brought the car to a hurried halt, realizing with some shock that the fort was not aboveground but below it. In front of her, Koenig's car had also come to a stop, and the general was already walking toward the fort.

A half dozen men emerged from the earth to meet the general. Looking around, Violet now saw half-buried vehicles parked in cavities cut into the hard ground.

"Jesus Christ, they've dug trenches," the colonel said, staring through the dusty windshield. He was a tall, rangy man with greying hair, flinty eyes, and a nose like a hook above the swath of bandages still wrapped around his jaw. At the moment, hunched over as he was, glaring at the view, he reminded Violet of a furious raptor.

"Goddamn trenches. It's like the last war all over again." He pushed open the passenger door without waiting for Violet to open it and climbed out.

Violet scrambled out of the vehicle as well.

"See where they want the vehicles put," the colonel told her. "I'll get further orders."

"Yes, sir."

The colonel stalked off, and Violet looked around with wide eyes. The column of trucks and vehicles behind them had ground to a halt.

Cautiously, Violet approached the warren of rabbit holes that was masquerading as a fort. More men had appeared out of the earth, and Violet approached the one closest to her. The soldier was caked with dust, leaning on a spade, smoking a cigarette, and watching their arrival with keen interest. He turned to greet her as she approached.

"Good morning," she said in English.

The cigarette fell out of his mouth.

"Colonel Clement has requested that I find out where I should have the vehicles parked," she said. "Can you give me some direction?"

The soldier blinked, bits of dust flaking from his cheeks.

Violet waited for a moment but he didn't answer. "Is this all that there is out here?" she tried.

The soldier jerked and rescued his cigarette from the sand. He yanked off his cap and doffed it.

"I thought you were a mirage," he said. "Make believe, like. The desert makes you see strange things." He had a thick Yorkshire accent. "Didn't expect a lass."

Violet stuck out her hand. "No mirage. Adjutant St. Croix," she said. "A pleasure."

The soldier shook her hand, his palm gritty and callused against hers. "Sergeant Williams of the One Hundred Fiftieth Infantry Brigade." He grinned suddenly. "Welcome to hell on earth." He seemed to catch himself. "Er, that's what we call it."

"Thank you, I think," Violet replied. "It's not what I expected."

"Aye. Thought it'd be a grand castle, did you?"

"Yes," she confessed.

"My CO told us this place used to be an ancient crossroads for the Bedouin caravans. Then the Italians built a fort on the site when they arrived." He looked around at the pitiful remnants that had long since collapsed and yielded to the elements. "Let's hope those fascist bastards fight out here as well as they build, aye?"

"Let's hope, indeed."

"A terrible place, yet perfect for war, no?"

"What do you mean?"

"Nothing to damage or destroy out here, aye? No beautiful buildings, no monuments to history, no cultural shrines. Just each other."

Violet nodded weakly. "I suppose."

"We've been waiting for you so that we can skedaddle."

"Where?"

He made a face. "'Bout ten miles north. We'll dig in near Sidi Muftah." Williams stuck his cigarette back into the corner of his mouth. "But we'll be getting a break in Tobruk first." He closed his eyes and sighed. "I miss the sea."

So did Violet.

Williams's eyes popped open. "You see any Jerries on your way here?"

Violet shook her head.

"Heard that Rommel's only a hundred kilometers west of here. But he won't get east. Not through us. The whole of the Eighth Army is making a line of defensive boxes from Gazala all the way here," he said. "The Jerries will try, but they won't get through."

Violet refrained from pointing out that the Germans had been getting through the Allied lines at a terrifying rate recently.

"Not likely you'll see much action here, though. Unless Rommel tries to go all the way around to get to Egypt. Don't expect he'll do that, though. Too far south to bring his supply lines from the ports, I reckon." Williams put his cap back on his head. "'Spose you're right lucky that way."

"Mmm." Violet made a noncommittal sound. It did not seem lucky to spend weeks or months out here in the blast furnace that was Bir Hakeim waiting for a Nazi generalfeldmarschall who might never appear. "The cars?" she prompted. "Where should we put them?"

"Right. I'll show you." Williams hefted the spade over his shoulder. "You can put whatever vehicles you have in the spaces we've already excavated." He eyed the line of trucks waiting beyond the fort and whistled. "But I think you're goin' to have to dig a lot more holes, lass."

★ ★ ★

Within hours of their arrival, the entire British 150th Infantry Brigade had vacated Bir Hakeim, leaving behind only a network of trenches and dugouts and two sandy, cracked cisterns filled partially with water. Within a few more hours, the new tenants had been deployed to start work on reinforcing the defences and expanding the underground grid, digging more trenches, gun pits, deep holes for equipment, and larger chambers that would be used as command posts. A hospital tent was erected in the center of the fort, a mess tent beside it, and a tent to be used as headquarters, surrounded by coils of barbed wire. Colonel Clement's lodgings were dug closer to the edges of the encampment with his staff's, excluding Violet. She suspected that she would end up sleeping in the Ford—not for the first time and certainly not for the last. There were far worse places that she could think of.

Once Violet had carefully stowed the colonel's car near his new underground quarters, she unloaded his personal belongings. His private papers she kept locked safely in the Ford, unwilling to leave them unsecured in his dugout. She had no idea when the colonel would be back and found herself wandering the honeycombed rubble under the merciless sun, trying to familiarize herself with the labyrinth.

"La Fleur."

Violet turned to find Private Picard standing just behind her.

"The sappers from the engineering corps have made a dugout for you," he told her, a shy smile on his face. "We were wondering if you might want to see it."

"A dugout?"

"Your own private apartment," Picard said.

A rush of gratitude tightened her throat. "Thank you. I'd love to see it."

"Perhaps don't thank us quite yet." Remy Picard's brown eyes danced with wry amusement. "It's not exactly Le Petit Trianon."

"Nor is it the back of a Ford." She laughed. "Sleeping in the car has given me a permanent crick in my neck. Please, lead the way."

She followed Picard back in the direction of the colonel's quarters. Just off to the side, away from the bulk of the men but within hailing distance, a rectangular hollow had been carved into the hard ground. It was perhaps four or five feet wide and ten feet long, lined on all sides with stacks of sandbags, and had a rolled canvas top secured at one end. Two painfully young sappers, stripped to the waist, were waiting with pickaxes near the edge.

"We hope you like it," the one closest to Violet said.

Violet hopped down into the waist-deep depression and looked around. Private Picard joined her, inspecting the sandbags.

"This is the most beautiful home I've ever seen," she told the sappers. It was ironic that after a lifetime of opulent villas and lavish manors that she had shared with servants and staff, this hole in the ground that she would share with sand and the occasional scorpion meant more to her than she could say.

"You can roll the canvas across the top during the day for shade and at night for privacy," they explained.

"Thank you," she said again. "For your hard work and your kindness."

Both the sappers smiled happily before swinging their pickaxes back over their shoulders and heading toward the center of the fort, undoubtably to dig another hole.

"I'll help you fetch your belongings," Private Picard said. "And set up your cot."

Picard helped her out of the dugout, and they retrieved Violet's meager belongings from the Ford. She left her tools locked up with the colonel's private papers but brought her camp bed, her duffel, and her tiny folding chair. The private helped her unpack.

"Thank you," Violet said again once they had finished.

Picard nodded. He seemed reluctant to leave.

"The sappers told me that they are to be laying mines once they're finished with the dugouts." Picard was toying with the edge of a sandbag. "They told me that they were going to lay fifty thousand around this fort. Maybe more. Anti-tank and anti-personnel. They talked about the plans. There will be specific, unmarked tracks through the minefields so that the supply convoys can get in and out."

"That sounds like a lot." Violet was content to let him talk. With days and weeks and months stretching before her and an uncertainty about how she would fill her time, it was nice to have some company, no matter how brief.

"And they have orders to dig in the seventy-fives and the Bofors anti-aircraft guns."

"Then we'll be well defended. That's a good thing." Violet bent and opened her duffel. She extracted both her books and her mess kit and put them all neatly on the seat of her folding chair.

She straightened, pleased with the results. It was a far cry from her father's library, with its shelves of books and crystal decanters, but it gave this space a homey touch.

"Do you like to read?" Picard asked.

"Yes. Very much." She pulled her greatcoat from the duffel and laid it over the foot of her bed. As much as the days were unbearably hot, she knew the nights would be uncomfortably cold. "It keeps my mind occupied during the empty days."

"I heard the Brits talking about the cockroach before they left."

"A cockroach?"

"No, *the* cockroach. The cockroach is what they called the desert madness. Otherwise strong men who are driven to insanity by the oblivion of this place. Like a cockroach burrowing around and around in your brain." He made a circular motion with his finger near the brim of his cap. "I think I'd rather fight Germans than slowly lose my mind all alone."

"Perhaps we will do neither."

"Perhaps." He didn't sound convinced.

"All we can do is look forward," she said, taking pity on the private. "Focus on the good things, not the bad things that haven't even happened yet."

"The good things?"

"Do you have a wife? Sweetheart?" Picard was probably close to her age. Maybe a little older.

"No." He twisted his hands wistfully. "Maybe one day."

"What about family?"

Picard shrugged sadly. "Not really. I'm kind of on my own."

Violet was regretting asking questions she didn't already know the answers to. "Well, you're not alone here." She pulled Dekalb's *Madonna of the Sleeping Cars* from the little chair. "Why don't you borrow this?"

The private blinked at her.

"You do read?" Violet asked, inwardly cringing and wondering if she had stuck her foot in her mouth all over again.

"Yes, yes, of course." Picard took the book and carefully turned it over in his hands. "Thank you. Are you sure that you don't mind me borrowing this?"

"Not at all." Violet smiled warmly at him. "It's the least I could do for all your help here."

The private blushed. "I hope…" He stopped.

"You hope what?"

"I hope that one day I have a wife just like you."

Violet cleared her throat, grasping for the appropriate response.

"I'm sorry. I shouldn't… That is… That was—"

"I'm flattered." Violet hastened to reassure him. "One day, when this is all over, I'm sure you'll meet someone and fall madly in love."

Remy Picard ducked his head and tucked the book under his arm. "Thank you," he said again. "I'll read this and return it right away."

Violet waved her hand dismissively at their bleak surroundings. She couldn't imagine much changing in the days and months to come. "I know where to find you."

George found Violet the next day.

"I heard a rumour that you had your own palace over here with the fancy officers but I didn't quite believe it," she announced to Violet without animosity. "I had to stop by before my shift to come see for myself."

Violet squinted up at her friend, who was standing at the edge of her dugout, her hands on her hips, the early morning sun behind her. "Please, do come in," she laughed.

George clambered down into the depression, careful not to spill the tin of tea she held in one hand. She took a sip and looked around. "I'm jealous."

Violet put her book aside. "Of the accommodations?"

"Of the solitude." George plopped down next to Violet on her cot. "I have to share with the other nurse."

"I wouldn't mind sharing," Violet told her.

"You would mind if the only other woman in this fort aside from you and me snores like a freight train. I woke up last night thinking that we were being bombed."

Violet snorted. "Oh, come on."

"I'm serious, Vi." George gripped her arm and rolled her eyes. "Rosalie is an excellent nurse and a pleasant enough person but I might start sleeping in the hospital."

"How is the hospital?" Violet asked.

"The boys are already setting up a better tent as we speak. More space, more organization. We need it. We're already bogged down with patients. Heat exhaustion, sand fly fever, yellow fever, dysentery. God help us if we actually have to deal with any Germans."

"I'm sorry I asked."

"Do you think they are going to come here? The Germans?" George said it lightly but Violet could hear the current of worry.

"I don't know. It's pretty far south from the coast and the ports. A long way to draw men and machines and everything that they need to fight." The British soldier she had spoken to earlier had made a good point.

"I'll be happy if we never see another German or Italian ever again. If we spend the rest of this war out here all by ourselves with no one shooting at us or bombing us."

"I think that might be a very distinct possibility."

"Did Colonel Clement say anything? About what the Germans might do?"

"No. He's with the general, and I can't imagine that I'll see much of him while we're here."

"Of course. Sorry. That was a foolish question."

"Not foolish." Violet leaned toward George, their shoulders touching. "I think we're all wondering the same thing."

"I'm glad you're here, Vi." George said suddenly.

"I'm glad you're here too."

"Did you think about staying behind?"

"What do you mean?"

"In Damascus."

"No." Violet traced a pattern on the cot's blanket between them. "I had that argument with myself in France once. I made my choice then."

"Henri told me what he did. Recommending you to the colonel, I mean. He also told me he apologized."

"And I told him that there was no apology needed." She paused. "Did you consider staying? You could have done just as much good in a hospital in Damascus as you could here."

"And leave Henri? Or you?" She shook her head. "Not a chance. This war has already torn too many families apart. The Legion is stuck with me patching them up for as long as you are both here. I know that we'll spend a lot of time passing each other like ships in the night but at least we're sailing together. Does that make sense?"

"Yes," Violet said thickly. "Corporal Gasquet once asked me who the person was who first believed in me. I told him it was you." She exhaled. "I don't know where I would be right now if I hadn't met you. Probably married to someone I never loved doing things that never made me happy."

"I think you're being hard on yourself."

"No, I think I'm being honest with myself. And I never thanked you for that. For believing in me, I mean. So thank you, George. For being a true friend."

"You've always made me feel braver than I think I am." George told her. "Because believing in each other works both ways."

The two women sat in a companionable silence for a long minute.

"I should probably tell you that, during our conversation, Corporal Gasquet also said that you were extraordinary," Violet said with sly grin.

"He did?"

"He did. And he blushed too."

"I'm not blushing," George protested. "It's a sunburn."

"Of course it is."

George stood and gulped down the remains of her tea. "I think I'm late for my shift."

"We wouldn't want that." Violet was still grinning.

"No, we wouldn't." She climbed back out of Violet's berth. "But with any luck, for the rest of our time out here in this no-man's-land, I'll never see another shrapnel or mortar wound again."

CHAPTER
20

Just before dawn, the sky exploded.

Violet jerked awake, blinking in confusion at the hazy twilight of predawn that lay like a blanket over the fort and around her tiny dugout. But it remained hazy for only the briefest of seconds before a searing flash of light penetrated the canvas above her head and a crashing boom tore across the ground. The earth around her trembled, and dust drifted down from the sandbagged walls.

Frantically, Violet rolled from her cot, disentangled the blanket from around the uniform she slept in, and staggered to her feet. Crouching, she rolled back the canvas and stuck her head aboveground. In other areas, men were surging from their own dugouts, illuminated by a steady series of bright flashes that marked gunfire and artillery. She hesitated briefly before she grabbed her helmet and climbed out to join them, heading directly for Colonel Clement's quarters. She had no idea if she would be needed but it was her job to be prepared. If the colonel needed to be evacuated or hurried to another post, she would be ready.

As it turned out, she was not the only one, and she joined a handful of his junior officers as the gunfire continued outside the periphery of the fort. The colonel was already striding across the rubble, heading toward the headquarters tent under a continuous

series of flares that flickered like a lightning storm overhead. Gunfire still chattered but more ominous was the chilling, underlying
squeak and rattle of tanks on the move.

"What the hell is happening?" Clement demanded to no one
in particular.

"The Third Indian Motor Brigade guarding the periphery has
engaged with the enemy just outside the wire, sir," said an officer
who had been sprinting across the rubble to meet them. "Southeast
of our position."

"Be more specific," the colonel growled. "Who and what have
they engaged?"

"Heavy tanks, sir. From the Italian Ariete Division. And some
German tanks as well." The officer was almost breathless. "Major
Amiel's patrol fell back at zero four hundred this morning, reporting enemy light forces approaching. Land lines have also been cut,
sir."

Another distant boom reverberated through the ground. She
was hearing landmines, Violet realized. Landmines detonating
under the heavy tracks of approaching tanks.

"What is the Third reporting in the south?" Clement
demanded.

"That the whole bloody Afrika Korps is drawn up in front of
them like a bloody review." The officer winced as he said it. "Sir."

Clement stopped short, bringing everyone with him to a halt.
"The bastards have really done it."

"Sir?"

"Elected to go around. To attempt to squeeze between us and
the goddamn Sahara." He scowled. "They'll not get past us," he
snarled. "Where is the general?"

"General Koenig is already at HQ, sir. Preparing the brigade
to stand to."

The colonel resumed his march, not pausing until they had
reached headquarters, where men ran in and out of the tent. The

colonel paused and barked a string of orders, sending his own officers running in a similar fashion. His gaze fell on Violet.

"Make yourself useful, Adjutant," he clipped. "But don't go far."

"Very good, sir."

"And for God's sake, St. Croix, put on your damn helmet." He
ducked into the tent before Violet could reply.

Violet jammed her tin helmet on her head and headed for the
hospital. There were very few options that existed for her to make
herself useful but the hospital was one. If the might of the Afrika
Korps was indeed bearing down on them, then there would be
casualties. And while Violet could not operate the heavy guns or
join the troops defending the perimeter of Bir Hakeim, at the very
least, Violet could help prepare for those who were.

The first face she saw in the hospital was George's. Her friend
had deep creases of worry carved across her forehead.

"What is happening out there?" she demanded.

"It seems that the Germans have engaged our forces to the
south."

George paled, and for the first time, Violet saw naked fear
clearly in her expression. It was unnerving.

"Is it bad?" George asked.

"I don't know."

"We've been told to prepare for casualties." George's posture
was rigid.

"I'm sorry I don't know more."

George shuddered. "I hate the sound of those tanks. It makes
my skin crawl. I hate that we're here, immovable, just waiting for
them to do their worst."

"I know." Violet shrugged helplessly. "But I'm here to help.
Whatever you need. Just tell me what to do."

"All right. Follow me."

Violet worked for over an hour, moving patients to create space
and making sure that the medical supplies that they had on hand

were ready to be used by the doctors and orderlies. The gunfire continued in bursts and light guttered and receded through the canvas roof like a fireworks display, but became less noticeable as the sky brightened into daylight. The distant detonations of land-mines continued, augmented now by horrifying whistling noises that ended in deafening crashes, these much closer. Violet under-stood that enemy artillery was close enough to shell the fort, but she kept working. If she was going to die, far better she die here working in the hospital than die cowering in her dugout.

Eventually, though, she ran out of tasks, or at least those that the doctors would allow her to do. Reluctantly emerging from the hospital, she shielded her eyes against the bright sunlight as she slowly comprehended the horrifying sight in front of her.

From the slight incline, Violet could now see the enemy that had approached from the south. There had to be at least fifty tanks crashing into the southernmost defences, firing indiscrim-inately and plowing their way ever closer. Behind them, farther back, another horde of tanks came on. The rattling and squeaking had grown to a stridency that sent icy rivulets of sweat down her back and sent her heart into her throat. On the perimeter of Bir Hakeim, the powerful 75-mm anti-tank guns that had been dug in fired in retaliation, finding their marks, and columns of black smoke were already rising from wrecks of ruined tanks. Yet more kept coming.

Violet crept forward, finding shelter behind a wall of sandbags, feeling utterly helpless. There was nothing she could do for the companies facing the approaching Italian tanks from behind their gun sights, or the men lining the trenches with their rifles, prepar-ing for the worst should the tanks break through the minefields and barbed wire. The air was clouded with eruptions of rubble and sand as the Axis shells found their targets. Dust from churning tank tracks and smoke from the guns and burning vehicles drifted overhead.

A shell exploded in the rubble a short distance from where Violet hunched, and she ducked, making herself as small as possible as sand and shards of earth rained down on her. When she looked up again, she saw that six of the tanks had managed to navigate the minefields and were bearing down on their outermost defences. An Axis shell blew away the top of a French company shelter just as the 75s opened up at close range. Men scrambled from the ruined dugout, and more Legionnaires surged from the trenches, sprinting toward the tanks. Violet watched in disbelief as they swarmed over-top of the closest ones, firing their revolvers through the observation slits. The tanks veered and ground to a halt, and as fast as the Legionnaires had attacked, they retreated, presumably waiting to do it all over again.

The enemy advance seemed to falter, and Violet could hear the shouts and jeers of men across the expanse. Many tanks burned, hungry orange flames licking at the wrecks, and Italian soldiers could be seen stumbling between them, many of their uniforms blackened and burned. The tanks at the rear of the advance reversed, and the jeers turned into all-out roars.

"Violet!" She heard her name through the din, and she turned to find George half running, half stumbling toward her, one hand clutching a helmet to her head.

"Does the colonel need something?" she asked.

George's eyes darted nervously past Violet toward the burning tanks. "No, but the doctors want to know if you can speak Italian. I remembered you said you could."

"I can," she replied.

"Good. Come with me then. There are going to be prisoners and casualties. They want you back in the hospital." George spun and hurried back toward the medical tent without waiting to see if she followed.

Violet took one last glance toward the south and the enemy that was circling and then hurried after her friend. She didn't for one moment believe that the retreating Italian tanks marked the end of anything.

★ ★ ★

Page forty-eight of *The Hound of the Baskervilles* had finally surrendered.

After having weathered too many hands and too many miles, the binding had lost its battle, and the pages had begun to fall away. Violet held the loose page in her hand, the book balanced on her knee, rereading the same paragraph for probably the fourteenth time. She had lit a candle against the encroaching darkness, and the flame guttered and spit. Outside, the guns had fallen silent, replaced only with the low voices of men and the occasional thunk or clang of ammunition or supplies being moved. Violet knew she should draw the canvas roof over her dugout and go to sleep—her body was exhausted—yet her thoughts would not settle. And reading was not helping at all.

Exasperated, she set the page back into the book and closed it with a sigh.

"Giving up on that chapter already?"

Violet jumped. She glanced up to find Henri standing at the edge of her quarters.

"Henri." She clambered off the end of her cot, her book forgotten entirely.

"Do you want me to tell you what happens on the next page?"

"No," she smiled at him. "I've read it so often, I have it memorized."

"Me too. May I?" He gestured at her dugout.

"Of course."

Henri lowered himself into the hollow. "I can't stay long but I come bearing gifts."

In the limited reach of the candlelight, Violet examined him head to toe, resisting the need to touch him. She'd seen only two French casualties being treated in the hospital from today's fighting but she had still worried. It seemed implausible that while the Italians had suffered so many losses, the French had suffered so few.

He caught her look. "I'm all right," he said. "I promise."

"There were a lot of tanks."

"Eighty tanks of the Ariete Division," he said grimly. "We got thirty-five of them. We'll take another thirty-five if they come back tomorrow."

Violet exhaled, pressing her fingers to her lips. "When. When they come back."

"The minefields did their jobs, and the gunners did theirs. My men did everything that they were supposed to do. No one buckled, and no one ran. If those bastards have come looking for a fight, then goddammit, they've found one."

"This is so much harder," she said.

"What do you mean?"

"Being at the mercy of the whims of your enemy. I don't know if anything could have prepared me for what I saw on the horizon this morning. I'm not nearly as brave as everyone seems to think. Today scared me."

"You can't be brave if you're not afraid first, Vi. That's what bravery is."

"I was scared for you. And the men."

"We were prepared," he reassured her. "And we will be again. Here," he said, holding the bundle in his hand out to her. "This should make you feel better."

"A blanket?"

"Yes. But unwrap it." Henri sounded inordinately pleased.

Carefully Violet unfolded the woolen sides. Nestled in the center were a tin of ham and two jars. "Where did you get these?" she breathed.

"Courtesy of our Italian guests," he told her. "We went through the Italian wrecks and saved what we could."

"I can't accept these. Your men should have these things—"

"My men have their share already. They were quite keen to share a little with you. The ham is from Corporal Gasquet." He gave her a crooked grin. "He wanted me to tell you that."

Violet set the blanket on the bed along with the ham and held up both jars reverently, reading the labels. "Plum and apricot preserves?"

"Yes."

She opened the jar of apricot preserves and inhaled deeply. "If I close my eyes, I might convince myself I'm actually in Italy, standing in an orchard, Vesuvius rising in the distance."

"Perhaps not the most opportune time to visit," Henri said dryly.

"True." She sighed and put the lid back on.

He held out another item. "It does, however, seem like an opportune time to give you this, though, given the state *The Hound* has fallen into."

Violet set the preserves down. "A novel?"

Henri handed it to her. It had a pale cover that was slightly singed at one corner with *Federigo Tozzi* printed in bold letters across the top and *Con gli occhi chiusi* in bright red lettering below.

"The lads in the hospital told me that you can speak Italian. They said that you were incredible calming the wounded prisoners brought in."

"Half of them thought they were going to be executed to save our water resources. I simply reassured them that we are not barbarians," Violet murmured distractedly, running her fingers over the cover. "In truth, it was the only thing the doctors would let me do. Not that I blame them."

"I didn't know you could speak Italian."

She looked up at him. "While you were growing up learning how to feed yourself and survive in the world, I was learning how to conjugate verbs in four different languages. Well, that and which fork to use first and the steps to a proper skaters' waltz." She smiled at him wryly. "For all the good it did me."

"You don't give yourself enough credit."

"Neither do you."

"Will you read it to me?" He held her gaze. "The story?"

"Yes." She didn't look away. "I'll read it to you, and I'll do you one better. I'll teach you the language if you like, so you can read it yourself."

"And the waltz?" His voice was low.

"What?"

"I don't know how to dance. Will you teach me how to do that, too?"

Somewhere in this conversation, the light banter that Violet had been so careful to keep between herself and Henri these last months had evaporated. She knew it, and she also knew that she should retreat and re-establish her distance. A distance she had chosen. This was the point where she needed to respond with a carefree laugh, a simple jest, or a deliberate dismissal.

"Yes," she heard herself say. "I'll teach you." Perhaps this was what happened when one watched death approach and then retreat.

She put the book down on the bed beside the rest of her treasures and held out her hand.

Henri's expression shifted in the soft glow of the candle. "Now?"

"I've got nowhere to be. Do you?" She gave him the choice. He could walk away.

He didn't. He stepped closer to her and placed his hand in hers.

"It's not so hard," she whispered, sliding her other hand over his shoulder, her fingers at the nape of his neck. "Put your other hand at my back."

Henri slipped his hand around her waist, his palm resting against her lower back. Violet shivered, and it had nothing to do with the cooling air of the night.

"There are four fundamental steps," she said. "The first is the walk."

It was patently absurd, she thought hazily. Waltzing in a tiny dugout in which they could barely move, surrounded by thousands of men who had survived this journey with them and, beyond that, thousands more who would see them both dead. Perhaps that was why she had said yes.

"Step forward," she instructed. "And then again but cross your back foot behind."

Henri took a minuscule step forward, and Violet matched it, stepping back. Another tiny step took them nowhere. She raised her head and glanced up at him, immediately regretting it because he was looking down at her, his jaw set and his eyes burning with desire.

She lowered her lashes and concentrated on keeping her breathing steady.

"Good," she croaked through a mouth that had gone dry. "Now the natural or right turn." Her voice sounded strange in her ears. She guided them in a circle that was more of a pivot. "And then the reverse." They went back the other way, their feet moving within the diminutive patch of earth.

A breeze floated across the ground, bringing with it the faint smell of gunpowder and scorched earth. The candle flickered and then extinguished, and they were plunged into darkness. Henri's hand tightened against her back, pulling her against him.

"Is that all?" he murmured.

"There will be music," Violet breathed. "And all you do is repeat those steps in time." She hummed a few bars, afraid that if she allowed a silence to fall, she would say something that would ruin everything.

They danced a few more steps, shuffling between her cot and the sandbags until they stopped altogether and simply swayed beneath the inky black sky and the carpet of stars scattered across the expanse. Violet stood with Henri, wanting to freeze this moment in time. Wishing that morning could be delayed, when the rising sun would inevitably bring more destruction and more death in ways that Violet knew she couldn't fully imagine. The tune died on her lips, and she lay her head against Henri's chest, listening to the steady beat of his heart instead.

"Do you miss home?" she asked.

"All the time. I miss the sunrise over the sea. I miss the silver of fish in my nets and the blue of the ocean beneath my boat. I miss the smell of my mother's apple strudel baking and the sound of my sisters' laughter." He shifted slightly beneath her. "And you? Do you miss your old life? The parties and the food and the cars and having everything at your fingertips?"

"No. Well, maybe the food. I can't say I'm enthusiastic about another tin of bully beef."

"You have a tin of ham now."

Violet laughed quietly. It felt good to laugh. "I do," she agreed. "And I'll be sure to wash it down with champagne."

Henri hummed. "I had champagne once."

"Once?"

"I was seventeen. A friend stole two bottles from one of the fancy hotels. We lay on the beach and drank them both. The bubbles went right to my head." He chuckled. "It was glorious."

"Promise me we'll do that one day."

"Get gloriously drunk?"

"Lie on the beach and drink champagne."

His laughter subsided. "I promise."

If Violet closed her eyes, maybe she could pretend that they were really back on a beach in Nice, the evening stretching out before them with promise. Maybe, if she tried really hard, she could pretend that they were out on the sea, the future stretching out before them with possibility. Maybe—

Somewhere in the fort, a man shouted something unintelligible, followed by the sharp bark of a Legionnaire's dog and the clanging of a truck gate being lowered. Reality intruded.

"I have to go." Henri's voice was hoarse.

"Stay." She wasn't ready to say goodbye again. "Just for a little while."

"I can't."

"Of course." She pulled away from him, embarrassed. "I'm sorry." She put some more distance between them, feeling foolish. What had she been thinking? "Thank you again for the book. And the food."

"Vi—"

"I should get some sleep. You should too. Tomorrow is going to come whether we want it to or not."

Henri looked like he might say something but, in the end, only nodded.

"Goodnight, Henri," Violet said.

"Goodnight, LaFleur," Henri replied.

And then Violet was left alone once again.

CHAPTER
21

27 MAY 1942
BIR HAKEIM, LIBYA

The spy seethed beneath the night sky.

If he had been given to fits of rage, he would have kicked something. Or perhaps hurled one of the salvaged bottles of eau de cologne that his comrades had scavenged from one of the Italian wrecks. Cologne, he fumed, along with novels and tins of meat and jars of sweets, was for picnics and not wars and were not going to win the fucking Italians anything.

For over three months, he had endured this godforsaken hell. Three months of choking down foul, brackish water trucked here from Tobruk and swallowing meager, monotonous meals. Three months of digging and drilling and doing it all under a relentless, molten sun that made the days insufferable in its presence and the nights miserable in its absence. Three months of waiting and dutifully reporting every single detail that was Bir Hakeim.

He had trusted that his messages were being passed on to the generalfeldmarschalls or whoever was in charge of planning the North African assault. But after watching the hapless Italians blunder straight into one of Bir Hakeim's largest minefields and then lurch directly into the jaws of the anti-tank guns that had been dug in for just that purpose, the spy had to wonder. Wonder if his intelligence was being used or if the Italians were just arrogant or incompetent or both. Germany was only as good as its allies, and the Italians were an embarrassment.

The spy took a deep breath, rolled his shoulders, and tipped his head back. Above him, the stars stretched as far as he could see. As always, they reminded him of his sister, and as always, he took comfort in their presence. They reminded him why he was here.

He'd waited impatiently as the fort had finally settled in for the night, only the occasional voice drifting through the darkness as the troops rested and prepared for the morning. The spy shuddered to think that tomorrow would bring a repeat of today, and the prospect of that had spurred him to risk sending another message. Satisfied that he was alone, the spy stole across the ground, navigating his way by starlight. He circumvented the coils of barbed wire that surrounded headquarters and made his way toward the holes that had been carved into the hard earth in an effort to protect the burlap-covered vehicles. Here, troop lorries and officers' personal vehicles were parked, sand drifted up to the tops of the tyres. He had a half dozen completely reasonable explanations for his presence here should anyone challenge him, but the sentries farther afield outside the perimeter did not even glance at him, their attention focused solely on the blackness beyond.

Silently, he slipped down the slope of a dugout that housed one of the Bedford lorries until he got to the very bottom. He dropped down to his hands and knees and scooped out large armfuls of sand in the near corner. He kept his radio buried, hidden in a sealed box here, where no one could accidentally stumble across it. The tall truck frame also provided a perfect cover for the antennae wire that needed to be run up the side while transmitting.

It took only a minute for him to set up his radio. The encoded message that he sent was brief: *Luftwaffe assistance required, targets: center HQ, supply convoys. Request permission for extermination of French command and internal sabotage.*

He had already sent artillery numbers and locations, minefield coordinates, and troop positions in dozens of messages long before this, and he did not have the time or patience to do so again. He had done his job—or at least the part of the job he had been ordered to do—and he was waiting for the generals out there to do theirs. Italian tanks alone were not going to destroy Bir Hakeim. It was going to take a far more concerted effort to annihilate this fort and the morale and men within it. He could help. He could begin the destruction and killing from inside the fort. All he needed was the order.

The spy waited for the brief signal that his message had been received. It came, and with it, a single word: *Denied.*

The spy cursed, and this time, he did kick at the sand, sending a soft shower against the truck's fender. He snapped the radio off in frustration without even confirming that he had received the response and cursed again. It was a full minute before he managed to collect himself, then he packed up his radio and reburied it, careful to leave no trace that the ground had been disturbed. He retraced his steps back out into the desert night and back in the direction of his quarters. His efforts were being wasted out here. He was risking his own life to provide this information, and the thought that it might be for nothing infuriated him.

He considered the radioed response. *Denied. Denied, denied, denied.* The word echoed unpleasantly in his head.

The spy hadn't responded. Hadn't given anyone any confirmation that he had received the order. And the desert was a vast place. Sometimes transmissions were lost or garbled. These things happened. What if that refusal hadn't reached him? There was no way to prove that it had. What if the spy finally took matters into his own hands?

He understood the need for order and obedience. He had been nothing but obedient for years. But the spy was quickly coming to the realization that the Abwehr was not all knowing. The officers and men making these decisions were not living his reality. They did not see what he saw. They did not know what he knew. Without immediate action, the spy very much feared that Bir Hakeim would become another failure like Dunkirk. And that was unacceptable.

Up ahead, the silhouette of the hospital tent loomed black against the starry night sky, where the beds were occupied by more Italians than Free French now. By the time he'd passed the hospital, he'd already made his decision. He'd start with sabotage. Weaken the French from within and cause as much chaos as he could. Assassinations would come next.

He considered his potential targets. Otto hadn't been wrong when he'd said that the death of a general would simply result in another man stepping in to take his place. That had been the way of war since the beginning of time. No, he needed a target that would break morale.

La Fleur.

It was a shame, he thought, not for the first time, as he absently caressed the hilt of his knife with his fingers. Had they lived in another time, in another place, the spy rather fancied that he might have genuinely pursued a future with her. As it was, every man in this fort who still possessed a pulse was at least partly infatuated with her. An anomaly that had somehow flourished with cunning, grace, and resilience in this hellish, merciless landscape. The coward de Gaulle could make as many rousing and impassioned speeches and pleas over the airwaves as he liked, but hiding as he was behind the skirts of the Brits, he could not do what this woman had done here. La Fleur made men *believe.*

And men with hope were dangerous indeed.

In the meantime, while LaFleur still lived, he would continue to extract what information he could. Perhaps he would ask her to question the Italian casualties about just how much they had known about Bir Hakeim before they had launched their disastrous attack. Framed correctly, she would think nothing of his request, and those sorts of questions coming from her wouldn't be inter-preted as anything other than feminine compassion and sympathy.

Perhaps he should have asked her tonight, he mused, and then decided that tomorrow would be early enough. In his experience, scared, injured men had very loose tongues, especially when tended to by kind, beautiful women.

The spy glanced over at the HQ tent nearby. There was still the chance that a well-placed bomb would relieve the garrison of its beloved general and whoever else was unlucky enough to be caught with him. For the next few days at least, the spy would avoid both headquarters and the hospital. If the Luftwaffe did indeed come to rain fire down from the skies, it would be difficult to hit one tent without the loss of the other.

Which, as far as the spy was concerned, wouldn't be a loss at all.

CHAPTER
22

Given the prospect of spending her days sitting hunched in her dugout in the heat and the dust with her thoughts and fears as her only company, Violet chose to report to the hospital instead. Here, those thoughts and fears were muted by the effort and distraction of the tasks at hand, however menial they might be. And here, that help went a long way to lighten George's load. In the last couple of days, George had been run ragged, Violet knew. Her friend's expression was now one of constant worry, and dark circles of exhaustion were carved beneath her eyes. Her usual quick smile was absent, her conversation taut and strained.

There were no floors to scrub in this hospital, just rough planks that had been laid down over the sand to form a patchwork of walkways and platforms. Headquarters, communications, and the mess had all been moved into dugouts, and the hospital was the only tent that had been left aboveground. It had been painted with a large red cross in the hopes that the German pilots would avoid it. So far, it still stood, though from sunup to sundown, it snapped and shivered as debris and shrapnel rained down on the canvas from the constant bombing and shelling.

As the guns thundered and Luftwaffe planes screamed down from the sky, Violet changed dressings, wiped fevered brows, emptied soiled buckets, and spoke words of encouragement in equal measures.

And many times, she simply read.

"Being a heavy stick, the dog has held it tightly by the middle, and the marks of his teeth are very plainly visible." Violet was reading from her fragile *Hound of the Baskervilles* to a captive audience of a Legionnaire whose femur had been broken by a bullet and a French Moroccan soldier who lay listless and weak with fever. "The dog's jaw," she continued, talking loudly over the constant din of the guns, "as shown in the space between these marks, is too broad in my opinion for a terrier and not broad enough for a mastiff." Violet glanced up to find that the Moroccan seemed to have fallen asleep but the Legionnaire was watching her with a fiercely thoughtful expression.

"So what sort of beast was it, then?" he demanded.

Violet hid a smile and dropped her gaze back to the page. "It may have been—"

A deafening explosion shook the ground and rattled the teeth in Violet's head. The book dropped to her lap as she instinctively ducked, throwing her hands over her head. They'd finally been hit, she thought, yet the canvas walls around her had not disintegrated, and the canvas roof above her head remained whole.

There were shouts of alarm, and doctors and soldiers scurried about, trying to ascertain what had happened.

"That was a damn ammo dump," the Legionnaire said from his bed. He was trying to heave himself up but Violet stood and pushed him back.

"What?"

"One of our ammo dumps must have been hit." He glared at her. "Let me up."

"To do what?"

"Something!"

"No," she snapped. "While I appreciate the intent, your leg is broken. Doing whatever it is that you think you are about to do will make it worse. You can hate it all you want but you can barely stand much less walk."

The Legionnaire slumped back in the cot. "Fuck."

"Agreed," Violet said with feeling.

"There are going to be casualties." He punched a frustrated fist into the bedding at his side. "I should be out there beside my brothers." He looked up at her beseechingly. "Please help them."

"I will." She stood and hurried toward the hospital's entrance.

She stepped outside into the fiery heat of the sun. Smoke was billowing up in a roiling, black column from the west side of the fort, and still the guns thundered incessantly. Violet's heart pounded, and a pressure coiled up tight like a wire in her chest.

Another shell detonated on the far side of the hospital, sending a plume of sand and debris high into the air. She wanted to scream at the guns to stop. Men were already being carried toward the hospital, emerging from the thick smoke and dust. Limp, bloody bodies ominously silent and others writhing in pain. Violet ran back into the hospital, where stretchers were being pulled from their stacks and sent outside. She joined those bringing the casualties in, putting pressure on wounds when she was asked or cutting charred uniforms away from the skin of those suffering horrible burns. And each time a casualty came in and she searched his face and he wasn't Henri, she felt glad and then guilty for it.

"Help us here." The order came from behind her, and she spun.

Henri and Corporal Gasquet were carrying a white-faced Legionnaire between them.

"Henri." His name slipped from her lips, and the overwhelming rush of relief made her entire body feel drained and unsteady, like she had just run a dozen miles.

"Are you hurt? Either of you?" She managed to direct the question to both men.

"No." Henri's face, along with his uniform, was blackened, his legs and boots caked with discoloured dust. "But this man needs off his feet, Vi," he added through gritted teeth.

Violet jerked into action, motioning them to the nearest empty cot. The Legionnaire's lower legs were a bloody mess.

"What happened?" she demanded.

"Ammo reserve was hit," Corporal Gasquet grunted breathlessly, confirming what the other Legionnaire had guessed. "It's a goddamn mess out there right now. Fires everywhere."

He and Henri lowered the man to the cot, and Violet snatched the blanket from the end, rolling it up and pushing it under his heels so that his legs were elevated. Blood pulsed and dripped from his wounds, pooling beneath him.

The Legionnaire shuddered, his face a mask of pain. "I didn't... hear it," he gasped.

"What?" Henri was trying to ball a thin pillow beneath the soldier's head to make him more comfortable.

"There was...no shell. I...didn't...hear it."

"What is he trying to say?" Gasquet had returned with a roll of thick bandage and was wrapping the man's legs in sure, quick movements. "God, this is bad." He glanced at Violet. "Is there plasma left?"

Violet shook her head. The RAF had tried to air-drop some earlier, but the bottles had all shattered upon impact.

"Shit. He needs a tourniquet," Henri said.

"I'm working on it." Gasquet was twisting a length of bandage above one of the man's knees in an effort to slow the bleeding.

"I'll fetch a doctor." Violet spun but the Legionnaire caught her wrist with his hand and pulled her back. His grip was unyielding.

"There...was no...shell. It didn't...get hit," he wheezed.

"Just try to relax," Violet soothed him. "We'll get you something for the pain and then—"

"You're not...listening. Germans...did not hit...dump."

Violet dropped to her knees beside the Legionnaire, his fingers still clutched around her wrist. "What did you say?"

"The shells, they...whistle before they...land. No...whistle. Just...explosion." His grip on Violet's hand weakened.

"I can't get the bleeding to stop," Gasquet panted.

Henri had dropped to a crouch on the other side of the Legionnaire and met Violet's gaze with his own. His red-rimmed eyes were a startling blue against his blackened, sooty complexion.

"There was..." The Legionnaire's voice was barely audible. "I saw—"

"Shhh," he said sharply to the Legionnaire, and put a finger to his lips. "Quiet. We'll take care of you."

"You...inside the..." The Legionnaire was fading.

"Stop talking. Save your strength," Henri told him.

"No...I...saw...on purpose..."

"Saw what?" Violet whispered.

"Saw..."

"What?" Violet demanded urgently. "Tell me what you saw."

The Legionnaire's fingers slipped from Violet's wrist, and his hand fell limply beside him as he lost consciousness.

Gasquet swore and yelled for a doctor.

Violet put her fingers on the unconscious soldier's neck, finding a thready, erratic pulse. Within seconds, it had stopped.

"He's dead," Violet said starkly.

Gasquet swore again and thumped his fist on the corner of the cot in frustration.

Henri stood and ran his hands over his head, bits of sand and dirt falling from his hair.

"What was he trying to say?" Gasquet asked. "Before he died?"

"That the ammo dump wasn't shelled," Violet mumbled.

"The ammo dump exploded by accident?" The corporal braced his hands on his knees and dropped his head in defeat. "Jesus."

"No," Violet said with a dawning comprehension that hit her like a punch to the gut. "Not by accident. I think he was suggesting that someone blew it on purpose."

"What?" Gasquet's head snapped up.

"Shhh." Henri came around the cot as Violet got to her feet. "Sabotage is an accusation that you can't walk back if someone hears you."

Captain Lipton of British intelligence had once asked her about sabotage. Sabotage and suspicious deaths. She'd had nothing to tell him then. Now she had both.

Violet stepped back. "But that's what he was trying to say, right? That this was sabotage?"

"I don't think so," Henri said. "He was caught in the explosion. He was in a lot of pain. It may very well have been an accident. A misfire. An errant shell. Or maybe he just didn't hear the actual shell that hit the dump."

"He's right," Gasquet said, straightening. There were bloody smears on his knees where his hands had been braced. "Anything else is insanity. Because even if someone did this on purpose, what good does it do them? Their fate is tied to all of ours. If we go down, so do they. If we die, so do they."

"But you were both there, right? Close by when it happened?"

"Yes, but—"

"Adjutant St. Croix, some help over here." The command was bellowed over the din by one of the doctors.

"Go," Henri said. "We need to get back out there too."

Violet managed to nod, the constriction in her chest tightening even further. She pressed a hand to her throat and tried to draw in a steadying breath.

"Hey, it will be all right," Henri said.

He reached for her but she pulled away, blinking hard against the emotion that was rising swiftly. Nothing about what had happened was all right. She glanced at the dead Legionnaire on the cot. What had he been trying to say? If Henri hadn't interrupted him, what would he have said?

Why had Henri not wanted him to speak? A horrible voice inside her head asked.

She shrank from that thought.

"Violet? What's going on?" Henri looked hurt and confused.

Violet shook her head, edging farther away from him. "It wasn't you," she whispered under her breath. "It can't be you."

Henri followed her gaze to the dead soldier. "It wasn't me. I'm still here."

They weren't talking about the same thing, and that little seed of doubt had opened up a devastating, yawning chasm that horrified Violet. What kind of person would think the worst of the best man she had ever known? She hated herself.

"Adjutant! Now!" the doctor roared.

"I'm so sorry," Violet said miserably. The apology was for more than her departure.

She turned and hurried toward the doctor barking commands, looking back only once. Henri stared after her, his expression pensive, before he, too, turned away.

"Hold his feet!" the doctor shouted at Violet, and she obeyed, pinning the man who was twisting and sobbing on the makeshift surgical table in front of her. The wounded soldier's upper body was badly burned, the skin red and blackened. Violet swallowed and fixed her gaze on the ground.

And beyond the hospital tent, the guns thundered still.

CHAPTER
23

30 MAY 1942
BIR HAKEIM, LIBYA

"Your orders are to retreat."

Violet stood in her dugout, a square of paper clutched in her hand. She stared at the young officer who had brought her the missive and who was now fidgeting in clear discomfort under her furious gaze.

"British High Command has ordered the immediate removal of all female personnel from the theater of war," he mumbled.

"Why?"

The officer stammered something indecipherable.

"Never mind. The nurses too?" Violet thought of George.

"Yes. All females. You are to leave Bir Hakeim and return to Tobruk."

"I see that," Violet said, crumpling the paper in her hand. "I can read."

"My apologies, La Fleur," he stammered. "I did not mean to suggest that you couldn't—"

"It is not you who should be apologizing," she replied tightly. The hapless officer was only the messenger. "Where is the colonel?"

"At the command post." He fidgeted some more. "Is there a reply you'd like me to deliver for you?"

"No." Violet tossed the order aside and climbed from her

dugout, heading in the direction of the command post. The early morning sun slanted long rays across the pockmarked ground, and she could already feel the temperature rising.

The officer had scrambled after her. "Please allow me to deliver your response—"

"No need." Violet didn't even pause. "I will speak for myself."

She found Colonel Clement exactly where the young officer had said he would be, in a hive of activity, surrounded by men hurrying back and forth, others seated at makeshift tables crouched over lists and tallies, and some who seemed to be gathering maps and documents. Even more men appeared to be in the process of preparing to deepen the headquarters cavity, wielding shovels and handcarts and toolboxes.

Colonel Clement winced as he saw her coming.

"A moment of your time, sir?" she asked with as much civility as she could muster.

"Of course, Adjutant. I expect I know why you're here," he sighed.

"A retreat, sir? You're ordering me to retreat? Now?"

"I apologize, Adjutant, I do, but the orders from British High Command are clear. They have been exceedingly specific that they wish all female personnel to be removed from Bir Hakeim, and your name is on their list. I cannot refuse them without risking my own position."

"If you stay, I stay, sir." It was an effort to keep her voice steady when all she wanted to do was shriek in frustration. She was well aware that more than a few men in the command post were listening closely.

"I am not happy about this either. If it were up to me, I would never have issued this order, but it's not up to me or even the French. The British are running this show and they have the final word. They think to take advantage of this window while the enemy licks its wounds and regroups because it's going to get much worse. We may have repulsed them for now, but they have taken our measure and, without a doubt, will return in an attempt to annihilate us." The colonel held up his hands to ward off her protest. "The supply convoy that arrived last night under the cover of darkness will return to Tobruk, taking with it the two nurses from the hospital, the wounded, and a small detachment of troops."

"And me."

"And you," he confirmed reluctantly. "You've been ordered to drive one of the ambulances with the wounded if that makes you feel better."

Violet despaired at the position she had been put in. Refusing to drive felt like turning her back on the wounded. Leaving the fort felt like turning her back on the Legion. "While I will execute my duty, it doesn't make me feel better at all."

"I understand, Adjutant, but my hands are tied. Collect your personal belongings and report to the convoy vehicles waiting by the northeast gate."

She took a deep breath and forced herself to think. Emotion would not get her what she wanted. "What else did the order say, sir?"

"I beg your pardon?"

"The missive that demanded my evacuation to Tobruk. Once I obey that order, ensuring that both you and I are clear from any accusations of insubordination, was there any further direction?"

It took the colonel a second to understand what she was asking.

"Why, no, there was not, Adjutant St. Croix," Colonel Clement said slowly. He strode over to one of the tables and sorted through a stack of paper, pulling a sheet from near the top. He scribbled something on the bottom of the order and returned, passing it to Violet. "There is, however, a new staff vehicle ready at the depot in Tobruk for one of our lieutenant colonels here in Bir Hakeim. I cannot imagine who in their right mind would object to the punctual collection and delivery of a critical liaison vehicle at such an important time."

"Very good, sir." Violet's frustrated anger cooled. She tucked the order in her uniform pocket. She was still being forced to leave but at least she had a way back.

"Please don't share that with anyone," Clement cautioned her. "And I mean anyone. I can plead a misunderstanding in a time of upheaval should it ever be required at some point, but not if it is common knowledge your return was planned prior. I think it would serve us all best if your return were as circumspect as possible."

"Understood." She wondered what she would tell George. "And thank you."

"I'm not sure that you should thank me. You'd be better off in Tobruk, where there will be a means to escape should the Germans break us." He touched the edge of the bandage that he still wore over the right side of his lower jaw. "But I owe you a life, Adjutant. Your life, on your terms."

Violet could only nod, the gratitude that she felt for his simple faith making it difficult to speak.

"The convoy is departing shortly," the colonel said. "I have selected a squad of men who will escort the evacuation to Tobruk and then join the returning supply convoy. The desert is still crawling with Germans and Italians and you are to avoid them at all costs. We are hearing reports that Rommel has advanced on the Hundred Fiftieth to the northeast." His expression sobered. "I know I don't need to tell you this but I'll say it anyway. There is a very real risk that you may be captured or killed. You may not make it back. And if you do manage to return, there might not be another chance to get out and away from here."

"You won't change my mind, sir."

"I didn't think so." The colonel cleared his throat. "If that is all?"

Violet hesitated. She hadn't slept well last night, the events of yesterday chasing themselves around in her head in a horrible circle. Should she mention anything to the colonel? Should she mention that a dying Legionnaire, delirious with pain, suggested that the destruction of the ammo dump may not have been a stroke of terrible luck but something more sinister? When she framed it like that, devoid of any real proof, she was half-afraid that the colonel might just retract her order to return and instead send her to the hospital in Tobruk to be treated for exhaustion and hysteria.

"Adjutant?" Clement prompted.

"Commandant Lavigne," Violet blurted. She had to say something.

"I beg your pardon?"

"Before we took Damascus, the commandant sent me to follow up with a British intelligence officer." She ignored the way the colonel's brows had climbed and forged on. "That officer suggested that there was a German spy working among the Legion." With as few words as possible, she recounted Captain Lipton's report. "The commandant was killed not that long after."

The colonel was frowning, the bandage on his chin bunching into wrinkles. "The commandant was killed in a robbery. I read the report when I requested your transfer. It was very clear and very thorough." Clement's eyes narrowed. "What are you suggesting, Adjutant? That Lavigne was killed by a spy?"

"No. Yes. I don't know. But yesterday, I was in the hospital when a Legionnaire was brought in. He'd been hit when the ammo dump exploded. He told me he didn't hear a shell before the explosion. He seemed to think that it had been sabotaged." She did not mention Henri's name.

"Sabotaged?" The colonel shook his head. "I find that very hard to believe, Adjutant. There were a lot of men around when that ammo dump went. No one else has mentioned that."

At least he hadn't dismissed her outright.

"This man who thinks the dump was sabotaged—where is he?" the colonel asked. "I'd like to speak to him."

Violet winced. "Dead."

"Of course he is." Clement's tone was flat. "He died from his injuries?"

"Yes. I apologize sir, and I know that this all sounds a little strange but the British suggested—"

"I am sick of British suggestions," Clement growled. "To be honest, Adjutant, I don't have time for *suggestions*. I don't have time for some vague cloak-and-dagger nonsense that may or may not even be real. What I must focus on is the goddamn whole of the Afrika Korps that is very real and right in front of us and will attempt to wipe us off the face of the earth."

Violet ducked her head. This had been a mistake.

"There are still over three thousand men here," he said. "And every single one of us is in the line of fire from whatever is coming over that horizon next. And I'm supposed to believe that someone here has been or is suddenly working to undermine everything we've managed to accomplish? Everything we've managed to survive?"

Violet didn't have a good answer for him.

"Look, I appreciate you bringing your concerns to me, Adjutant." Clement sounded like he was trying to be patient. "But I think you would be best served by focusing on the real matters at hand. Not improbable conjecture. Especially not British conjecture," he said with feeling.

"Yes, sir."

He put his hands on his hips. "Are you certain that you still wish to return to Bir Hakeim?"

"Yes, sir." Violet looked him straight in the eye. "If you stay, I stay. It is my job." And if there was a spy here, working against them, she could not simply run away. Even if no one believed her, even if she couldn't prove anything yet, she owed it to these men to keep trying.

"I need to know that you can stay focused, Adjutant."

"I can, sir."

"Very well. Consider this matter resolved, understood?"

"Yes, sir."

"Was there anything else? Because if there is not, I need to get back to work."

"No, sir, nothing else, sir."

"Very good. Godspeed out there, Adjutant."

★ ★ ★

The journey to Tobruk took a day and a half.

It was completed in near silence, conversation restricted almost exclusively to driving decisions or the needs of their patients. This was not a pleasure trip to the coast but a harrowing exercise in avoiding marauding Germans who continuously patrolled the tracks that connected the string of forts and defensive boxes along the Gazala Line. George rode with Violet in the front of her ambulance, and Violet was grateful for the company. By the time that they reached the marked crossroads that would take them east to Alexandria or west to Tobruk, she felt like she had been driving for weeks. Her eyes were gritty, her neck was sore, and her fingers that gripped the wheel of the heavy vehicle had gone numb a long time ago.

Violet rolled her shoulders and relaxed fractionally as they approached Tobruk. She checked to make sure the second ambulance was still behind her and then glanced over at George. Her friend had been uncharacteristically silent almost the entire journey and was now staring out her window.

"I have to ask you something, George," Violet said, adjusting her grip on the steering wheel. The journey had taken all of her concentration, but now that they were closer to Tobruk, the thoughts that Violet had wrestled with since the day the ammo dump blew kept crowding into the edge of her consciousness.

"All right." George didn't turn away from the window.

"Does Henri ever talk about Germany to you?"

"What?"

Violet hated herself for the question, hated that she was even thinking this way, hated the thought that her best friend would be well within her rights to tell her to go to hell if she determined what Violet was really after, but she couldn't help it.

"I was wondering if Henri ever visited Germany when you were growing up. When he got old enough to travel on his own. If he still had connections there."

George was staring at her, her exhaustion momentarily replaced with confusion. "Why are you asking me that?"

Violet's nails were digging painfully into her palms where they were wrapped around the wheel. "I, uh… It was just something that…" She couldn't do it. She couldn't bring herself to ask George if she thought her brother might be a spy. Not without real proof. "Never mind. It's nothing."

"It's not nothing or you wouldn't be asking."

Violet squirmed in her seat. "I was just thinking that this is hard for him. He was born in Germany. But for a choice that your mother made, a choice that he had no control over, he might have grown up there. He might have considered himself a German." It was a clumsy attempt to deflect, and Violet cringed at the accusation she still heard in her own words.

"Oh." George turned back toward the window. "No," she said. "No?"

"He's never gone back. Not that I know of, anyway." George's answer was listless and distracted.

It seemed that she had not heard Violet's question as an accusation. Violet almost wept with relief.

"He rarely admits to anyone that he was born there. He hates what they are doing," George mumbled.

Violet nodded, guilt and shame making her feel ill.

"I feel so guilty and ashamed," George said suddenly, as though she were reading Violet's mind.

Violet glanced sharply at her friend, flustered. "What?"

George looked down at her hands clutched in her lap. "The closer we get to Tobruk, the worse I feel."

"What can you possibly have to feel guilty and ashamed about?" Violet was pretty certain that she had the upper hand on guilt and shame.

"That I left Bir Hakeim."

"Don't feel guilty," Violet reassured her. "Your patients will understand why you left. You were ordered to leave."

"No." George pulled at a hangnail on her thumb. "That's not what I feel guilty about."

"What?"

A drop of blood welled on George's thumb where she had torn the skin. "I feel guilty because I am glad that we left." Her voice was a whisper. "The Germans aren't going to walk away from Bir Hakeim. And I don't want to die. Not yet."

Violet guided the ambulance around a rough crater in the road. "Don't feel guilty."

"I'm running away. And I left my brother behind." She sounded like she was on the verge of tears.

"You're following orders. And Henri can look after himself. He'll be fine." Violet didn't know that but it was what George needed to hear.

"Henri told me the same thing. He was glad we were leaving. He told me never to come back."

Violet bit the inside of her cheek and said nothing.

"Am I a bad person?" George asked miserably. "Because all I

feel is relief that I'm not there, waiting for the next round of tanks and bombers and wondering if I'll see another sunset."

"You're not a bad person." Violet briefly tore her eyes away from the road to look at her friend. She shifted uncomfortably in her seat. She still hadn't told George she was going back. She wasn't sure how she was going to. What she was going to say. "You're not a bad person," Violet repeated. "You're an incredible friend, an amazing nurse, the most loyal sister. You've been there for your patients and sacrificed a lot along the way. Wanting to survive does not make you bad. It makes you human."

George sniffed and wiped the drop of blood from her thumb on her shorts.

The ambulance bounced and lurched, and Violet was forced to focus back on the road. They had reached the outskirts of Tobruk, and Violet couldn't help but stare. The harbour was filled with ships and boats, though a number of them had sunk and been abandoned where they were. Debris floated in the water and was caught up on shore and at the base of jetties. The pale, blocky buildings that lined the harbour had been shattered in places, piles of rubble existing where a structure had once stood. Palms that might have once lined the streets had been reduced to charred stumps. And all around her, chaos reigned.

After months of the isolation and emptiness of Bir Hakeim, the sheer number of men and vehicles and artillery moving about Tobruk was overwhelming. Violet was sure that *vital urgency* was the phrase that the commanding officers were using to describe the action in the port. Disordered confusion was what Violet saw. After months of waiting, the Germans were finally at the door, and an underlying panic was almost palpable.

Violet navigated her way to the hospital. She brought the ambulance to a stop just outside, her muscles suddenly fatigued beyond reason. With a monumental effort, she opened her door and slid to the ground for a moment, feeling like she was a hundred years old. Her job was done. For now.

George had exited the vehicle as well, and staff from the hospital were hurrying toward the ambulance to begin unloading. She hauled her duffel from the cab and swung it over her shoulder, arching her back and examining the low-slung building and the fortifications of sandbags that had been stacked around it to protect the pale white walls.

"I suppose this is home sweet home for the next few days," George said, making a clear effort to inject some positivity back into her voice. "At least it's not a tent."

"Mmm." Violet ducked back into the cab of the ambulance and retrieved her own duffel. The ambulance would be moved once the unloading was complete but it was no longer her responsibility. No, her next responsibility, according to the orders concealed in her pocket, lay parked somewhere in a warehouse or workshop nearer the port.

She hoisted her bag across her shoulders and joined George, careful to stay out of the way of the men unloading stretchers.

"I'm glad you're here with me, Vi," George said.

Violet flinched.

"Shall we go and see where they want us?" She started toward the hospital entrance but stopped and turned back when Violet didn't move. "Are you coming?"

"No."

"No?" George's face was pinched with confusion. "What do you mean?"

"I'm not joining you and the other nurses here."

"If you're worried about scrubbing floors, it won't be that bad, Vi, I promise. You have a lot more experience than you had before—"

"No, it's not that." Violet took a deep breath. "I'm going back."

"Back?"

"To Bir Hakeim."

"What are you talking about? You can't go back." George's duffel slid from her shoulder and landed with a thud.

"I have orders to pick up an officer's car here and return."

"No. We have orders to be here. You can't go back to that place," George said again.

"I'll be all right."

"You won't." Her friend was blinking back tears. "I want you to stay with me. We've been in this together since the beginning."

"I'm still with you," Violet said, gripping her hand. "This is no different than any other time you were in a hospital and I was out on the road somewhere. Nothing has changed."

"Everything has changed," George cried. "I don't want you to die."

"I don't want to die either. But risk is nothing new out here for either of us."

"Don't go back, Vi." George grabbed her arm. Her eyes were brimming with unshed tears. "It's bad enough Henri is still there. I can't lose you too."

Violet covered George's hand with her own. "Do you remember the day of the boat accident? The day you told me that you would stand behind whatever decision I made, so long as it was mine? Mine and no one else's?"

A tear slipped down George's cheek.

"This is my choice."

George wiped away her tears with the back of her sleeve.

"I'll see you again, I promise," Violet told her, ignoring the fact that no one could make any sort of promises like that out here. "I'll be back to scrubbing floors and emptying bedpans and getting reprimanded for my terrible nursing skills before you know it."

"I always thought you were braver than me, you know," George told her though her tears.

"There are many who would say going back is stupid and not brave."

"I'm not talking about today. I'm talking about the day you volunteered."

"You volunteered too."

"But when I volunteered, I had the support and blessing of my whole family. I had people all around me who were proud of my choice to fight for my country. You didn't. And to do what you did knowing that, in choosing to join the fight, you might lose everything and everyone in your life, was the bravest thing I've ever seen anyone do."

Now Violet was crying. "I didn't lose everyone. I still have you."

George enveloped her in a fierce hug. "I love you," she whispered against Violet's ear. "Come back safe."

CHAPTER
24

3 JUNE 1942
BIR HAKEIM, LIBYA

Violet had driven the lieutenant colonel's new car back to Bir
Hakeim in the dust and the dark behind the supply trucks carrying water and ammunition, reaching the fort just after midnight,
though it seemed like most of the garrison was awake waiting for
their return. Their arrival back at the fort had taken on a celebra-
tory feel, not surprising in circumstances where there were very
few things left to celebrate.

Violet had since resumed her duties in the hospital, where
the colonel felt she would be safest. Bir Hakeim was completely
besieged on all sides now. They had all watched Rommel's feared
Panzers gather like a storm to the northwest, though no one had
panicked. The guns on the fort's perimeters along with the raiding
Jock Columns from the garrison had thus far kept them at bay, and
the men seemed fiercely determined to continue to do so come hell
or high water. France may have fallen but this small patch of earth
would be defended to the death, if not by dwindling water and
ammunition, then by pride.

This morning, like so many others, had started off with a mist
sitting thick and heavy over the fort and surrounding area. As the
sun climbed into the sky, the entire garrison had waited on tenter-
hooks for the inevitable attack that always materialized as the mists

dissipated. But this morning it hadn't come. She took advantage of the reprieve to return to her quarters, thinking that she might find an extra hour of sleep in the quiet.

She was brought up abruptly by the sight of a man crouched in the dugout, his back to her, examining her books. She stumbled to a stop, small rocks cascading over the side and making the man turn.

"Adjutant St. Croix, I presume." He was tall, with blue eyes set above a square jaw, and spoke with a faint accent.

"Colonel Amilakhvari." She hadn't met him but knew who he was. Everyone knew who he was. The handsome Georgian prince who had served with distinction in Norway, who had joined de Gaulle without hesitation, and who was adored by his men here.

"You know who I am." He seemed delighted with this revelation. He bounded out of the dugout with the grace of a gazelle. "I offer my sincere regrets that I have not had cause to make your acquaintance earlier." He offered her a courtly bow and a charming smile.

Violet could understand now how the nurses had been reduced to excited giggles whenever his name was mentioned. She, however, was far less amused and far more alarmed.

"Was there something specific that you were looking for in my personal effects?"

"Ah. My apologies for the intrusion." He didn't sound overly apologetic. "I volunteered to fetch you and saw your books."

Violet ignored the matter of her breached privacy for the moment. "Fetch me for what, sir?" Colonels did not fetch people. They had junior officers for that.

"General Koenig has requested your presence. Immediately."

Violet blinked. "General Koenig?"

"Please follow me, Adjutant." He didn't give her a chance to respond but simply headed in the direction of headquarters.

Violet followed him as they wound through a series of trenches, her trepidation growing. Everything about this was highly irregular. Amilakhvari finally stopped, letting her precede him into a large dugout that had been cratered into the ground and lined with row upon row of sandbags. Tables had been set up and were covered in hastily thrown burlap, hiding whatever documents were stacked on the surface. A half dozen men stood around, all unsmiling and grim, and Violet was brought up short when she realized that two of them were in an Italian uniform. Even more peculiar, both of the Italians were blindfolded.

"Adjutant St. Croix." A tall man was walking toward her, his hand extended. He had light hair beneath his cap and grey-blue eyes. Exhaustion was stamped into the lines of his face yet his gaze was direct and uncompromising, and his handshake was like steel.

Violet swallowed, unsure whether she should be saluting him or shaking his hand, but since he was already gripping hers, the choice seemed to have already been made. She'd not met the general in person before, though his aura of confidence and utter authority was unmistakable.

General Koenig released her hand. "When was the last time you slept or ate something, Adjutant?" he asked, looking at her critically.

"Probably about the same time you did, sir," Violet told him. She was too tired to care if that sounded too familiar for addressing a general.

He seemed to find that amusing. "I'd offer you something to drink but we're a little short."

"I won't complain if you don't, sir."

"No," he said slowly, appraising her. "I don't suppose you will. Come." He gestured for her to approach the table where the two Italians waited.

"I confess I've heard a great deal about you, Adjutant St. Croix," he said. His voice was rough from thirst or exhaustion or both. "The men speak very highly of your service to the Legion, and now I understand why."

Violet tried not to stammer. "Thank you. And likewise, sir."

General Koenig simply nodded, any pleasantries dismissed. "I've been made to understand that you speak fluent Italian."

"Yes, sir."

"I require a translator, one who is both precise and able to maintain complete discretion. May I rely on you, Adjutant?"

"Yes, sir."

"Very good. Lieutenant Colonel Masson, if you will?" He gestured at one of the officers standing near the table, and the man hurried to remove the blindfolds from the two Italians.

The two men blinked against the light. They looked around curiously and then focused on the general. Both saluted him. Koenig returned the gesture.

"These two gentlemen are Italian officers who have entered the grounds under the flag of truce. From what we understand, they have indicated that they wish to relay a message from their generals." Koenig spoke rapidly to Violet.

Violet studied them, wondering just how much they might already know about Bir Hakeim. Wondering if somewhere among the men still here they had an ally. The older of the two Italian officers stepped forward, and Violet forced herself to focus. He was short, with heavy jowls and deep pouches under his eyes, and used his hands with abandon, making sharp, cutting gestures in the air as he spoke.

Violet listened carefully.

"He thanks you for your reception," she said when the man stopped to take a breath. "And he is here to request your complete, unequivocal surrender." It was hard to keep her voice steady and devoid of emotion.

"Indeed." The general did not sound surprised.

The Italian officer began speaking again, more urgently than before.

"He advises us that we are completely surrounded by the combined Italian and German forces and to surrender now will prevent an unnecessary effusion of blood."

"I am well aware that we are surrounded," Koenig replied drily. "They are hard to miss."

Violet translated.

The Italian officer took another step forward, his expression one of distress. His spoke again, his tone almost pleading.

"He says it will be much better for you and your garrison if you surrender to the Italians. You will be treated fairly, you have his word. The Germans will be much harsher in their treatment of the garrison. They have sworn to exterminate us if we do not surrender now."

"'Exterminate us'?" General Koenig appeared unmoved.

Violet waited for his response, afraid to move. Afraid to breathe. She glanced around but the men in the dugout with them seemed equally frozen, awaiting their general's response.

"Please translate this, Adjutant," Koenig finally said, turning to the Italian officers. "Please thank your generals for their pleasant conduct but tell them that there is no question of surrender. My troops have arms and ammunition and are prepared to fight."

Violet did so, with the precise, dispassionate bearing that her father had always demanded when she had stood in front of him, reporting and recounting her accomplishments and failures. It was an odd feeling, knowing the full wrath of Rommel's Afrika Korps would likely descend on Bir Hakeim after the general's refusal to surrender, but the dread and trepidation that she might have expected to accompany that knowledge was wholly absent. Perhaps it was because a clear decision had been made, and all speculation and ambiguity had been removed. The Axis forces had demanded surrender, and the French had defied them. And even Violet could recognize that that defiance was a salve to the humiliation and shame of the French capitulation and surrender two years ago.

Both of the Italian emissaries started speaking at once, beseeching the general to reconsider. Violet dutifully translated the garbled entreaties but General Koenig waved his hand, effectively silencing everyone.

"That will be all. We will not surrender." He gestured at the Italians. "Lieutenant Colonel Masson, please have these men escorted back to the perimeter so that they may return to their own lines."

"Yes, sir."

The Italian officers were blindfolded once again and were led out of the command post by Colonel Amilakhvari and the remaining French, leaving Violet alone with Koenig.

"Thank you for your service, Adjutant St. Croix," he said to Violet. "And thank you for your proficiency and composure. I trust that you will keep what transpired here confidential until I can make my own announcements."

"Of course, sir." Violet saluted him and turned to go.

"Tell me, Adjutant St. Croix," the general said, stopping Violet in her tracks. "Did I do the right thing?"

Violet turned around slowly. "The right thing, sir?"

"Refusing to surrender."

Violet blinked. "I'm not a general, sir. I am only an adjutant."

"Which is precisely why I asked you." The general pulled the burlap off the table, revealing a collection of maps and documents. "The task of defending this fort falls to you and the thousands of souls here, none of whom are generals. You, and every man here, are the heart of France, and what I may ask you to do will be beyond bravery." He leaned heavily on the table, suddenly looking weary.

Violet could understand why this general was so beloved by his men. Because he saw them as such. He did not see them as a means to an end, or pieces to be moved around a deadly chessboard, or subjects to be commanded callously by their king.

And she would answer him not as a general but as a man. "I cannot speak for everyone here but I will speak for myself."

"Please."

"I could have surrendered before I ever volunteered. I could have believed the people who told me that I would never last a day." Violet looked the general directly in the eye. "But the problem, sir, is that no one truly knows for certain what tomorrow will bring, no matter where or who you are. But what I know without a doubt is what I will bring to tomorrow. Tomorrow is for the brave, who had the chance to surrender their convictions and beliefs a long time ago but did not. None of us got here by accident, sir. We chose this. We did not choose surrender but chose tomorrow, whatever that may look like."

General Koenig stared at her for a long moment.

Violet did not look away.

"Thank you, Adjutant," he finally said, and his voice was hoarse.

"You're welcome, sir."

Violet saluted him once again, and the general returned it.

CHAPTER
25

7 JUNE 1942
BIR HAKEIM, LIBYA

German Junkers had joined the Stukas and Messerschmidts in the attempt to annihilate Bir Hakeim.

The high-explosive bombs that they delivered shook the ground, compressed the air, and added searing flames to the already barbarous heat. A cloud of sand and dust hung perpetually suspended over the garrison, making it hard to breathe and coating already parched throats. The RAF harried and harassed the enemy but were outnumbered and overwhelmed. The crews working the dug-in Bofors anti-aircraft guns were their only other defence against the relentless attacks and, as such, were constant targets for the Luftwaffe. It became a deadly game, and one that the Free French were beginning to lose.

The fort's dwindling supplies of water had become dire. Violet had temporarily left the hospital to help a company of sappers move the garrison's remaining water trucks into deeper, more secure dugouts where they would be better protected from the constant bombardments.

Near the edge of the fort where the garrison's vehicles were secured, including her Ford, the sappers had secured two of the trucks the day before in deeper trenches. Each had been moved a measured distance from the others to reduce the odds that a single bomb would destroy all three water trucks. The sappers were almost finished with the trench for the third water transport, and Violet was waiting to back the heavy truck into its new cavity. While she waited, she ducked into a narrow space between a bulky Bedford truck and a trench wall, trying to find respite from the sun and the scream of the planes above.

She almost ran into Christophe Gasquet.

"Corporal," she spluttered in surprise before she smiled, welcoming the sight of a familiar face.

"Adjutant St. Croix." He returned her smile. "Whatever are you doing here? I was sure you'd be in the hospital."

"Moving water trucks," she said. "Somewhere where the Stukas and shells can't get them. What are you doing?"

Gasquet tapped the bonnet of the Bedford. "Captain sent me to make sure that the wireless in our company's Bedford still works, in case we needed it in the next few days. Though it doesn't," he added. "I'm going to have to come back with parts."

"Your captain thinks we're going to be driving out of here?" Violet tried not to sound incredulous.

"Don't know." He wasn't smiling anymore. "I'm just following orders."

"Sorry."

"Don't be. Corporal Chastain had the same reaction. I think anyone would."

Violet ran her fingers over the rough wall of the trench. "How is Corporal Chastain?" she asked. "I haven't seen him for sometime." If she was being honest with herself, she'd been avoiding him. Or at least places where she might bump into him. That knowledge made her feel guilty and ashamed all over again but she couldn't seem to stop.

"Raiding out on Jock Columns with Colonel Amilakhvari almost every day. He's outside the wire again today." Gasquet leaned against the truck. "He was upset you returned, you know. He thought you'd stay in Tobruk."

"You can tell him that his sister is quite safe."

"I think it was you he was worried about."

"He is not my CO. And you can tell him that I'm quite safe also."

"Right."

Violet pushed herself away from the trench wall. "I should go and see if the sappers are finish—"

An explosion suddenly shook the ground and compressed the air around her. She was thrown off-balance, scraping her temple against the trench wall. She straightened and pressed her hands to her ringing ears.

"What the hell was that?" Gasquet's voice sounded muffled.

Violet touched her forehead and winced when her fingers came away bloody. From beyond the shelter of the Bedford, men were yelling.

"Something was hit." Her voice sounded hoarse. She forced her feet into action. The scene that met her was not so different from the one she'd seen when the ammo dump had been hit, though there were no fires. She could see at least a half dozen sappers were lying where they had fallen, some unmoving, some writhing and groaning in pain. Others were swarming in the direction of the water trucks.

"No, no, no," Violet moaned. Even from where she stood, she could see the shattered wreck of a precious water transport that they had moved yesterday. The remaining water gushed into the ground, where it vanished almost instantly, and the sappers were helpless to stop it. She blinked away a warm stickiness that was clouding her vision and stumbled forward. Gasquet caught her arm.

"Let me go," she cried. "I have to help."

"You're hurt," he said. "Your head. You can't even see properly right now."

Violet wiped at her eyes, realizing that the warmth in them was blood dripping over her brow. She wiped her hand on her uniform with a slight shudder but her attention was still on the sappers. "It's nothing."

"It doesn't look like nothing."

"I'm a nurse, remember? Scalps always bleed."

"Go to the hospital. Get it cleaned and stitched. I'll stay to help."

Violet wiped at her stinging eyes again. She wanted to howl with frustration and anger.

"Go," Gasquet told her, pushing her firmly in the direction of the hospital. "Take care of yourself first, so when these men get to the hospital, you're there and ready to help take care of them."

Violet nodded. Gasquet was right, whether she liked it or not.

"Be careful," she told the corporal and then hurried away.

★ ★ ★

Violet had been in the hospital only long enough to temporarily bandage her own head with a length of gauze when a gunner staggered in. He was weaving in pain and clutching his left arm. His breath whistled between clenched teeth, and his complexion was grey and pasty even beneath the dust caked across his face.

"Goddamn bosches," he wheezed as Violet rushed to help a medical orderly hoist him onto a bed.

Someone had wrapped his arm with a uniform shirt, and as the orderly peeled the fabric away, the gunner groaned. Violet forced herself not to look away from the bright shard of bone that had pierced the skin of his upper arm or the blood that had sheeted the skin beneath.

"What's your name?" she asked.

"Smith. Horace Smith." He struggled to sit up.

Violet pushed him back down. "Relax. We'll take good care of you."

"Goddamn bosches," he said again, his head falling back. "They got Davis. And Zip too."

"Who?" Violet asked as a doctor elbowed his way in to examine the gunner's arm.

"The fellas in my crew." He cursed, his lips barely moving. "They're going to need help."

"Is someone bringing them here?" Violet asked.

"No." He closed his eyes. "They're still on the gun. They won't leave their posts. Can't leave their posts. Too many goddamn planes." He opened his eyes and looked beseechingly at the doctor. "But they're in a bad way. You need to go help them. Davis was bleeding bad."

"Out of the question." The doctor was already motioning for the orderly to move the gunner out into one of the boxy vehicles they were using to conduct surgeries. "Can't leave. Not if you want to keep this arm."

"Please," the gunner gasped, jerking upward in pain as he was shifted. "Help them. Not me. Send medics."

"Stay still," the orderly snapped.

"We don't have medics to send," the doctor told him with regret. "They're attending a crew of sappers. Heard two of our water trucks were hit."

"Two?" Violet gasped. She'd only seen the first. "How?" They'd dug those trucks in deep.

"Don't know. Don't have time to wonder."

The orderly threw the bloodied uniform shirt to the side with far more force than necessary. "Would have been better if the bosches had hit another ammo dump."

"It would be better if they weren't hitting anything at all."

"Please help my crew," Horace whimpered from the bed, interrupting the two men.

"I'm sorry," said the doctor. "Truly. But I can't help. Not right now."

"I'll go," Violet told him.

The doctor and orderly looked at her askance.

"To the batteries?" the orderly asked, his jaw slackening. "Good Christ. Do you know what's happening out there?"

Violet glanced back at the wounded gunner. "I have a pretty good idea. I also know that if those guns fall silent, it's going to get a lot worse for many more." She looked back at the orderly and doctor. "I can't do surgeries but I can do first aid," she said quickly. "You're both needed here but I am not. You can spare me."

"You look like you're wounded already."

"It's nothing. Scalp wound. It can be stitched later."

The doctor grunted. "Very well. Not my decision but I won't stop you. Take a field kit from whatever is left of the supplies."

"Surely someone else could go?" the orderly protested.

"Who?" Violet demanded.

The orderly threw up his hands.

"Go," said the doctor.

"Thank you." She crouched beside the gunner. "Tell me where to find your crew."

★ ★ ★

This close, Violet could feel the power of the guns all the way through her body each time they fired. The 75s and 25-pounders roared incessantly at the encroaching tanks and artillery while men sweated and swore beneath the beasts. She held her helmet to her head as she wove her way through the network of trenches and dugouts, a field kit of first aid supplies strapped across her chest. She followed the gunner's instructions with help from a handful of Legionnaires along the way who gave her stunned looks but nevertheless simply pointed her in the right direction. Violet found his crew exactly where he said they would be, manning one of the big, swivelling Bofors guns dug into the southwest corner. And their comrade had been right. They were in a bad way.

The two Legionnaires who sat on the pointer and trainer seats on either side of the long cannon were slumped behind their sights, and for a moment, Violet was afraid that they might be dead. She glanced up at the sky, but miraculously, there were no Stukas in sight. She wasn't sure how much time she had before that changed, but it wouldn't be long. Another member of the gun crew was sitting propped up against a stack of ammunition crates, naked from the waist up, and it was he who saw Violet coming first.

He struggled to his feet, swaying.

"Please do sit back down," Violet said, eyeing the blood that had dripped down his bare chest and soaked the waistband of his shorts. "Before you fall down."

The gunner obeyed with a groan and collapsed back against the crates. The top of his bony shoulder was badly burned, the skin red and raw, and beneath that, lacerations striped his ribs. One of his eyes was completely swollen shut, the other nearly as bad, and the side of his face was already purple and puffy. He had lost his helmet, or perhaps had never had it to begin with, and his shaggy hair was matted with more blood. The two other gunners had stirred at the sound of her voice and they stared down at her from their perches, blinking rapidly.

"You are Davis?" she asked as she crouched beside the badly bleeding gunner. She opened her field kit. There wasn't much she could do for the burns or the swelling at this very moment but she could at least slow the bleeding across his ribs.

"La Fleur." He sounded dazed. "You're real."

Violet started. She would never get used to being recognized by men she hadn't yet met. "I am quite real," she confirmed, pulling out a packet of gauze. "Horace sent me to help. And I'm assuming it was your uniform he was wearing wrapped around his arm." She had nothing to wash or disinfect his wounds—those supplies had run out yesterday—but the flies were already at the lacerations.

"Yes." Davis was watching her out of his one eye, though he seemed to be having trouble focusing. "I thought I had maybe died."

"Not yet." Violet gave him a quick grin. "But this is going to hurt." She began winding the bandages around his ribs.

Davis cursed.

Violet winced. "Sorry. One of you Zip?" she asked over her shoulder.

"That's me," said the soldier sitting in the trainer seat. His voice was like gravel.

"You hurt?"

"Not enough to get out of this seat."

"Be more specific," Violet said. "Your man in the hospital seemed to think you'd been injured."

"Ankle probably broken," he said tightly. "But I don't need it to work the hand wheel swivel. Petey over on that side does all the firing with the pedals. I just get the gun pointing in the right direction."

Violet glanced up briefly. "And you, Petey? Injured?"

"No." Petey sounded like he was sixteen. "Horace and Davis got it worst."

"All right." She returned her attention to Davis and the wrappings she was applying. "God, I hate blood," Violet muttered.

Davis's head jerked up to stare at her before he started laughing, a slightly hysterical, rasping sound.

"What's so funny?" she asked, ripping the end of the bandage with her teeth.

"I hate guns," he wheezed. "Always have. And yet here you are with the bandages, and here I am with a cannon that can shoot a plane out of the sky."

"You win," Violet said, and that sent the gunner into another round of gasping mirth.

She tied off the end of the dressing and sat back on her heels.

His laughter faded. "Merde. My head. I can barely see, and what I can, there are two of." He slumped back.

"You need to get to the hospital," Violet told him.

"Can't. Bastards will be back. Gun doesn't work without someone loading it."

Violet scowled. "You can barely sit much less stand."

"I can—"

"Listen." Petey had twisted in his seat. "Do you hear them?"

Violet did. The distant shriek of Stukas.

Davis lunged to his feet, only to go down in a graceless pile, landing on his hands and knees.

"Merde," said Zip.

Petey leapt from his pointer seat. "Davis. You got to get up. We need a goddamn loader."

Davis mumbled something unintelligible and promptly collapsed.

Zip cursed again. The approaching Stukas became louder.

"Tell me what to do," Violet demanded.

Petey gawked at her for a heartbeat before he scrambled up onto the loading platform behind Zip. Violet followed him.

"These are the clips," he said, pointing to the stacks of shells. "Four shells in each clip."

They looked like any other bullet, except these were longer than her forearm.

"All you gotta do is feed them into here." He showed her the channel for the shells. There was already a clip loaded. "Clip on the left, pointy end to the front. We're short a guy to hand you clips, so you're on your own. Do your best. But don't stop."

"Right."

"Here." He reached into his uniform pocket and pulled out a wad of cotton. "For your ears."

"Get in your goddamn seat, Petey," Zip shouted over the increasing scream of the Stukas.

"Don't stop," he said again to Violet. "No matter what. Zip will be working the swivel, and I have the cannon angle and fire pedals. Keep feeding the gun until I tell you to stop. Do you understand?"

"Yes." Violet stuffed the cotton in her ears.

Petey clambered off the platform and threw himself back in his seat.

"Coming in from the northwest," Zip barked. "First formation, three."

Violet snatched a clip from the stack as the platform swivelled beneath her feet. Her heart was pounding so hard that it felt like it was going to come right out of her chest. Both Zip and Petey were working the wheels behind their sites as they lined up the approaching planes, and the cannon rose to meet the trajectory of the planes.

"Come and get us, you bastards," Zip shouted just as Petey engaged.

The Bofors roared as Petey fired, and Violet pushed another clip into the channel as the shells disappeared. The planes screamed overhead and around the battery, and sand and earth erupted, leaving columns of drifting dust and debris in the air. Violet snatched another clip and then another and then another until her world had been reduced to nothing more than a desperate race to keep the gun fed.

A thump and a muted explosion followed by an exultant shriek from Petey told her that at least one of their shells had found their mark. One of the Stukas dropped sharply in altitude, trailing black smoke behind. Violet did not have time to see if it went down because another formation was already in front of them.

"Where the hell are these bastards going, Zip?" Petey yelled.

"I don't— Oh, Jesus." The gun paused, and an explosion boomed into the momentary stop. "They're bombing the hospital."

"Bastards!" Petey screamed, and the Bofors thundered into action again.

Violet wanted to stop, wanted to see if the Luftwaffe had really gone after the tent with the bright red cross, wanted to cry, wanted to be sick, wanted it all to go away. Instead, she kept feeding the gun, her breath coming in great, heaving gulps, her arms aching, her hands raw. She lost track of time, and it wasn't until she became aware that the platform was no longer swivelling below her feet and the sound of the Stukas was fading once again that she allowed herself to look up, over the edge of the battery's dugout.

Across the expanse, where the hospital tent had once stood, fires raged. She could make out men running in and out of the smoke, presumably in an attempt to assist. She wobbled off the platform and fell to her knees before regaining her footing. Without looking back, she started running through the trenches in the direction of the hospital.

★ ★ ★

The swarm of Stukas that had veered deliberately away from the minefields and the batteries and taken aim at the hospital tent and surgical theater vehicles, all marked clearly with bright red crosses, had done so with expert accuracy. The patients suffering beneath the canvas roof, including gunner Horace Smith, who had sent help to his crew, and the Legionnaire who had enjoyed *The Hound of the Baskervilles*, were killed instantly. Three orderlies that Violet had worked side by side with perished. The remaining reserves of medicine and medical supplies were also destroyed as the Luftwaffe completed their carnage. By the time the sun started its descent in the west, the sky singed an unnatural purple-orange from the dust that still lingered in the air like a fog, Violet felt spent, heartsick, and helpless.

She leaned against the colonel's Ford, resting her forehead on her arms, careful to avoid the row of stitches that snaked along her hairline. She hadn't known where to go or what to do in the wake of so much destruction and devastation, so she'd come here and spent an hour digging out the tyres. She had no idea if the Ford would ever be driven anywhere again or if it might just be pounded into dust in the coming days that were as bleak as they had ever been. With the destruction of the two water trucks, their water supply had reached critical levels. Ammunition was dwindling rapidly, and the hospital and all its supplies were now gone.

"What the hell were you thinking?"

Violet raised her head to see Henri striding toward her. In four long steps, he had reached her and, without pausing, he pulled her against him, his arms like steel around her.

"What the hell were you thinking?" he mumbled again against her ear. He tightened his embrace. "I thought you were dead."

"I'm not dead." She allowed herself to lean into him, just for one moment putting all the dread and the doubt and the horror out of her mind, because she was too exhausted and too broken to resist. For a moment, she just wanted to pretend that everything was different.

Henri released her and pulled back, his hands running over her shoulders and down her arms, his eyes searching her face. "I thought you were in the hospital," he rasped. "I thought you'd been killed, but when I got back all I heard from every Legionnaire in this damn fort was that you weren't at the hospital at all but somewhere out on a goddamn perimeter battery. On a goddamn Bofors with a crew that had been hit, knocking Stukas out of the sky. And then I wondered all over again if you were dead because no one seemed to know where you were." He was rambling, his words almost nonsensical and tripping over each other. "And they all called you some sort of avenging angel and I was terrified that you might actually have become one. An angel, I mean, a real one, a dead one, and you scared me, Vi. You could have died out there. They target those batteries."

"They targeted the hospital too." She stepped back, away

from him. "They're trying to break us. And they might just have done it."

"No," Henri said. "We won't break."

"We lost two water trucks this morning," she said dully.

"I heard."

"They exploded. Five men died. Fourteen more were wounded."

"What do you mean, exploded? They were hit by a shell?"

"I don't think so." The odds of two separate trucks, dug deep into the ground, being hit by two separate shells were low. Violet slid down the side of the Ford, putting her head in her hands. She felt, rather than saw, him lower himself beside her.

"What does that mean? What the hell is going on Violet? I need you to tell me," he croaked.

She understood that she was at a crossroads in this moment. That she had to make a choice.

"Let me help. Please, Vi."

Violet lifted her head and met his cerulean gaze with her own. "Before he was killed, the commandant sent me to British intelligence." In halting words, she recounted everything that Captain Lipton had told her. "He asked if there were any suspicious deaths or any suspicious acts that could be sabotage. Patterns or events that would suggest that there was a spy working against us from within."

Henri leaned back against the side of the Ford, silent.

"He suggested that the most likely suspect would be among those with ties to Germany." She didn't look away from him.

"I have ties to Germany," he said presently. "My father, who fought for the kaiser, was killed in the last war. My mother was born in Berlin."

"I know."

"You thought I was a spy. I could easily be one."

"I didn't want to think that."

"But you doubted me."

She couldn't lie to him. Nor could she bring herself to answer.

"Do you still think I'm a spy?"

"No." She almost wished he would yell. Tell her that her doubt was unforgiveable and that he was angry and hurt. Instead he continued speaking in a controlled, impassive voice.

"Why?"

"Because I have to believe in something out here, Henri. And I choose to believe in you."

He dragged his fingers through the sand, making uneven channels. "You think the commandant, the ammo dump, the water trucks are all connected." It wasn't a question.

"Yes. But I have no proof."

"You wouldn't."

"What?"

"If the Abwehr has had a spy embedded in our ranks somewhere for as long as you're suggesting, then he is a very patient and very dangerous man. He won't leave proof behind."

"I saw Gasquet today."

"I beg your pardon?"

"He was near the trucks. Said he was checking on a radio." This had weighed on her mind, festering like a weeping desert sore that wouldn't heal.

Henri inhaled sharply.

"He was close to the hotel when the commandant was killed. He was in the fort when the ammo dump blew. And he was there, right where we had dug in those water trucks." She didn't add that he'd insisted that she retreat to the hospital. The hospital that had been bombed.

"Christophe Gasquet is a good soldier and a better friend. He has a wife and two small boys waiting for him at home that he speaks of often. We were at Dunkirk together." Now he sounded angry. "He's not a traitor."

Violet ground the heel of her palm into her eyes, despair

and regret and helplessness making it hard to think clearly. "But what if—"

"What? What is it that you think Corporal Gasquet is going to do next?" Henri demanded. He was still angry. "Hmm? Because he's running out of targets. We have almost nothing left here."

Violet stumbled to her feet. She wished that she had never started this conversation. This had been a terrible mistake. "I should never have said anything. I'm sorry, Henri. I'm sorry for doubting you. I'm sorry for not trusting you before now. I'm so, so sorry. For everything."

She fled back in the direction of her quarters. Henri was wrong. If there really was a spy in their ranks, someone who was determined to destroy them from within, he wasn't running out of targets at all.

And the most obvious ones had stars and stripes on their sleeves.

CHAPTER
26

8 JUNE 1942
BIR HAKEIM, LIBYA

The sandstorm rolled in late in the afternoon.

There were signs that it was coming—a strange shift in the pressure of the air and the frantic swarming of the flies that always preceded those storms. But still, the guns thundered, the distant artillery of the Germans answered by the French, as if this entire contest could be won or lost by mere ammunition expenditure before the blinding clouds of dust could descend.

The stalemate was infuriating the spy. He was in a precarious position—his fate was still tied to the fate of the garrison until they either surrendered or were overrun and occupied by the besieging forces, but neither of those two things seemed to be imminent. Three different and humiliating attempts to draw a voluntary surrender from Koenig had been rejected and had only served to buoy the seemingly unbreakable morale of the French.

The Luftwaffe had finally targeted the marked hospital, after days of pounding impotently at Bir Hakeim's guns and the perimeter defences. It had shaken French resolve but not broken it. His calculated destruction of the garrison's remaining water supply had had a much greater impact. Yet General Koenig refused to back down. Still, Germans died outside the periphery of the fort while the Free French somehow survived inside.

There were new rumours that the Allied 101st Transport Company, a company that had already delivered fifty trucks' worth of water and ammunition almost a week ago and evacuated the prisoners and seriously wounded back to British lines, would attempt another convoy. Given the thick German noose of tanks and infantry and artillery that had been tightened around Bir Hakeim, the spy had assumed that no supply column could get through. But as he eyed the dark, ominous smudge that seemed to breathe and grow with each passing second on the horizon, and the lack of any Luftwaffe presence in the sky, he agonized. Planes could not fly in storms like this. Tanks and guns could not find targets amid clouds of blinding sand.

Yet trucks could still navigate and drive.

He needed to send another message. He would again transmit the necessary intelligence alerting the Axis forces to the possibility of a convoy but he would not ask or wait for further instructions. He already knew what was required next. Mere sabotage would be paused for systematic assassinations in the days to come.

The spy wound his way through the trenches snaking across the fort. He'd reconsidered and come to the conclusion that the general needed to die. La Fleur would die first, of course, to break morale, but afterward, he would work his way through the ranks. The officer who was unlucky enough to take Koenig's place would die next, and then the one after that. It mattered not how many men stepped forward—they would all die and, with them, the resolve and capabilities of the Free French.

The spy emerged from the trenches and once again made his way toward the fleet of lorries covered in burlap and hidden away in their hollows, making sure he wasn't followed. He had never sent a message in the daylight, always waiting for the cover of darkness, but with the approaching storm, he couldn't wait. Once again, he extracted his radio from its concealed hole that had since been joined by a jerrycan of water. He took a quick moment to refill his empty canteen and then poked his head up above the sunken Bedford truck and glanced around, but there was no one near. On the horizon, the smudge was now a menacing wall, the storm rolling closer and faster than he had anticipated. He needed to send his message and be back in his dugout with the canvas top rolled across before it hit.

Within minutes, he had the radio uncovered and connected to the antennae. He attached the battery, turned on the transmitter, and adjusted the dials with practiced motions.

Target potential relief convoy to BH from 101, he transmitted, his molars grinding.

The guns still thundered, and shells still crashed into the earth around him but more sporadically. The hum and buzz of swarming flies aboveground filled in the pauses. He just needed a minute to—

"What the hell are you doing?"

The spy froze where he was. The demand had come from behind him.

He turned slowly to find Corporal Gasquet between the Bedford and the dugout wall, a heavy toolbox in his hand.

The spy considered kicking the radio under the truck but that was pointless. The corporal had already seen it. He was staring at the box, an expression of horrified incredulity unfolding across his face. He looked up at the spy, and the incredulity turned to fury.

"You fucking traitor," he said.

The spy said nothing, only stood slowly. His pulse raced, and he focused on maintaining calm. He needed to be able to think. He carried his revolver at his side but he despised using firearms to assassinate men. They were loud and messy and invariably attracted attention. But he might not have a choice. This was not the same situation as the commandant's room. Here, he faced a dangerous adversary, and it would not serve him to underestimate Christophe Gasquet.

"It's not what you think," the spy said. He was in a terribly vulnerable position. Trapped, the wall of the dugout behind him and the bulk of the truck beside him. The only way out was past this man.

"It's exactly what I think." Gasquet dropped the toolbox with a crash. "My God. I trusted you. We all trusted you. We trusted a goddamn traitor. A goddamn *spy.*"

The spy needed time. Time to figure out what he was going to do. How was he going to make this look the way he wanted? For right now, he needed to keep Gasquet talking. "I can assure you, I am only doing my duty, same as you. I am only a soldier, same as you." An inane thing to say but it had the desired result.

"You're not a soldier, you're a monster. A fucking Nazi," Gasquet shouted. "You massacred my mother's entire family at Babi Yar. My aunt, my uncle, my grandmother. My four cousins, the oldest of whom was only six years old. *Six.*"

The spy wasn't entirely sure what Babi Yar was, though he suspected it had something to do with the extremists who could be found in the upper ranks of the Nazi party. But he was well acquainted with dead family and dead children.

"And your country murdered my sister and my father," the spy replied evenly. "So perhaps we are even."

"We are not even close to fucking even," Gasquet roared.

A distant gun boomed, and seconds later, the earth erupted with a mighty crash somewhere nearby, sending sand and debris raining down on them. Gasquet flinched and ducked, and the spy took the opportunity and threw himself forward, knocking the corporal to the ground. He fumbled for his revolver but Gasquet reared up and shoved the spy backward, hard enough that the side of his head banged painfully against the bulk of the truck. For a moment, he saw a bright haze of stars. In the next moment, his vision cleared, and he realized that Gasquet was grasping a heavy hammer from the toolbox.

The spy scrambled away, his fingers finally closing around the smooth handle of his weapon, but Gasquet wasn't coming for him. With a dawning horror that came too late, the spy understood his intentions.

Corporal Gasquet had turned the hammer not on him but on the radio that still sat exposed on the ground. The heavy hammer flashed in the light as he brought it down with all his might on the little boxes. The spy raised the revolver and pulled the trigger, and the corporal crumpled to the ground, but it was all too late. The blow from the hammer had shattered the tubes and dials and connections, now fragments scattered across the sand around the ruined radio.

The spy dropped to his knees beside his destroyed radio and put his head in his hands. He forced himself to think. The radio was beyond repair. Even if he had the spare parts, which he didn't, the damage was simply too severe.

The sound of urgent voices approaching and then fading made him freeze, but only for a second. He was entirely too exposed here. Outside, the sound of gunfire had died, and the wind had started to howl. The sky had darkened in the strange and eerie way it always did before a storm consumed them. He didn't have long.

Corporal Gasquet had obviously been sent here for something, and when he didn't return, someone would eventually come looking for him. Trying not to panic and working quickly, the spy yanked the wire antennae down from the truck and then gathered the broken remnants of the radio, raking them together with his fingers. He shoved everything back into the hole they had come from and covered it all back up with armfuls of sand.

The corporal was going to be the bigger problem. The bullet had caught Gasquet at the base of the skull, killing him instantly and leaving a noticeable bullet wound that had bled into the collar of his uniform. It would be obvious to anyone that he had been shot with a handgun. Quickly, the spy evaluated his options. He had neither the time nor the tools to dig a hole and hide a body. Here, near the vehicles and away from the front lines, it was unlikely that someone would believe he had died from accidental friendly fire. He couldn't move the body without someone seeing. He was going to have to leave the dead corporal where he was.

However, like he had with the commandant, the spy could muddy the waters.

Another shell whistled overhead and detonated close by. The ground shuddered and shook, and more rubble and rock rained down around them. Making a quick decision, the spy lunged for the hammer lying in the sand and picked it up. He brought it down on the base of the corporal's head, where he had been shot, crushing the base of his skull and disguising the bullet wound. He scrubbed the hammer clean with sand and replaced it neatly in the toolbox. He selected an orange-sized piece of broken rock and pressed it to the wound on the dead man's head, leaving it bloody, and let it fall to the ground beside his ear.

Unless one looked very, very closely, the corporal no longer appeared as a man who had been murdered but simply a man who had been in the wrong place at the wrong time and become another unlucky victim of flying shrapnel and rock from the constant shelling. It was the best the spy was going to be able to do. Without a radio, cut off from Berlin, and uncertain what was going to happen in the coming days, the spy could not afford suspicion. He still had work to do, whatever that might look like. But for now, his only job was to get far away from the dead corporal.

The spy stood and stumbled back the way he had come, the storm on top of them now. Whatever visibility there had been minutes ago was gone, the choking, blinding dust now whipping through the air and stinging his exposed skin. He focused on putting one foot in front of the other, leaning into the wind, trying his best to retrace his steps back in the direction of HQ. The sun had been obscured, and the earth around him seemed to undulate in shifting waves of shadow as he walked. The side of his head throbbed from where it had hit the truck, and the pain seemed to worsen when he thought of the lost radio.

He squinted through the eerie light and stopped abruptly as a figure seemed to waver in front of him. A figure with long dark hair and pretty eyes and a smile that she had always worn when she'd told him stories about the heavens. She was smiling now, her face blurring and coming back into focus as his head pounded. The spy reached out to touch her but she vanished, replaced with swirling sand. He blinked frantically and rubbed his face. A hallucination, the rational part of him might have suggested, something that almost every man had suffered out here at some point in time or another. But in his heart, he knew it was a sign. A sign that he still had much left to accomplish.

He stumbled forward again, and a coil of barbed wire abruptly checked his progress. He staggered to a stop, nicking his hand but feeling an immense measure of relief as he recognized that he was just outside HQ. His dugout wasn't too far. He would retreat there.

Forty-eight hours, he decided. Forty-eight hours he would give Rommel to defeat this garrison and haul Koenig and all of its officers away for extermination. After that, if the Desert Fox could not accomplish that, then the spy would have to do it for him.

CHAPTER
27

9 JUNE 1942
BIR HAKEIM, LIBYA

The duck was served with orange sauce.

There was lamb with mint and marinated salmon garnished with capers and lemon. There were plates of chocolate soufflé and raspberry macarons, and best of all, glasses of crisp, citrusy chardonnay and a smooth, smoky, cabernet sauvignon. The tables were set with white linen, gilt mirrors on the walls reflected the candlelight, and in the background, Charles Trenet crooned softly about love and loss. Henri was waiting for her at the table, dressed in a midnight dinner jacket, his sandy hair combed back from his face, his sea-blue eyes never leaving hers. Violet's favourite rose satin gown swirled against her legs, cool and decadent.

"Violet." Henri stood and pulled her chair out for her.

She smiled at him and reached for a wineglass. She lifted it to her lips, anticipating the way the cold bubbles would slide down her throat and tickle the roof of her mouth.

"Violet."

She frowned. She didn't want to leave the food and the drink and the dream. Not yet.

"Violet. Wake up."

She opened her eyes, disoriented. The candlelight was gone, replaced by a weak torch beam. The gilt mirrors were replaced by sandbags, and the glass of chardonnay that she'd held had vanished altogether. But Henri was still there on the edge of her dugout, and her mind struggled to understand why. She hadn't expected to see him ever again after their last conversation, when she had all but admitted to once believing that he was a spy and then accused his friend of the same.

"What time is it?" She'd fallen asleep leaning against the sandbags on her tiny folding chair.

"Almost midnight."

"Oh." She looked down. She was still clutching her pocketknife. It was a miracle she hadn't stabbed herself when she'd fallen asleep. Or woken up, for that matter.

Henri lowered himself into her dugout. "I—what have you done to your hair?"

Violet did not look at him. "I'm cutting it." Or rather, she had started and then stopped, unable to continue. It would seem she had succumbed to exhaustion before she could force herself to finish.

"Why?" He sounded aghast.

She ran a hand over her newly shorn locks clipped close to her scalp at the front. It had been a long time since she had cared about her appearance, but sitting in front of Henri at this moment, looking as she imagined she must, she had to fight the sudden urge to cover her head. In the next instant, she hated herself for her vanity. Instead, she lifted her chin and gripped another hank of hair near her neck and sawed through it, letting the short curls fall to the ground.

"Stop." Henri seized her hand with the knife.

Violet didn't resist. Nor did she resist when he gently pried the knife from her grip.

"What are you doing, Violet?"

"I don't want to surrender, and I don't want to admit that we are at the end of this fight, but I am not a fool. We have lasted almost fourteen days against a formidable foe but we have gone as far as we can go. We have done all that we can. If I am not killed outright and am taken as a prisoner of war, I thought it best that I not be immediately identified as a woman. I am not so deluded to think that there will be any sort of courtly chivalry offered by our enemy on this field of battle." She made it all the way through those sentences without crying, and for that she was proud of herself.

"Jesus, Violet. I won't let that happen."

"I appreciate the sentiment but that will be far beyond your control." She'd had time to think about every possibility in the last twenty-four hours.

The garrison had reached the end of its supplies needed for survival, and no more would be coming. Violet was down to an inch of sludgy water in the bottom of her canteen, a single biscuit crawling with weevils, and a can of bully beef. Out on the batteries, there were no shells left for the 75s, and the remaining ammunition was almost exhausted as well. The German and Italian tanks had gained so much ground surrounding the fort that they had paused their constant firing across the open expanses for fear of hitting each other. German infantry attacks had been repulsed and bodies were heaped and strewn on the very edges of the perimeter, but the defenders were holding on only by threads of desperation.

"Please give me back my knife." The last word hitched.

Henri didn't reply.

"Please don't make this any harder than—" She stopped at the feel of his hands in her hair.

"I'll do it," he whispered. "So you don't have to."

Violet closed her eyes as he shifted closer behind her. She didn't move as he lightly brushed the remaining hair back from her face and off her shoulders, combing it away with his fingers. Slowly, he worked the blade through the strands, taking great care not to pull or tug too hard. Violet remained motionless, even long after he'd finished.

"Thank you." She could barely get the words out.

"You look lovely."

She opened her eyes to find him crouched in front of her. The back of her throat was burning. "Hardly." He'd said this to her once before, in a fishing boat that had belonged to a different lifetime.

"True. At this moment, you don't look lovely, you look breathtaking. I mean it."

Violet choked back a sob.

He reached for her hands.

She stared down at their linked fingers, trying to sort through the fear and the hope that clashed within her. "What happened to your thumb?" His left thumb, where it pressed into her palm, was wrapped with a strip of gauze.

"It's nothing." His fingers were clutching hers with an almost painful grip.

"I'm glad you're here," she whispered. "I didn't know if I was ever going to see you again. Thank you for coming back."

"You were right," he said.

"No, Henri, I was wrong. I never should have doubted you. And I never should have cast accusations—"

"Christophe—Corporal Gasquet is dead."

Violet's stomach lurched. "How? When?"

"His body was found this afternoon. In the dugouts for the trucks." He pulled away from Violet. "He had gone to fix the radio in the Bedford."

"What happened?"

"Struck by blast rock from a shell."

"In a dugout?" Violet regretted the question the instant it was out of her mouth. She had been here long enough to know that death found one when death was good and ready and there was little one could do to stop it.

"I didn't find him. I only saw…his body afterward. It was partially buried by sand, which means he would have died before the storm yesterday."

"Henri?" Something in the way he spoke made Violet uneasy.

"I missed it, Vi."

"Missed what? What are you telling me?"

"This was lying underneath his arm when they found him." In the dim torchlight between them, Henri passed Violet an object.

It was a dial, housed in a small metal casing that fit in Violet's palm. The casing was dented and broken, as though it had been torn from its moorings, though the dial was whole, with tiny numbers inscribed along the curved edge.

"Oh, God." Violet understood what she was looking at immediately. "It's from a radio, isn't it?"

"Yes."

"One of ours?"

"No." The torchlight extinguished. "Not ours."

Violet swallowed against the queasy dread that had settled into her bones.

"You were right." He sounded sick. "The soldiers who found him didn't recognize the dial," Henri said. "They gave it to me in case it was important."

She pressed the backs of her knuckles to her lips hard enough to hurt. "Where is the rest of it?"

"What?" Henri's voice was muffled.

"Where is the rest of the radio?" Violet turned the dial over in her hands. "This is a broken piece. Where is the rest of the radio?"

"I don't know. I went through all of his things, and there was nothing for me to find. No notes, no radio, no code books. Nothing at all. He could have hidden those things anywhere. He had probably replaced the radio part before he was killed. We would never have known it if he hadn't suffered horrible luck."

Violet ran her fingers over the numbers inscribed on the edge of the dial. "Did he ever mention a connection to Germany? Or Italy?"

"No. Not one that I remember."

"What do we do now? We can't just do nothing until we're forced to surrender and the Germans arrive and—"

"I need you to listen to me, Vi. We're not surrendering."

"What?" She tried to read his expression in the shadows of the night.

"Do not speak a word of this to anyone yet. But we're going to get out of here."

"How?"

"We'll use the darkness."

"We're to get through the Germans?" Violet repeated dumbly, thinking of the overwhelming firepower that had the entire fort surrounded. "Undetected?"

"Through the southwest gates," Henri told her. "Our sappers will clear a path through the minefields for the troops and the vehicles carrying the wounded and heavy equipment. Three battalions of troops led by Legionnaires will follow to deal with any resistance."

Violet tried to imagine what that would look like. And then she tried to imagine surviving it. "We're going to sneak out? In the dark? All of us?" When she said it out loud, it sounded just as insane as it did in her head. It sounded like a far-fetched plot in one of her adventure novels.

"The Germans are expecting us to surrender. They won't be expecting this."

"This path through the minefields that the sappers are clearing—how wide can they possibly make it?"

"Wide enough for each vehicle to get through. They're going to mark it."

"And what if it's not wide enough? What if a vehicle hits a mine? What if a vehicle breaks down and gets stuck? What if the corridor becomes blocked?" Violet paused as she pictured the entire garrison of Bir Hakeim stranded in a long line, unable to move forward, unable to move back, and trapped on either side by the minefields. "Henri—"

"It's not a perfect plan but it's the only one we have. We all know the risks. And we all know what will happen to us if we're still here, out of water, out of ammunition, and out of options when the Germans finally overrun this position."

"Oh, God."

"Colonel Clement will be sending you orders shortly to get the vehicles ready. You'll be driving him out in a convoy along with the other officers. You'll use one of our Jock Column routes once you're clear."

"Route to where?" Violet rasped. Where could they possibly go that would be safe?

"We're heading to a British-held rendezvous point twenty kilometers south."

"And where will you be?"

"My company is going to be right behind you. We'll be with the ambulances and the wounded. Making sure they get out safely."

"And you'll meet us at the rendezvous?"

"Yes."

"Is this really going to work?" she asked in a small voice.

"It has to. This might be the end of this battle but it is not the end of this war. It cannot be the end of this war. We will not surrender. Not now, not ever. The Free French will fight again." He turned her hands over in his. "We'll fight again."

"And what about Gasquet?" Violet asked. "Should we take the matter to General Koenig?"

"I thought about that," Henri replied. "But he's consumed with planning our retreat. And what would we tell him? That there is a dead spy in the corner of the fort, now stacked with the rest of the bodies needing burying by our digging parties before we escape?" Henri stood and paced the small dugout. "That this spy might have been feeding our enemy information that has brought us to this point? But that solves nothing, does it? That changes nothing. Perhaps what needed to be done had already

been done by fate. He's dead. He can do no more. He can no longer work against us."

Violet watched him pace.

Henri stopped. "If he died before the sandstorm, then whatever radio access Gasquet may have had yesterday, if he indeed
had it, came long before the general made any decision about our
plans for tomorrow night." He exhaled loudly, seeming to come
to a decision. "I don't think we should bother the general with
this now. His focus needs to be on what is to come and not what
has already passed. If we survive tomorrow night, we will tell him
what he needs to know. A dead spy is no longer a threat to anyone.
Certainly not more of a threat than the Panzers and artillery and
infantry and God knows what else is waiting for us out there. Can
you live with that?"

Violet nodded even as fear skittered down her spine at the
reminder of what they would soon face.

"You need to be ready for tomorrow, Vi. Use the sandbags
from your dugout to line the colonel's car. They'll protect you both
in case you come under fire. Make sure that you get whatever you
need from the mechanics. Don't take no for an answer. I know
there's almost none left, but load extra water and extra petrol,
whatever you can get, in case you get separated from the column
and it takes you longer to get back to the rendezvous point. Promise me you won't take any chances—"

"Henri." Violet finally stood. "We'll survive this. We've come
too far."

"No matter what happens, I'll be with you out there. You
might not see me, but I've got your back. That I promise."

"I know." She reached up and touched the side of his face.
"And I've got yours."

CHAPTER
28

I've been ordered to smash all the windscreens in all the officers' vehicles."

It was a secretary from the general's command post who informed Violet of this. He stood next to the shiny new Ford, hammer in hand, with an unsmiling face.

"Now?" She glanced up at the darkening sky.

"Yes."

Violet edged in front of the Ford as if she could protect it. "And why would you do that?" she asked as pleasantly as she could.

The secretary blinked, and Violet realized that the hand that was holding the hammer was shaking. "Because if bullets strike the windscreen, the glass will crack and shatter and you will not be able to see out of it," he recited.

"If bullets strike the windscreen, I will not be able to see out of it because I will likely be dead," Violet told him. "Along with anyone else riding in the front of the vehicle."

"I have my orders."

"Have you seen what a Messerschmidt does to a vehicle when it is strafed?" Violet pressed.

The secretary shook his head.

"I have. Trust me on this. A piece of glass will do nothing to stop death if it comes for you tonight."

The secretary's face paled in the encroaching twilight. "I'm sorry, La Fleur. I have my orders from the general's command," he insisted. "I must carry them out. Please do not try to stop me."

The hammer in his hand was trembling even more noticeably now.

Violet sighed. "Do what you must then." She left the Ford to fetch the last of the colonel's belongings. She winced as a dull crack echoed behind her. By the time she had returned with the colonel's personal items, the glass in the Ford was gone, tidied away like it had never been.

She examined the car again, checking the tyres for the seventh time, and for the seventh time, found them intact. The day had crawled by, minutes feeling like hours and hours feeling like days. There had been little else for her to do to prepare for tonight other than make sure the Ford was ready to be driven. As night fell, she had finally started the car and driven it out of its dugout for the last time. She wove her way across the shell-pitted expanse and parked in the line of HQ vehicles that would move out. Now there was only more waiting.

Violet rested her head on the steering wheel, willing the car to do everything she would ask it to do tonight. It had not really been driven since she had delivered it from Tobruk, and she was well aware that the extreme heat of the days and cold of the nights, along with the countless sandstorms, were not kind to engines. But the gauges had indicated that the vehicle was as ready as it would ever be.

"La Fleur?"

Violet straightened and turned to find Private Picard waiting near the vehicle's front fender. He had a wooden ammunition crate in his arms.

"Private." She smiled at him and extricated herself from the front, hugging her greatcoat closer around her. This night promised to be a cold, moonless one.

"Corporal Chastain sent these over. They are some of the battalion's small arms and remaining ammunition, and he asked that I give them to you in the event that you might need them."

"Thank you, but I have my own weapons prepared and ready." She touched the revolver she had strapped to her waist beneath her coat. "I'm sure your battalion could use these more than I."

"He thought you might say that. In the event that you refused to accept them, he ordered me to destroy the lot so that they are not left behind for the bosches."

"That would be wasteful and unnecessary."

"Corporal Chastain also said that you would say that. Which is why he is sure that you will accept them."

Of course he did. An ache twisted in her chest. She thanked Henri silently for the gesture and the thought and hid a small smile. "Very well. We can put them in the car."

Private Picard grimaced. "I've also been ordered to join you and Colonel Clement in the HQ column as opposed to travelling out with the other orderlies."

"Indeed?"

"I am an excellent shot and a reasonable navigator should you require assistance tonight."

"Should I require assistance? You mean if I am wounded? Or killed?"

"Yes," Picard said simply. "Three sets of hands and eyes are better than two. If you are wounded, I will do everything in my power to make sure you and the colonel survive. As I know you have already done for every man here."

"I've only done my job. Same as you."

Private Picard nodded. "Where would you like these?"

"Let's put them in the boot. We need to keep some room for you in the back." She helped the private stow the guns in the already crowded compartment. When they were done, he peered into the rear of the car.

"You are ready." It was more of statement than a question from the private as he examined the sandbags that lined the rear and lower edges of the car's interior.

"I don't know if anyone can really be ready for this," she said.

"No, I don't suppose they can, but your preparations make me feel better." He straightened. "Thank you for coming back from Tobruk," he said suddenly. "When you didn't have to. You have given every man here more hope and more inspiration than any general ever could."

Violet closed the car door and turned to face the private. "And you and every man here are an inspiration to me, Private." She held out her hand.

Picard reached out and took it. "I will meet you at the forward assembly position at H hour," he said, and released her hand, giving her a smile.

Violet returned it. "See you at midnight, Private."

* * *

The night had become bitterly cold as midnight approached.

The entire garrison had fallen into a taut silence that Violet imagined could be sliced like a ribbon were one to wave a blade through the air. Above her head, a wide swath of stars had blanketed the velvet sky, providing meager starlight for the men who toiled below. Violet waited, sitting silently in the front seat of the Ford, *The Madonna of the Sleeping Cars* clutched in her hands. She wasn't reading—it was much too dark for that and she knew the story by heart anyway—but holding on to the book made her feel like she was holding on to a little piece of home. A little piece of hope. A little piece of what the future might hold should she survive this.

A burst of machine gunfire erupted, and she jumped. Given

that she had been expecting it, she felt more than a little foolish. Some of the garrison's last ammunition was being used to cover the sound of so many vehicles being brought to life, and it was her signal to turn the Ford over. The staff car caught and idled obediently, and Violet forced herself to take a few deep breaths.

The brief gunfire ceased, and quiet once again descended, only the low rumble of engines breaking the stillness. She guided the Ford forward ever so slowly as the column crept into the night. The Bren carriers vanished into the darkness ahead of them along with the Second Battalion as the sappers worked to clear their path through the minefield. The HQ column stopped at their designated assembly point as planned, waiting until the corridor was ready.

Violet climbed out of the car, the forgotten book tumbling from her lap. She bent and retrieved it as she scanned the point looking for Colonel Clement and Private Picard. Around her, in the starlit dimness, she could make out the shapes of men all down the line of vehicles waiting as she was. Some were smoking, some were fidgeting, and some were as still as death. Violet offered an encouraging smile and wave at a few of the men closest to her, more for her sake than theirs, even if she couldn't entirely make out their faces in the darkness. It was still reassuring to feel connected to another human life, if only for a second or two.

She reached through the open window and returned the novel to the front seat of the car and made a last trip around the Ford, checking the tyres one more time. All was well. All was ready. Or at least as ready as she could make it.

She rubbed the back of her neck before jamming her hands deep into her pockets against the chill of the night. She thought about the German cannon and guns that awaited them outside the wire in the consuming blackness. She thought about the minefields that they would need to navigate and what those mines did to vehicles and their drivers should they detonate. She'd dressed the bloody stumps of the legs and feet of men who had been unlucky enough to drive over one. She thought about the enemy infantry that waited to cut down men. She thought about the unforgiving desert that would simply swallow them whole and erase their very existence should she fail to navigate properly.

And then she forced herself to think of nothing and deliberately offered another smile to the men moving across the ground, dark shapes falling into line. The gesture felt unnatural but she refused to give in or show the fear that was crawling through her.

"Adjutant St. Croix."

Violet turned at the sound of her name, uttered quietly. Colonel Clement was approaching the car, bundled as he was in his greatcoat.

"Sir." Violet swallowed hard against the lump in her throat and the pressure that was squeezing her lungs.

He stopped directly in front of her and suddenly held out his hand. With stiff movements, Violet shook it, his fingers as icy as hers were.

"Whatever happens tonight, Adjutant St. Croix, please know that it has been a privilege and honour to serve with you," he told her in hushed tones.

"And you, sir. And thank you for affording me the opportunity. You didn't have to."

"Oh, but I did," he told her with a wry note. "I don't actually wish to consider the odds of getting out of here in one piece, but if I were a betting man, I'd put my chips on La Fleur. We all would." It was the first time he'd called her anything other than *Adjutant*.

"I'll do my best, sir."

"I know." He fumbled for his pipe and jammed it between his lips though he didn't light it. "There are three rings of German lines around this fort now, each less well defended than the last. But I want you to focus on getting past the first one. Once we do that, we'll reset and reevaluate. But whatever happens, don't stop driving. Stay in the safe corridor and don't stop for anything or anyone, understood?"

"Understood, sir. I will follow the plan."

"Follow the plan until the plan goes awry, La Fleur. I trust you to do whatever necessary if and when the time comes." He took the pipe from his lips and stared at it, as if surprised it wasn't lit. He frowned and put it back in the side of his mouth. "General Koenig will be directly behind us, along with Colonel Amilakhvari and the rest of the officers. The trucks and ambulances carrying the wounded are behind them. It shouldn't be long now." Clement gave her a strained smile and then moved away toward the far side of the vehicle, seemingly wishing to be alone with whatever thoughts he might have.

A movement near the rear of the Ford caught her eye and Private Picard materialized out of the darkness.

"There you are," Violet whispered as he approached. "I was beginning to think you found a better ride."

"Never." Picard offered her a smile that was just as strained the colonel's had been. "This is exactly where I'm supposed to be. Should I get in?"

"Not yet. We're to wait outside the vehicles. They'll give us the signal to get in."

"Ah."

Violet leaned back against the driver's door and slid down the side, perching on the running board. She wrapped her arms around herself and tipped her head up to look at the silver swath of the stars above them. Picard joined her, both of them content to sit and study the constellations. She was relieved that he didn't seem to want to talk about the escape or wonder out loud if they would survive this night. For these precious minutes that were still hers, she wanted to forget everything that lay outside waiting for them. She didn't want to be La Fleur. She didn't want to be a driver or a soldier or a Legionnaire. Right now she just wanted to be a girl sitting under the night sky in the company of a friend.

"There are so many stars," Violet murmured under her breath. "It's incredible. Right up there, it looks just like a band of light splitting the sky in two."

"That's the Milky Way," Picard whispered back. "So many stars that you can't distinguish them individually. The ancient Greeks believed that it was created after Zeus placed his infant son, Heracles, on Hera's breast while she slept so that he might drink and become immortal. When Hera woke, she pushed the baby away in surprise, spilling some of her milk and creating that band of light in the sky."

Violet turned her head to look at the private. "I would be surprised too. How do you know so much about the stars?"

Picard's eyes were still trained above them on the heavens. "My sister loved the stars. She was the one who told me stories about the constellations and how each civilization believed they had come to be. She would have loved to see the desert sky."

Violet returned her gaze to the sky. That he had spoken in the past tense was not lost on her.

"You miss her," she whispered.

He jerked a little beside her. "Yes."

"Tell me about her."

For a moment, Violet wasn't sure he would.

"She was older than me. She had beautiful hazel eyes, a voice like an angel. She was always protecting me, teaching me, including me in everything she did. She was the one who taught me how to read. How to write, how to swim. I loved her more than anything." His voice, though a whisper, was hoarse with emotion. "And no matter what I did, no matter how much I loved her, I couldn't keep her from dying."

"How did she die?" Violet ventured.

"Retribution." The emotion had been replaced with cold certitude.

Violet waited for him to go on but he didn't.

"I'm sorry you lost her," she said. "But you were lucky."

"Lucky?"

"To love and to have been loved like that, even for a little while." She shifted slightly so that she could better see him in the dimness.

"Yes." His thoughts sounded faraway. "I suppose I was. She made me the man I am now."

"Do you have a photo of her?" It was something that Violet often asked the men she cared for in the hospitals. It was always a welcome distraction and got the men speaking of happier things. "Would you show me?"

Picard hesitated. "Why? Why are you asking me about her?"

Violet hugged her arms a little more tightly around herself. "At a moment when the future is so uncertain, it is sometimes good to remember just how rich we really are." She grimaced. "I'm sorry. You don't have to tell me or show me anything you don't want to."

"No," he said. "I don't mind at all. It's almost...poetic, really. That you should see her tonight."

Violet wondered at the choice of words but he was already pulling out a small leather wallet. He opened it and passed it to Violet. His lighter snapped open, and a flame jumped, protected against the night by his cupped hand. He held it close to the photo so that she could see.

"That's us when we were young. I was maybe three in that photo. She was twelve. It's the only photo I have."

Violet examined the small black-and-white image of two children standing in front of a broad, leafy tree, sunshine making both squint. The girl was crouched, her arm slung over the small boy's shoulders, and both had been caught laughing. A dog lay in the grass beside them among a sea of wildflowers. "She was beautiful." Violet smiled with wistful envy. "You both look so happy together."

"We were."

Violet tipped the photo slightly so that she could make out the writing on the bottom corner of the photo. *Remy & Liesl, August 1913* had been neatly printed in fading blue ink.

Violet went still.

"Her name was Liesl?"

"Yes."

"How lovely." A queasy sensation roiled through her, leaving her skin icy cold. Prickles of awareness raised the hair on her arms, and it suddenly became even more difficult to swallow.

Captain Lipton's words resounded through her mind with a discordant crash. Liesl *is used in each transmission.*

Picard closed his lighter with a snap. As if watching herself from a distance, Violet handed him his wallet, making sure her lips were pulled back over her teeth in a facsimile of a smile. The private tucked the wallet into his coat pocket while Violet's mind raced.

There were many women in the world named Liesl. Thousands upon thousands, she guessed. It could be a coincidence. It had to be a coincidence. Surely, a spy would never use a call signal with personal ties. Surely, the—

"Adjutant." It was Colonel Clement addressing her.

Violet shot to her feet.

The colonel was standing next to the passenger-side door. He met her gaze over the roof of the Ford. "It's time. The route is ready. Let's go."

Violet's eyes flew to the front of the column, where vehicles were already rolling forward once again. She nodded, fear and panic threatening to choke her. Clement opened the door and slid into the front. Violet took her place behind the wheel, her heart racing as fast as her thoughts.

The rear door opened, and Private Picard settled himself into the back. Clement twisted and frowned.

"Who are you?" he demanded. "And why are you in this vehicle?"

"Private Picard, sir. I am to serve you and Adjutant St. Croix tonight in any way needed, sir. The orders were approved by HQ."

The Bren carrier in front of Violet began to move forward. Violet put the Ford in gear. She gripped the wheel as tightly as she was able, if only to keep her hands from shaking.

The colonel was scowling. "I was not advised of this."

"I'm sorry, sir." Picard sounded flustered. "Should I get—"

"Never mind." Clement turned back to face the empty windshield. "Not your fault, given the hectic nature of the last twenty-four hours. Happy to have you with us, Private. Keep your head down."

"Yes, sir."

Violet concentrated on the track ahead of her, trying to keep focused in the darkness. Should she say something to the colonel? And if she did, what could she possibly say? That she thought Private Picard might be a spy? That this man who was now in this vehicle, part of a desperate, insane attempt to escape, was loyal to the Nazis? If that were true, then how had Gasquet been involved? Had they been partners before Gasquet had been killed accidentally? Or maybe Gasquet hadn't been killed accidentally at all?

Questions were buzzing through her head like a fly dashing itself against a windowpane in an effort to escape, and as hard as she tried, she couldn't make sense of any of it. If Picard really was a spy, why on earth would he be in this vehicle? Why would he not simply stay at Bir Hakeim and wait for the Germans to flood into the compound at dawn, at which time he would simply ride away with them? Why not make himself a target of German artillery and German infantry that might cut him down out here as easily as they would herself?

What purpose could he possibly have out here that would

prompt him to risk the relative safety of the fort and venture into the minefields and—

"Watch the Brens, Adjutant," Clement growled. "Don't want to drift outside the lane, do we?"

"No, sir." Violet adjusted her grip and leaned forward, staring hard into the night. They had reached the bottom of the slight slope and advanced into the minefield, stretched out single file down the narrow, marked corridor that had been cleared by sappers. An error a few feet either way would get everyone killed. So far, the night remained dark and silent.

"Jesus Christ, this might actually work," muttered Clement as they continued to creep forward ever so slowly. "Steady on, Adjutant."

"Yes, s—"

An explosion shattered the silence and rocked the Ford as all hell seemed to erupt in front of them. Flames from the blast roared and lit up the darkness, making Violet throw up a hand to shield her eyes against the sudden, disorienting light and illuminating the column stretched out over the minefield.

"Goddamn Brens have drifted into the minefield," Clement wheezed.

Which was true, but more horribly, the rest of the column, including Violet, had followed them. In the flickering, angry light from the burning Bren carrier, she could see that they were outside the safe corridor marked by the sappers. She brought the Ford to a lurching halt, and Violet sat frozen, afraid to move, afraid not to move. Beneath the undercarriage of the Ford and spread out in all directions lay an entire array of mines designed to blow vehicles just like hers to kingdom come.

An eruption of gunfire suddenly tore through the night, and the sky exploded in a bright mass of red and green flares, bathing the entire column in an eerie light. Any pretence of stealth was gone. German artillery banged away as the gunners woke and scrambled to their posts and selected their targets. Tracer bullets began zinging across the corridor in a macabre arc, deadly missiles seeking targets.

"Get us the hell out of here, St. Croix," Clement roared.

"I don't know where the mines are," she shouted.

"You'll have to take a chance—"

A second Bren gun exploded in a ball of fire. A third carrier, trying desperately to reverse course, was hit, and a shower of sparks burst before a new fountain of flame shot into the sky.

Bullets thumped into the side of the Ford.

"Drive!" the colonel yelled. "Go right around this—"

Another explosion ended his words, and Violet recoiled, her ears ringing. They'd been hit, she thought desperately, and in the unnatural glow of the flares, she saw blood splattered across the passenger-side door. The colonel was slumped forward, his head lolling against the dash, his body unmoving.

"Colonel!" Violet gasped, though she could barely hear herself. She threw the car into gear, worked the clutch, and stomped on the gas pedal in frantic, unschooled motions. She had to get them out of this killing field. She veered around the burning carrier and managed to swing into the safety of the marked corridor. They had to—

Whatever else she might have thought vanished as pain flared across her throat. She tried to scream, tried to breathe, but a band of fire around her neck prevented her from doing either. She twisted and writhed, her hands trying to get beneath the cord that was wrapped around her throat. The car bucked and bounced over the uneven ground. Tears streamed from her eyes as she understood that she was going to die.

"Take your foot off the goddamn gas, and I might let you live," Remy Picard snarled in her ear from behind. "Stop the goddamn car."

Spots danced before her eyes but she still understood what he wanted. He wanted the corridor blocked. He wanted the general's car behind them boxed in. He wanted every officer and every Legionnaire trapped like rats in a maze, where he could kill them or simply let the Germans annihilate them with artillery. In a single stroke, using her car as a stopper, he could orchestrate the destruction of the Free French and the heart and hope of France.

He had risked his own life and waited until they had been drawn from the safety of their trenches and defences. He had waited until they were all exposed. He was not going to let her live. That she knew with the very bottom of her heart and soul. She thought about the general who had refused to surrender. She thought about Henri, somewhere behind her, who had believed in her. She thought about every man who had defended this position for months, putting the needs of their country above all else. None of those men deserved to die in a corridor of German fire because she didn't do her job.

For the last time, Violet reached for the wheel and yanked it to the side, mashing the gas with all the energy she had left. The Ford veered and leapt forward into the darkness, away from the marked corridor and directly into the minefield. She would die this night, but she would die knowing that she had done her job.

CHAPTER
29

He needed her to suffer.

He needed La Fleur to suffer the same way Liesl had suffered at the end, wracked by unbearable pain, knowing she was dying slowly and painfully and unable to stop it.

It would have been easier to shoot La Fleur once she had brought the car back into the marked corridor from the field—it would have been smarter to shoot her—just as he had shot the colonel, but something had come over him. Perhaps it was that all hell had broken loose and that he knew that there was a very good possibility that he wasn't going to survive this night. Perhaps it was vanity, or insanity, or arrogance, or frustration that he had been denied justice for so long. Whatever it was, it came with a rage that he embraced and revelled in.

Behind this vehicle was General Koenig's car, trapped in the melee, unable to move forward, unable to move back, exactly where Remy had known it would and needed to be. Remy would get to the general next, but for right now, he needed to snuff out the light of France. To extinguish the Free French's symbol of hope and resilience. He had been waiting far too long to do this to deny himself the satisfaction now.

"Take your foot off the goddamn gas, and I might let you live," he yelled, bracing himself in the back seat and pulling the garrotte tight against her neck. They were in the center of the corridor, pyres of wreckage burning on either side of them. "Stop the god-damn car."

She would do what he told her to, he was sure, because women were, above all, survivors and not given to idiocy and suicidal hero-ics. She had survived this long. And she would do as he asked for a chance to survive a little longer. He wouldn't give her that chance but she couldn't know that. All she had to do was stop the car.

She didn't.

Instead, the Ford accelerated and veered wildly to the left, plowing past the burning hulk of a Bren carrier and gathering speed across the empty minefield. Tracer rounds came directly at them in a hypnotizing pattern, like they were driving into a deadly snow-storm. The spy swore as he was thrown against the car door. Pain lanced through his shoulder, and his grip on the garrotte slipped. Yet still, she didn't slow down. The car was charging wildly now across the rocky ground littered with divots from shelling, the undercarriage banging and grating as it careened toward a German battery. Too late, the spy understood what she was doing. Too late, the spy understood that she would sacrifice a chance at survival for the survival of the men behind her. After all this time, he had underestimated her. Liesl would have been furious with him.

He fumbled for his pistol, which had bounced away from him in the back seat somewhere when the car had veered to the side. He would have to shoot her after all and turn this car around to block the corridor himself. He glimpsed his pistol near his foot and transferred the garrotte to a single hand. He knew the pressure was slipping but he had no choice as he strained toward the weapon on the floorboard. The Ford was weaving erratically now, and he was being thrown back and forth. His fingers brushed the smooth metal of the pistol before closing around the barrel.

He released the garrotte altogether, heard La Fleur suck in a breath, coughing and gagging, but it didn't matter anymore. He lifted the pistol, turning it in his hands as the car pitched and rolled, struggling to cock the hammer. The Ford banged in and out of a hole, and the gun slipped again. Tracer rounds were thumping into the front grill of the car with loud, discordant bangs. The spy yelled in frustration. La Fleur was hunched forward behind the wheel, only the top of her head above the dash. The wind whipped through the car, cold and cutting.

And still she didn't stop.

Remy finally managed to straighten the pistol in his hand and he clung to the back of the driver's seat. He cocked the hammer and lowered the barrel toward the back of her blonde head. He prayed that the car would slow as soon as she was dead but he was prepared to launch himself into the front seat as soon as he fired if necessary. His finger tightened on the trigger.

And then everything went black.

It felt like a mule had kicked his chest, and for a moment that seemed suspended in time, he hung in the air, unhindered and untethered. He flailed helplessly until a deafening crash jarred through his very bones. He tried to protect his head with his hands as he was tossed sideways like a ragdoll. The wind was knocked out of him, and pain lanced through his shoulder and neck. And then, as abruptly as it had all started, it stopped, and he was left gasping for breath, blind and disoriented.

He lay still, trying to get his bearings, blinking and spitting sand from his mouth. He wasn't blind after all, he realized, it was simply blood that had run into his eyes. On either side of him, he could still make out the grisly glow from burning vehicles. Except the car he was in no longer rested on its tyres but on its roof, and he was lying on his back inside, the bulk of the Ford above him. They had hit a mine, he realized, and the explosion must have had launched the car into the air and flipped it.

Groaning in agony, he rolled to the side, pain running like

liquid lightning through his left shoulder. It was either broken or dislocated, he knew. Blood was running down the side of his face from a gash near his temple, and it splattered onto his arm as he moved. He clawed forward, propelling himself through the side window. At the front of the car, in the depths of the disembowelled engine block, flames were crackling and spitting. Tracer rounds still winged their way above his head, and the thunder and rattle of the guns hadn't lessened. Nearby, men shouted and screamed and died. The scrape of blades and bayonets rang beneath the guns, punctured by the sharp bangs of detonating grenades. From this vantage point, it looked like Legionnaires had thrown themselves at the batteries of German gunners in an effort to save their comrades.

Fools.

He dragged himself completely free from the Ford and lay on the cold ground, the warmth from the day long gone beneath his cheek. The dying engine of the car ticked and pinged and popped as the flames became greedy. The front tyres still spun. He closed his eyes, fighting against the pain and trying to decide what he would do next. La Fleur had taken away too many of his choices but there was little to do about that now. He needed to make some new choices if he was to survive this. But first things first.

There was a body crumpled just ahead, and in the ghostly flare light, he could see that it was the body of Colonel Clement. He pushed himself to his knees. Where was La Fleur? Was she dead? He couldn't be sure that he had shot her when he had pulled the trigger. Had she been thrown clear of the car or killed in the explosion or crushed beneath the wreck? The spy crawled over to the colonel's body and yanked the man's pistol free from his holster. Breathless with pain, he checked to make sure it was loaded. It was.

He staggered to his feet, bent double at the waist. He peered into the interior of the Ford, but the driver's seat was empty, ghoulish green shadows pulsing and fading as the flares sunk slowly through the sky. She couldn't be far—

He caught the movement out of the corner of his eye but it was too late. La Fleur caught him with her shoulder, her head down, rushing him like a rugby flanker. He didn't have time to react before she knocked him off balance, nearly jarring the pistol from his hand, the horrible pain from his shoulder making his vision go blurry. A new, searing sting across his thigh brought everything back into focus, and he realized that she had a knife in her hand, though it was far too undersized to do significant damage. He staggered back, his good arm extended, putting a distance between them, the pistol levelled at her.

"You killed them all." She wasn't looking at the gun but at him. "It was you."

He couldn't tell if she was angry that she was about to die or angry that she hadn't figured out what had been in front of her for so long. But it didn't really matter, did it?

"Of course I did. I only wish I could have killed more." A strange, almost hysterical euphoria was flooding through him now, perhaps a symptom of battle or a symptom of the knowledge that he would win. "More doctors, more colonels, more officers, more men. I should have blown up your entire world, not just pieces of it. Should have killed you and your precious general long ago. Reconnaissance was never going to be enough for me. It just took me this long to realize it."

La Fleur would not beat him. Could not hope to triumph over him. Not now. Not here. He had the upper hand and they both knew it. The fates had deigned to offer him a second chance to kill her and, in doing so, balance the scales for his country and, more importantly, his sister. And once he had killed her, he would continue killing until everything that represented France, until everything beloved by the French, had been reduced to nothing.

"You don't have to do this." Now her eyes were trained on the gun in his hand.

"But I do. You killed Liesl," he growled. "You stripped our humanity from us. She died starving in the streets like an animal."

"I didn't kill anyone," she cried.

"Neither did Liesl, and yet your country wanted her dead anyway. She did nothing to deserve it."

"It was a war," she panted. "Terrible things happen in a war."

"The war was over," he roared. "Yet France was not satisfied. France wanted to revel in our suffering." He cocked the hammer on the pistol. "And now I will revel in yours."

CHAPTER
30

10 JUNE 1942
OUTSIDE BIR HAKEIM, LIBYA

The shot, when it came, buckled Violet's knees and sent her sagging to the ground.

She waited for the pain, for the shock, for the darkness, or whatever was supposed to follow. Except all she saw were the phosphorescent suns still sinking from the sky, the burning vehicles strewn at the edges of the minefield, the tracer fire that seemed to have become more concentrated, and the fleeting shadows of men as they ran across the open ground. All she heard was the rattle of gunfire, all that she smelled were dust and burning petrol, and all that she felt was simply a dulled terror. Death, it seemed, was not that much different than life.

"Violet." Hands grabbed her roughly and pulled her partially upright so that she was resting on her knees.

She twisted and found herself looking at Henri, his features washed pale by the flares. She tried to understand what she was seeing but her wits seemed to have deserted her. "Are you dead too?" she asked.

"Not yet. And neither are you." His arms were tight around her. "I saw your car go. I saw you hit that mine."

"I'm all right." Her mind felt sluggish, reality lagging behind her all-encompassing terror. She'd hit a mine. She had been travelling at speed. The damage would have been to the rear. Her head snapped up. "Picard—"

"Is dead."

Violet twisted back the other way and saw that the private had also crumpled to the ground next to the burning Ford, but unlike her, he was no longer moving. He was staring up at the flares in the sky, his eyes wide and unseeing. "You shot him."

"Yes. He was going to kill you."

"He was a spy," she croaked, trying to make herself think. Her left wrist was throbbing, and if she examined her right hip, she was quite certain it would already be purple and blue.

"I know. Too late, I knew." He tugged on her arm, dragging her to her feet. "We have to go."

"The colonel is dead."

"I know."

"Picard shot him. In the car."

Henri swore.

"And then he tried to kill me." She put a hand to her throat, feeling the raised welt on her skin where it burned.

Henri rested his forehead against hers. "But he didn't. He didn't," he repeated, and Violet wondered if that was for his sake or hers.

She looked at him. "Where is your company?"

"Still with the ambulances. Some are dead. One of our trucks was hit." He pulled her forward.

"And now we're in a minefield." Her ears were ringing, and her thoughts wouldn't seem to settle. She balked, her feet sliding on the rocky ground. "Stop, Henri. We have to stop. We can't get back."

"We can. Follow your tyre tracks back. It's how I got here. It's how we'll get back out."

Violet's breath was coming in shallow gasps. "I don't want to die."

"Neither do I." He touched the side of her face. "Trust me, Vi. And trust yourself. We'll get out of this together."

She nodded, and Henri crouched, running low across the uneven ground. Violet followed, her step hitching as pain laced her hip, but she did not take her eyes off the tracks in front of her. Like Henri's, each one of her footfalls landed in the tread of her once-beloved Ford.

It seemed like it took a lifetime to recross the ground that Violet had covered in the car, and all around them was utter chaos. The once carefully planned, stealthy escape had devolved into a street war, men fighting hand to hand while bullets whined and vehicles burned. A handful of officers' cars that had been close to the front near Violet's were swinging away and accelerating into the night. She hoped that the general's car was one of them. But still far too many trucks and vehicles remained unmoving, either destroyed, damaged, or without a driver.

Up ahead, Violet could see a boxy ambulance truck that had stalled on the edge of the corridor, backlit in a grotesque silhouette by flames. Wounded men, those who were at least partially mobile, were struggling from the back, the canvas sides shredded and torn.

"No! Stay there!" Violet tried to scream at them, but nothing came out of her mouth except a raspy croak.

The first patients staggered away from the truck, directly into the minefield on the far side. Violet watched in horror as an explosion threw a plume of rock and sand into the air, the soldiers dying instantly.

Violet reached the ambulance, her chest heaving, feeling like she might vomit. "Stay," she begged, more with her hands than her voice.

Henri was pushing the terrified men back into the truck, the ones that had seen their comrades die in the minefield looking stunned and panicked. Bullets whined and pinged. He grabbed the arm of a soldier running by. "Why aren't we moving forward?" he demanded.

"They're shooting the drivers," the man choked. "To keep the trucks stalled."

Henri cursed.

"We need to move this truck," Violet panted. "The rest can follow."

"They're shooting drivers." Henri had gripped her arm.

"They're shooting everyone," she retorted. "You need to get in. I'll get us out of here."

"Can you drive this?"

"I can drive anything," she wheezed. She'd follow the direction the HQ cars had taken, and with luck, the remaining trucks and ambulances that were still operable would follow her in turn.

She limped around to the driver's side and yanked open the door. The previous driver, a thin man with a bushy beard, fell lifelessly out of the truck, and in the flare light, the bullet hole through his forehead was unmistakable. Violet pulled him aside and climbed up thinking that once upon a time, surrounded by snow and ice, she'd had to pull another dead man out from behind the wheel of an ambulance. Only then, she hadn't yet known what she was capable of.

She turned over the engine and nearly cried when it rumbled to life.

Henri clambered in beside her, a rifle gripped in his hand. She didn't even wait until he had closed the door before she jammed the truck into gear and accelerated into the darkness. The truck bounced mercilessly, and the revving engine and the constant explosions still weren't able to drown out the screams of pain from the wounded men in the back. Violet shut it all out and pressed down on the accelerator even harder. To go slow would mean that they would all die. Their only hope was enough speed to break through the enemy cordons before the vehicles were hit irreparably.

Beside her, Henri was gripping the door and staring straight ahead as the ambulance banged its way across the ground. Behind her, more trucks and ambulances followed her lead. They broke through the first line of defences, but now a new tide of tracer bullets and machine gun fire erupted, these next defenders long alerted to the attempted escape. A bullet thumped into the interior just behind her head and Violet flinched. Sparks danced across the bonnet like firebugs where more rounds glanced off steel.

And yet the confusion and chaos that had spread seemed to work in their favour. With so much destruction, so many vehicles burning and men running and guns firing, no one seemed to know exactly where anyone else was going or where they were headed. Bullets still struck the sides of the ambulance and Violet still hunched behind the wheel, making herself as small as possible, but the farther they went, the fewer the bullets, and Violet spent more time dodging boulders than shell craters. She pressed on ruthlessly, using the stars for direction, Henri guiding her from time to time with his compass.

She drove endlessly, ignoring time. The glow from the flares had long ago faded and the darkness was almost absolute once again, save for the meager starlight. The screams from the wounded men in the back had been reduced to whimpers and sobs. And still she drove on. It wasn't until the mist that always preceded dawn crowded in that Violet was forced to slow and gear down, finally bringing the truck to a halt.

"I have to stop," she said. "I can barely see anything anymore."

Behind her, a ragged line of French trucks closed the distance and followed suit. For a moment, she was afraid she was no longer capable of moving, with her fingers wrapped so tightly around the wheel and her head drawn between her shoulders like a frightened turtle's. Every muscle in her body was cramped, every fiber contracted in a deathlike rigour. Her wrist still throbbed, and when she shifted, a searing pain erupted in her hip. Yet all of that meant that she was still alive. The pain and discomfort meant that she hadn't been beaten yet.

She and Henri stared out at the vaporous clouds that had now completely obscured their vision. The presence of the mist told her that she had been driving for hours. It felt like days. She didn't turn the truck off, terrified that if she did, she might never get it started again. And there were too many souls in the back relying on her to take that risk.

"Do you know where we are?" she whispered. Her voice was completely gone.

With painfully slow movements, Henri studied his compass and withdrew a crude map from his pack. "South," he rasped.

"How far south?"

"I'm not sure."

"Past all the Germans?"

"I don't know. Maybe."

"They will not take prisoners," she said. "Not in the desert."

"No," Henri agreed. "They won't."

"They will make an example out of us, won't they?"

"I reckon they will."

Violet looked out her window at the blackness. "And the rally point that we're looking for? What's there?"

"A stockpile of petrol drums. Supplies. A mess tent. Maybe a few others. The British Seventeenth Motorized Brigade is supposed to be there. Waiting to see action."

"That's it?"

"That's it."

"Not a crusader castle."

"Definitely not a castle." He paused. "Do you have your pistol with you?"

"No, I lost it in the wreck."

He handed Violet his. "Take mine."

Silently, she accepted it.

"Violet—"

"Don't say it."

"Make sure you save a round, Violet."

Her jaw was rigid. "We've made it this far. I've made it this far. I will not give up now."

"There are stories, Vi, of what they might do to—"

"We should form square," Violet cut him off. She would not consider defeat until it stared her full in the face.

Henri choked out what might have been a humourless laugh. "Expecting a cavalry charge, Napoleon?"

"Maybe." Violet peered ineffectively into the darkness. "For all we know, we're on top of a German command post. If we're surrounded, we can at least use the trucks to defend ourselves for as long as we can. We won't be able to outrun a mobile unit. Not with the wounded."

Henri stuffed his compass and map in his pack and pushed the door of the truck open. "I'll see it done." He vanished into the mist, and his voice drifted back disembodied and muffled as he spoke to the other drivers. The rumble of engines rose and then fell, and with guidance, the trucks maneuvered themselves around Violet's vehicle.

Henri returned after what seemed like an eternity. "Formed and armed. I've seen that whatever ammunition and guns remaining have been distributed. Whatever comes with the dawn, we will be ready. Every man capable is willing to fight to the last."

They sat in silence for another while, surrounded and cocooned by the mist. She tried not to think about the men behind them, the ones who had followed her out and were relying on her to find the rally point. She tried not to think about what might happen if she failed to do so. But she couldn't stop thinking about everything that had come before their final flight.

"You saved my life," Violet said into the darkness. "In that minefield."

"And you saved mine in this truck. I think we're even."

"You didn't send him, did you? Didn't send Picard to me with guns or have him reassigned to the colonel? To me?"

"No, Vi, I didn't. And by the time I found out, by the time I understood, it was too late." Henri reached for her hand in the dark, his fingers finding hers. "I should have known. I think Gasquet did, too late."

"We've already had this discussion. If he was good at what he did, then nobody knew."

"I'm sorry I wasn't there."

"You were there when it mattered." She shook her head. "He kept talking about his sister. He showed me a picture. Her name was Liesl. That's when I knew." She shuddered. "He blamed me for her death. Blamed France for her death after the Great War. Said she died in the streets like an animal, starving."

Henri didn't answer right away. And when he did, he was subdued. "We called it the hunger blockade," he said. "Aside from the reparations the Allies imposed, the naval blockade that they enforced targeted civilians too. I read somewhere that a million Germans starved to death after that war. I am inclined to believe it. I saw it firsthand. Picard—or whatever his name really was—could have been me."

"Yet it wasn't. You fight for France," Violet said.

"No. I fight for humanity," he said quietly. "And what Germany, what the Nazis, are doing to people is wrong, and that wrong transcends borders. Hate cannot be allowed to flourish and triumph. We all lose if that happens. My mother was the one who taught me that."

Violet stared out the windshield at the mist. "He said that reconnaissance was never going to be enough for him. That he should have killed more. That he wanted to revel in our suffering."

"Then I feel badly for him. To have nothing to embrace in life but hate is an empty, unhappy life indeed."

"I'm glad he's dead," Violet confessed. "I don't know what he stole from us or how many deaths he might have caused, but he can't do that anymore." She looked at Henri across the cab. "This is never going to stop, is it?"

"This war?" He sighed. "It will. Eventually. I have to believe that."

"What will happen to us?"

"We'll keep fighting. For as long as it takes."

"If we survive this day, I don't know if I can say goodbye to you again."

"You won't have to—"

"Stop. I've done nothing but say goodbye to you. In France. In Syria. In Libya. I'm tired, Henri. I don't want to say goodbye anymore." Violet pulled her hand from his and slumped back against the driver's-side door. She ran a hand along the edge of the seat, pausing when her fingers found a neat hole punched into the side. A new tide of horror rose with the knowledge that if that bullet had struck a handful of inches either way, they would not be having this conversation. One of them would likely be dead.

Henri covered her fingers with his again, pulling them away from the bullet hole. "Do you remember where I moor my boat?"

"What?"

"Do you remember where my boat is?"

"Of course I remember—"

"Good. I will meet you on the beach there," he said. "We will watch the sun set and drink champagne and you will do a better job of teaching me how to dance properly."

"Henri—"

"I'm not finished. I will impress you with my newfound knowledge of Italian, and then we will discuss the latest Sherlock Holmes novel, and you will come to understand that I was right all along that Doyle writes a superior mystery. After that, I will undress you and you will undress me and we will swim in the sea under the moonlight. And when we tire of swimming, I will make love to you until you can't remember your name. We will watch the sun rise over the sea from the bow of my boat. And then we'll do all of that all over again."

"What else will we do?" she whispered.

"We will have afternoon naps in the shade. We'll pick olives and apples. Sit up on the cliffs and watch thunderstorms roll in. I'll sip lemonade and watch you repair my outboard." He threaded his fingers with hers. "Sound all right?"

Wordlessly, Violet nodded.

"Good. Then no need for goodbyes if we're going to meet again."

"When do I get lemonade?" Violet asked, the words twining with a tearful laugh.

"You can sip lemonade and watch me pull nets."

"Without your shirt."

"Without my—" Henri chuckled. "Oh, I see how it is now."

Violet smiled and sniffed and rested her head on Henri's shoulder. "I'll meet you there."

"Promise?"

"I promise."

They stayed like that as the minutes slipped by. A faint pink glow finally appeared, signalling the end of the darkness and heralding the arrival of morning. Henri shifted away from her and pulled his field binoculars from his pack. Violet gripped the wheel, preparing herself for whatever fate was waiting for them beyond the walls of mist.

The sun rose, flooding the desert with light and carving holes in the mist. Plateaus and sloping hills appeared, a tapestry of amethyst and indigo. Violet scanned the horizon in front of them. No Germans. No British. Only rock and sand broken by clouds of white and an endless expanse of sky above.

"Violet." Her name was spoken urgently.

Her pulse spiked. "What?" She turned to find Henri shoving his door open and clambering down from the truck again. "What is it?"

He braced himself against the truck door and brought a pair of binoculars to his eyes. "Vehicles. Men."

In the spaces in the drifting mist, Violet could see what Henri saw. In the distance, wavering on the horizon, a row of trucks sat dark and silent, small forms moving in between them.

"German?" Violet tried to keep her voice matter-of-fact but dread was rushing in like a tide.

"I don't know. I can't tell."

The sun crept higher, and the mist tore into greater tatters. Unable to stay still, Violet slipped from the cab of the truck and came to stand beside Henri. Other men had done the same, standing like silent sentinels as their fate was slowly revealed.

Henri made a funny sound in his throat.

"What is it?"

He didn't answer, only kept the binoculars jammed to his eyes.

"Henri. What do you see?" There was a bubble of hysteria caught in her chest, expanding up and out.

He lowered the binoculars and bent double, his hands on his knees, his shoulders heaving.

"Henri!"

He passed her the binoculars without speaking. Violet brought them to her eyes. The sky and earth swung wildly in her field of vision. She finally settled them and, within seconds, found the shapes of the vehicles. Small figures moved between them, and their actions seemed to flow back and forth in an orchestrated symmetry. And then, in the long, golden rays, Violet saw what Henri had seen.

A ball, flying up in the air and back to earth, bouncing between the silhouettes as they chased it forward.

"They're playing football," she said, stupefied.

"Yes." Henri straightened.

"There are men playing football in the desert."

"Yes."

The ramifications of that slowly unfurled in her mind like a banner. "They must have water," she mumbled. "And they have time. They are not fighting, not this morning." She followed the ball through the lens. "Only the bloody English would play football in a desert."

"Those men are the British Seventeenth." Henri wiped his face with the bottom of his uniform. "We found it. We found the rallying point."

Violet sagged back against the truck, relief making her weak and boneless. The binoculars dropped from her hand, and she bent to retrieve them, though her fingers were shaking so badly it took her two attempts. She laughed then, a raspy, dry wheeze that came from the bottom of her lungs and spilled out unchecked until it morphed and meshed with what sounded more like sobs.

Henri didn't say anything, simply put his hand on her shoulder and left it there, and disjointedly Violet wondered if his touch was the only thing keeping her from shattering into a million tiny pieces.

She wasn't sure how long it took for her to compose herself and calm the emotions ricocheting through her, but when she did, Henri was still beside her. She took three deep breaths and handed the binoculars back to him.

"Get in the truck," she finally said. "I'll drive."

CHAPTER
31

The St. Croix villa looked unchanged.

Violet stood in front of the wide carved doors, contemplating the building. On either side, blooms cascaded over the edges of clay pots the way they always had, and the step had been swept neatly, the way it always was. The stucco was the same pale honey colour, trimmed with cream, and the small stone fountain that sat in a place of honour in front still burbled. She stepped forward and raised her hand to knock and then let it fall before she could do so. Strange that she should feel an interloper in front of a house she had lived in for most of her life. Strange that she should feel the need to announce her presence at all. She pushed the doors open and entered, closing them quietly behind her.

The blinding, bright heat of the day vanished as she stepped farther into the cool, dim interior. She left her pack near the door and straightened the top of her simple dress. She hadn't worn her uniform in some time now, though it was carefully folded in the bottom of her bag. She'd bought the dress she was wearing secondhand outside of Marseille because she'd fallen in love with the azure cotton that reminded her of the sea. It was the first thing she had bought after the war had ended, and it had taken her longer than she had expected to feel entirely comfortable in it. It had been a strange transition, this return to a different way of life.

Low voices drifted from the direction of the dining room, and Violet headed toward the sound. Her footsteps echoed off the tile as her eyes slowly adjusted, taking in the villa's interior. Here, there were subtle changes—a painting no longer gracing a wall, a sculpture gone from its pedestal, a piece of ornate furniture absent from its corner. Yet as she entered the dining room, the scene was as familiar as if the years had never passed.

Her father sat at one end of the long, walnut dining table, her mother at the opposite end, separated by an embroidered table runner, a glass vase of arranged flowers, and an assortment of bowls with breads and fresh fruits. Her father was reading a paper, her mother was picking at her food, both studiously ignoring each other. A woman Violet had not seen before but who was wearing the familiar uniform of a dark frock and apron was the first to notice Violet standing in the door. She uttered a small squeal of alarm and nearly dropped the silver carafe in her hands.

The commodore looked up from his paper with annoyance. His gaze caught on Violet, and his brows drew low over his eyes.

"You've finally decided to come crawling home, have you?"

Violet wandered into the room, studying the man at the end of the table. He looked so much older than she remembered, as if the five years that had passed had instead been counted in multiples of those years. His hair was nearly entirely white above the Home Guard uniform he still wore. He seemed...smaller. Diminished. The usual trepidation and anxiety that Violet had always experienced when addressing her father was absent. "It's good to see you, Father." She meant it.

She turned to the other end of the table, where her mother sat, her fork frozen halfway to her mouth, a full glass of cognac sitting in front of her. Like the commodore, her mother also seemed to have shrunk. Her hair was still immaculately coifed, her makeup carefully applied. Though like her father's, there were a few more lines on Audrey's face, carved in deep, bitter grooves. "And it's good to see you too, Mother."

"What have you done with your hair, Violet?" her mother demanded. "It looks terrible. And your dress. My God. You look like a peasant."

Violet ran her fingers through her loose curls that now kissed the bottoms of her ears. She pulled out a chair and settled herself on the long side of the table between her parents. The housekeeper hurried over with a plate, a set of silverware, and a cup filled with steaming coffee. "Thank you." Violet nodded her appreciation, and the woman hastily retreated.

Her father was still staring at her over the top of his newspaper. "Why are you here?"

Violet took a sip of her coffee, blowing on it first to keep the rich brew from scalding her lips. "I wanted to make sure you were all right," she said. "My letters I wrote to you were returned."

The commodore grunted. "Do not presume to play the victim with me, Violet. You should be grateful that I am currently allowing you to remain here. I made clear the consequences of your choices."

"You did." She set her cup down. "In truth, I am a little surprised to find you here."

"The house in London was destroyed. I've been stuck here in this infernal heat. Don't know when I'll be able to get back."

"Hopefully soon," her mother muttered.

"I'm sorry to hear that," Violet remarked.

"It's been awful," Audrey complained. "The rationing has been dreadful. Unbearable sometimes, if you must know. The things I've had to do without."

"I'm sorry to hear that as well." Violet reached for an orange and lifted it to her nose, inhaling the tang of citrus.

"Violet," her father admonished sharply, "what has happened to your manners?"

Violet didn't respond, only began peeling the orange with her thumb. She was struck by the surreal nature of this conversation, understanding that the true horrors of the war seemed to have entirely bypassed this villa and the people trapped within.

"Are you back for good?" the commodore asked.

"Perhaps." A piece of orange peel fell to the plate.

"Perhaps?" Her father's brows lifted. "I'm afraid to inquire about your vacillation on the matter," he said. The pages of his newspaper snapped in his hands. "Though I suppose I must now ask how your war was."

Another strip of peel dropped as Violet considered her answer. Over two thousand of the Free French that had defended Bir Hakeim had escaped and slipped through the German lines, living to fight another day. Afterward, Violet had been sent first to Egypt, where she had resumed her duties of ferrying a dizzying array of officers wherever they needed to go. From there, the Free French had been absorbed into the US Fifth Army and landed in Italy, where Violet once again found herself behind the wheel of an ambulance. The fighting had been horrendous, the destruction unimaginable, and there had been days when she had railed against the universe, unable to do anything except watch men die under her care. But slowly, the Nazis had yielded, Italy had given way, and in the last months of the war, Violet's duties had finally propelled her onto French soil in an old American Dodge ambulance that boasted mulish steering and an unfailing transmission.

"Illuminating," was the word Violet decided on. "My war was illuminating."

"Now that that nonsense is behind you, you'll need to start thinking about your future if you expect to stay in Nice." Her father grunted again. "I'm assuming that is why you're here? To beg forgiveness and entry back into your old life?"

"My future?" Violet popped a piece of orange in her mouth

and closed her eyes briefly in bliss as the juice and flavour burst over her tongue.

"Augustino—Mr. Leblanc is still in town," her father told her. "He's become very wealthy. His factories did quite well in the war. These last years have been very profitable for him."

"Ah." Violet chewed slowly.

"He hasn't married, and he might be persuaded to take you back." The commodore pursed his lips. "Provided that you apologized."

"And did something with your hair," Audrey added.

"For what?" Violet considered the woman sitting at the end of the table, feeling as though she were gazing at a stranger.

"Because you look atrocious," her mother drawled. "You don't seem to have taken any pains at all with your appearance, and I don't know how you expect to find a husband when—"

"No, Mother. I meant, for what would I apologize?"

The commodore's hand thumped to the table, making the silverware bounce and clatter. Her mother jumped.

"For being selfish," her father barked. "For leaving him to run off for whatever charade you've fancied yourself a part of these last years. You'll be lucky if he forgives you. I'm not sure I can."

Violet reached for her cup. The coffee had cooled enough for Violet to finish it in three swallows. It really was good coffee. She wondered where her parents had managed to get it.

Her mother glanced at her father and seemed to recover. "The good news is that many have left France." She reached for her cognac glass. "Not all have returned and most probably won't remember your faux pas. You'll be accepted back into the fold of society provided you behave. No more…outbursts."

"No." Violet split another section of orange with her fingers.

"No?"

"No," Violet said. "I don't think I will apologize. For anything."

Juice dribbled down her wrist, and she licked it before it could drip onto her dress.

"Violet!" Her father's breath whistled through his teeth in outrage.

"This is your fault, Robert," her mother snapped. "She's always been difficult but this is beyond the pale."

"I don't know what you are playing at here, Violet. You should listen to your mother. You are still young. You still carry our name, and though I'm not sure if that means anything to you anymore, it still means something to others. It still has value to others."

"I'd like to think that my service these last years has imbued the St. Croix name with both courage and honour."

Her father leaned over his paper. "You forgot your place, Violet. You defied me, and you defied a man who was willing to be your husband. A man willing to look after you for the rest of your life. If you are ever to have another opportunity for a respectable future, you need to desist this sort of behaviour and this sort of attitude immediately."

"You're wrong, Father." Violet finished the last piece of orange.

"I beg your pardon?"

"I didn't forget my place." Even now, she felt none of the anger or resentment that she might have expected given the conversation. Instead, a sense of peace had descended, an acknowledgement of her own truth. "I didn't forget my place at all," she repeated. "I finally found it."

Violet stood and wiped her sticky hands on a snow-white linen napkin with perfect etiquette. She went to Audrey first and pressed a kiss to her cheek. "Goodbye, Mother. I wish you all the best." She went to the commodore next. "Goodbye, Father. I love you both."

"Robert, do something," Audrey shrilled from her chair. "You can't just leave, Violet."

"I had never planned to stay." Violet headed for the dining room door.

"I don't even know who you are anymore. I don't even recognize this person you've become," her father called after her.

Violet paused at the door and turned. "But I do. I know exactly who I am."

★ ★ ★

The sun was sinking steadily in the west when Violet nosed the battered Citroen onto the shoulder of the road. The Citroen was the second thing she had purchased, and it had taken a fair number of hours to get it running. Violet still hadn't managed to work out all the quirks but she loved it more than anything she had ever driven because it was hers.

On the other side of the pavement, a lone light mounted to the side of a familiar square building flickered on ahead of the encroaching night. Violet hefted her pack over her shoulder, skirted the row of thick shrubbery, and started down the twisting path to the sea. On the smooth, pebbled beach, a half dozen boats had been hauled from the water for men to labour over their hulls. Still more fishermen were gathering nets that they'd spread out for repair, the dying light signalling the end of their work until tomorrow. The small pier that jutted into the sea was festooned with boats secured by rope, buoys bobbing alongside each.

"Bonsoir, Mademoiselle Violet." An old man, his face dark from the sun, a cap pulled low over his eyes, met her as she stepped onto the beach.

"Monsieur Martin." Violet smiled warmly at him. "Bonsoir."

The fisherman doffed his cap. "You are here to watch another sunset?"

"Yes."

"Ah." He twisted his cap in his hands and glanced at the other men who were heading back up and away from the water. "We are done for the day. Would mademoiselle like some company?"

"Thank you for your kindness, but no," she said. "You have

family who have been waiting for you to come home since sunrise. You should go home. Spend time with them."

"But who is to spend time with you?" He was looking at her sadly.

"I am waiting for someone too."

"Mmm." He replaced his cap back on his head with gnarled hands. "You've been waiting a long time."

"I will keep waiting until he comes along, Monsieur Martin."

The old fisherman looked down at his sandaled feet and then nodded. "Then enjoy your sunset." He paused. "Perhaps we will see you here again tomorrow?" he asked hopefully.

"You need me to look at an engine?"

"Mmm." He looked heavenward. "Perhaps Gustave might have mentioned something to that effect."

"Then perhaps Gustave can come and ask me tomorrow himself." Violet laughed. "And I'd be happy to take a look."

Monsieur Martin smiled. "And so he shall. Au revoir, Mademoiselle. And merci."

Violet waved as he headed up the slope. She did the same with the other familiar faces as she approached the water's edge.

She let her pack drop gently onto the beach and sat down, stretching her legs out in front of her. Here, the air was salty, the breeze coming off the water cool against her heated skin. The stone beneath her skin was still warm from the day, and she closed her eyes, tipping her face toward the sinking sun. The beach became quieter as the fishermen left, leaving only the seabirds above her head for company and the steady crash of waves as the water curled into the shingle to fill the silence. And then she waited.

She had last seen Henri three years ago. She had left him on the side of a dusty road in Alexandria but she had not said goodbye. She had thought of him every day since. She had scoured the casualty lists that she was able to pilfer from officers and doctors, her heart in her throat until she reached the ends of the columns of unfamiliar names. Henri's parents had received no word of him save for a single letter that had somehow found its way to France from Tunisia. Nothing after that. Violet chose to believe that that was a good sign. And every day since the war had ended and she had returned to the south of France, she had come here to this beach. Come to keep her promise.

The sun had become a blazing orb of gold and swathed the sky in hues of topaz and amethyst, the kaleidoscope of colour reflected in the clouds and the crests of each wave. It was painfully beautiful. In the distance, along the coast, lights were starting to come on among the homes and hotels crowding the edge of the ocean and twinkled between the palms and the roofs. People dotted the promenades, and cars glided down paved streets. Life had continued on, the passing of time indifferent to the insignificant struggles of those who marked it.

A gull wheeled low, shrieking its presence as the day finally surrendered to twilight. Violet watched it soar against the encroaching indigo of the sky. The moon was now visible, a faint crescent emerging from the cover of colour and, aside from the gull, her only company. She leaned back on her elbows, letting her senses fill with the beauty of the evening.

Behind her, footsteps punctuated the sound of the sea, a clatter not unlike a windchime as the smooth stones were disturbed. She didn't turn around, afraid that if she did, she would find that she was imagining them.

"Buona sera, signorina," he said.

Violet kept her eyes on the bird high above her head, diving and rising with the wind.

"Sei in ritardo," she replied.

The footsteps stopped beside her yet still she didn't look.

"Mi dispiace per questo." The stones rattled as he lowered himself to sit beside her. "There were matters in Paris that needed some attention. I came as soon as I was able."

Violet sat up and reached for her pack. She withdrew a bundle from inside and gingerly unwrapped it, revealing a dark glass bottle with a rich gold label. Her hands were shaking. With care, she placed it on the pebbles between them. "Did you know that the Veuve Clicquot cellars once sheltered over a thousand civilians from the bombardments during the Great War?" she asked.

Out of the corner of her eye, she saw him reach for the bottle. "So this is why you chose this champagne for the evening? For the valour of the vineyards?"

"No." Violet smiled out at the sea. "I fixed the carburetor of a Renault outside of Lyon in June for a farmer, and he insisted on paying me."

"In expensive champagne?"

"Turned out the Nazis had stashed five hundred bottles in his barn. The war ended before they could load them on a train back to Germany." She let her fingers trail over the smooth beach stones. "I've been saving it since, waiting for you."

"I never wanted to keep you waiting. I'm sorry." He put the bottle back on the beach.

Violet moved then so that she was kneeling in front of Henri. She threaded her fingers into the hair at the nape of his neck and kissed him. He stilled for the briefest of seconds before he caught her face in his hands and kissed her back, carefully at first, as if he was afraid she might pull away, and then not so carefully. He gathered her into his lap, his fingers sliding over her back. When Violet finally broke the kiss, they were both breathing hard.

"I've wanted to do that for years," Henri whispered.

"What were you waiting for?" Violet rested her forehead against his.

"You," he said simply.

She kissed him again, a soft brush of her lips against his. The kiss spoke not of goodbyes, of stolen moments, or of fear that it might be their last. This kiss promised hope and joy and dreams.

This was a beginning, not an end.

"I love you," he said. He smoothed a piece of hair back from her forehead, his touch soft. "I've loved you from the moment I met you. No, that's not true. I was bleeding and angry then." His hand slid over her hip. "It was probably a few days later that I fell in love with you. For sure by the first time I saw you pick up a wrench."

"I love you too." Violet ran a finger down his cheek, tracing his jaw and coming to rest on his lips. He watched her, the muscles beneath his skin flexing under her touch. He looked almost the same as he had the night she had met him—messy, sun-streaked hair, tanned skin, strong shoulders, and sea-blue eyes. Except there were lines etched into his face, a weariness to his eyes, and scars marring his skin, all things that hadn't been there before.

Every time she looked in the mirror, she saw the same. They both had them.

"You're Italian is quite good," she whispered.

"I don't know that much. Italy was...hard." He words stuck.

"I know." She brushed the hair back from his face. There would be time to talk of those things. Time to talk about the memories and the nightmares and the recollections that sometimes made everyday things seem difficult. Later. She reached for the champagne, and with deft motions, uncorked the bottle. The liquid fizzed and dribbled down the side.

"You're very good at that."

"I've had a lot of practice." She offered him the bottle and watched him bring it to his lips, drinking deeply.

"I have something else for you," she told him, reaching for her bag without leaving his embrace.

"What is it?"

She pulled out a creased envelope. "A letter. For you. From George."

He snatched it from her hand. "Where is she? Is she all right?" He tore the envelope open.

"She's quite all right," Violet said, hiding a smile. "She sent me a letter too."

He was unfolding a single sheet of paper, the action made awkward between them. Neither made an effort to move.

His eyes scanned the top of the page. "Perth."

"Mmm-hmm."

"She's in Perth. Australia." His eyes raced over the page and then back to the top. "She's married."

"He's a doctor," Violet interjected helpfully. "They met in Tobruk. Apparently, she saved his life, though I haven't been provided with all the details. I've asked," she assured him, "in my last letter."

A muscle in his jaw worked. "I have not met this doctor."

"No."

"How am I to know that he's good enough for my sister?" he demanded.

"Because she's George. And it must be one hell of a man who can keep up with her."

"She says she's happy."

"Then believe her. And be happy for her."

Henri set the letter down. "I'm going to miss her terribly."

"Me too."

They sat in a contemplative silence for a moment before Henri passed the champagne back to her. Violet took a drink, wrinkling her nose as the bubbles burst and tickled. She wiped her mouth with the back of her hand.

"What?" she asked, catching him looking at her with an intensity that sent heat rushing to her cheeks.

"You're so incredibly beautiful." His voice was hoarse.

Violet leaned forward and kissed him again, tasting the champagne on his lips. "Thank you. Though I'm not dressed for dancing."

"Dancing?" His hand slid up her back.

"It's what you promised next." She took another sip of champagne. "We watch the sunset, drink champagne, and I teach you how to dance properly. Do you remember?"

"Oh, I remember." He took the bottle from her fingers and set it aside. "I don't think I want to dance. Not tonight."

Violet shivered as his fingers played with the small buttons on the back of her dress.

"I'd like to skip ahead, I think."

"Ah." She shivered again and glanced around. Twilight was giving way to the rising moon, the shadows of the palms and shrubs lining the beach deepening. Only a suggestion of gold remained, dusting the froth of the sea where it hissed back against the shore.

"You wish to convince me that Sir Arthur writes a superior mystery?" A button slipped open. "I've read *The Valley of Fear*," she managed as another button on her dress was released.

"Yes. Though that's a discussion for another time, I think." Henri's breath was hot against her skin. Her dress slipped over her shoulder.

Violet's head tipped back.

"Would you like me to stop?" Henri asked.

"No. Don't you dare."

"Good." He pressed a kiss to the bare skin along the side of her neck. "I want to swim under the moonlight first."

"And after that?" she asked.

"Then you can decide."

"Decide what?"

Henri cupped her chin with his fingers, an impossibly gentle touch. "What you do next. Where you go next." He kissed her. "You have a lot of things to do in this part of your life not yet lived, Violet St. Croix. And I'd like to be by your side every step of the way, if you'll have me."

"Yes. Yes to it all." Violet wrapped her arms around him, not caring if she was squeezing too hard.

He embraced her just as passionately.

"Would you help me tomorrow?" she whispered, barely able to form the words because he was holding her so tight, and not caring at all.

"With what?"

She extricated herself, and now it was her fingers that went to work on the buttons of his worn linen shirt.

"I have an outboard to fix." She smiled up at him. "And after that…I'll decide then."

ACKNOWLEDGEMENTS

One of the most common questions that I receive as an author is "What do you like most about your job?" There are a myriad of things that I adore about being an author, but one of the most valuable aspects of writing these stories is the privilege I have of listening to and reading the accounts of the courageous men and women who have gone before us and shaped our world with their incredible sacrifice and bravery. I'd like to offer a sincere acknowledgement of gratitude to those who faced extraordinary and sometimes incomprehensible challenges and left behind a record of it, so that their efforts would not be lost to history. The world is a better place because of them.

I'd like to thank every reader who has chosen one of my books because I am grateful for the opportunity to be able to share these stories with you. A heartfelt thank-you to my family for their support and encouragement. To my editor, Alex Logan, once again a sincere thank-you for making each one of my stories better, and thank you to the entire team at Forever who work tirelessly on my behalf. And to my agent, Stefanie Lieberman, thank you for your continued support and invaluable advice.

Reading Group Guide

YOUR
BOOK
CLUB
RESOURCE

HISTORICAL NOTE FOR
TOMORROW IS FOR THE BRAVE

Tomorrow Is for the Brave is a work of fiction and produced entirely from my own imagination. The inspiration for this story, however, came from the lives and experiences of real people and includes real events that took place during the years in which this novel is set. The character of Violet St. Croix was inspired by the life and experiences of Susan Travers, the only woman to officially become a member of the French Foreign Legion. I first discovered Ms. Travers's extraordinary story while researching the Allied North African campaign of 1942 for my previous novel, *The Garden of Lost Secrets*.

Born in England and raised primarily in the south of France, Travers first persuaded her parents to allow her driving lessons when she was seventeen. When war broke out in 1939, she volunteered for the French Red Cross, hoping to be assigned to the front lines. She could drive a car and shoot a rifle, and she reasoned that she would be most useful as an ambulance driver. To her dismay, she discovered that she needed to complete her nursing diploma first. In her own words, Travers described herself as "completely hopeless as a nurse," and the bungled operation that Violet mentions in this story was drawn from Travers's own experience.

In March of 1940, Travers joined the French Expeditionary Forces that travelled from Paris to Finland to assist in the war against the Russians. After France surrendered to Germany in June of 1940, she returned to London to join the Free French forces under the command of General de Gaulle. From there, she travelled to Sierra Leone, Cameroon, and the Republic of Congo, where she served as a (reluctant) nurse.

Finally, Travers headed to North Africa, and it was there that she was moved out of the hospital and assigned as a driver for Commandant Lotte, a medical doctor for the Free French forces. On June 17, 1941, Susan Travers was assigned to (then) French Colonel Marie-Pierre Koenig, whom she would continue to drive throughout North Africa until after the siege of Bir Hakeim.

Violet's service in Finland was inspired by the Red Cross volunteers who served as nurses during the Winter War. The French did send nurses (including Susan Travers), though not until March 3, 1940, and by then the Winter War was over. For the purposes of this story, I imagined that my character of Violet accompanied the armed French force sent to Finland eight weeks ahead of the Red Cross volunteers. She would have joined Swedes, Danes, Norwegians, Ukrainians, Estonians, and many others who all travelled to defend Finland against the Russians.

Most of the characters in this novel are completely fictional. However, the story is certainly sprinkled with real people. Aside from the nonfictional military appearances of General Koenig and Colonel Amilakhvari, Lady Enid Furness appears as herself in this novel. She was a tall, beautiful woman described as adventurous and seductive, and her sexual assignations and affairs were infamous. Equally as infamous were the men Viscount Furness hired to keep tabs on his wife and the cheetah she kept.

But as notable as she was for what was perceived as frivolous behaviour, there was nothing frivolous about her bravery in the face of war. She really did drive an ambulance during WWI. And in June of 1940, when France signed an armistice with Germany, Enid did not return to England but remained in

France. There, along with her fourteen-year-old daughter, Enid began giving away her rations to prisoners of a nearby detention camp in Eze. Once the viscount died in October of 1940, she began helping prisoners escape, using the family's villas as safe houses.

The Black Code that my spy stumbles across in this novel was real, though his discovery of it is completely fictional. In truth, the Black Code (also known as Military Intelligence Code No. 11) was a secret code used by American military attachés, and it was compromised not in a hotel room, but stolen from a US embassy in Italy. Axis intelligence agents attained the keys to the embassy, broke in, and copied and replaced all the documents without anyone the wiser. The Germans were thus able to decipher American communications.

Much of Violet's fictional experiences as a military driver were inspired by real situations and circumstances that Susan Travers faced. Air raids were common, and the destruction that they wrought was severe. The lack of water was always an impediment, and keeping vehicles running under extreme environmental conditions was nothing short of miraculous. Travers described the dangers and hardships of driving in a desert environment in great detail, and I tried to pass on these struggles to my characters.

In February of 1942, the newly formed 1st Free French Brigade (into which Susan Travers had been incorporated) was posted at Bir Hakeim, at the southern end of the Gazala Line. The Gazala Line was a defensive line of "boxes," or forts designed to prevent the Germans and Italians from breaking through in their push east to capture Cairo and the Suez Canal.

In May, as Rommel's forces advanced, Bir Hakeim came under siege. Susan Travers was with the forces defending the fort, and on the night of 10 June, 1942, when the garrison escaped through enemy lines, she navigated minefields, tracer fire, artillery, and the rough terrain to eventually deliver General Koenig to the rendezvous point the following morning. Her vehicle, when she examined it later, had dozens of bullet holes that had damaged the engine and sheared off pieces of the bodywork. One round had passed directly between Travers and her passenger. She described the escape as "an amazing feeling, going as fast as I could in the dark towards what looked like a mass display of beautifully coloured fireworks dancing towards me, bringing what seemed almost like certain death. This was what I had come for—to feel what it was like to be a man, in the very heat of battle."

Afterward, Travers remained with the French Foreign Legion and served in the Italian Campaign, on the Western Front (Germany and France), and later in Indochina. By the end of her military career, she had been awarded the Legion d'honneur, the Croix de Guerre, Officier de l'Ordre de Nichan Iftikhar, and the Médaille militaire. At the age of ninety-one, she wrote her memoirs, titled *Tomorrow to Be Brave: A Memoir of the Only Woman Ever to Serve in the French Foreign Legion*. The title of her memoirs inspired the title for this novel, and the story she tells is as extraordinary as the woman who tells it.

The siege of Bir Hakeim by Axis forces lasted two weeks. Many of the events during this time that are depicted in my story were drawn from the history books. It was true that Bir Hakeim was built almost entirely underground, and when Rommel's forces finally entered the fort after the French retreat, they discovered over 1,200 separate dugouts for men, guns, and vehicles. Veterans of WWI made regular tactical comparisons between Bir Hakeim and the trench warfare two decades prior.

I did, however, take some small licence with dates to fit my fictional account. The crippling sandstorms were real, but the significant storm that I describe in June actually took place in May. The ammunition dump that explodes in my story was actually hit five days earlier, and there is absolutely no evidence that the dump was destroyed by anything other than an unlucky Axis shell. The sabotages of the ammunition dump and water trucks were pure imagination on my part.

It's extraordinary but true that two Italian officers approached Bir Hakeim under a flag of truce and were guided into the fort blindfolded. In the first of three attempts to convince Koenig to surrender, the Italian officers (who spoke little to no French) and the French officers (who spoke little to no Italian) engaged in a parley. That I could insert Violet as an interpreter seemed too good an opportunity to pass up and is fictional, of course. In actuality, the gist of the message was made clear, and Koenig's response clearer still. The message that he sent to his officers afterward said, "General Rommel has asked us to surrender and has threatened us with extermination. I have refused. Do your duty."

Also accurate is Koenig's decision to retreat from Bir Hakeim nearly a week after the first demand for surrender came, by which time the ammunition, supplies, and water had been exhausted. Of the 3,600 men and officers originally stationed there, approximately 2,400 escaped through enemy lines in the dead of night. What started as a single-file, silent retreat devolved into a chaotic, carnage-filled battlefield, marked by heavy artillery fire and hand-to-hand combat through and across minefields. When the tallies were finally taken, 763 were reported missing and presumed dead, 72 dead, and 21 wounded. But both General Koenig and Colonel Amilakhvari survived and made it to the rendezvous point, driven through the horror by Adjutant Susan Travers.

Violet and Henri's discovery of the rendezvous point in the early morning hours as the mists cleared was inspired by the real experience of Pierre Iehele, a French officer in charge of several ambulances who had managed to get his vehicles free and clear beyond enemy lines. Navigating in the darkness as best he could but having no real idea how close he might be to the rendezvous point (or a German patrol camp), he formed a square in the desert, prepared to fight until the last man. When the sun came up, his men spotted a camp in the distance lined with trucks and vehicles, but Iehele was unable to tell if they were English or German until he saw them playing football. "They must be English!" he concluded, and he was right. He had managed to get his group within a few hundred yards of the rendezvous point.

Though Bir Hakeim ultimately fell to Rommel's Axis forces, the tenacity of the Free French bought the British Eighth Army a critical window of time to recover and regroup after suffering debilitating losses. It also forced Rommel to extend his fragile supply line south around Bir Hakeim at a significant cost to the Germans, both in supplies as well as men. It was an important victory for the French from a morale perspective, proving to the world and the Allied forces that the French could contribute to the fight against Germany. Rommel, famous for his military and tactical skill, conceded later that "Seldom in Africa was I given such a hard-fought struggle."

FURTHER READING

Atkinson, Rick. *An Army at Dawn: The War in North Africa (1942–1943)*. Vol. 1 of the Liberation Trilogy (Holt Paperbacks, 2007).

De Courcy, Anne. *Chanel's Riviera: Glamour, Decadence, and Survival in Peace and War* (St. Martin's Press, 2020).

Ford, Ken. *Gazala 1942: Rommel's Greatest Victory* (Osprey Publishing, 2008).

Harper, Glyn. *The Battle for North Africa: El Alamein and the Turning Point for World War II* (Massey University Press, 2017).

Hasey, John F. and Dineen, Joseph F. *Yankee Fighter: The Story of an American in the Free French Foreign Legion* (Arcole Publishing, 2017).

Holmes, Richard. *Bir Hakim: Desert Citadel* (Ballantine Books Inc., 1971).

Kagan, Neil. *The Secret History of World War II: The Spies, Code Breakers, and Covert Operations* (National Geographic, 2016).

Kundahl, George. *The Riviera at War: World War II on the Côte d'Azure* (I. B. Tauris, 2017).

Mitchelhill-Green, David. *Rommel in North Africa: Quest for the Nile* (Pen and Sword Military, 2017).

Travers, Susan and Holden, Wendy. *Tomorrow to Be Brave* (Simon & Schuster, 2000).

Tucker-Jones, Anthony. *The Battle for the Mediterranean: Allied and Axis Campaigns from North Africa to the Italian Peninsula, 1940–1945* (Arcturus, 2021).

Windrow, Martin. *French Foreign Legion, 1914–1945* (Oxford Press, 1999).

DISCUSSION QUESTIONS

1. Bravery is a theme throughout this novel. Who do you think was the bravest character and why?
2. Parents often put significant expectations on their children throughout their lives. Do you think the expectations that Violet grew up with were reasonable? At what point in the story do you think those expectations might have changed? What sort of expectations did you grow up with and how did you deal with them?
3. Did you know who the spy was during the story? Did you suspect Henri, and if you did, how did that colour your view of his character and his relationship with Violet?
4. The North African theater of war is not as well-known as the campaigns carried out on the European or the Pacific fronts. Were you familiar with the history of the area and the impact it had on later battles?
5. Friendship is an important focal point of this novel. How did the friendship between George and Violet impact each of their lives? And how did the friendship

between Violet and Henri evolve? Was George's or Henri's influence greater by the end?

6. George is relieved when she is ordered to retreat. Does this make her less brave? How do you think you would have reacted, given the situation? What choice would you have made?

7. Violet and the rest of the garrison endure hunger, thirst, heat, cold, fear, and illness. Could you visualize the hardships that they endured? What element would you have found the most difficult to contend with?

8. The young Violet that we meet at the beginning of the story is quite different from the Violet that we see at the end, after the war. At what point in the story did you feel that Violet found the courage to truly embrace her own sense of self and purpose? Why?

9. Were Tino and Violet's father being fair by refusing to allow her to volunteer for the Red Cross? Do you believe that they were genuinely concerned for her safety, or do you think that they had other motivations to keep her from training?

10. Books are featured as a connection between Henri and Violet that continues throughout the story. Have you read any of the novels that Violet and Henri trade? If so, which ones, and which was your favourite?

11. Violet meets Lady Enid early in the story. What influence do you think that her advice had on Violet? Do you think her title, wealth, and lifestyle would have had an effect on society in real life?

12. Grand prix racing is still as popular in Europe today as it was during this story. What do you think made

Violet fall in love with it? Have you ever been to a race? Which part was your favourite?

13. This story was inspired by the real life of Susan Travers. Had you heard of her before reading *Tomorrow Is for the Brave*? Are there other women that you are aware of who served during WWII in a combat role?

14. Henri and Violet's relationship evolves slowly over time. At what point in the story do you think that Violet fell in love with him? Do you think that he fell in love with her before or after that? Do you think that their earlier differences actually brought them closer together?

ABOUT THE AUTHOR

Award-winning author Kelly Bowen grew up in Manitoba, Canada, and attended the University of Manitoba, where she earned bachelor of science and master of science degrees in veterinary studies. She worked as a research scientist before realizing her dream to be a writer of historical fiction. Currently, Kelly lives in Winnipeg with her husband and two sons.

Learn more:
www.kellybowen.net
Twitter @kellybowen09
Facebook.com/AuthorKellyBowen